MW00603309

I MADE IT OUT OF CLAY

I MADE IT OUT OF CLAY

BETH KANDER

/‖MIRA

/II MIRA™

ISBN-13: 978-0-7783-6812-0

I Made It Out of Clay

Copyright © 2024 by Beth Kander

Recycling programs
for this product may
not exist in your area.

All rights reserved. No part of this book may be used or reproduced in any manner whatsoever without written permission.

Without limiting the author's and publisher's exclusive rights, any unauthorized use of this publication to train generative artificial intelligence (AI) technologies is expressly prohibited.

This is a work of fiction. Names, characters, places and incidents are either the product of the author's imagination or are used fictitiously. Any resemblance to actual persons, living or dead, businesses, companies, events or locales is entirely coincidental.

For questions and comments about the quality of this book, please contact us at CustomerService@Harlequin.com.

TM is a trademark of Harlequin Enterprises ULC.

Mira
22 Adelaide St. West, 41st Floor
Toronto, Ontario M5H 4E3, Canada
MIRABooks.com

Printed in U.S.A.

For my father, and everyone who loved him (and loves him still).

We all have chapters where grief surpasses gratitude.

But the love, the laughter, the pride—that's the real story.

MONDAY

1

The soft growl on the train is coming from me.

I flush with shame at the insistent rumbling of my stomach. Thankfully, the Monday-morning brown line is too crowded with bundled-up commuters for anyone but me to notice the sound. If someone does somehow clock it, they'll probably assume it's coming from the pigtailed pregnant woman I gave my seat to at the last stop.

The train lurches, and I nearly drop my peppermint mocha. Technically, you're not supposed to have open food or beverages aboard, but no one follows that rule. You'll only get in trouble if you spill on someone. Nobody really cares what's going on in the background until the mess impacts them.

When my stomach rumbles yet again, the pigtailed pregnant woman gives me a conspiratorial look. Everyone else on the train might think it's her, but she knows it's me. She isn't judging, though; her expression is friendly. Surprisingly kind and intimate in a maternal sort of way. I take in her pert nose, amused hazel eyes, and the beautiful coppery shade of her two neat, thick braids. I want to tell her *I bet you're gonna be a great mother*—but who needs to hear that from a stranger? Besides, maybe she already *is* a mother. This might not be her first rodeo.

Another grumble from my midsection cues me to return my attention to myself. I smile weakly, averting my gaze as I take a slow sip of my mocha, attempting to temporarily silence my stomach's demands. While I've always had a healthy appetite, lately it's like I'm haunted by this constant craving. I can take the edge off sometimes, but I'm never really satisfied.

My granddaughter Eve, oy, let me tell you, she can really eat, my grandmother used to say with pride. But it wasn't a problem when I was a kid. I was just a girl who liked food. Now, it's like I can never get enough. I've been trying to tell myself it's seasonal. The weather. Winter cold snap making everyone want to hibernate and fatten up like all those rotund city squirrels. But I think it's something more than that.

Like, say, losing my father a year ago.

Or my looming fortieth birthday.

Or my little sister's upcoming wedding.

Or the growing conviction that I'm going to die alone.

Or, most likely, all of the above.

Rather than sift through all the wreckage, it's easiest to just blame my hungry malaise on December—and specifically, Christmas.

Holidays make excellent emotional scapegoats, and I've always had a powerful love/hate relationship with Christmas. I'm pretty sure that's just part of growing up as a religious minority in America. The holiday to end all holidays is an omnipresent blur of red and green, a nonstop monthlong takeover of society as we know it, which magically manages to be both inescapable and exclusionary. It's relentless. Exhausting.

But at the same time, dammit, the persistent cheer is intoxicating, and I want in on it.

That's why I do things like set my vintage radio alarm to the twenty-four-hour-carols station that pops up every November for the "countdown to Christmas." It's an annual ritual I never miss, but also never mention to any of my friends—the literal definition of *guilty pleasure*, which might just be the most Jewish kind of enjoyment ever.

From Thanksgiving all the way until the New Year, I start every day with the sounds of crooning baritones, promises of holiday homecomings, and all those bells—silver, jingling, carol-of-the. I can't help it. My whole life, I've loved all the glitzy aspects of the season. The sparkling lights adorning trees and outlining the houses and apartment buildings throughout Chicagoland always seemed so magical to the little Jewish girl with the only dark house on the block. And as an adult, God help me, I cannot get enough of seasonal mochas. (At the same time, I feel a need to assert my Hanukkah-celebrant status, resenting the default assumption that everyone celebrates Christmas. Because humans are complicated.)

One of the best and worst things about the holiday season is how much more you wind up chatting with other people. Wishing total strangers *happy holidays*, commenting on their overflowing shopping bags, chitchatting with people in line for the aforementioned addictive peppermint mochas. I'm not in the mood for it this year as much as in years past, but once in a while I'm glad to take advantage of the holiday-related conversational opportunities.

For instance, there's a new guy in my apartment building. He moved in a few months ago. He has a British accent, thick dark brows, muscular arms, and a charming tendency to hold the door for everyone. I haven't crushed this hard on someone since high school. We said hello a few times over the fall, but December has opened the door to much more lobby banter.

Hot Josh—which is what I call him when he's not around, and am absolutely doomed to someday accidentally call him in person—has been getting a lot of boxes delivered to our lobby. Which, for better or worse, has given me multiple excuses to make stupid jokes. Most recently, a huge overseas package arrived; it had clearly cost a fortune to ship. Hot Josh made some comment about the overzealous shipper of said holiday package, rolling his eyes at the amount of postage plastered all over the box.

It's better than if they forgot to put on any stamps at all, I said. *Have you heard the joke about the letter someone tried to send without a stamp?*

Uh, no? Hot Josh replied, raising an eyebrow.

You wouldn't get it, I said, and snort-laughed.

He just blinked. Apparently, for some of us, all those cheery holiday conversational opportunities are more like sparkling seasonal landmines.

At the next train stop, only a few passengers exit, while dozens more shove their way in. The handful of departing passengers include the pigtailed pregnant woman. She rises awkwardly from her seat, giving me a *hey-thanks-again* farewell nod as she indicates I should sit there again.

I look around cautiously as I reclaim my seat, making sure no new pregnant, elderly, or otherwise-in-need folks are boarding. It's only after I finish this courtesy check that I notice I'm now sitting directly across from a man in full Santa Claus gear.

He's truly sporting the whole shebang: red crushed-velvet suit with wide black belt and matching buckle, epic white beard, and thigh-high black boots. His bowl-full-of-jelly belly is straining the buttons on the jacket, and I honestly can't tell if it's a pillow or a legit beer gut.

I'm not sure how to react. If Dad was here, he wouldn't hesitate. He'd high-five Santa, and they'd instantly be best friends.

But I never know where to start, what to say. Like, should I smile at the guy? Refer to him as "Santa"? Maybe, like, salute him, or something?

I gotta at least take a picture and text it to Dad. He'd get such a kick out of this guy—

My hand automatically goes for my phone, pulling it swiftly from my pocket. But my amusement is cut off with a violent jerk when I touch the screen and nothing happens. That's when I remember that my phone is off—and why I keep it off.

My rumbling stomach curdles. Even after a whole year, the habit of reaching for my phone to share something with my father hasn't gone away. I'm not sure it ever will.

Shoving my phone back into my coat pocket, I ignore St. Nick and just stare out the filthy train windows instead. Even through this grayish pane streaked with God-knows-what horrific substances, the city is beautiful. I love the views from the train, even the inglorious graffiti and glimpses of small backyards. And now, every neighborhood in Chicago has its holiday decorations up. This Midwestern metropolis, with its glittering architecture, elegant lakefront, and collection of distinct neighborhoods sprawling away from the water, knows how to show off. Most people think downtown is prettiest. But if you ask me, it's hard to beat my very own neighborhood, Lincoln Square.

In the center of the Square is Giddings Plaza. In summertime the plaza's large stone fountain is the bubbling backdrop to all the concerts and street festivals in the brick-paved square. But in wintertime, the water feature is drained and becomes the planter for a massive Christmas tree. Surrounded by all the perky local shops, the plaza is cute as hell year-round. When you add tinsel and twinkle lights and a giant fir tree that looks straight out of a black-and-white Christmas movie, it's almost unbearably charming.

We haven't had a proper snowfall yet, so the natural seasonal scenery has been lacking a little. But even with the bare tree limbs and gray skies, the stubbornly sparkling holiday decor provides a whispered promise of magic ahead.

I really want to believe in that magic.

The light shifts as we rattle beneath looming buildings and trees, and I briefly catch my reflection in the dirty window. Dark curls crushed beneath my olive green knit cap, round cheeks, dark eyes, no makeup except a smear of lip gloss I bought because it was called Holiday Cheer. The details are all familiar, but I barely recognize myself. I wonder if I'll ever feel like the real-me again, or if grief has made me into someone else entirely.

Last month marked the one-year anniversary of losing my dad. A whole year, and it still doesn't feel real. Most days, it seems like I'm in the wrong version of my life. Or like everything around me is just some strange movie set I wandered onto and can't seem to escape. I keep waiting for things to feel normal again. For me to feel normal again.

Hasn't happened yet.

But somehow, a year passed—the days dragging, the months flying—and it was time to return to the cemetery. "Unveiling" is one of a thousand strange and powerful old Jewish traditions. For the first eleven months after someone dies, their headstone is covered. It allows the family to ease in to their new reality, as if *easing in* is possible. When the first yahrzeit—anniversary of death—approaches, there's a formal unveiling of the headstone. The next step in the painful, protracted process of accepting that your loved one is really gone.

It was a simple event, held graveside at Beth Shalom cemetery. A quiet corner, shaded beneath a tree, not too near any other headstones. When we buried my father last year, we also purchased the adjacent plot for my mother.

There's a discount if we get them both now, said my mother. *Your father would approve.*

Nobody laughed or cried when she said it. We just nodded.

None of us have shown true emotion since Dad was ripped from our lives. The shock of the loss rendered us wooden. We move through the world like marionettes, walking and talking, but no longer real girls. In the days leading up to the unveiling, I had been readying myself for a long-delayed emotional outburst. Hoping someone would finally crack. The first dam would break and set off a chain reaction. Those of us who knew Dad best would finally let our sorrow burst forth like Niagara Falls.

I could almost see it, a holy moment of release: my mother would wail, then my younger sister, Rosie, would join in, and that would give me permission to howl as well. The Goodman women would all let out the mournful keening yearning to break free.

But nope.

Instead, as I stood graveside between my mother and my little sister, all three of us remained dry-eyed. Ana, my sister's fiancée, was the only one periodically sniffling. The Goodman women simply said the prayers, acknowledged the moment, and that was it. One more mourning to-do item checked off the list, and the marionettes lurched off again.

The unveiling service for my father was almost identical to the one for my grandmother—except at Bubbe's unveiling, Dad was there, with silent tears sliding down his face. Squeezing my hand. Putting his arm around my mother. Kissing the top of my sister's head. Showing his emotions and granting the rest of us permission to mourn. With him at our side, we all cried at the graveside when her headstone was revealed, then laughed over lunch at the nearby diner while we shared our favorite Bubbe stories. My father was the one who knew how to be fully human in a way the rest of us just don't. We tried to make that clear on his headstone.

DAVID MOSHE GOODMAN
APRIL 10, 1950–NOVEMBER 25, 2023

BELOVED FATHER, HUSBAND, BROTHER, FRIEND.
HE NEVER MET A STRANGER
(OR A SANDWICH)
HE DIDN'T LOVE.

HIS MEMORY WILL ALWAYS BE A BLESSING.

It was strange to gaze at those simple letters. Even with their attempts at heart and humor, the words on his headstone were insufficient. Seeing the graven memorial didn't open me up. It just added another dead bolt to the door I'd firmly shut on my emotions.

Not good enough, I thought, and turned from the stone.

We were also supposed to light a yahrzeit candle in Dad's memory, or so I thought. The flame would have brought a warmth and brightness my father would have appreciated. But no one mentioned lighting a candle, and I wasn't sure when or how to bring it up. So I just kept my mouth shut.

When I left the cemetery, hastily thanking the rabbi and making excuses to skip out on post-unveiling socializing, all I could think about was how much my father would have hated our stoic gathering. How much more he would have hated me skipping out on the chance to have lunch with my mother and sister after the service. But also, how he would have loved all the blithely cheerful Christmas decorations along the road beside the memorial park.

The inappropriate Christmas crush was something he and I shared: two Jews gazing starry-eyed at every wreath and poinsettia. He would have adored the shimmering streetlights decked with massive, sparkling snowflakes. Mom and Rosie eye-rolled all things Christmas. Dad and I were the holiday apologists in the family, gleefully singing along with "Let It

Snow" and "Walking in a Winter Wonderland" and "White Christmas." Our rule was that we could belt out at full volume any and all of the Christmas songs that don't directly mention Jesus.

You know, all the best Christmas songs were written by Jews, my father liked to remind anyone who cared to listen, which mostly meant me. He was so damn proud of this little factoid. The thick Wilford Brimley mustache he'd cultivated in the eighties and insisted on maintaining ever since twitched above his smile. *Irving Berlin, Johnny Marks, Mel Tormé…any Christmas song worth singing, I guarantee you, some nice Jewish kid wrote it.*

Could've written some more Hanukkah songs while they were at it, my mother would always interject, as if irritated that all the musically inclined Jews gave the good melodies to the other holiday. Mom was the keeper of the faith, the stalwart, the one worried my little sister, Rosie, and I would drift away from our Jewish heritage if she wasn't ever-vigilant. For Dad, being Jewish was easy. It was just a built-in part of his identity, no need for maintenance. For Mom, it was a handful of holy sand that she was determined to never let slip through her fingers.

Not a big enough market, Dad said cheerfully. *They wouldn't've made a dime.*

And then he went back to happily humming "I'll Be Home for Christmas," off-key.

God, he was a terrible singer. I'd give anything to hear him butcher "Walking in a Winter Wonderland" one more time.

The holiday season has sharpened the dull knife of my grief, twisting it into my side with every unwelcome reminder of my loss. My fortieth birthday is barreling toward me, and I can't stop thinking about all the things my father has already missed, and all the things he's about to miss. Milestones like my birthday. And Rosie's Hanukkah-themed wedding, which Dad would have paid for while rolling his eyes relentlessly. His love of Christmas cheer was the one exception to his general rule of poo-pooing anything over-the-top. He was a jeans-and-baseball-cap guy, a Chicago-dog and deli-sandwich aficionado, a lover of deals and cheap thrills. It was Mom and Rosie who loved spotlights and splurging. Birthday parties and weddings were always moments for them to shine—and for Dad and me to retreat.

He would have loved walking Rosie down the aisle, though. Even if a big holiday wedding with hundreds of guests would have seemed extravagant to him, he would have been delighted to see Rosie have the wedding of her dreams. His greatest joy was seeing his family happy. That was it; that was all. At every recital, soccer game, graduation, he was always there, dabbing at his eyes and grinning from beneath his massive mustache.

But he won't be there to get teary-eyed walking Rosie down the aisle. Or to walk me down the aisle, if I ever manage to get married.

The thought hurts, but it's also a moot point, since I haven't had a steady boyfriend in years. It seems doubtful that my string of bad relationship choices, and current tactic of flirting with my hot new neighbor by cracking third-grade-level jokes, will lead to me standing under a chuppah anytime soon.

We're approaching the Southport stop, which means an even larger crowd of commuters will press onto the train. For once, I'm grateful for the incoming crush of additional bodies. Maybe harried holiday travelers will distract me from my darkening thoughts. My stomach rumbles again as the crowd in front of me shifts, riders preparing to either exit or reluctantly make room. Santa once again comes into view. The automated voice calls out that we're approaching Southport. Closing my eyes briefly, I can almost hear what my father would say to the Santa across the way.

Hey, buddy, this your stop? All the way from North Pole to Southport, huh?

I open my eyes and decide to just go for it. What the hell.

As the doors slide open and people pour from the train, I raise my festive cup in greeting.

"Merry Christmas, Santa," I say.

Santa Claus stands up and lets out the longest, foulest belch I've ever heard in my life. The stale smell of booze nearly makes me gag. He looks at me with wet, bleary eyes and grabs his red velveteen crotch, leering at me before stumbling out onto the platform.

Ho, ho, ho.

2

"*There* you are!"

When I get off the train at Merchandise Mart, Sasha is waiting for me on the platform. That's unusual in and of itself, because Sasha is always at the office early, knocking items off her to-do list, never exiting the building unless she has a client pitch or remembers she should maybe eat lunch. But what's really throwing me is the fact that she's not wearing a coat.

Something's definitely up.

Sasha grew up in Los Angeles, and her hatred for the cold knows no bounds. She bundles up in sixteen layers as soon as it dips below fifty degrees and stays in her cocoon of coats, scarves, and good fleece leggings until April. But today, she's standing there in her sharp orange blazer and dark fitted jeans, no hat, no scarf, shaking in her trendy but well-lined Canada Goose winter boots. I enjoy living in a snow globe, but Sasha hates it. Her arms are wrapped around herself, teeth chattering. Even her waist-length dreads look frozen.

"You okay?" I ask, hurrying over to her and unwrapping

my scarf from my neck to offer it to her. "Where's your coat? You get mugged or something?"

"Did you not get my text?" Sasha says, taking my scarf and grabbing me by the elbow.

I haven't told Sasha that I still keep my phone off most days, only turning it on when absolutely necessary. She knows that was a thing I did right after the funeral, but she doesn't know it's *still* a thing.

"No," I say instead. "You know I never hear my phone on the train—"

"Shit's going down at the office."

"What?"

"Hurry, it's cold as hell and we can't be late for this meeting," Sasha says, rushing me through the turnstile.

"I don't have any meetings until ten thirty," I protest.

"Wrong," she says.

Sasha and I have only been coworkers for a few years, but we've been close friends for more than a decade. We met at a party when we were both still relatively new to the city—she was a shivering transplant from California, I was a sort-of-local trying to find my way around the city. I'd just finished a graduate program in marketing at Michigan and had returned to the area to try to launch my career. It was my first time living in Chicago proper, though I grew up less than an hour away from the city.

We hit it off right away and started exploring the city together. We discovered we were both diehard *Buffy the Vampire Slayer* fans, which came in handy when the weather got too cold for us to want to do anything but binge our favorite show. We both loved our gin martinis extra dirty, preferred savory over sweet, and loved nothing more than making a whole meal out of an array of appetizers: salty, cheesy, deepfried. We both worked in advertising and had mixed feelings about being really good at convincing people to buy things they might not actually need.

We bonded over our miserable dating lives and our wholesome childhoods. Sasha Green was the daughter of two psychiatrists in LA, while I was the product of a high school physics teacher and a real estate agent in suburban Chicago. Sasha was the iconic best friend I never had in high school or college. We finished each other's sentences and joked that we shared the same brain. It felt like ours was a fated friendship, meant to be.

Plus, we were both Jewish—something that I didn't initially assume, since apparently the Ashkenormativity (aka the default assumption that all American Jews are of white European descent) was strong with me back then. I was stunned when she invited me to a seder at her apartment. Turns out her mom's Sephardic and Ashkenazic, and her dad was raised in the Black Baptist church but converted to Judaism. Sasha was not only Jewish but also had the same damn bat mitzvah portion that I did. It was truly *basheret*: a match made in heaven.

Sasha was the one who told me about the opening at Mercer & Mercer when I was looking for a bigger agency. She'd been an account executive there for several years, and had some pull. I was working for a cute boutique firm, doing marketing and copywriting and soup-to-nuts services for small clients. I loved it, but as I hit my mid-thirties, I was ready for something that was a little less "cute" and a little more "matches contributions to a 401(k)."

Sasha gave me the heads-up about the senior copywriting job at M&M before the position was even posted. I applied early, even though I felt underqualified. I called my father for a pep talk.

You've got this, Evie, he assured me.

It's what he always told me, no matter what. And while sometimes he was wrong—I didn't get every job, every audition, every opportunity I went after—every time he said it, I felt like at least maybe it wasn't impossible.

So I sold the hell out of myself at all the interviews, and got the job. For the last three years I've been working my ass off, sometimes putting in ten- or eleven-hour days. I still feel sort of middle of the pack at the office. Not particularly special, selected for promotions like Sasha, or beloved by my supervisors like our favorite coworker, Bryan. I'm barely on the radar for anyone with any real influence at the agency. One of the senior executives still calls me Neve, having misheard my name on day one. She was far too powerful for anyone to correct her that day, let alone at this point.

But my salary is solid; I've actually been able to pay down my student loans and even start beefing up my modest savings account. It's been good. Every other area of my life could use improvement, but I'm not looking for any big changes on the job front. Which is why the look on Sasha's face this morning is making me very, very nervous.

"There's a meeting at nine," Sasha says. "All staff. Email went out at eight thirty. Seriously, how do you not keep up with your email while you're on the train?"

"What's the meeting?" I ask, sidestepping her question. I don't want her giving me any more static about how much I still avoid my phone.

"Something big. Someone from corporate flew in for it."

"What? Why?"

Corporate means *New York.*

The Chicago office of Mercer & Mercer occupies two full floors of the August Building, a sleek office complex near Merchandise Mart. We look like a behemoth, but we're just a satellite. The hallowed Mercer & Mercer headquarters is in Manhattan, and has a much larger footprint. They only send someone to Chicago when there's a huge client pitch—or bad news to deliver.

We aren't prepping any huge new pitches this close to year's end. We're just in maintenance mode before we dim the lights from Christmas through New Year's. Which means that odds are, this is a bad-news visit.

"Not sure," Sasha says. "But it can't be good."

"Maybe we're all getting bonuses," I say hopefully.

No one has gotten a bonus in five years, thanks to a few little things like oh, pandemics and global supply chain shortages and the world generally being a dumpster fire all the time. The whole company was going to "continue indefinitely tightening the proverbial belt while celebrating every success," as the corporate office said in a clichéd email to the whole company last year. Apparently even though the world was back to normal—whatever that means—most employers retained a general sense of impending fiscal doom, and weren't feeling generous.

"Yeah, right," Sasha says flatly, waving my words away and killing my optimism with a flick of her slender wrist. "If anything, it's gonna be cuts. All the managers are losing their shit, trying to get their teams in on time."

Creatives, as a rule, are not known for their punctuality. Technically, Mercer & Mercer opens at eight thirty, but only the admin team is ever there that early. Those of us on the creative and account side who really want to be taken seriously, like Sasha and me, are there by nine. But a lot of the graphic designers and web folks don't roll in until closer to ten.

"Is Bryan in yet?" I ask, nervous.

Bryan Walsh-Alvarez is the third musketeer in Sasha's and my small social circle at work. He's a couple years younger than we are, which he never lets us forget. He's also the only one of us who's married. His husband, Carlos, is a doctor, which is another thing that Bryan makes sure to mention approximately every five minutes. Bryan's life and finances are secure, even if he were to suddenly find himself unemployed, which is one of the many reasons he's generally lax about getting to work on time. Legal weed now being readily available at a dispensary across from his building doesn't help, either.

"Actually, yes," Sasha says. "Julie got the heads-up last night and texted him at two in the morning."

Thank God Bryan's creative director, Julie, likes him so much, and knew to text him at two in the morning, when he'd still be up playing video games. Texting him at eight would have done nothing, because he would absolutely sleep right through it.

"Come on," Sasha says, as if I'm dawdling. I'm not, but I am struggling to keep up, because my long-legged friend hasn't let up on the pace for a single second. We're practically running up the sidewalk, our breath coming out in chilled cloud puffs, hard and fast. Have I always been this out of shape?

"Do you think there will be bagels at the meeting?" I ask.

"No," says Sasha.

"Killjoy," I pant, by now sweaty and freezing at the same time. "You sure you don't want my coat?"

"No, I want you to hurry your ass inside," Sasha says, stepping up the pace even more.

Three minutes later, at nine on the dot, we're squeezing ourselves into the conference room on the fifth floor—thankfully the elevator doors were opening just as we made it inside the building. It seems like everyone else from our office is already there. Every seat around the long mahogany conference room table is taken, so Sasha and I flatten ourselves against the wall just as a slick businessman in a suit that probably cost more than my monthly rent clears his throat, leans over, and raps three times on the table.

Everyone flinches.

Straightening up again, the suit smiles and steeples his fingers in front of his chest like he's about to announce his plans to stop Batman. His white hair is buzzed military short on the sides, oddly gelled and spiked on top. He's in his seventies, so he would've been much too old for frosted tips in the nineties, but I bet he had them anyway.

Across the room, Bryan catches my eye.

His freckled face is pallid, his reddish hair and button-down shirt both rumpled. I self-consciously smooth my own dark curls and give him a sympathetic look. Bryan is unaccustomed to being awake before nine, let alone being at work by then. He's also usually in ringer tees and ripped jeans, so the nice-ish shirt and khakis look bizarre on him. Julie must have told him to look presentable for the morning's big announcement. I wonder if the clothes actually belong to Carlos. And if maybe Carlos wore them yesterday, since they definitely have a picked-up-off-the-floor look. Bryan may have just grabbed them in a blind panic trying to get here on time.

Welcome to hell, Bryan mouths.

For real—where are the fucking bagels? I mouth back, and he struggles to hold back a snort.

"Thank you all for meeting on such short notice, such short notice," says the suit. He speaks quickly but inefficiently, repeating certain words and phrases in a way that sets my teeth one edge. "I'm Barry Ellis—Barry Ellis from the New York office. East Coast team sends their best, as always, as always. All right, all right! Let's cut to the chase."

Sasha and I exchange a glance.

Not much of an opener.

"Summer was a strong quarter. Nice work, nice work, good numbers, that's what we like to see. Well done," he says, with a bland cap-toothed smile too big for his tanned face. He looks like someone who just lost a senate race and refuses to concede. "Well done. But I'm not gonna sugarcoat it, Q3 was rough and Q4's looking worse. We might lose the Java-Lo account. I'm not saying we will, but we might. We might."

Shit.

The Java-Lo account? This makes everyone shift nervously in their seats, the low buzz of anxiety humming louder through the room. Java-Lo has been one of our biggest clients for years—a coffee company that most people on the street couldn't name, but whose industrial coffeemakers were in basically every hotel, restaurant, office building, and wealthy private kitchen in North America.

I don't know all the details, because I'm not on the official Java-Lo creative team. But it's the single biggest revenue line in the Chicago satellite budget. From packaging design to coffee-cocktail holiday guidebook copy to robust international marketing, literally everyone in our office touches it occasionally. It's in Sasha's primary portfolio. And Bryan's one of the lead designers for Java-Lo.

Bryan shoots me a nervous look.

I give him what I hope is a reassuring nod, but probably looks more like some sort of random twitch.

"So what we do wanna see is some real energy this month," says Barry, with a loud clap that makes one of the interns yelp aloud and quickly try to cover it with a coughing fit. "Some real energy! I know it's the holidays and blah blah, but this isn't the time to slack off, it's the time to double down. Show 'em what we're made of. And consider that we'll be looking at hours and impact if we have to make some tough calls in the New Year. In the New Year…if not before."

"Jesus," Sasha says, under her breath. "Is he seriously talking about firing people right before the holidays?"

I shake my head, mouth dry.

"All right, so," Barry says, looking around the room like a shark deciding what fish to rip through first. "Any questions?"

The room is clearly full of questions, but no one's going to open their mouth to ask one. Bryan mouths a silent one to me: *What the actual hell?*

Barry nods, satisfied. Like by keeping our mouths shut, we got the answer right.

"Good," he says. He claps his hands again, grinning that artificial grin. "Good. All right, back to it, then, team—and hey, hey! Merry Christmas!"

3

"So, who's polishing up their résumé?" Bryan asks as he refills his coffee from the gleaming spigot of a stainless steel Java-Lo 3000.

The futuristic machine was a gift from the company when we first landed the account. The slick logo—the engraved letters *JL* with three threads of stylized steam rising from them—is practically a foot tall on this massive thing. The Java-Lo 3000 is apparently a ten-grand coffeemaker. Turns out, there's a whole world of companies and mansion owners out there that can drop ten thousand dollars on a coffeemaker. Which is kind of stomach turning, but is also the reason I'm able to pay my bills.

I dig around in the office fridge and find a fruit tray someone shoved in there, leftovers from a client pitch yesterday afternoon. I put some pineapple and melons on a paper plate, but they look too sad to eat.

"Guess we all should be," I say, trying to make light of it. "High-turnover industry anyway."

Bryan raises an eyebrow. He's taken a few personal days

lately, and I wonder if he's already been out there chasing another job. Maybe my comment hit a little too close to home if he's keeping it close to the vest for now. He doesn't say anything else, but it makes me feel mildly better that maybe he has one foot out the door already, much as I'd miss him as a coworker.

"I cannot lose this job," Sasha says, looking grim.

Her perfectly lined eyes are closed, like she's warding off some unseen evil. Her high cheekbones look sharper than usual. Everything about her is more angular than it used to be. Sasha's always been pretty fit—she's a marathon runner who doesn't have a car and walks or bikes everywhere in good weather—but this seems like a new level of svelte. It's hard to tell under all her winter layers, but she must have dropped at least ten pounds. When did she lose that weight?

I know we shouldn't comment on bodies, so I decide not to ask her about it. Not right now, especially. And meanwhile, here I am, eating again. Ugh. I should really go to the gym. No one's seen my cheekbones in years, and the word *angular* has never once been used to describe me. *Zaftig* is a more apt descriptor.

I look at my plate of sad fruit, which is somehow empty. I set it down and wrap my arms around myself self-consciously. I suck in my gut a little, but almost immediately give up.

"I get it," Bryan says sympathetically. "Losing your job would totally suck. It's not like you have a real cushion. Like, say, being married to a doctor, which I highly recommend—"

"Shut up, Bryan," I say, elbowing him and giving Sasha a reassuring nod. "Hey. Sash. You're not gonna lose your job."

"You don't know that, Eve," Sasha says, shaking her head. There are dark circles under her eyes, another detail I somehow hadn't noticed earlier. She must not be sleeping well. Maybe I *will* ask her about it. The sleep stuff, anyway. When we're not at the office.

Although lately, I pretty much only see her at the office.

She was dating this guy Emmet for a while, and when they got together we saw less and less of her. After close to a year, she and Emmet split sometime this summer, thank God. She's been more present the last couple of months, but still hasn't fully emerged from her ghosting phase.

"Java-Lo's the biggest thing on my docket, by far. It's like eighty percent of my portfolio," Sasha says, voice low.

I can tell she's genuinely upset, but I'm not sure why she, of all people, is so nervous. Sasha's at the top of her game, and everyone knows it. She's constantly headhunted by other agencies. She's smart about money. Sure, she has a penchant for expensive clothing, and she bought a gorgeous, overpriced condo in a doorman-guarded upscale Lakeview building last year. She has some pretty steep expenses. And she enjoys fancy dinners and going out on the town—or at least she used to, up until she went into hermit mode with her now-ex-boyfriend. I don't know if he was a full-on asshole or just a real homebody, but when they were together, social Sasha disappeared from the scene.

Bryan and I were pretty sure her boyfriend must have basically moved in with her and cajoled her into Netflix-and-chilling nightly. We joked about it, but the fact was that it really stung. Especially since she wasn't there for me when my dad died. She came to the funeral, but that was it. No shiva visit. No showing up with ice cream to just let me cry. Those first few months, I was reeling, and she wasn't there to catch me.

But she broke up with Emmet months ago. And I recall reading a highly scientific article in *Seventeen* magazine a thousand years ago that said it should only take you half the time you were in a relationship to get over it. Together less than a year? You should be over it in under six months. She's got to be over the breakup by now, and she'll survive whatever cuts Mercer & Mercer may make. Personally and professionally, Sasha is my friend who will always be fine.

Whether he realizes it or not, thanks to Carlos, Bryan is also now more financially and emotionally stable than I am. I wonder if any of my friends are aware of how much I'm struggling these days. Probably not, since I've deliberately failed to mention it.

"It's not the *only* thing on your docket," I point out. "And we haven't lost them yet. And the whole leadership team loves you."

"Yeah," Bryan agrees. "If any of us are getting cut, it's probably you, Eve."

"Bryan!" Sasha snaps. "Don't say that."

"What? It's true. Last in, first out," Bryan says, matter-of-fact.

"I've been here three years," I say. My inferiority complex about being a non-standout employee suddenly flares like a dangerous fire in my chest. "I'm not the 'last in.' Nancy just started here, like, three months ago! And there are interns, and that new receptionist whose name we haven't even learned yet, and…and I'm not even *on* the Java-Lo account."

"Yeah, but everyone working on Java-Lo's been here *forever*," Bryan says. "They'll probably want to move our copywriters over to other clients, and cut someone else from some other team to make room for them. And Big Boss Denise still thinks your name is Neve."

"Shit," I say, a lifetime of culturally ingrained paranoia making me think, *Oh my God, Bryan's right.* Our agency moves people from account to account all the time. Maybe I really am expendable in this scenario, even if I'm not on the struggling Java-Lo account.

I look desperately around the kitchen. Despite having already inhaled all of the fruit, I very much want a doughnut.

"You're going to be fine," Sasha says, although she doesn't sound super convincing. "We're all going to be fine, we just…

just need to keep our heads down. Generate some good work this week. And keep showing up on time."

She looks at Bryan.

"What?" Bryan says. "I get to work on time! The office opens at ten, right?"

Sasha and I snort in stereo, and I'm grateful to Bryan for managing to lighten the mood.

"Okay," Sasha says, refilling her mug from the Java-Lo machine and tilting her head toward the door. "We should get back to our desks and just...get through the day."

"Thanks for the pep talk, coach," Bryan says, saluting.

The rest of the workday is blurry. A series of email responses, a kickoff meeting for a new but small-budget client, drafting some copy for another small client's local radio spots, all with the buzzing backdrop of coworkers whispering about who might get cut.

Mercer & Mercer occupies the seventeenth and eighteenth floors of the August Building, and the layout on both of our floors is exactly the same. Bryan and I are both on the eighteenth floor, with all the other copywriters and designers. His seat is six down from mine. Sasha is on the seventeenth floor, with the account executives, media buyers, and administrative team.

Our office is the open-concept style popular with so many agencies, even though employees universally hate it because you have zero privacy. The executives have private offices tucked into the corners, near the breakroom and the conference rooms where client meetings are held. The peons, though, are seated in ergonomic chairs at long, wide, gleaming-chrome tables in the center of each floor's massive main room. We have partitions around our workspaces, but they're clear. So it cuts down on sound, just a little, but you're totally visible to your colleagues on either side of you at all times—and also to the person directly across the table from you.

The outer walls of the building are floor-to-ceiling windows, which adds to the fishbowl feeling of the place. The open floor plan and copious panes of glass make for pretty minimal interior design options—ironic, for a creative agency. On our limited wall space, the decor consists of framed prints from our flashiest ad campaigns and the gleaming awards we've won for said campaigns, which feels self-congratulatory and totally cringe.

"Invitation to the holiday party!"

I look up from my desk, confused. Nancy is beaming down at me. She's a new hire, a media buyer who came from Ogilvy and has a ton of good contacts but is annoying as hell. She's what my bubbe would have called a *kibitzer zhlobeleh*—a gauche little gossip.

Nancy is a box blonde, a few years older than I am, which puts her squarely in her forties. But she dresses like she's in her twenties, and aggressively so. Today she's in thigh-high black leather boots and a red-and-green pleated minidress. Her hair is pulled into two messy ponytails on each side of her head, and she's wearing a red Santa hat.

Last in, first out, I remember Bryan saying.

Here's hoping.

"We're doing a river cruise!" Nancy crows.

"A river cruise...in December?" I ask, raising an eyebrow dubiously and wondering how long she's lived in the Midwest. "This is Chicago. That sounds terrible."

"Oh, it'll be *fun*," Nancy says, beaming. Her big white teeth are distractingly bright. Can't be a home whitening treatment. She must pay a dentist for that. "And we're all going to wear Santa hats to keep us warm. It's Friday night. The invitation is tucked into the brim. Ho ho ho, here you go!"

Before I can stop her, she jams a Santa hat on my head, then prances off to torture Talamieka, the designer to my immediate right. Talamieka is a talented artist who doesn't suffer fools, and I almost want to hear whatever cutting response she might shoot at Nancy. But I'm also suddenly really tired. I glance at the time on my computer. It's after five.

I'm going home.

I walk past Bryan's desk, but he's already gone. No surprise there—if forced to come in early, Bryan would absolutely feel justified in leaving early. The dude is devoutly opposed to putting in a full workday. He was a quiet quitter before it was cool. Which makes me nervous. I know he'll ultimately be fine if he's let go, but I'd miss the hell out of him. He's a pain in the ass, but he's also the only person who can get me to smile when I'm in a foul mood. And he's good at his job, which means everyone wants to work with him. So hopefully he'll be okay. But I can't help wishing that for once, Bryan would take something as seriously as the rest of us do.

While it's not a shock that Bryan exited early, I'm surprised that when I swing by Sasha's desk downstairs, she's already gone, too. She never leaves before I do. Most days I'm begging her to leave while she insists she just has to send "one more email." I'm glad she's not tied to her desk today, for once, although I wish she would've buzzed up to my desk to see if I wanted to sneak out with her. I think, again, about her hollow cheekbones, and hope my best friend is doing okay. I think about texting her, seeing if she wants to grab a drink.

But it's cold outside, and I didn't sleep well last night. My own social muscles are still pretty atrophied from my past year of grief and lethargy. Sasha probably has other plans, anyway.

I'll do it tomorrow, I think, and head for the train.

4

By the time I board the train at half past five, it's pitch-black outside. It's typically dark by four thirty this time of year, which is one of the worst things about living in the Midwest. I dread daylight savings every year. "Fall back" feels like a personal attack on anyone with even a mild touch of seasonal affective disorder. Whenever I got the winter blues and asked my father why the hell he'd settled our family in one of the coldest regions of the country, he'd always grin and say, *Because Florida has alligators.*

"Merry Christmas!"

A disheveled woman steps onto the train, jingling a red bucket. Everyone on the train collectively shifts in their seats, averting their eyes. This time of year, Chicago's homeless population embarks on the CTA more often than usual, escaping the cold and hoping for generosity from commuters in a holiday mood.

Determined not to be ignored, the woman shakes her bucket again. The sparse coins within rattle, and a harsh metallic sound echoes through the train car, making me wince. The bucket woman looks around, eyes wet and beady, hoping at least a few of the sluggish evening commuters crowding the train car will toss some money her way.

"Come on, come on, s'almost Christmas," rasps the panhandling woman. "Christmas! Remember Christmas? I'm talking about Christmas…"

Feeling guilty, I dig around in my pocket. I try to be subtle about it, not wanting to call attention to this action. I almost never have cash, and don't want to get the woman's hopes up.

When my fingers close around a stray quarter at the bottom of my pocket, I hesitate. Giving just a quarter seems shitty. Plus, my apartment building has coin-op laundry, and I need six quarters to run the washer and another six for a dryer cycle. Twelve quarters for every single load of laundry. Sasha jokingly calls me a quarter hoarder. I'd honestly rather give this woman a ten-dollar bill, but I don't have any paper money. Only one lonely coin.

My quarter lands with a dull clunk in the bucket.

The woman looks up at me. Her skin is leathery, and her small blue-black eyes bore into my own. Patchy gray hair pokes out from under her black knit cap, and a few wiry strands twist up from her chin. She's wearing several layers of ratty clothing, but no actual winter coat. I look down, trying to avoid her penetrating gaze. Her shoes are worn through at the toes, and the sight of her stocking feet poking through them sends shame coursing through me.

"Look up," she says.

Her voice sounds different. Accented. Unexpectedly familiar. It's hard to tell in just two syllables. But her words are a command I cannot ignore. I look up, and startle.

The old woman's face is no longer her own.

Her eyes have shifted from cobalt to the steely shade of an overcast day. Her puckered lips look thinner, primmer. She holds her head more erect, looking at me with a firm, tender regard. My vision blurs and I choke back a strangled cry, because all of a sudden the old woman isn't some random panhandler.

She's my grandmother.

"Bubbe?" I gasp.

She nods, ever so slightly. Her eyes meet mine and they're all I see. Everything else fades away, watercolor and shadow, insubstantial, gone. My grandmother's gaze is familiar and determined. She has something to say and she wants to make sure I hear it.

"Make..." she says, so soft that only I can hear her.

"Make what?" I whisper, terrified.

"Make—"

The train lists sharply around a curve in the track, and I stumble backward, head dropping toward my chest as I fumble for my footing. When I look up again, my grandmother is gone. There is only the wary panhandler, staring at me with unfamiliar eyes, blue-black and watery. A stranger.

"Nothing, nothing, nothing," she mutters, looking briefly into the bucket before snapping her head back up toward me, disgruntled. "That's all you got?"

Her hard glare makes me flinch, but I'm still so struck by what's just happened that I don't look away from her.

"Bubbe?" I whisper again, trembling.

"I know you got more on you," says the woman, who doesn't seem to hear me at all.

"Sorry," I say, taking a step back, the spell fully broken. Or maybe nothing had happened at all, and I imagined the whole thing.

I haven't been sleeping well, and my mind *has* had a tendency to drift this past year. Could I have possibly nodded off while standing there on the train? Maybe. My heart is still hammering away in my chest, telling me that something is wrong, but honestly—everything feels wrong, all the time. So it's hard to trust my gut these days.

"You got more," demands the woman.

"I don't have any cash," I mumble, still reeling. "Not on me."

"Yeah, right. Where's your Christian spirit?"

Well, *that* officially confirms that this old woman isn't my grandmother.

"I said, where's your Christian spirit, asshole?" she repeats, louder.

It must be a line she uses a lot. I bet it works on some people. I bite my tongue, because saying *actually, I'm Jewish*, would confirm: *yep, I'm an asshole.* Or worse, it might make *all* Jewish people sound like assholes, thanks to the constant representative responsibility all minorities carry. When I instead say nothing, she shakes her head, disgusted.

"You got plenty more. I can tell."

I want to insist that I really don't have any more, not *on* me. If I had more, I'd give it to her—honest to God, I would. Even though she's nothing like my grandmother, she might be someone's grandmother—and even if she has no family, she's still a person. Still worth something. There's a very real part of me that wants to tell her that. A part of me that knows she's only yelling and cursing because she's tired, hungry, not getting the mental and physical healthcare she deserves. I want to tell her that I know that, and feel awful about it.

You are worth something. I'm sorry your life is hard. I know how it feels to be invisible. I know how it feels to be lonely. I'm sorry I don't have any cash. I have credit cards, though. Come with me and I'll buy you dinner.

That's what my father would have done. He was always helping people out, doing the right thing even when it wasn't the easy thing. For a slim half second, I think that maybe I, too, can do hard things.

But the panhandling woman is already pulling open the

door that connects our train car to the adjacent one, rattling her bucket for a new audience. A cutting breeze rushes into the car. I hear the old woman call "Who's a giver here?" as the door slides shut behind her. She's gone.

Everyone's gone, I think.

Then my stomach gurgles another loud request for food. A request I'll be able to fill, over and over, while others go hungry. The thought makes me hate myself. I put my hand over my middle, ashamed of my hunger, my stasis, my utter inability to do anything that might actually make a difference. This season doesn't feel merry or bright.

It just feels cold.

5

By the time I make it home, I'm already envisioning an evening spent in full-on goblin mode. The awful day of office tension, bookended by strange encounters on the train, has sent me spiraling back toward the moody dark corner I've spent too much time in this past year. My stomach rumbles yet again, solidifying my plans for the night: put on sweatpants, order takeout to be left in the lobby, and avoid any and all further interactions with actual humans.

Crossing the threshold into my building allows me to finally breathe a small sigh of relief. Imperfect as it is, I love my apartment building. Tucked right on the border of the Lincoln Square and Albany Park neighborhoods, it's more than a hundred years old. Fifty units, brick exterior, the split structure forming a U-shape around a haphazardly maintained courtyard.

There were some renovations to the property twentyish years ago, so the bathrooms and kitchens are dated but mostly fine. The basements and subbasements—each section of the U has its own—are scary as hell. That's where our washer and dryers are. The coin-op situation sucks, but at least they're in the building and I don't have to haul my laundry to a laundromat like when I rented a crappy studio apartment in Andersonville.

I have two keys, one for the exterior door, one for my own apartment. Somehow I always mix them up, jamming the interior key in first, cursing and realizing my error each time before successfully sliding the exterior key into the lock. I've lived here for three years, and it still happens every damn time. Sighing as I pull the wrong key out of the hole for the hundred-thousandth time, I'm startled when the door handle pulls back from me.

"Locked out?"

I look up, and all the fatigue and frustrations of the day melt away. Intense brown eyes, sheltered by thick black brows, are looking down at me. The eyes are set above a strong nose and a perennially five-o'-clock-shadowed jaw, and beneath a full head of thick black hair I badly want to touch.

This is the knee-weakening face of my new neighbor, Hot Josh.

"No, I just—wrong key," I say, like the idiot I am. "I always try the wrong one first, they look just the same—"

"You need a color cover," he says, and I stare at him blankly. What the hell is a color cover? He holds the door open a little wider. "Come on in, then, it's cold."

His British accent nearly makes me pass out. It's so crisp, making every sentence he utters sound confident and well-informed. Even when he uses words or phrases I can't quite parse, like *chuffed*. Or *color cover*. There are all sorts of words I'd love to hear him say in that sexy, proper accent—particularly improper ones, like *May I rip your clothes off, luv?*

I step into the cramped lobby of our building. Hot Josh has a fistful of envelopes and grocery circulars in his hand; he's obviously down here to retrieve his mail from the dingy silver mailboxes lining the wall. He's not wearing a winter coat, just a tight black T-shirt that shows off his muscular chest. The cold breeze blowing in along with me causes him to wrap his arms around himself, biceps flexing. He's not tall—not short, but not tall—and he's built as hell. Seeing him this close up always gets me flustered. I try not to stare at the curls of dark chest hair peeking out of the deep V-neckline of his shirt.

In every encounter I've had with Hot Josh since he moved in here, I'm pretty sure I've come off as mentally unwell. I've tripped over nothing, laughed maniacally when he told me he moved here from Milwaukee—why the hell would I find that funny?—and reflexively deployed my most pathetic introduction when we first exchanged names.

Hello, I'm Josh, he said, like a normal human being.

I'm Eve, I said, *like the woman blamed for the entire downfall of humanity.*

Ah, he said politely. *Well, I'll…certainly remember that.*

And now on top of all of that, I've proven that despite being a long-term tenant here, I somehow still don't even know what key unlocks which door in the building.

"Heading upstairs, Eve?" Josh asks, raising one of those thick, dark brows. His arms are still crossed over his chest, hand still clutching his mail. He looks mildly amused, but also cold. And inquisitive. I love the sound of my name in his mouth.

Which is why I gaze at him for another thirty seconds before I realize that when I'd clomped in from outside, I'd positioned myself in the doorframe leading from the lobby to the stairwell, totally blocking his way.

"Sorry," I say, blushing hotly as I step aside. I wish I could think of something clever to say, but I can't. The burning in my cheeks feels ridiculous. This isn't middle school. I am thirty-nine years old and a professional copywriter, for God's sake. I should not get all tongue-tied just because there's a cute guy in the vicinity.

But there's something more than just good looks when it comes to Hot Josh. I can't put my finger on what it is, but there's—something. An electricity snapping in the air as soon as he's nearby. All of a sudden I'm thirteen again, crushing on a boy too cool for me but secretly believing he'll someday realize I'm more interesting than the cheerleaders. When he's around, I always feel like something's about to happen.

Of course, nothing has ever happened.

If my track record is any indication, nothing ever will. It's rare for me to crush so hard on a stranger, though. I'm more prone to falling for a close friend, pining silently for years, then buying him a super nice wedding gift when he inevitably marries someone else. Which is probably why until recently, my other go-to move was going home with some random guy I met at a bar or party, not because I was into him but because it was better than going home alone.

But for the past year, love and sex have just been off the table. I've heard that some people try to screw their grief away, but I went in the opposite direction. The idea of romance has just held zero interest for me. My body wants food, and sleep, and to be left alone. It definitely has *not* wanted to be touched, or explored, or seen naked. Honestly, the idea of hooking up with anyone has seemed both exhausting and disgusting.

Until I saw Hot Josh.

So maybe he can end my long, miserable streak of solitude. Maybe he'll also break my pining-or-settling patterns. After all, he isn't a close friend, and he isn't some rando at a bar. He's something exciting and in-between, someone I see daily but barely know.

I've picked up precious few details about him, scattered here and there. He moved here from Milwaukee—though his delicious British accent means he clearly didn't grow up in Wisconsin—and works in consulting, whatever that means. He travels sometimes, but I don't know if it's for work or a long-distance relationship or what. Technically, I don't know if he's single. Although I do know he moved in alone, and no one else has been in or out of his place in the two months he's been there.

Not that I'm constantly monitoring his place.

I'm just observant.

And home most evenings.

"Yep, going upstairs," I say.

"Small world, upstairs is where I'm headed as well," says Hot Josh.

I bite my tongue hard to keep another maniacal laugh from flying out of me. I wish I had some cute slim-girl giggle. But I don't. Just the zaftig guffaw I inherited from my father. It's a truly unsexy laugh that lands somewhere between hyena and Homer Simpson.

Remaining mercifully silent, I just give Hot Josh a tight little nod. I'm going to have to learn how to keep my shit together around this guy, because he didn't just move into my building; he moved directly across the hall from me. These unexpected encounters are going to keep on happening. And I can't just be constantly swallowing my braying chuckle. I'll eventually choke.

Just then, Hot Josh leans in toward me. For one insane second I think he's going for a kiss. I squeeze my eyes shut— *just let it happen just let it happen just let it happen*—then after an awkwardly long moment, I open them. That's when I see that Josh was only leaning over me to push open the stairwell door, and is now holding it open, to let me go first. Waiting for me to move my stupid ass.

I walk past him, under his arm, like we're doing the limbo or something. We're so close we're almost touching. Taking the first step into the stairwell, cheeks burning, I realize that Josh is going to be walking behind me up the two flights of stairs to our second-floor apartments. Grateful that at least my puffy winter coat means he won't get much of a show, I hurry up the stairs. I'm sweaty and fighting not to pant aloud by the time I reach my door. Fumbling for my key, I jam it into the lock—and, of course, it's the wrong damn key.

Dammit.

"Door stuck?" Josh asks from behind me.

"Yep, just sticky, that's all," I lie. I turn around and give him a stupid little wave. "All good, thanks."

"See you around, then," says Josh. "Oh, and someday you'll have to tell me what it's like in the North Pole."

I stare at him blankly for a moment.

Then my fingers go slowly to my head. I'd completely forgotten about the freaking Santa hat Nancy had assaulted me with earlier. It's still perched jauntily on my head, probably making me look like a deranged elf. Josh smiles before smoothly slipping the right key into his lock on the first try, and disappearing into his apartment.

6

I head straight for the fridge before I even take off my coat. My encounter with Hot Josh has my stomach churning. I haven't put in a take-out order yet and it's past six; delivery will take at least an hour at this point. Maybe I won't order in tonight. Maybe I'll actually cook something. At the very least, I need a nosh to take the edge off.

Everything feels better with a full belly, I can almost hear my grandmother say. *Have a little bite.*

When I was a little girl, Bubbe constantly slipped me food. An extra slice of toast in the morning. A second sandwich hidden beneath the first one in my lunch box. Apple slices tucked in a napkin, placed carefully into my pocket, in case I needed a little something on the way to school. Even though I didn't need it, I always took the food she offered because I saw it for what it really was: a way for my brusque immigrant grandmother to say *I love you.*

A day like today, I really wish I was coming home to Bubbe.

God, what I wouldn't give right now for a snack and some solid advice from her.

My bubbe was a woman with slate gray eyes, a spine of steel, and blue-inked numbers on her papery arms. Her years as a child in one of Hitler's camps had left their mark on her in more ways than one. She had no ability to express affection verbally. She made sure that I knew she cared about me by always being there. Listening with such rapt attention that it was almost unsettling. And relentlessly ensuring that I was well-fed; that before my stomach could even express interest in sustenance, it was already full again.

In the twenty-plus years since her death, she's still someone I think about daily. She's right up there with my father, vying for the dubious distinction of being the most influential person in my life. Bubbe was my greatest protector, Dad my greatest source of unconditional love. With both of them gone, it feels like I enter every situation without a shield or shepherd.

I love my mother, but we've never been as good at connecting with one another. Dad and Bubbe were the ones who could intuit my fears, tell me what I needed to hear—make me laugh, in the case of my father, or light a fire under my ass, in the case of my grandmother. Both were valuable contributions. Now that they're both gone, I feel rudderless. That's probably why I keep having dreams about Bubbe. My mind must be trying to find some way to comfort itself.

But I've never hallucinated a vision of her on the train before.

Make... the woman on the train—or in my hallucination—had said.

Make what, though?

Make something of your life.

Make me proud.

Make a difference in the world.

Whatever this vision of my grandmother was telling me to do, I guarantee I haven't been doing it. Unless she was going to tell me to *make a sandwich* or *make sure to remain alone and childless*. In which case, I've been doing Bubbe proud.

My thoughts are interrupted by another growl from my stomach, right on cue. Why am I still hungry, when I had breakfast, lunch, and snacked all day at the office? I hate how quickly something I've already taken care of can come back. Appetites are like weeds, or zombies. Cut them down and they spring right back up again.

Hunger, it's a powerful thing, Bubbe once observed, watching me wolf down my fifth or sixth snack of the day. *Hunger knows what it wants. Hunger has teeth.*

I wondered how hungry she had been when she was a young girl, starving in the camps. How brutally hunger's teeth had ravaged her small stomach. She knew all too well what the pangs of actual ravenousness felt like, and never wanted me to feel anything like it.

Trying to tamp down all my guilty memories of too many meals consumed, I stare into the fridge to see what I can throw together for dinner. Empty milk jug, some expired condiments, a half-full jar of peanut butter, one lonely Sketchbook brewery growler. Looks like in spite of my momentary motivation to cook, I'll be ordering Thai.

Again.

I dig into my pocket for my phone, giving silent thanks for food delivery apps, the only reason I like to turn my phone on these days. I know eventually I'll have to start more reliably keeping my phone on, but I'm not ready. Besides, only my mother really knows how often it's off. She calls me, but everyone else texts and just thinks I'm slow to respond. I know it bothers my mother; she's worried that in an emergency, she won't be able to reach me.

Sure enough, when I turn my phone on, there are three new voicemails—all from my mother. HOT MAMA RENA is how her name appears, every time she calls or texts. It's the name my father entered for her when he gave me my first thick-brick phone in high school. That's how I've had her in my contacts ever since.

My rumbling gut momentarily clenches at the sight of that name, over and over. A little over a year ago, the Saturday after Thanksgiving, I was out with my friends and left my phone at home. When I got back to my apartment, I had five missed calls from Mom, along with a text saying 911 CALL NOW. When I called her back, I found out about Dad's heart attack. She could barely get the words out to tell me he was already gone.

It's the sort of thing that should have made me better about keeping my phone close by, but it's only made me even more phone averse. I always hated the phone, and my loathing for the modern ball-and-chain has deepened over the past bitter year. I tell my friends it's a moral stand: *I wish society didn't expect us all to be so constantly available; I don't want to be controlled by this stupid little thing.* But the truth is, I can't remember the last time a phone call brought me good news, so I'd rather just chuck the thing out the window and be done with it.

I open the fridge again and pull out the peanut butter jar. If I have to call my mother before ordering dinner, I need something to tide me over. I dig a spoon out of the one and only drawer in my tiny kitchen. Then, steeling myself, I call my mother.

"Eve, call your sister," Mom says as soon as she picks up, bypassing any actual greeting.

"Hi, Mom," I say stubbornly.

"Hello," she retorts. "Call your sister."

"Why do I need to call Rosie?" I ask, confused. "I don't have any messages from her. *You're* the one who called me three times."

"To tell you to call your sister!" Mom says, already exasperated. "Did you even listen to my voicemails?"

"Mom, come on," I say. "You know my policy. I never listen to voicemails. No one should. Barbaric practice."

"For Christ's sake, Eve," Mom says with a massive sigh.

It's a familiar sound.

I can picture her in her kitchen in Winnetka, shaking her head of silver curls, perpetually baffled at my ineptitude. If she knew that at this very moment, I was standing in my still-zipped winter coat eating peanut butter out of a jar while planning my next take-out order, she would be appalled. For her dinner, she's probably sipping a plant-based shake, pulled from her pristine, carefully curated fridge. When Dad was alive, the fridge was always full of leftovers—he was a hell of a cook—and the pantry was full of snacks. Now that he's gone, there's never real food in the house. My mother is terrible in the kitchen. She exists primarily on green drinks, prepackaged salads, and vague memories of meals gone by.

The kitchen isn't the only thing in her life that she's reduced to practically nothing. My mother has stripped the whole house of its once-charmingly-cluttered glory. Immediately after our week of shiva, she cleared out Dad's stuff from every closet, every drawer, every last corner. She joined the JCC gym, dropped twenty pounds, and is now training for a half marathon. She keeps the house and herself immaculate, not wanting to bring in anything that might add clutter or character. I imagine right about then, she's smoothing a nonexistent wrinkle from a tailored pastel pantsuit, looking around to make sure there's no mess she somehow missed.

"I'm sorry I'm so exhausting," I tell my mother around a mouthful of peanut butter. I wonder if I can put her on speaker so I can pull up the Grubhub app while we chat. "I know how tired I make you. Maybe you should go lie down."

"Hilarious," says my mother. "I can't, I'm having the house photographed tomorrow. He's coming first thing in the morning. The photographer my office always uses is so busy these days, he's really doing me a favor, but he wanted to come by at seven so I have a bunch of staging to do tonight."

"You're...having the house photographed?"

"I have to, if I ever want to get it listed."

This takes me aback. Even though I know Mom should ultimately sell the house and get a condo or something, the idea of her actually taking a step toward getting rid of my childhood home stings. I wonder how soon she's planning to make this happen. I try to keep my tone casual.

"When are you thinking about listing the place?"

"Not yet," my mother says, her own tone unreadable. "I just figured—can't hurt to get the photos done. While it's clean and all. Looking its best."

"When does it not look its best?"

With her as its only inhabitant, the house is always immaculate. It's also inarguably a nice piece of real estate, even if some of the design is distinctly dated. It's in a neighborhood that's become incredibly expensive, and it will definitely go for a stupid amount of money if Mom decides to sell. But it was cheap when she and my father bought it as newlyweds. *A real bargain*, Dad always said with pride.

The last time they did any renovation was right after my grandmother died. Just like with my father, there was no keening or wailing from my mother when we lost Bubbe. Just a stoic week of sitting shiva, then Mom rolled up her sleeves. Without consulting the rest of us, she quietly purged all of my grandmother's old-world doilies, afghans, and antique lamps from the house. Next, her grief manifested as a deep need to gut rehab the spaces where Bubbe had loomed largest. Which obviously meant she had to start with the kitchen.

I need something modern, she said when convincing my father to start getting quotes from contractors. *This place feels haunted, David, and I swear to God I can't live with all her ghosts anymore.*

So, they redid a third of the house in the late nineties: the kitchen, the dining room, the bedroom and bathroom that had been designated as Bubbe's when she moved in with us. After that, they never updated anything again.

The pristinely preserved rehab job is why Sasha calls my parents' house a "*Friends*-era time capsule." The kitchen is full of particularly strong choices. It has large black-and-white tile flooring, cherry red curtains blooming like poppies in the windows, all-white cabinets, and black Formica countertops. It's a definite vibe.

Not that I should judge. It's not as if I'm some revolutionary interior designer. My apartment has "vintage charm," which is to say it's very old, but has some character. All the doorways are arched. There are built-in bookshelves on each side of the bricked-over fireplace. The crown molding is original to the building, which is lovely, but so are the windows, which means the place is freezing eight months out of the year. I have cozy blankets scattered throughout my apartment, since I'm in constant need of a little extra warmth.

My apartment has made its way to shabby-chic, though its inhabitant remains merely shabby. A few years ago I finally got rid of my cobbled-together living room furniture and bought a modest but matching mint green sofa and love seat. Sasha gifted me some accent pillows in celebration. And at Bryan's insistence, for my birthday last year I framed the small collection of art prints from local Chicago artists—including Bryan—that I'd purchased at various art fairs and small-dollar charity auctions over the years. Bryan and Carlos helped me arrange them artfully on the wall. *Never turn down a designer willing to help elevate your look*, Bryan wisely advised.

Life- and decor-wise, I get by with a little help from my friends. But I wish, sometimes, that I had some of my grandmother's things. That my mother hadn't gotten rid of them all. Come to think of it, my apartment looks a helluva lot like my bubbe's old house. An actual item from her collection would complete the look.

But thanks to my mother, it's all gone. And now she'll also be selling my childhood home. Something deep in the pit of my stomach shifts uncomfortably.

"But, like," I say, chewing my lip, "are you really going to sell the place?"

"Eventually," says my mother. "*Any*way. Call your sister."

"Why am I calling Rosie?" I ask.

"She needs you."

"She hasn't called me."

"You're her maid of honor," Mom says. "And the wedding is this weekend."

"If she needs something, she'll let me know," I say, hearing the snap in my voice.

I can't help it. My little sister has never once had a problem advocating for herself. The only time she ever calls me is to ask for a favor. *Hey, can I get a ride? Hey, do you mind if I borrow your car? Hey, can you pick me up from O'Hare?* Now that I think about it, almost all of the favors have to do with using my Subaru.

Rosie is six years younger than I am. It's a big enough gap that we barely grew up together. When I was ten, she was four; when I was starting high school, she was still getting visits from the tooth fairy. She hadn't even had her bat mitzvah yet when I left for college. Some part of me sees her as perpetually twelve. Her tendency to unabashedly whine when she isn't getting what she wants, to ask for yet another favor without ever saying thank you for the last one, and to somehow still always be everyone's favorite, doesn't help alter that perception.

Plus, she's blonde.

And thin.

And getting married while I remain terminally single.

"Just call her," my mother says.

"Fine," I sigh.

"Are we still on for lunch tomorrow?"

"Are you still paying?"

"Ha-ha," Mom says, clicking her tongue. "Don't be late, please, I have to get my nails done after we eat. It's a busy week. Speaking of which, you gonna tell me who you're bringing to the wedding?"

I wince.

When I sent in my RSVP to the wedding, I was a little tipsy. That's a lie: I was shit-faced drunk on half-off well vodka after a night out with Bryan and Carlos. In spite of Sasha telling me for weeks that it was a terrible idea, I had, in my alcohol-soaked state, RSVP'd to the wedding with a plus-one. Even though I had no idea just who that plus-one would be.

Didn't matter, because the idea of attending my little sister's wedding solo was more than I could stomach. After all, I was coming out of the worst year of my life. Losing my father, putting on almost twenty pounds of grief weight, world affairs being an ever-growing dumpster fire, Sasha ghosting me while she was with Emmet, and feeling fully abandoned as my fortieth birthday approached. Everything was already too awful. Showing up alone to the big family wedding was not an option.

I'll find a date, dammit, I promised myself.

Rosie's impending nuptials have made me feel deeply insecure about my singlehood. I wasn't expecting it to be so bruising. After all, Rosie was always the social butterfly—queen of her summer camp cabin as a kid, president of her sorority in college, popular fitness instructor now. I've always been more introverted than my baby sister. But despite all her extroverted joiner tendencies, Rosie was also the one who swore up and down she'd never get married.

My childhood was the one spent fantasizing about my wedding, my future children, my life as a wife (and veterinarian/investigative journalist, two other life goals that have yet to materialize). I was the one with the steady high school boy-friend, Marc, who broke my heart when he told me he didn't want to do the long-distance thing in college. I was the one who found another steady boyfriend in college, Derek, who I truly thought was The One—right up until he spent his ju-nior year abroad and emailed to let me know about his new Spanish girlfriend, Sofia.

In spite of all the early heartbreak, it was me who kept put-ting herself out there for years, trying to meet someone. It's not fair that I'm the one who wound up sad and alone. And Rosie's the one getting married. On the eve of my fortieth birthday, barely a year after we lost our father. All things considered, at the very least I needed a goddamn wedding date.

Even if he wasn't *The* One, I needed *Some*-One. That's why I RSVP'd for two. Besides, I had plenty of time to find a date, I told myself. Six whole weeks.

That was five weeks ago.

Since then, I've tried literally everything. I went on three first dates in rapid succession, none of which led to a second date. I called two exes, one of whom mumbled some bullshit excuse about work travel, the other of whom awkwardly in-formed me he was recently engaged. I congratulated him and hung up, wondering what his stupid fiancée had that I didn't. The next night I was out at the bar and some young ruddy-faced Irish guy told me I was "an exotic beauty," and instead of laughing in his face I asked him if he had a favorite Jewish holiday. He stared at me blankly and then walked off, presum-ably to hit on someone a little less "exotic."

I even asked Bryan if he'd be willing to play my straight date for the night. He gave me a very sad look, and a kiss on the cheek, and told me that there was no way he could pull it off once he hit the dance floor. Which, I had to admit, was a fair point.

I've got no one.

"It's a surprise," I tell my mother, who snorts in response.

"A surprise."

"Yep."

"You're lucky it's buffet and not a plated dinner."

"That's what they call me, Lucky Eve," I say, stomach rumbling louder at the sound of the word *buffet*.

I jam the last spoonful of peanut butter into my mouth. I can barely track what my mother's saying at this point. All I can think about is what I'm going to order for dinner tonight. Pad Thai? No. Pad Se Ewe? Maybe. Or Panang Curry. Yes! Curry.

"And how's work?" Mom asks.

"We can talk about it tomorrow," I mumble, not wanting to get into that mess right now, either. It's already been a long damn day. I just want to curl up, eat takeout, and binge whatever Netflix recommends.

I finally manage to put my mother on speaker and open up the Grubhub app. Dammit—it's less than an hour until closing time at my favorite Thai place, and they're not taking online orders anymore. But I bet if I call them, I can get an order in. My stomach raises its volume, urging me to get this done.

"Don't be late tomorrow," my mother is saying. "I've got a packed schedule—"

"Yeah, got it," I say to my mother. "Me, too. So I should get going."

"Am I on speaker phone? Why am I on speaker—"

"Okay, love you but I gotta go, lots to do, apparently there's some big family event this weekend—"

"Call your sister," says my mother loudly.

"Yep," I say. "Will do."

And then instead of calling Rosie, I call Green Leaf Thai.

TUESDAY

7

"...outside is frightful
But the fire is so delightful
And since we've no place to go
Let it snow! Let it snow! Let it snow!"

Dean Martin croons through my radio alarm, the chorus of the classic Christmas carol waking me up in a pleasant haze of hope that maybe there really will be snow outside. A winter wonderland of glistening snowflakes might actually revive whatever cheer is still buried in my increasingly Grinch-like heart.

But when I check the weather, no luck. All we have in store is more of the same freezing temperatures, without a single predicted flurry in the forecast. In other words, all the winter with none of the charm: cold, gray, snowless. The crappy weather piled atop the suffocating combination of strange train encounters, looming office layoffs, my baby sister's wedding imminent, and my fortieth birthday means I'm fresh out of fa-la-la-la optimism.

Forcing myself to turn my phone on for a brief morning check-in of missed alerts, I scroll through all the notifications. Emails I'm not going to read until I'm at my desk, some probably inane Instagram tag from Bryan, a neighborhood newsgroup alert about swastikas spray-painted on a bunch of garages in Albany Park—yeah, it's too early for me to deal with the world. I start to set my phone down when it dings, a text popping up.

Hey call me plz

Rosie.

Guilt tugs at me. After ordering my dinner last night, I really did think about calling my sister. But then Netflix asked me, "Are you still watching?" And I said yes, and that was that. No phone calls, no nothing, just me and my *Gilmore Girls* marathon.

My desire to call my sister has not increased since then, nor will it. I'm already feeling sour and surly. I want coffee, I want breakfast, and I *don't* want to talk to Rosie. But I can't keep ignoring her like this. My mother is right. Rosie's wedding is in less than a week, and I'm her maid of honor. But only *technically*, because while I hold the title, Rosie's best friend, Layla, has done all of the maid-of-honor heavy lifting.

Layla is the one who lives in St. Louis, where Rosie and Ana live, and therefore had the ability to spend weeks poring over magazines and Pinterest boards with Rosie. She's the one who planned the bachelorette weekend in Lake Geneva. The one who came in to Chicago with Rosie and Ana to sample cakes, meet with the rabbi, select a rehearsal dinner spot, and go bridesmaid-dress shopping. They invited me to join, since that was the right thing to do—but no pressure, of course, said Layla's text.

I read between the lines, and politely declined.

Truly, Layla has taken every single maid-of-honor duty off my plate except for making a toast at the wedding. Rosie claimed this was all just so we wouldn't have to work around my pesky office day-jobber schedule. Rosie and Layla have been fast friends since the day they met in college. Layla recently took a pause on her Ph.D. program, and now she and Rosie are both Peloton, SoulCycle, and Pilates instructors in St. Louis. Which means not only that they have a lot in common, but also that they share a lot of literal and figurative flexibility.

But I'm pretty sure the real reason Layla has played a bigger role than me has less to do with geography and more to do with personal dynamics. Layla and Rosie consistently get along, whereas Rosie and I have a far spottier track record. We've never been close, and this past year hasn't brought us any closer.

When we lost Dad, I thought Rosie might reach out. Might step away from her social media and SoulCycle for long enough to have a real conversation. Might think to invite me to spend a holiday with her and Ana. Something. Anything. But she never did. She just kept posting sunny selfies, and got engaged, and went on Insta-worthy road trips with Layla and the girls. Honestly, I don't know why Rosie isn't just talking with Layla right now, and leaving me out of the whole thing.

But I suck it up and call my little sister.

"Eve! Hi," Rosie says, picking up immediately.

She's talking in that bright, perky tone that means other people might be listening. She's probably about to lead a spin class or something, pacing outside the workout room. She's doubtless wearing tight dark yoga pants and a loose but flattering workout top, her clavicle-length honey-blonde hair pulled into a low ponytail.

"What's up?" I ask, already exasperated.

"Just checking in on a few things before we hit the road and head your way. Ana and I are driving in tomorrow. We're gonna stop at camp on the way, just do sort of a walk-through, then we'll be in Chicago 'til the big day. I'm going to stay with Mom, Ana's gonna stay with her parents in Skokie—"

"Sounds great," I say. "Hey, I have to get ready for work, so—"

"Right, work, that's what I'm calling about, actually," Rosie says, and for a hot second I wonder if somehow she knows about the layoffs threatening my office. But no: "You took Friday off, right?"

"Um, no—"

"But it's the day before the wedding!"

Her voice is lowered, her tone shifting, but she's still got a little performative pep in there. She must have stepped into a side room or something so she could drop the upbeat demeanor. I'm sure there's still a tight smile plastered on her face in case anyone walks in on her. Rosie enjoys her reputation as the ever-cheerful fitness coach. She apparently even does YouTube videos or something that have gotten kind of popular. Mom was telling me about it recently, but I wasn't really listening.

"And?"

"And, there's, like, a million things to do that day. Plus the rehearsal dinner."

"Right, I'll be there for that at six—"

"Oh my GOD, Eve, it's not at six, it's at five so that the rabbi can come, she has to be at the temple for services at seven so we had to do an early dinner, you know this, I know you know this—"

"Rosie, God, take a breath," I snap, pushing myself up on my elbows, still in bed and already exhausted. "I'll see what I can do."

"Okay. Okay, good," she says, sounding relieved. Like she can finally check me off her to-do list. "Oh, hey, and while I've got you—are you getting your hair and nails done with us Friday afternoon, before dinner? Layla needs to confirm the numbers and she said you never texted her back."

"Sorry, I thought the random number asking me about a salon appointment was spam."

"Ha freaking ha," Rosie says, and I can hear the eye roll in her voice. "Text her back."

"Yep. Will do."

I definitely will not be texting Layla.

"Good." Rosie pauses. "Are you…still planning to mention Dad in your toast?"

My stomach clenches, an invisible fist grabbing my guts and twisting them into violent braids. Last night's Thai dinner rolls around threateningly. I swallow hard, banishing any tremble from my voice.

"Yeah, I said I would."

"And you'll mention Bubbe, too?"

Another hit straight to my miserable gut.

Why was I the one who had to do all the emotional labor here, memorializing our dead relatives? Bubbe and Dad were the two family members with whom I'd been closest. Neither of them would be there to serve as my buffer or guide me through my bumpy little life. Going to the wedding alone *and* standing up in front of the assembled crowd to give a speech about the two people I wished most were there feels like a special kind of hell.

"Yeah, I'll…mention Bubbe," I say, voice flat and cold.

"Maybe a funny story about when she moved in with us," Rosie suggests.

Bubbe moved in with us when we were kids—well, when Rosie was a kid, and I was racing toward adolescence. I was thirteen; Rosie was only seven. Our grandmother lived with us until she died, when Rosie was a senior in high school and I was a struggling young adult. She loomed so large, not only in our lives but in family lore. She was our direct connection to the Old World. I'm hard-pressed to think of *funny* stories featuring her, though.

Had Rosie found her funny?

I adored my grandmother, and was also always a little frightened around her. Not because *she* was frightening, but because she had seen so much of the world's darkness. She bore witness to too much of the world's cruelty. She was a tough-as-nails woman who made her way to a new world, learned a new language, married, had a daughter—my mother, her only child—and raised her alone when her husband died of a stroke in his thirties.

All the trauma she endured seemed to cling to her, an invisible dybbuk that never left her side. She was unapologetically superstitious, spitting through her fingers, throwing salt over her shoulder, warning us not to tempt the evil eye. She always wore a *hamsa* necklace, a small gilded silver hand intended to ward off malevolent spirits. She was untrusting of strangers, fiercely protective of family, ever vigilant. She tried to instill these traits in all of us, although it seemed that most of my family merely humored her when they nodded along to her stories or threw in a "God forbid!" after referencing any possible tragedy. They didn't take her seriously.

I did, though.

Whenever she spoke, I hung on every word.

You have to remember what matters, bubbeleh, she'd say to me, eyes gazing off into the middle distance, steely and determined. *And then do whatever you have to do to protect it, keep it safe.* Farshtay? *You understand?*

I understand, Bubbe.

Good girl, she said, and slipped me a butter cookie.

I'm not sure I actually understood even half of what Bubbe meant when she shared her strange statements and stories, but I always knew the answer that was expected: *Farshtay—I understand*. Comprehension. Solidarity. Total agreement. A promise to make her proud.

A promise I haven't kept very well.

"Yeah, sure," I say. "A funny story."

"Good," Rosie says, all the sunshine brightness returning to her voice. "Okay, and I gotta know—who're you bringing to the wedding?"

"It's a surprise," I say, and end the call.

8

"So what are we doing for your birthday?"

Bryan grins wickedly at me over his morning cup of coffee. He's on his first mug of the day, having just arrived at the office, even though it's almost ten. Apparently the urgency of yesterday has already faded for him. Sasha started texting him at nine warning him to get his ass downtown, but Bryan cannot be hurried.

"Absolutely nothing," I say, spreading a thick schmear of chive cream cheese on my everything bagel. One of our clients had dropped a platter off this morning. Since my days at Mercer & Mercer might be numbered, I'm not passing up a single free snack from here on out.

"Aw, come on!" Bryan protests, looking at Sasha to back him up.

Sasha, who brought her computer into the breakroom so she could keep working while we snacked and snarked, actually does look up from the screen for a minute.

"It's a big one," she says. "We should mark the occasion. You only turn forty once—"

"Do not say the f-word!" I hiss. "It sounds so old."

"It *is* old," says Bryan, voice dripping with faux sympathy. He gives me a little pout. "Do you have a good medical team, for when things really start falling apart? My husband's a doctor, if you need any referrals for hip replacement surgery or—"

"You are only three years younger than I am," I say, swatting at him.

"And always will be," he says, dodging me gracefully and batting his eyelashes.

"Shut up, Bryan," Sasha says pleasantly. "E, come on. We want to celebrate you."

"No need," I assure my friends. "Seriously. I'm a Hanukkah baby. My birthday always got swallowed up by the holiday—which I hated as a kid, but honestly? I love it for me now. Takes the pressure off. Keeps me young."

Bryan snorts.

"Besides," I say, offering up my ultimate excuse for birthday avoidance this year, "Rosie's getting married this weekend, remember?"

"I still can't believe your sister scheduled her wedding for your birthday," Sasha says, shaking her head.

"Your *big* birthday," Bryan adds unhelpfully.

"Don't call it my *big* birthday," I say, exasperated. "It was the only day they could get the venue. And it's technically the day *before* my birthday."

Rosie and her fiancée, Ana, met at Camp Heller-Diamond, a Jewish overnight camp an hour outside the city, when they were twelve. They didn't start dating right away or anything. They were just kids. Bunkmates and besties. Who later worked as camp counselors together. Then wound up in the same sorority at the University of Wisconsin. Then fell in love, left the sorority, got an off-campus apartment together their junior year, and the rest is history.

So, when it was time to tie the knot, they wanted to go back to where it all began. Summer was obviously a no-go. But even spring and autumn weddings are tricky at a summer camp; they're always packed with youth group retreats or family minicamp weekends or tie-dye-wearing artists on a creative retreat. But it turns out that if you beg the director long enough, you just might be able to schedule the Hanukkah wedding of your nerdy Jewish summer-camper dreams.

"Still!" Bryan says. "Tacky!"

"Yes," Sasha agrees. "Tacky as hell."

"Um, the whole wedding is Hanukkah-themed," I inform them. "Candles on every table. Some sort of weird latke-vodka cocktails. I don't think 'tacky' is something my sister is trying to avoid."

"My God," says Sasha. "Who has a *theme* for their wedding?"

"All the kids are doing it these days," Bryan says knowingly, doubly smug as the sole married person in the room *and* the youngest among us.

"Oh really?" I ask. "What was your theme?"

"True love," Bryan says, and we all groan. Then he lifts a brow. "Got a date yet, Evie?"

"She's not taking a date to the Camp Hanukkah wedding," Sasha snorts. But then, when I say nothing, her eyes go wide. "Eve! You didn't!"

"Oooh, you didn't tell her?" Bryan gasps.

"I told you not to RSVP with a plus-one!" Sasha says, and she seems genuinely upset. "Why would you do that?"

"It's aspirational!" I say, rushing to my own defense since no one else will. "I am manifesting something good, see? I will manifest the perfect date for this wedding—"

"Don't say that—" Sasha says, looking stricken.

"Manifesting? Must not be going well," Bryan interjects.

He turns to Sasha with a smirk. "Poor baby already asked me to go. I had to turn her down."

"Asshole," I mutter, wondering why I'm even friends with him.

"Yes!" Sasha says, without a trace of sarcasm. "That's perfect! Bryan, go with her."

"What? No," Bryan says, making a face. "I hate weddings, I almost skipped mine."

"I'm going to ask Hot Josh," I say loudly.

And for half a second, this shuts everyone up.

But only for half a second.

"Sexy British neighbor guy?" Bryan grins. "Nice!"

"It's Tuesday," Sasha says. "You think this guy doesn't have Saturday-night plans?"

"Do either of *you* have plans for Saturday night?" I ask.

"No, but I'm a boring old married guy," Bryan says, before quickly correcting himself. "*Young* married guy. But still boring. We never go out on Saturday nights. Too crowded."

"And I hate going out, period," Sasha says. Before I can remind her that wasn't always the case, she adds, "And seriously, there's nothing wrong with going alone—"

"Okay, I have to go do some actual work," I say, roughly shoving my empty paper plate into our office compost bin.

"Aw, Evie, come on," Bryan says. "We're only teasing."

Bryan is fake-pouting again and still looks playful. But Sasha is quiet, and there's something unreadable in her expression. She doesn't look like she's teasing. She looks worried.

"Stay in here 'til I finish my coffee," Bryan wheedles, taking a dramatically slow sip. "And we'll talk about something else. Like, are we all about to get fired? Did I miss any updates on that, any emails, any morning meetings…?"

"No meetings this morning, but you should still get here on time," Sasha says. "For real. This could be really bad—"

"Jesus Christ!" I interject, able to participate in the conver-

sation again now that it's not about my pathetic personal life.
I've really started resenting the feeling that joy can be taken
down as easily as holiday decorations, boxed up and tucked
away for the season. I know I'm usually the one bringing the
mood down, but maybe I should try to lift it up. "Enough with
the doom and gloom. It's the holidays. Let's try to lighten the
mood a little. Want to come over to my place tonight, drink
some eggnog, watch some Christmas movies…?"

"I am loving the big Christmas energy from the Jewish girl,"
Bryan says. "But obviously tonight is out."

"Plenty of Jews like Christmas," I say, wondering what he
means by *tonight is out*.

Is there some event I forgot about? The stupid office cruise
isn't until Friday. Which is also when Rosie's rehearsal dinner
is, so I guess at least I'll have a legit excuse to skip the frigid
boat party.

"Not like you do," Sasha mutters.

"Oh, come on, it's basically just another American holiday.
Besides, did you know that all the very best Christmas songs—"

"—were written by Jews," Bryan and Sasha say in unison,
since I have told them this a million times.

"I'm just saying, there's precedent for Jews getting in on the
Christmas cheer."

"Not me," Sasha says, returning to her laptop. "I hate Christmas."

"See, now *you're* a good Jew," Bryan says, reaching over like
he's going to pat her on the head. She raises a hand in warning and he backs off. Instead, he sets down his mug of coffee,
then claps his hands together in a bizarre parody of Barry from
yesterday. "Anyway! *Obviously* we can't do eggnog and movies tonight, because…"

"Because…?" Sasha echoes.

Bryan barrels on, mercifully not realizing her question is
genuine.

"The Big Gay Christmas Concert!" Bryan crows, pumping the air with his fist.

Sasha and I lock eyes in a shared panic.

We both one hundred percent forgot about the concert.

Bryan is a proud member of the Chicago Rainbow Chorus, and their annual holiday concert is the highlight of his year. Which means it has become a nonnegotiable event on our December calendars, as well.

A few years ago it was just a handful of enthusiastic chorus members singing in a sparsely decorated Unitarian church basement. But now it's become quite the extravaganza. Three-hundred-seat concert hall in Boystown, standing room only. Big Broadway numbers, a toy drive for the local children's hospital, warm mugs of cocoa served either "virgin" or "a lady never tells." If Bryan realized we actually forgot about his big night, he would murder us.

"Oh and I tagged you in the Insta post about it, but! Remember to wear your best ugly Christmas sweater for drink discounts. Or best Hanukkah sweater, whatever, as long as it's tacky as hell, obviously."

"Obviously," says Sasha.

"Obviously," I repeat, vaguely remembering an Instagram tag I'd ignored.

"Obviously what?"

Nancy walks in, garish in a yellow floral baby doll dress over thick white pantyhose paired with chunky heels. She's wearing the stupid Santa hat again, too. I guess she's still doling out invitations to the Freeze Your Ass Off River Cruise.

"Obviously, we should all get back to work," Sasha says coolly, and we do.

9

The rest of the morning flies by in a blur of project briefs and pitch preparations. I edit some copy. I respond to some emails. I roll my eyes when Nancy pipes up at a staff meeting that matching team shirts would really make us stand out at the next client presentation. I show up to every meeting and finish everything I'm supposed to get done before lunchtime, but it's truly a morning of half-assing it all. No chance I've elevated my B-student status at the office today.

I can barely focus on my tasks, because now that I've committed aloud to inviting Hot Josh to the wedding, it's all I can think about. I haven't made any actual decisions or taken any risks like this in so long. The whole thing feels impossible.

How am I going to ask him?

What do I do when he inevitably says no?

And God, what do I do if he says yes?

There are no good options. If he turns me down, perpetually running into my across-the-hall neighbor will be excruciatingly awkward. I'll probably have to move. If he says yes, well, hell. I don't even know what to do in that unlikely scenario.

The trick is going to be making the ask hyper casual.

Like I don't even care, one way or the other.

Hey, Hot Josh, oh my God hahahahaha WHOOPS, I mean JOSH! Want to go to this wedding with me? No big deal. Super chill. Whose wedding? Oh—haha. Funny you should ask. I mean of course it's someone I barely know. I mean, well. My little sister actually. But we're not that close. Although I am the maid of honor. But like, kind of not really, there's this other bridesmaid Layla who—never mind, never mind. Anyway I swear, it's all, like, SO CHILL, not a big deal, oh hey, did I mention it's also my fortieth birthday this weekend? Big milestone, not at all anxious about it, hahahahahaha! WAIT, COME BACK, WHERE ARE YOU GOING?!

This is a terrible idea.

Just then, another email message hits my inbox. It's from my creative director, Amy, saying she might have "extra" assignments for me toward the end of the week. Weird. I'm not usually her go-to when she needs something extra. I'm just the bread-and-butter gal, churning out copy for steady but unexciting frozen food and pharma clients. Most of what I do, I can crank out pretty quickly, without even thinking about it. I can often multitask, catching up on my personal emails or scheduling a haircut while I brainstorm new headlines.

That's why I'd planned to write a draft of my wedding toast between this morning's meetings. But between actual work and dreaming up stupid ways to ask Hot Josh out, I never got around to it. But it's fine. It's only Tuesday. The wedding is Saturday. Plenty of time.

Time—oh, shit.

I look up and see that it's nearly noon. Time to meet my mother for lunch.

Instead of taking the train to meet my mother, I decide to walk the half mile from Merchandise Mart to Macy's. It takes the same amount of time, unless you catch the train just right. Still, when it's cold out I usually take transit just to get out of the wind for a few minutes. But today, I appreciate the blustering gusts.

I feel my cheeks reddening, my muscles contracting in quick shivers and hurried steps. Lord knows I can use the exercise, and Mom will approve. She's been more critical of my weight lately, which grates on my nerves. She's not usually a stereotypical Jewish mom about bullshit like that, but she's hypercritical these days. I hope that maybe she'll decide to go easy on me today, but the odds are rarely in my favor.

"Jesus, Eve! Did you walk here?"

My mother looks genuinely shocked. She stares as I unbundle myself at our table. She's seated and already has a swiftly cooling coffee in front of her. Her shining silver curls are stiff with product to eliminate all frizz. She's wearing neutral lipstick, lots of mascara, and one of her many pale pastel pantsuits, the chosen uniform for female real estate agents of her generation.

"Yeah," I say. "Trying to get those steps in."

"Good for you, but careful you don't catch cold," Mom says, frowning and wrapping her arms around herself, rubbing her upper arms as though I brought a draft in with me. "With the wedding this weekend, that's really tempting fate."

I can't win.

I drop into my seat across from her and pick up the menu, cheeks still stinging from the cold wind scraping at them.

"I'm going with the Walnut Room salad," my mother says. "They have great salads here. Really great salads. You should get one. So good. Very filling. I always wind up taking home leftovers."

I don't say anything. But I'm definitely ordering actual food and skipping the allegedly amazing salad. I'm pretty sure that there has never in the history of the world been a "really great salad." There have only been moderately sad salads, and very sad salads. Exhaling, I look around, hoping the cheer of the place will distract me from the irritation I'm already feeling toward my mother.

The Walnut Room is the restaurant on the seventh floor of the historic Macy's on State Street in downtown Chicago. It's been there for more than a hundred years, and feels like stepping into a bygone era, with its alabaster arches and high ceilings, white tablecloths, the constant buzz of cheery shoppers below offset by the quiet chatter of the mostly older crowd of diners within. Large white Macy's bags boasting their iconic red star logo sit beside most tables, like well-behaved dogs perched by the owners' feet.

The already-heady vintage atmosphere is heightened at this time of year, thanks to the holiday decor. The bubble-gum-bright, over-the-top holiday decorations are breathtaking. There's a forty-five-foot-tall Christmas tree in the middle of the room, resplendent in lights and colorful decorations. The tables all radiate out from there, ensuring everyone a view of either the gorgeous tree or downtown Chicago.

Our table is in the main dining area. It's one of the farthest from the tree, and we still have a good view. Holly, tinsel, brightly painted nutcrackers, a six-foot stack of massive pink, green, and yellow macarons, and a thousand Christmas tchotchkes dazzle everywhere you look. I even see a delicate silver menorah on a small table display in the far corner. (Spot-the-menorah: a holiday I-spy game inadvertently played by every Jewish person in the world.) My gaze drifts past the menorah, though, lingering instead on the Christmas tree looming over us.

Dad would love this.

Something catches in my throat, and I try to cough it away. At this sound, my mother furrows her brow.

"So how are you doing?" she asks, suspicious. Like I've already caught a cold and I've been hiding it from her, and now Rosie's wedding will be ruined.

"I'm doing fine, Mom," I lie easily. "How are you doing?"

"I'm doing," she says with a noncommittal shrug, and returns her gaze to the menu even though she already knows what she's ordering.

Check-in complete, I guess.

I think about completely moving on from anything personal. I could ask her what reality shows she's watching these days, or how her marathon training is going. But I'm so sick of meaningless conversations with my mother. Ever since we lost Dad, we both feel the need to spend more time together—*it's what he would have wanted*—but never know what to do with that time. What to talk about. We usually stick to superficial topics, and we always avoid talking about the one person we're probably both thinking about. It's been that way this whole painful year. But today, I decide to suck it up and ask about one semi-meaningful thing.

"Yesterday, when you were talking about selling the house," I say, choosing my words carefully. "Do you think you're really…ready for that?"

"Oh," my mother says, uncomfortably. "I don't know. I mean, look, it would be stupid not to at least consider it. I'm watching how fast all my clients' homes are getting snapped up, feels silly not to think about. It's a seller's market, and it might just be, you know…time. To downsize. It's more space than I need, it's not as if Ana and Rosie would ever want the place…"

And it's not as if I'll ever have a family that might want it, I think, trying not to be wounded by the things my mother does and doesn't say.

"Right, sure," I say.

"Anyway," she says. "We'll see."

"We'll see," I echo, sipping my water and wishing it was wine. I try to keep my voice steady. "Just seems like a…a lot of big changes, and…not easy stuff, so…"

My mother heaves her trademark sigh.

"I know this isn't easy for you," she says, flexing her fingers.

They're painted pale pink, gleaming and flawless. I'm not sure why, exactly, she needs to go get another manicure today. But what does my raggedy-nailed self know? "Rosie getting married, the whole thing. Everything. You know."

My mother is not usually the one to have heart-to-heart chats with me. That was always my father's job. I'm sure she wishes he was here right now, to handle this for her. To handle *me* for her.

Yeah, well—me, too, Mom.

"I'm thrilled for Rosie," I say, a little too loudly. "I love Ana. It's going to be a beautiful wedding."

"I know it's not ideal that it's also on your birthday—"

"It's not on my birthday. The wedding is on Saturday and my birthday's on Sunday," I say, hoping I sound breezy but probably sounding bitchy. "Honestly. Mom, you should know when my birthday is—"

"I know when your birthday is—"

"I know, I'm just teasing—"

"Well, it's sometimes hard to tell when you're teasing—"

"It's not actually that hard to tell when I'm teasing—"

"Honey, please," Mom says, biting her lip, a shiny wet spot of lipstick clinging to her front tooth. "We're all…we're all trying the best we can, right?"

She's trying to stop our sniping from escalating into an argument. She's trying to be gentle while she does it, which is a stretch for her. She's usually the tough-love parent, the no-nonsense real estate agent who calls it as she sees it, for her clients and for her children. A good investment, a bad paint job, she'll always just tell it like it is. I can see she's making an effort. It's just not enough.

But I don't have the energy to fight.

"Right," I say, making peace. "Sorry. I'm just hungry."

"The salads are good," my mother says.

"So I've heard," I say, eyeing the pot pie on the menu.

"Have you been following your sister on the TikTok?"
Mom asks.

"What?"

"I told you last week, she has this TikTok. Fitness videos.
They're very good, very popular. Some weirdos on there give
her a hard time, but it's mostly been very good for her. She's
making money for 'influencing' or something, I didn't really
understand it. But she had me get on TikTok so I could follow
her. You should follow her, too. It helps with the algorithms."

"What do you know about algorithms?" I ask incredulously.

"That they help your sister," my mother says sternly. "Follow her, please."

"Fine," I say. I pull out my phone and turn it on.

"Was your phone off again?" Mom asks.

I ignore her and open up TikTok, which I wasn't even sure
I had on my phone. I think Bryan insisted on it at some point.
I do a quick search for my sister's name, and find her account
immediately. "GoGo-RoRo" is grinning on a stationary bike
in the first preview video. I hit Follow, then power my phone
down again.

"Followed," I say.

"Thank you," says my mother.

She looks like she wants to say something else, but she
doesn't.

"Sure thing," I say, grabbing the menu again. "So how's the
wedding stuff going? How much shit do you have to get done
the next few days?"

"Not too much, all things considered," she says with a wave
of her well-maintained hand. "Rosie and Ana are both so organized, we're in good shape. And Ana's parents have picked
up a lot of the slack. Nice things about two brides. Less conventional approach as far as who's supposed to do what. Breath
of fresh air."

As her hands move gracefully to accentuate her words, I notice with a pang that she's no longer wearing her wedding ring. Instead, on her left ring finger is a gleaming emerald, which I recognize as a ring my grandmother used to wear. I think there are Hebrew letters engraved on the inside of the band, although I can't quite remember what they are.

For some reason I want to take the ring, to see the Hebrew letters, to slip it on to my own finger. I want to ask my mother why she's wearing it, and why she's not wearing her wedding ring. I want to ask her where she put the ring my father gave her.

Instead, I hear myself ask, "Do you think I'm going to die alone?"

My mother freezes. She stares at me for a long moment, then blinks slowly and seems to recover. She waves her hand in the air again, maybe summoning a server, maybe shooing away my question.

"What a question," she mutters, and doesn't answer it. "But that reminds me. Your date, for the wedding. You still won't tell me who it is?"

"Still a surprise," I say, relieved when a server appears to take our order.

The server has bright red curls cropped short in the back, long in the front, and a pert button nose. In her festive white-collared button-down shirt, she looks like a modern-day little orphan Annie, all grown up.

"Hi, I'm Annie, I'll be taking care of you today," she says, and I immediately feel bad for her. Her name really is Annie? I can only imagine how many times she's been asked if the sun will come out tomorrow.

Mom asks for the Walnut Room salad, dressing on the side. I order Mrs. Hering's 1890 Original Chicken Pot Pie, flaky, buttery crust and all, and ignore the sharp intake of my mother's breath. I'm a grown-ass woman and I'll do what I want. And if I have to buy some Spanx to fit into my brides-maid's attire, so be it.

We avoid eye contact for a long moment after putting our orders in. I look around the holiday scene. Since it's a Tuesday, it's busy, but not as bustling as it will be over the weekend. Families will come in from the suburbs to have actors in cheap purple chiffon fairy costumes sprinkle magic dust in their children's hair, give them wishing stones, and promise them that Santa will bring them what their hearts desire.

There are no sugarplum fairies here today, though, and even amid all the bright seasonal decor, I notice a fracture in the alabaster molding in the wall near our table. And above that, rusty water stains line the ceiling. This place must have been stunning when it first opened its doors in the early 1900s. It's still beautiful, but there are cracks in the facade. It's easy to miss amid all the hustle and bustle, glitter and ornaments—but the place is long past its original glory days. The old girl could use some work—not just a surface-level touch-up, but some deeper, more foundational repairs.

"Anything else going on with you?" Mom asks at last. "Since you won't tell me who your mystery date is."

I thought I saw Bubbe on the train the other day, I think, thoughts tumbling around my brain like a washing machine reaching the height of its spin cycle. *Which probably means I'm losing my mind. And there's still no one special in my life. Plus I can't seem to stop eating. No professional achievements to report. Basically, I'm feeling like a failure on every front. Oh, and hey, remember that guy who died last year? Do you think maybe, just maybe, we can finally talk about Dad?*

"We're expecting some layoffs at work," is what I actually say.

I immediately regret this disclosure, even though it had seemed like the least worrisome thing I could share. I was hoping to distract my mother from the whole date thing, especially since I'm sweating now just thinking about asking Hot Josh to go with me. But as soon as I see her eyes widen, I realize my mistake.

"Oh my God, you're losing your job?"

"Not me," I say quickly, but the damage is done. I've inadvertently activated full-on Worried Jewish Mother Mode, and there's no easy off switch for that setting once the switch has been flipped. "Some people might, but we don't really know who—"

"What are you going to do?"

"I'll be fine—"

"How's your résumé? Do you need me to take a look at it? I can talk to my colleague Joan, her son works in advertising— or maybe it's marketing, is that the same thing? Anyway, she says he makes a very nice living—"

"Mom," I interrupt. "I'm fine. Everything's fine. We're all fine. Okay?"

"If you say so," she says, looking slapped. She flexes her fingers again, examining her nails, and looks away from me.

This is the point in the conversation where Dad would step in, if he were here. Any time things turned emotional, my father was the one to take the wheel. My mother is organized, loyal, reliable, absolutely full of redeeming qualities. But she's always been shit at acknowledging tension or, God forbid, difficult feelings.

Rena, let me in a little, my father used to say, gently tapping on my mother's forehead. *What's going on in there?*

I wonder if she ever actually let him in, or if she always just let out that great big sigh. She sure seems to keep the door locked when it comes to me. My whole life, it's been hard to talk to my mother about anything emotional, but this past year it's been impossible. We've never talked about my father since he died. None of us. We barely mention him at all.

It was so sudden, and we were all wrecked—Rosie, Mom,

me. We were briefly united in the shock of our loss. For the strange blur of days in the immediate aftermath, we shared a common language. Our grief was unspoken but palpable. It was all we had. We held each other up, clutching elbows, hands on backs. We only wanted to be around each other. No one else understood just how much we had lost.

But after the funeral and seven stiff days of sitting shiva, we all retreated to our corners and busied ourselves with anything that allowed us to focus our minds somewhere else. I threw myself into work, started eating everything in sight, and stopped making any decisions. Rosie swiftly got engaged to Ana and began planning the wedding, making as many big, bold decisions as possible. Mom never stopped moving: aerobics classes, marathon training, house showings, manicures, book club. We all avoided talking about the one person we were so desperately missing; the one person who had tied us all together, and in whose absence we had begun the inevitable process of drifting apart.

"I want you to be happy for Rosie," my mother says.

"I am," I say, the words turning sour in my mouth.

"She needs you," my mother says, again. I start to ask her what she means by that—what, exactly, she thinks Perfect Rosie needs from me. But I keep my mouth shut. "Anyway, the wedding is going to be lovely, it really is. Out at the camp, all that nature. Should be really nice."

"Yep."

"I'm glad it's at the camp," Mom says, taking out her lipstick and reapplying it without the aid of a mirror. "I'd be worried if it was at the temple, what with all the *mishigas* lately."

"What *mishigas*?" I ask. Mom rarely uses Yiddish, since it evokes her own mother. But this is one of our favorite words, since it sounds like what it is: *mishigas*. Messiness, craziness, utter foolishness.

"You didn't hear?" Mom asks, and for half a second I think she's going to tell me about some stupid drama about whether or not to allow bar mitzvah kids to twerk on the dance floor or something, but then she lowers her voice and says, "We got another bomb threat."

I nearly fall out of my chair.

"Another—"

"Some bread for the table," our little server Annie blithely interjects, approaching with a warm basket. "And some butter—"

"We don't need all that," my mother starts to say, but I'm already slathering a thick, creamy pat across a warm and comfortingly crusty roll.

The ginger waitress nods at my mother apologetically. *Too late now.* Then she winks at me and vanishes again.

"The temple's gotten multiple bomb threats?" I ask around a mouthful of bread.

"Yeah," my mother says, and I'm genuinely unsure if the mildly disgusted look on her face is regarding the antisemitic threat or my inhalation of the evil carbs. "Last year it was just an email. The FBI said it was not credible or whatever. But this time, some neo-Nazi asshole called up the office during Sunday School last week."

"During Sunday School? Holy shit. So there were kids in the building—"

"They evacuated everyone. SWAT team came, the whole bit. There wasn't a bomb. Just a threat. But still, with all these troublemakers, maybe not the greatest time for a wedding, big crowds, all that…"

"Holy shit," I say again, not sure what else to say. "How was this not in the news?"

"I guess because we didn't actually get bombed," Mom says. "But, you know. When they're really going to bomb you, they don't usually call first."

"That's not funny," I say, but my mother just shrugs. Somehow this response unsettles me even more. I shake my head, still stunned. "Is there going to be a cop car in the parking lot from now on, like at the high holidays?"

For the biggest holidays on the Jewish calendar, Rosh Hashanah and Yom Kippur, more people pour into synagogues than at any other time of the year. Throughout my childhood, I didn't think anything at all about the fact that on those days, there were always two or three squad cars on hand, directing traffic into the parking lot, watching everyone enter the building, being visibly present.

It didn't occur to me until I was well into my twenties that this security measure wasn't one taken by all religious groups. The megachurch right across the street from us never had a police presence back then—although I'm pretty sure they have an armed guard these days. I guess it's just the world we live in, which is a brutal thought.

But my mother is shaking her head.

"No, actually," she says. "No police presence. That was the decision. We had a town hall about it right away—the next morning. It's a diverse congregation, you know. Diverse community, Evanston. So. People were saying how not everyone feels safer with police around. Which hadn't even occurred to me, if I'm being honest."

"Oh," I say, not admitting that it hadn't initially occurred to me, either.

"We wouldn't want one of our Hebrew High teens to show up, 'look suspicious,' and have a bad interaction with the police or something," Mom continues, twisting her white cloth napkin in her pale, painted fingernails. "We wouldn't want someone getting hurt, just because someone else felt nervous."

"Yeah," I say automatically. "Of course. But so…what are they going to do, then? To keep everyone safe?"

"They're bringing in some security expert to do some trainings or something, and we're updating the locks and whatnot. But no cops. For now."

I nod, feeling sick at all the hard decisions my mother's community is having to make. *My* community, even if I haven't been very involved lately. I can't separate myself from this fear, but it feels surreal. There have only been a handful of times in my life where I've felt threatened for being Jewish. Antisemitism buzzes in the background of my life, ever present but usually brushed away like a pesky fly. Sure, people make stupid jokes and ignorant assumptions. Sure, it sucks to be a Jew on the internet, but it also sucks to be a woman or gay or Black or a hundred other things on the internet. Sure, synagogues are targets of bomb threats now and then.

But it's not supposed to happen at the synagogue where I had my bat mitzvah. The building where my parents spent every single Friday night, for the entirety of their marriage. The community that meant so much to my father that he served as the congregation president for a decade, his portrait hanging in the hallway with all the other past presidents of the temple. I imagine his picture in the hallway and my mother sitting in her pew, alone, prayer book in hand, one eye on the door. My gut clenches.

"Are you…still going to services Friday night?" I ask.

"Every week," my mother says, tilting her chin defiantly. "No chickenshit neo-Nazi schmuck's gonna take away my temple."

For the first time in a while, I smile at my mother.

She can drive me up the wall, but she's tough as hell.

I wish I had half her chutzpah.

"Maybe I'll join you sometime soon," I say.

"You should! Rosie and Ana came last Friday night," Mom says. "It was nice. Rosie did one of her TikTok things about coming home for Shabbat at her childhood synagogue. We all went out to dinner after services."

"Oh," I say stiffly, a spiraling stab of jealousy twisting through me.

I only live half an hour away, but this was the first I was hearing about dinner and services last Friday. Or the bomb threat on Sunday. If Dad were still alive, I would have been included in all of those updates, good and bad. It's hard not to feel resentful at all the obvious ways my remaining family is excluding me.

"Anyway," Mom says, lifting an eyebrow. "If you come for services, any chance it'll be with your mystery wedding date? I can drive you both, I'm going straight from the rehearsal dinner to the temple, and the rabbi's going to do a blessing for Rosie and Ana—"

"We'll see," I say, and then I remember. The stupid cruise. Which I still want to skip, but it's also occurring to me that doing so might be a bad look. "If the rehearsal dinner gets out in time, there's actually this office party I should probably go to. Doesn't seem like the time to skip out on office socializing, with the cutbacks and all."

"Oh," says my mother, looking doubtful. "Well…if you're worried about losing your job, I guess, but…it's the wedding weekend…"

"And I'll be at everything I need to be at," I say, a little sharper than intended.

"I just…" says my mother, then she exhales and seems to change course. "Where's the office party? Is it near the restaurant?"

"Not far," I say, since the rehearsal dinner is at a nice new-American place in the Loop. "It's on a boat. River cruise."

"In December?" Mom says, appalled.

"Yep," I confirm.

"That's crazy."

"I know."

She points a finger at me.

"You be careful. And do *not* catch a cold."

10

I barely have time after work to trek home before the concert. But I have to go home to get my ugly Hanukkah sweater—which, of course, I would have just brought with me that morning if I'd remembered the concert was that night. I can't show up without it, or Bryan will know I forgot about his big event. This week is messy enough; I don't need to piss off one of my closest friends.

Hurrying into my apartment, I dig through the back of my closet, and there it is: a royal blue sweater with a big gold Hanukkah menorah sprawling across the chest. And the best part: I push a small button near the lower edge of the shirt, and voilà. The tiny lights representing the flames at the top of each candle in the menorah begin twinkling obnoxiously. Nine little lights blinking cheerily, right there on the chest. And beneath the menorah, in English letters shaped to look like Hebrew, are the yellow-gold words LET'S GET LIT.

It's gloriously over-the-top, as if some drunken Jewish designer was told that no one could top the tackiness of ugly

Christmas sweaters, and said with miraculous confidence, "Hold my Macca-beer."

I pull the sweater over my windblown curls. It's tighter on me than it was the last time I wore it. Two years ago, it was still sort of baggy. Now it's hugging my boobs so much that the fabric stretches, warping the menorah. But the lights are still twinkling and it's not uncomfortable. Besides, I don't have any other ugly holiday shirts on hand, so snug light-up menorah it is.

I grab my keys, throw a scarf around my neck, try to make sure I'm not forgetting anything else. Then, catching a glimpse of myself in the mirror, I gasp.

For a half second, a few stray curls spilling over my cheek and the scarf lending a more elegant element, I look like my grandmother in her younger years.

Bubbe always said I looked like her. Whenever she said so, I scoffed, because I just couldn't see it. She was so crisp, sharp and well-dressed, while I was always messy and soft around the edges. But after she was gone, and I went through a bunch of old photographs of her, I started to see what she meant. Now, every now and then, in the right light, I see the shadow of my grandmother in my face. It's not just the shared jawline, easy to miss because of my fuller cheeks. It's our skin, the arch of our brow, and most of all, it's our eyes. Big, dark, and questioning. I always assumed hers held more answers than mine, but maybe they didn't when she was my age.

My vision swims a little, and I lean closer to the mirror. The face staring back at me is mine, but then for a second, it isn't. My heart stutters. It's me in the glass, it has to be—or is it my grandmother? Like on the train?

Suddenly, the lights cut out in my bedroom.

An eerie swath of moonlight slices downward through my window and onto the mirror, providing just enough illumination to see the haunted reflection still staring at me. My stomach rumbles, and the darkness behind me seems to shift.

Like there's something lurking behind the woman in the mirror.

Something lurking behind *me*.

There's a whining buzz in my ears. With a sharp intake of breath, still facing the mirror, I raise my gaze and see a shadowy figure looming over me. The buzzing in my ears grows louder. Louder. Looking back in the mirror, I stare at the terrified face of my grandmother—myself—my grandmother—

I close my eyes—

The buzzing stops.

I open my eyes, and everything's normal. The lights are on. It's just me in the mirror. Just me, standing there, the menorah stretching across my front blinking expectantly. I let out a shaky breath, and pull the scarf from my neck. I don't need it tonight. My coat will be enough.

I turn on every light in my apartment, trying to stop my heart from flying into my ribs like a deranged bird. Usually I'm a stickler for green living, turning out all the lights, unplugging small appliances, conserving energy. But tonight I need to literally lighten the atmosphere. I'm going to leave the lights on when I head out so my apartment will welcome me with brightness instead of darkness.

The little lights on my Hanukkah shirt twinkle in solidarity. My heart is beating more regularly now. I'm ready to head out—all dressed up with somewhere to go. The stupid shirt really does make me feel better about everything. Although I can't help but wonder what Bubbe would think of this outfit. I can almost hear her voice, the thick Slavic accent, the clucking of her tongue.

Oy, Eve, she'd say, shaking her head in well-coiffed disapproval. *That shirt…it's a lot.*

My father, on the other hand, thought it was hilarious. He

was the one who bought it for me, almost ten years ago. Saw it at a TJ Maxx and couldn't resist. He bought it on sale, post-holidays, for ten bucks. This memory calms me, slows my racing heart, makes me feel like myself again. I recall how my father made a big show of giving the tacky Hanukkah sweater to me when I came home for Passover, that walrus mustache of his twitching with glee.

Um, I cannot pull this off, I told him.

Sure you can! Dad beamed. *You've got this, Evie! And if you don't bust this thing out for Hanukkah, I'm going to be very disappointed.*

And so I have, every year since. Except last year, when I was still too sad to wear it. But now the sweater's back on, bright and cheesy as ever—and while one of the family ghosts haunting me might roll her eyes at it, the other would high-five me.

God, I miss them.

I turn on my phone to check the time. *Shit.* I'm supposed to be in Boystown in half an hour, and even if I drive, parking will definitely make me late. I'm probably going to have to get a Lyft. I'll walk outside and call for one at the corner—I don't like ride-share drivers picking me up from my actual address. I probably have Bubbe to thank for all my paranoia.

My apartment is sweltering, but since I'll need my coat later, I tuck it under my arm when I head out the door. Swiping my lips with some more Holiday Cheer lip gloss, I step out into the courtyard and nearly run smack into Hot Josh.

"Wow," he says, taking a hasty step back. "That's…quite the jumper."

"Oh," I say, flushing and wishing I'd put my coat on already. I look down at my blatantly twinkling chest, the fabric pulled so tight that it looks like I'm wearing a light-up holiday billboard advertisement for my boobs. "Yeah, uh, yep."

"Off to a party, then?"

"Concert, actually," I say, glad that at least I really am going out and not just hanging around my apartment, alone and weird in my battery-powered Hanukkah apparel.

"Concert," Josh says, amused. "What concert, exactly?"

"Rainbow Chorus."

"Oh," says Josh, with what seems like recognition. I guess Bryan's singing group has gotten pretty popular. He gestures vaguely with his hand, like he's trying to find the right words. "So, er, are you—"

"Gay? No, although I mean I definitely believe we're all on a spectrum and—" I blurt hastily, completely steamrolling over the end of Josh's question and hearing the final word of it way too late:

"—Jewish?"

"Yes," I squeak, face burning with the blazing intensity of a full eighth-night Hanukkah menorah. "I'm Jewish."

"Cool," says Hot Josh. "Me, too."

Then he walks into the building, like he didn't just upend my universe.

11

Hot Josh is Jewish?

I stare open-mouthed long after he disappears into the building. This unexpected insight erases all the strangeness of this week. It erases everything, if I'm being honest. I don't know anything anymore, other than the fact that my hot neighbor is Jewish.

I stand there at the curb, stunned, for the full three minutes awaiting my ride. When my Lyft arrives, it's a comically small Toyota, and I don't even care. I clamber into the back seat, still in shock. Trying to process this information.

Hot Josh is Jewish!

I haven't dated anyone Jewish since college. Learning that Josh is a member of the tribe hits me in an unexpected way. Honestly, I've never been sure that it's important to me that my future partner be Jewish.

But I'm not sure it's *not* important.

And maybe having this in common with him will give me a leg up on the competition. (Surely, there must be competition. The guy is a smoke show.) Now I won't just be his weird neighbor; I'll be his weird *nice Jewish girl* neighbor.

Still reeling, I wipe some sweat from my brow. The heat is cranked up so high in this Lyft that the approximate temperature is July-in-hell. But my Lyft driver is rocking out to some sort of Bangladeshi pop music, and I don't feel like yelling over it to ask him to adjust the temperature. Glad I kept my coat off, I hope that between the blasting heat and the swooning over Hot Jewish Josh, I don't get too *shvitzy* on the ride to the Big Gay Christmas Concert.

When we pull up to the event venue, I'm taken aback by how many people are waiting outside in the cold to get in. Bryan had mentioned something about selling out the main floor and balcony and rush tickets being offered on a first-come, first-serve basis to people willing to do standing room only. But I honestly thought he was full of shit. Since I already have a ticket, I head inside, grateful to bypass the giddy hopefuls trying their luck.

"Eve! Over here!"

Sasha waves at me from inside the crowded concert hall, holding an elegant hand aloft so I can see her through the merry mayhem. There are concertgoers everywhere, almost all of them in tacky Christmas sweaters, laughing and hugging. A disco Christmas mix is pumping over the lobby loudspeakers. It's intense.

I make my way toward Sasha as quickly as I can, nearly getting knocked over three times by all the enthusiastic revelers milling around the lobby.

"Oh my God, it's so crowded. How'd you see me?" I ask.

With a smirk, she points at my chest. Although I'd put my coat on when I exited the Lyft, I was still warm enough that I hadn't zipped it. Framed by my puffy down winter wear, the twinkling menorah adorning my chest is on full display, like a big Jewish beacon.

"The only Hanukkah boobs in Christmas Town," Sasha says.

"I like to think of them as my lit tits," I say.

"Classy," she says, shaking her head, but she's smiling.

Sasha's not donning anything nearly as brazen as I am. Instead, she's wearing a sleek red blazer over an evergreen camisole and tight black pants with red stilettos. The girl is Jewish, but her sleek Christmas cosplay is on point.

"Rocking the sexy-elf look," I tell her.

"I do what I can," she says. "But for real, though, I want to bail on this so bad. Did you see the lines outside? We could probably get a hundred bucks for our seats."

"Are they good? I haven't looked at the email confirmation."

"I'm not sure. All I know is that Carlos texted me and said his seat is right next to us and that he's 'eagerly awaiting our arrival.' Come on, let's get this over with."

We squeeze our way past chatty concertgoers, out of the lobby, and into the main concert hall. There are wreaths and lights everywhere, and everyone is laughing, embracing, buzzing with a collectively festive mood. And although I undoubtedly look like a frumpy cheeseball next to chic Sasha, there's no need for me to feel out of place. There are reindeer antler headbands, light-up red noses, and ugly Christmas sweaters galore. I'm relieved and weirdly proud to find that my attire is entirely appropriate.

"This is fun," I tell Sasha.

"This is the opposite of fun," she informs me. "Can we just send Carlos an apology, tell him we suddenly have a very bad case of being on our periods…and then scalp our tickets and go get a drink somewhere? Pretty please?"

"Aw, come on," I say, hooking my arm around her elbow. A bit of the old Christmas cheer is sliding down my proverbial chimney, and I want to enjoy it for as long as I can. It's been so long since I had fun of any kind. "We haven't been out together anywhere in forever. Don't you want to get in some good quality time with your friends?"

The question makes her wince, and I get it. We've both been hermits for so long—her while she was in the relationship, and in its aftermath; me in my wallowing sorrow. Bryan and Carlos started dragging me out a few months ago, and thanks to them I'd grudgingly rejoined the world, at least a little bit. Sasha is the one who really hasn't.

"I'm not sure I'd call this quality time," Sasha says, and then she's interrupted by a shrill whistle. Startled, we both look in the direction of the sound.

Carlos lifts a hand and waves at us, grinning. Bryan's husband is not only a five-star doctor (internal medicine, patients love him, great Yelp reviews), he's also a model-hot first-generation Cuban from Miami whose dazzling smile can melt ice.

And apparently he can whistle like a freaking lifeguard.

Several people are looking enviously at the attractive man beckoning us toward the seats beside him. Seats that happen to be located in the first damn row.

Sasha gives me an oh-hell-no look.

"I am not sitting in the front row," she hisses.

"We can't leave now. He already saw us."

"Maybe he's waving at someone else. Maybe he doesn't even know we're here, and we can still bail."

"Pretty sure he didn't miss these," I said, indicating my lit tits. "And you said he already texted you."

"Eve! Sasha! Over here!" Carlos calls, pointing to the seats beside him.

"Shit," Sasha mutters.

Two minutes later, we're seated beside Carlos as the lights go down in the amphitheater, and everyone cheers. Hooting, hollering, the whole shebang. The energy is infectious. It feels less like a concert and more like Christmas-themed gay disco meets Deep South church tent revival.

Carlos, seated to my right, has a rolled-up concert program in his hand. As the curtain goes up on the stage, he taps the program excitedly against my shoulder.

"This is going to be so good," he says, beaming. "And I love your sweater!"

"Thanks." I grin, and look over at Sasha, seated to my left. She's slumped down into her seat like she's trying to disappear. I squeeze her knee. "Try to enjoy yourself."

"Bah humbug," she says.

A spotlight slams on, and there's Bryan, center stage. He's wearing his own ugly Christmas sweater: green-and-red plaid, with a giant brown felt gingerbread man sipping a martini. Bryan grins, and when he opens his mouth, it's not just his voice we hear: from the darkness behind him, the whole choir sings in unison, and the spotlighted lip-synching effect is jarring.

"JOY TO THE WORLD!"

A rainbow of other light specials is thrown on, revealing the rest of the singers and evoking delighted shrieks from the crowd. Above their heads, neon lights flash the words Big Gay Christmas Concert. The singers open their mouths in unison.

"THE LORD IS COME!"

12

"They get better every year, I swear!"

Carlos is beaming from ear to ear, one arm around Bryan, the other beckoning for a waiter to come take our drink order. We're at a super hip queer bar across the street from the concert hall. Carlos made reservations for one of the private tables there several weeks ago, before the place filled up. It was a good call, since every table is taken, and just like at the concert, the rest of the place is standing room only.

"Seriously," Carlos says. "You guys were so good."

"Aw, thanks, babe," says Bryan.

"It's true! And I'm the biggest fanboy. So, so big."

"So, *so* big," Bryan agrees, smirking suggestively.

"Why aren't you in the chorus, Carlos?" I ask, kicking Bryan under the table.

"Oh, I'm one hundred percent tone deaf," Carlos laughs.

"It's true," Bryan says, wrinkling his freckled nose. "But luckily he's hot."

"And a doctor, don't forget," Carlos says.

"I never do," Bryan says. "And so, so big…"

"Shut up, Bryan," Sasha and I say in unison.

"And a good Catholic schoolboy to boot," Bryan adds sweetly.

"Were you really a good Catholic schoolboy?" Sasha asks.

"I had them all fooled," Carlos assures her. He gives Bryan another squeeze, then asks him, more seriously, "Hey, did you see the text from Monica? Can you go in for the paperwork tomorrow?"

I exchange a glance with Sasha.

Do we know who Monica is, and what this paperwork might be?

Sasha lifts an eyebrow.

We don't.

Bryan gives a small shake of his head, clearly indicating to Carlos that they should talk about this later. It must not be anything super important; the two of them are clearly genuinely happy. Carlos nods and kisses Bryan's cheek.

My stomach rumbles.

"Is there any food here?" I ask.

"Oh, honey, no," Bryan says. "But don't worry, we're gonna fill up on drinks."

An hour and two rounds of cocktails later, we're all laughing and relaxed. The dance floor is packed and we're eyeing it occasionally, remembering what it was like when we were the ones pressing ourselves up against strangers and grinding the night away.

"I was a little nervous heading into the concert this year," Bryan confesses. "There was gonna maybe be a protest, according to the socials. Some Klanned Karenhood types saying this was immoral, going after us like with the drag brunches and stuff."

"Are you serious?" Sasha asks. "They're trying to pull that shit here?"

For a half second, my mood darkens again. It's sometimes

easy to forget in a city like Chicago how fragile everything is for so many of us, all the time. The uptick of ugliness. The looming threat of those who don't want to allow room for anyone unlike them. The sort of monsters I was taught to fear as a child in Hebrew school, while being simultaneously assured that world peace was a realistic goal.

"So they said," Bryan says, then grins. "But no one showed up to their little protest, so cheers to that!"

"Cheers!" we all yell, and Carlos orders another round.

Soon the momentary darkness is drowned in a sea of vodka and buried in a landslide of cackling over inside jokes. It's the best night I've had in such a long time. Even Sasha seems to be enjoying herself. She sips her third martini and nudges me.

"Okay, Eve. You gotta tell Carlos about Rosie's Camp Hanukkah wedding theme."

"Do what now?" Carlos asks, confused.

"Oh, yeah, this is good," Bryan agrees.

"My sister's getting married this weekend," I say, with an over-the-top roll of my eyes. "At a Jewish summer camp. And she's, like, making it kind of a big candles-and-latkes Hanukkah-themed extravaganza. Ancient festival of lights meets modern lesbian wedding. It's a whole thing."

"That sounds fun," Carlos says.

"But it's also Eve's fortieth birthday, so it's kind of brutal," Bryan says with a look of faux sympathy.

"Can we please stop mentioning my birthday," I sigh. "And the wedding is the day before, it's not the exact day, okay?"

"The big four-oh!" Bryan says, ducking to avoid me dousing him with the last drops of my drink.

"I crossed that bridge last year, it's not so bad," says Carlos.

"That's because you look twenty-five," I tell him. "And you're married. And a doctor. If I had even one of those things going for me—"

"Okay, okay, no pity party," Sasha chides.

"Did you ask Hot Josh yet?" Bryan chimes in.

"Hot Josh?" Carlos says.

"Cute British guy, just moved into her building," Bryan explains. "She's gonna ask him to be her date to the wedding."

"I didn't ask him yet," I say. "But…"

"But…?" Sasha asks, taking the bait.

"But it turns out he's Jewish."

They all squeal.

"What!"

"OMG!"

"British *and* Jewish? Unicorn! We have a *unicorn*, people!" Bryan yelps, which is hilarious, since his pale Irish Catholic ass would never have known this was something to be excited about until Sasha and I came into his life. "No—wait—oh my God, he's a *Jewnicorn*. Oh, girl, this is *fate*."

"Jewnicorn? Jesus, Bryan, that sounds like a foot disease," Sasha says. "Evie, how did you not lead with that when you got to the concert?"

"I was just way too excited about all the big gay Christmas joy," I say with a grin.

"Fair," Bryan says, sipping the last of his gin and tonic. "Okay. Who wants to dance?"

"Not me," says Sasha. "I'm about to tab out."

"Boo, no fun!" Bryan says, pouting.

"I got the tab tonight," Carlos says.

"No way, you always—" Sasha starts to protest, but Carlos silences her with a peck on the cheek.

"Always, nothing!" he says. "You haven't even been out with us in a year! Let me get this. I'll be right back."

"Thanks, Carlos," Sasha says, then blows a kiss to all of us. "I'm gonna call a car. See you kids at the office. Don't get into too much trouble."

"Aw, stay a little longer," Bryan pleads, but Sasha's already headed for the coat check. As she exits, and Carlos makes his way to the bar to settle the bill, Bryan grabs my hand. "Looks like you're my dance buddy, Evie Goodman!"

Before I can put up any sort of resistance, he hauls my ass to the dance floor. I let him. The night is tinged with holiday magic and good drinks, and some part of me really does just want to dance. It's also kind of refreshing to know that no one here will wind up asking me to go home with him, seeing as literally every dude here is gay. At least for a little while, the pressure's off. I can just cut loose, like in the old days.

Within seconds, Bryan and I are flailing around like drunken Muppets to old-school Madonna dance remixes. It turns out that it's '90s Night, which just makes this already-delightful night even better. Bryan and I know the lyrics to every single song and scream along at the top of our lungs. We're probably the oldest people actually dancing, sweating in our ugly holiday sweaters while everyone else is dressed to impress. But we don't care. We're having fun. And it feels so damn good.

"You getting tired?" Bryan yells over the pounding bass line.

"I could do this all night!" I yell back, shaking my menorah-lit tits at him.

Just then, I'm doused with something cold and wet.

"Oh shit! I'm so sorry!"

A kid who looks barely eighteen, with a dyed-pink faux-hawk and huge kohl-lined eyes, is looking down at me sorrowfully. They just spilled an entire cheap gin drink all over the front of my menorah-boobs.

"No big deal," I say, dabbing at my chest. I hit the button to turn off the lights so I don't wind up electrocuting myself or something. Death-by-ugly-Hanukkah-sweater-on-gay-bar-dance-floor is just not the way I want to go.

"You okay?" Bryan asks.

"Yep," I say. But the buzzy spell is broken, and I'm realizing how late it is and how tired I am. Dancing at a bar past midnight just isn't my speed anymore. I suddenly want nothing more than my sweatpants and pillows. "I think I'm gonna head home, though. Past my bedtime."

"You sure?"

I nod and turn to go. But suddenly there's Carlos, with three tequila shots in hand. He's grinning like the mischievous schoolboy he once was. Before I can even protest, he's handed one of the shots to me, another to Bryan, and is holding his own aloft.

"Yassss," says Bryan.

"*¡Salud!*" Carlos cries.

"*L'chaim!*" I yell.

And we take the shots.

13

After that last shot, I probably should've called a car. But transit is one of the reasons we all claim city living is ideal, so I usually guilt myself into taking the train when I can. Besides, the sign outside the station says there's a brown line approaching in two minutes. And for the first time in forever, I don't feel the ominous undercurrent of dread and stasis pulling me down. I feel happy—and, yes, tipsy, but not so drunk that I'm falling on my ass or anything. So, I take the L toward Lincoln Square, humming Christmas songs under my breath as the train rattles through Chicago.

"Nice shirt."

Ready to accept the millionth grinning compliment of the night on my gaudy holiday sweater, I look up with a liquor-eased smile of my own.

But the man looking down at me isn't smiling.

He's a thin white guy. Young, maybe in his late twenties. He's wearing a denim jacket, not nearly warm enough for this chilly night, but a cavalier attitude toward the cold is typical of Midwestern guys. He could be a grad student at DePaul or Loyola or something, with his crisp-cut blond hair and bland good looks. But there's something unnerving about him.

It's the way he's looking at me.

Like I somehow pissed him off.

My smile freezes, along with the rest of me.

There's an ominous tint in his pale blue eyes. My whole body has gone taut with a fear that feels ancient, familiar. I know men like this; a shadowy echo in the back of my mind agrees in a whisper: *We have always known men like this.*

"Fucking Jew," he says, and spits on the floor of the train.

It lands, wet and bubbly, just to the left of my scuffed winter boots.

Everything suddenly feels hyperreal, every detail vivid. I'm looking around and realizing that there's no one else in the train car. It's just me and the skinny white guy, and this isn't a hallucination.

Shit.

My heart has become a battering ram trying to bang its way right out of my menorah-clad chest. A thousand thoughts slam into me. There's a reason they call antisemitism the oldest hatred. It's ancient and omnipresent. It has never been eradicated, and periodically metastasizes like the cancer it has always been.

Think think think—just this week: the bomb threat at my family's synagogue, the NPR piece about a record number of hate crimes this year, the world still reeling from recent tragedies and dreading the next ones, the phone alert from our neighborhood group about swastikas painted on all those garages in Albany Park.

How did I think none of this would ever directly impact me?

I'm sickened by my own stupidity. A single woman, taking the train alone, after midnight. Drunk. Flaunting my Hanukkah shirt, exposing my identity to the whole damn world.

Having no backup, no protection, not even the mace I used to keep on my keychain when I first moved to the city.

My stomach audibly rumbles.

Now?

Seriously?

The man in the denim jacket's lip curls. He looks disgusted, and I'm not sure if it's because he heard my stomach or just finds everything about me vile. He takes a step toward me, flexing his fingers. His knuckles crack loudly, and I flinch like it's a gunshot. His lips are forming a smirk now. He can tell I'm scared. He's enjoying it. He swings his arms upward, catching the handrail above my seat, leaning over me. I can smell his too-heavy cologne and something bitter and oniony on his breath.

Just then, the train lurches to a stop, and I use the excuse of the motion to slide one seat over, then stand up like I'm about to exit. But I don't know if I should—what if he follows me? The door slides open, and I'm flooded with relief when a whole crowd of Christmas carolers steps onto the train.

They're in full Dickensian costumes, all clad in jewel-toned hooded overcoats and wide skirts, hand muffs, top hats on the men. There are at least a dozen of them, laughing and speaking in broad, fake Cockney accents. They fill the train with their voices and bodies, swarming around us, blessedly oblivious to the ominous encounter they've just interrupted.

"Sorry, guvnah," a broad-shouldered caroler says as he accidentally bumps into the thin blond man. "Bit of an oaf, I am."

The man in the denim jacket takes a step back as the other carolers mill around, mercifully filling the space between us. I stand up, zipping my coat and gripping one of the poles for balance, ensuring I'm firmly locked in to the crowd of carolers. I give them a watery smile, mutter hello, and nod my head idiotically up and down, trying to look like I know them. Trying to do whatever I can to become part of the group. There's no greater protection than being claimed.

As the train bumps along, I keep half an eye on the man in the denim jacket. He's pulled out his phone, and most of the times I glance his way he's looking down at it. But twice I catch him staring at me. I shudder and look away, repositioning myself even closer to the nearest caroler, but never fully turning my back on the threat.

When the train pulls up to my stop five minutes later, I'm weak with relief to see that the caroling group is also exiting here. I practically cling to their petticoats as we all step out of the train, spilling out onto the platform. I'm able to walk with them for a full two blocks before they begin bidding each other farewell, breaking off into smaller groups of one and two. Should I try to stick with one of the pairs, or will that make me the creepy stalker now?

Glancing over my shoulder, I verify that there's no one behind me. The man who spit at me must still be on the train, rattling toward the Francisco stop. But I decide I'm not going to take any more stupid chances, and I run the remaining block and a half to my apartment building. I already have my keys in hand, a weapon at the ready, and God help me, I'm going to put the right key in the exterior lock on the first damn try tonight.

When I finally make it into the lobby of my apartment building, a single tear rolls down my cheek. My breathing is ragged, my lungs seizing. I put my hand to my heart, and it presses damp fabric. Very damp—it's more than just sweat. I hold my hand up to my nose and the sharp smell of alcohol makes me cringe.

Dammit.

I'd forgotten the whole reason I hadn't zipped my coat up earlier—my sweater was soaked with gin. My coat, my shirt, everything reeks of body odor and alcohol. I could put off washing the Hanukkah sweater, but I'll need the coat in the morning. It's my only good winter coat, and tomorrow is supposed to be frigid. Even if it fully dries overnight, I can't show up to the office smelling like a frat house. I'm going to have to do a load of laundry.

Swearing and still shaking, I make my way up to my apartment. I change into my comfiest red plaid pajamas and grab a laundry basket, quarters, detergent. Already unsettled, I'm dreading the trek down to the creepy basement. I've never wished I had in-unit laundry as much as I do right now.

But I tell myself I'm being childish. The laundry room isn't that bad. I don't have to go outside, and the lobby door is securely locked—I made sure to pull it shut tight behind me. I'm home. I'm safe. I'm an adult. I can wash a stupid load of laundry.

Still, when the dank smell of the lower level hits my nostrils, my stomach tightens. I hate it down here. It doesn't feel like the rest of the apartment. It feels like a dungeon, where malevolent prisoners are just waiting to lunge.

The basement reveals the true age of the building. What's that Nora Ephron quote, about how some features give away your secrets? "Our faces are lies and our necks are the truth." When it comes to really showing its age, the basement is definitely the neck of the building.

The walls are cemented-in brick, the floors poured concrete. There are cobwebs in all the corners that no one ever bothers to brush away. While everything aboveground has been renovated at some point or another over the past century, the basement has not. It's sectioned off, lurking beneath each of the sprawling arms of the courtyard apartment.

The U-shape of the building makes for three even sections, a really popular old Chicago residential-architecture style. Each section has its own utility room with a washer and dryer. Just one per section, which means you often have to wait on someone else's load to finish before you can wash your clothes. But it could be worse. It could be one washer and dryer for the whole building. Or, like my last apartment, no on-site option at all.

I set my laundry basket down on the cement flooring so I can dig the quarters out from my pajama pocket. A clinking sound makes me gasp, and I drop one of the quarters.

Chill out, Eve. You know that's just the steam heat clinking in the pipes.

I crouch down to see where my quarter rolled. If I can't find it, I'll have to go all the way back upstairs. Thankfully, it didn't get too far. The basement had a lot of water seepage after the big storms this fall, and our super did a low-budget patch job with some construction clay he bought on clearance. After finishing his half-assed repairs, he had several bags of the stuff left over, which he shoved into the basement corner. The abandoned bags of clay had stopped my little quarter in its tracks.

Retrieving the coin, I wrinkle my nose. The sour dampness from the repeated water damage permeates the whole lower level of the building. Nothing down here is ever really repaired or replaced, just jerry-rigged and shoved back into place. The ancient washer and dryer down here, coin-operated and buzzy as hell, are easily older than I am.

Don't make 'em like that anymore, Dad said when he first saw them.

He'd been helping move me in, and squirted mustard all over his shirt when we got Chicago dogs for lunch, so he bought a T-shirt from the hot dog joint and threw his own dirty shirt in the washer when we got back to my new place. He beamed as the beige-colored washing machine shuddered to life.

Lookit her go! Nowadays appliances like that crap out after ten years. These babies are vintage! Quality! They'll outlast us all.

I never expected they would outlast him.

It's stupid, but it's hard not to resent shit like that. The week after my dad died, I found a half gallon of milk in my fridge that had yet to reach its expiration date. I threw the whole damn thing against the wall, screaming *Fuck you!*

Then I silently cleaned up the mess, poured the remaining milk down the drain, put the jug in the recycling bin, went to bed at five in the afternoon, and didn't get up until nine the next morning. I haven't screamed at unexpired milk since then, but the inclination to despise anything that shouldn't have outlasted my father is still there.

Shoving my feelings down deep as I stuff my laundry into the washer, I slam the lid and hit the start button. With a loud buzz, the washer starts shaking awake. For no good reason, I kick the damn thing. Then I turn around and gasp.

Someone's standing in the shadows, watching me.

14

It's the man from the train, I think wildly, pressing my back against the dully thudding washing machine. My heart is ramming into my ribs like a city bus with a drunk driver behind the wheel. *Shit, he followed me, how am I going to—*

But then the figure emerges from the shadows, and my heart slows its panicked pace, if only slightly. It's not the man from the train.

It's Hot Josh.

He's holding a massive basket absolutely overflowing with dirty laundry. Linens are piled so high he's almost completely hidden behind the mound of fabric.

"Sorry, sorry, didn't mean to startle you," he says, tilting the basket toward me as if to indicate *I mean you no harm.* "And I don't know what that washer did to tick you off, but if she shrank your favorite trousers or something, you've made your point and I'm sure she's sorry."

"You scared me to death," I say, still not quite able to catch my breath.

"Saw that," Hot Josh says, sheepish. He shakes his head, boyish and apologetic. "Sorry, again. You, er, just put that load in, then? Before giving her a little kick, showing her who's boss?"

"Yeah," I say, embarrassed anew that he saw me kick the stupid old machine. I look down and realize I'm clad in plaid from head to toe, wearing my cozy but unflattering red flannel pajamas with my clunky winter boots, and my embarrassment deepens. "Sorry, if you need the machine, it'll be about forty-five minutes, but—"

"No, no worries," says Hot Josh. "Not a problem. I'll come back down in a tick."

He turns to go, and I want him to stay. Not only because he's attractive and funny and I somehow enjoy being around him even though I always wind up making a fool of myself… but also because I can't take being down here alone anymore.

"Hey," I say, emboldened by the last lingering alcohol in my system. "I can, um, text you. If you want. When I'm ready to put my load in the dryer? We could come back down together, I'll put my clothes in the dryer, you'll put yours in the wash, it'll be…efficient…"

Oh God, I'm babbling.

"Oh, ah," Josh says, looking mildly uncomfortable. "I can always do my wash tomorrow, it's no rush, I don't want you to have to bother with—"

"Here," I say, shoving my phone at him. "You can just put your number in. I'll text you when I'm ready to come back down. Seriously, it's not a bother, it's…it's kind of creepy down here. I don't actually like coming down by myself."

Throwing in that vulnerable bit of honesty at the end makes the feminist in me wince, but Josh nods.

"Creeps me out, too," he says easily.

Then he sets down his basket. It really does have a shocking amount of laundry in it; he must go weeks in between washes, which strikes me as odd for someone who seems so otherwise fastidious. He takes my phone, and looks puzzled.

"Battery's dead," he says.

"Oh, no, it's just—off," I say, flustered.

"Ah," he says, nonplussed. He turns the phone on, and we stand there awkwardly for a moment as it comes to life. He hands it to me to enter my passcode; after I do that, he swiftly punches in a number. His pocket immediately buzzes.

"Calling myself. Now I'll have your number, too."

"Cool," I say, taking my phone back and hardly believing my luck.

I just got Hot Josh's number!

Sasha and Bryan are going to plotz.

"Cheers," says Josh, picking up his basket and turning to go upstairs. Then he looks over his shoulder at me. "Coming up, then?"

"Yep—yes," I say, putting my empty basket on top of the rumbling washer.

As I follow him upstairs, I groan inwardly. He probably thinks I'm deranged. There's no need for me to get his number and text him. He lives across the damn hallway. I could've just offered to knock on his door when it was time to go downstairs and swap the loads of laundry.

Then again, either that hadn't occurred to him, making us equally foolish, or it had…and he'd given me his phone number anyway. The tiniest seed of hope takes root in my chest, extending tentative tendrils.

Maybe he *wanted* me to have his number.

Maybe I really should ask him to be my date to the wedding, right now. It's already super last-minute; the wedding is just four days away. There's truly no time to waste.

Then again, if I ask him now, and he says no, our rendezvous in forty-five minutes to head to the basement will be supremely awkward. And this day has already done a number on my nerves.

Tomorrow, I promise myself. *I'll ask him tomorrow.*

WEDNESDAY

15

"...beginning to look a lot like Christmas
Toys in every store
But the prettiest sight to see is the holly that will be
On your own front door..."

My radio alarm goes off, and I blearily rub at my eyes. I barely slept last night. It was almost two in the morning before my laundry was done—Josh went downstairs with me when I swapped my load from washer to dryer, but I had to dart down alone to grab my clothes when the dryer cycle was done. Even after its time in the dryer, my Hanukkah sweater was still damp. Possibly ruined, since I'm not sure if full-out laundering is something the cheap little battery pack can handle.

I should have just dry-cleaned it. Instead, upon realizing my mistake, I hastily draped my once-cheery sweater across the rickety white plastic drying rack some tenant had abandoned in the basement years ago. I touched it gently, thinking of the grin on my father's face when he gave the sweater to me. My heart twisted painfully at the memory.

Hoping the poor garment might recover, I'd grabbed my mercifully dry coat and hurried back upstairs. Burrowing under my covers, praying to finally sleep, I kept tossing and turning. I was too wired, too anxious. I couldn't stop thinking about the cold-eyed man on the train. His hateful stare, boring into me from that carelessly handsome face. His spit hitting the floor by my boot.

Fucking Jew.

The vision of my grandmother on the train earlier in the week had felt like a warning, and now it's hard not to feel like this is exactly the sort of thing she would be trying to warn me about. If anything was going to summon the spirit of a Holocaust survivor, surely it was this rising neo-Nazi tide. But a warning isn't enough. I'm already scared. I don't need an alert; I need a plan.

Bubbe, what am I supposed to do?

When I finally did drift off to uneasy sleep, my mind tossed me from one nightmarish scene to another. Bubbe made an appearance at some point. Even while I was sleeping, the feeling that crept through me felt exactly the same as on the train, when the panhandling woman morphed into my grandmother. A fog of dulled dread, hope, and a desperate but futile desire to understand what was happening. She was saying something to me again, something I still couldn't quite understand.

"Make..." Bubbe repeated, voice firm. *"Make..."*

Her rasping voice sounded just like the woman on the train— and then, my grandmother became the homeless woman. Just as the homeless woman had become her. She went from being my beloved Bubbe to being a stranger who didn't even recognize me, which gutted me. And then she rattled her bucket. When I looked down into it, there wasn't a coin.

Instead, there was a ring.

Emerald and diamond, gold band, something engraved on the inside that I couldn't quite read. The ring was familiar; with a sudden jolt of recognition, I realized it was the same one my mother had worn to lunch at the Walnut Room. I reached down into the bucket, trying to grasp the ring—but then everything went dark, and I woke up.

Now it's seven o'clock, and I think I maybe got four consecutive hours of sleep.

Today's gonna suck.

There's no good breakfast food at my place, so I get an egg-and-cheese croissant from the bakery near the train station. I practically swallow it whole before my train even arrives, and immediately wish I'd gotten two. Stomach still rumbling, I get on the train, and keep my head down for the whole forty-minute ride to the Loop.

After the mercifully eventless train ride, I head directly to my desk. I keep my head down there, too. The threat of layoffs is still hanging like a heavy cloud over the open-office layout. I open up a blank document and stare at it for a while. I still haven't written a single word of the toast I'm supposed to give at the wedding Saturday night. My maid-of-honor speech. Even if delivering it will be hard, writing it should be easy, shouldn't it? I'm a copywriter. This is what I do for a living.

But writing a line that will convince someone they need to pick up a bucket of chicken on their way home is not the same as finding a meaningful way to memorialize my father and grandmother while wishing my sister and her bride much happiness as they begin their new life together.

And somehow making it funny.

I'm starting to realize how little I know about everything—including, and maybe especially, Jewish weddings. I Google "why break glass Jewish wedding" and spend a few minutes reading through the first half-dozen results. *This is just like researching content for copywriting,* I tell myself. I exhale and force my fingers to move across the keys.

At Jewish weddings, it's traditional to step on a glass. I've known about this ritual forever but never really knew why we did it. Why do we shatter something in the middle of a celebration? Well, as I learned in a deep and meaningful 15 minutes of internet searching, it turns out there are many powerful and poetic reasons people ascribe to this ritual. So much symbolism. So many stories. But there's this one big theme that really resonates: we shatter the glass to remember past pain and let it exist alongside current joy. We acknowledge that even in the moments of our greatest joy, sorrow still exists. Maybe that also means that even in our moments of greatest sorrow, joy will still exist.

I stare at the words on the screen.

"They're going to think I'm full of shit," I mutter.

But I do hit Save before closing out of the document.

Looking down at my phone, I see a text from Rosie reminding me to take the day off on Friday so I can run errands for her. And a calendar invitation to the five-o'clock rehearsal dinner downtown. Then a work email pings through—an invitation to another all-staff meeting Monday morning.

I heave a sigh, and decide I'm not going to ask for Friday off. It just seems too risky with the threat of layoffs still looming. But I'll email my group creative director, Amy, and ask her if I can work remotely that day. Amy rarely says no to remote-work requests, seeing as she works remotely from Austin. She moved there during the pandemic, and when Mercer & Mercer reopened the Chicago office, she convinced them that she could help land some high-potential Southwest clients if they let her work from Texas. So she's still there, and not in much of a position to tell others to show up at the office.

By lunchtime, I still haven't crossed paths with Sasha or Bryan. Not too unusual on a busy Wednesday, but today it unsettles me. I want to lay eyes on my friends, to make sure everyone's good after our night of mild debauchery. My train ride home had been unexpectedly terrifying. Sasha took a car home, so she was probably okay, but what if some assholes had messed with Carlos and Bryan?

They're fine, I try to assure myself. *It's just your fatalistic thinking thanks to this past year of hell. They're fine, and they'll be excited to hear that you got Hot Josh's number.*

Cheeks heating at this thought, I turn on my phone. I saved the fresh new number as "Hot Josh," since I don't actually know his last name. His mailbox still has the previous tenant's name on it—Helen Pulaski. Feeling like a silly schoolgirl, I reread our exchange from last night. There's nothing deep or promising about it. It's three stupid lines. But it still makes me smile.

Me: K ready to head down.

HJ: Cool. I'll be in the hallway in a minute, assuming traffic's not brutal.

Me: *(I initially typed "lol" but mercifully erased it before actually sending the slightly more cool)* Ha

"Hey, Eve."

I startle, and look up to see Nancy. I'm immediately wary, wondering what new team bonding activity she's about to propose, or what bad news she's here to deliver. She's dressed in relatively tame attire, for Nancy: black wrap dress, super wide electric-yellow belt. She low-key looks like a bumblebee.

"What's up?" I ask.

She looks over her shoulder, like maybe someone's watching us, and mouths something I can't quite catch. I shake my head, confused. I've always been a terrible lip-reader. She heaves a sigh, leans toward me conspiratorially, and stage-whispers, "Barry's back."

It takes me a second to remember who Barry is.

Oh, shit.

Corporate asshole suit guy.

"He's holed up in the conference room for the day," she says. "Anyone who gets called in there… It's not gonna be good."

"I saw an email about an all-staff meeting Monday. I figured it'd be quiet until then," I say, uncharacteristically engaging with Nancy. Eagerly lapping up my unexpected conversational contribution, Nancy drops her voice even lower.

"We all hoped that. But they're gonna rip off a few Band-Aids before the weekend. That's what I heard, anyway."

I wonder who her sources are, but I don't ask.

"I hope you're wrong," I say instead.

"Me, too," Nancy says with startling sincerity.

Then she flits off to keep pollinating the office with her hot gossip.

For the next hour I'm on pins and needles, dreading a conference-room summons. The office has gone oddly quiet. I'm sure Nancy has successfully spread the Gospel of Downsizing, and everyone else is in the same purgatory, every position feeling precarious. I pull out my phone to try texting Bryan and Sasha. I'd forgotten to turn it off after rereading my exchange with Josh, so I immediately see an alert from TikTok.

I never use that stupid app, and should really take it off my phone. But then I remember I'd opened it yesterday at my mother's insistence that I follow my sister, and I see that the alert is indeed letting me know that user @GoGo-RoRo has posted a new video I might want to see. Against my better judgment, I tap to see what my little sister is telling the world.

The video is soft-focus, using some sort of romantic filter. Rosie is aiming the camera down at herself, ensuring a flattering angle as she strolls the grounds of Camp Heller-Diamond hand in hand with her fiancée, Ana. Poor Ana, the corporate lawyer who absolutely abhors social media, is probably less than thrilled to be in this video. But she's smiling dutifully, gripping Rosie's hand. She's going to be a very patient wife, which is what my sister needs.

"So hiiiiiiiiiiiiiiiiii," Rosie says, beaming at the camera. "It's just FOUR DAYS until I get to marry the love of my life, right here at our favorite place on earth! And in the place where we first met! I know…if you had told me ten years ago this would be my life, and this would be my WIFE, I'd be like…WHAT! And I mean, getting married at a Jewish summer camp? Come on! I'm not even, like, that Jewish! You know? But it just feels so right!"

I roll my eyes.

Not even that Jewish.

What is that supposed to mean?

My sister and I are so different, but I always thought being Jewish was one of the few things we had in common. Apparently even that was something we experienced differently. For me, it's something humming through me all the time. A connection to my family, the foods I eat, my humor, my paranoia, my commitment to social justice, the way I interact with the world. I'm not particularly religious, per se, but I'm unapologetically Jewish.

For Rosie, it's apparently even less intrinsic. A summer camp activity, a factoid about herself she remembers now and then. But somehow she's the one marrying a nice Jewish girl. The three boyfriends I've had in my thirties—two of whom, if I'm being honest, were basically just long-running hookups, and one of whom was a truly toxic asshole—were, coincidentally, all lapsed Catholics.

There was Kirk, when I first moved to Chicago. A tall, mustached volunteer firefighter who "wasn't into commitment" but sure was into going down on me. When that flame was finally extinguished, there was Miguel. A short, muscular actor and cater-waiter who had me run lines with him before auditions and always brought over tons of free food from his catering gigs. He was sweet, but we didn't have much in common other than a love of hot sex followed by the cold leftovers he always provided. I'm ashamed to say that in the end, it was harder to break up with all the free food than the guy.

And most recently, for two solid years, there had been Eric. A psychiatrist with a stunning penthouse apartment in the West Loop. He called me his "Wednesday Girl," telling me that he met with patients most nights, but had blocked off Wednesday for me. I was flattered that such a successful, overscheduled man prioritized weekly time with me. Every Wednesday, without fail, we went out for a fabulous dinner followed by athletic, sweaty, back-arching, tit-bouncing sex that made me see stars. He was charming, brilliant, and had blue eyes that took my breath away. I truly thought he might be the one.

But apparently, so did all six of the women he was sleeping with.

Turns out "Wednesday Girl" wasn't a cute nickname acknowledging his hectic work schedule and sweet commitment to prioritize our weekly quality time. Nope: in addition to his Wednesday Girl, there was also a Tuesday Girl, Thursday Girl, Friday Girl, Saturday Girl, and Sunday Girl.

I guess he took Mondays off to stretch, or something.

After calling it quits with Eric more than a year ago, I haven't seen anyone seriously. The idea of diving back into the dating pool makes me shiver. Swiping left and right and wondering who was swiping me made me feel sad even before I spiraled into true depression. Dating is the worst. I sometimes wonder if the old-schoolers have it right. Not matchmaking, necessarily, but courtship. Family introductions. A nudge in the right direction. I'm all about my empowered feminism and everything, but Jesus, trying to find love on your own is brutal these days. It honestly doesn't feel worth all the trouble.

I was already edging away from the dating game when the ground beneath me crumbled. And now it's been more than a year since I went to bed with anyone. Which seems impossible. Achieving an entire year of celibacy? I'd never have taken that bet a few years ago. But here I am, and seeing as I still have little interest in intimacy, there's no end to the streak in sight.

"So anyway!" Rosie continues, golden hair gleaming as she giggles theatrically from her cultivated little corner of TikTok. The camera has shifted slightly, so you can't even see Ana anymore. "The whole thing is going to be so rustic and gorgeous. Mason jars, flowers, and so many candles, SO many candles, you guys— Ugh, sorry! Not *guys*! *Folks! Friends!* Oof, look at me, still washing the patriarchy out of my mouth, sorry sorry sorry— Ahh okay, here we are, look!"

The camera goes from selfie mode to forward facing, showing a bland wooden building with an angled roof.

"This is the *tayatron*, that means *theater*, that's where the wedding ceremony will be. And then over here—" she swings the camera dizzyingly from the first wooden building to a second indistinguishable wooden building right beside it "—this is the cafetorium, where we're going to have the dinner and dancing. Doesn't look like much on the outside but the decorations are so fire, friends. So. Fire! And the food is gonna be upscale camp buffet."

The camera view is on selfie again, Rosie's face filling the frame, lashes perfectly mascaraed, blue eyes wide.

"Let me tell you, the honey-pomegranate-glazed free range air-fried chicken is so mind-blowingly—"

"What are you watching?"

I startle and practically throw my phone, instead managing to click it off and shuffle it under some papers on my desk. Bryan raises a knowing eyebrow.

"Little sister on the Gram?"

"TikTok," I admit.

"Ooh, Old Lady Eve's finally trying the TikTok," he teases. "I'm shocked."

"You're the one who made me get this stupid app."

"We work in advertising. We gotta know what sells."

"We do know what sells."

"Good luck convincing the leadership of that, Neve," Bryan teases, then furrows his brow. "Hold on, you said you were watching *your sister* on TikTok?"

"Yeah?"

"But you were just watching GoGo-RoRo."

"Yeah…?" I say, mouth twitching at how stupid that name sounds out loud.

"Your sister is GoGo-RoRo?"

"Um, I guess…?"

"Shut up."

"What are you—"

"Shut! Up! She's, like, a star. I mean not like a Beyoncé-level star. But, like a fitness influencer that basically every gay I know follows. Plus every woman. And even some straight whack-a-do guys. She has like a million followers."

"You've got to be kidding," I mutter.

"I'm totally serious. She's your sister, for real? The one getting married this weekend? I take back my rejection! I want to go! Take me with you!"

"Too late, Bry."

"Please?"

"Ask me again and we're not friends anymore."

"Fine," he sighs. "But now that I know you're GoGo-RoRo's sister, I'm definitely sneaking along for a family shindig one of these days."

"Please stop saying 'GoGo-RoRo.' It sounds like baby talk. You're not allowed to do that until you and Carlos decide to have a kid."

Bryan momentarily freezes; I guess he still gets flipped out when anyone mentions parenthood. Then he shakes his head and asks, "They drag you over to the Java-Lo account yet? Rumor has it it's about to be all-hands-on-deck!"

"No, not yet," I say, wondering if it's a good thing or a bad thing that I haven't been tapped to help that team yet. "How's the pitch coming along?"

"My junior designer's freaking out, but we're making progress," Bryan says with a shrug. "We'll get there. Hey, I didn't ask, how was lunch with your mom yesterday?"

"It was…you know. Lunch with my mom."

"Was GoGo-RoRo there?"

"Bryan, I swear to God…"

"Okay, okay! So…did you ask hot what's-his-British-butt to the wedding yet?"

"Not yet," I say. "But I'm asking him tonight. Swear."

"Way to eleventh-hour it."

"We call it 'Jewish time,'" I inform him.

"Uh-huh," Bryan says, rolling his eyes. "You seen Sasha today?"

I shake my head.

Before either of us can say anything else, Bryan's group creative director, Julie, appears at his elbow. Julie is a tough advertising broad, in her early sixties with dyed-blue hair cut pixie short. She never looks nervous.

Except now.

"Bryan, there you are," she says, and her voice is too bright. Too warm. I can hear the anxiety fraying its edges. "Can I, uh, talk with you for a minute?"

"Sure," Bryan says, shooting me the briefest of *oh-shit!* looks. "Everything okay?"

Without answering him, Julie gestures forward, toward the conference room. The room where Barry is holed up, deciding our fates. Bryan doesn't even have time to give me another look before Julie, biting her lip, escorts him down the hall.

16

Sasha and I sit beside each other at the wide mahogany bar of the Heron Hotel. The hotel is right across from our office, and its warm, friendly bar is the default rendezvous point for Bryan, Sasha, and me whenever we have a bad day. Sasha and I had hoped to find Bryan here, since neither of us has seen or heard from him since he was laid off a few hours ago. But he's not here.

It turned out Sasha was off-site at a client pitch this morning, and by the time she got into the office after lunch, Bryan was already gone. I didn't see him after Julie escorted him down the hall. It was Nancy, unsurprisingly, who found Sasha and me to confirm the bad news. She barely held back tears when she told us, voice shaking, *They let him go.*

"Bry text you back yet?" Sasha asks for the thousandth time.

"No," I say, sighing, and wishing the bar had a food menu. "I'm going to try Carlos."

"Good idea."

Sasha slowly twirls the bottom of her elegant red wineglass as

I text Carlos. This all feels so wrong. The Java-Lo pitch hasn't even happened yet. If Bryan has already been let go, what does that mean? Are we all on the chopping block?

My phone lights up. Several messages come in, one after the other.

Carlos: Hey hon.

Carlos: B is in for the night.

Carlos: Reeling a bit. But he'll be ok.

Carlos: Talk soon. Xx

I show the text to Sasha, who bites her lip.

"Damn," she says.

I send Carlos a quick reply, thanking him for the update and telling him to reach out if they need anything. Then I turn my phone over face down on the bar and take a long sip of my pinot noir.

"This doesn't feel real," I say.

"And right before the holidays," Sasha says gloomily.

"You think we're next?"

"Probably."

"God," I say, wondering if this week can get any worse.

My litany of woe is overwhelming at this point. Still mourning my dead dad. Unsettling visions of my dead grandmother. Scary train encounters. Shitty workweek. Childhood home about to be sold off. Terminal singlehood and a full year of celibacy. Little sister's hokey Camp Hanukkah wedding to look forward to over the weekend. Bomb threat, evidently not for the first time, at my mother's synagogue. Whole world remains a dumpster fire.

And the cherry on top: happy birthday to me; this weekend I turn forty.

This is the first milestone birthday to bother me. Thirty was no big deal. I was pretty proud of where I was at that point. But I seem to have been treading water in the decade since then, and more recently, slowly drowning. I was already insecure enough about being forty, childless, and single. With everything else pressing in on me, how am I supposed to feel anything but bereft?

I should try to share some of this with Sasha.

Instead, I order us another round.

And then another.

Two hours later, Sasha and I are both drunker than we've been in years. Way, way drunker than at the Christmas concert after-party last night. I can't remember the last time I went out for drinks two days in a row. It feels awful, and it feels wonderful.

"I've missed you," I tell Sasha.

"Yeah, yeah," she says, waving away my words.

"No, I mean it," I say. "We should do this more often."

"Get hammered?"

"Spend time together."

"Yeah," she says. "You're right."

"We should reinstitute Bestie Brunch!"

"Bestie Brunch," Sasha says, closing her eyes dreamily. "It's been, what, a year?"

"More than that," I say.

Sasha, Bryan, and I used to get together almost every Saturday for Bestie Brunch. Even when one of us was seeing someone, the time was sacred. No dates allowed. Just the three of us, drinking bottomless mimosas, eating eggs Benedict, and telling each other everything. But after a solid two-year run, the dedicated time started slipping down our priority lists. Life kept causing each of us to have to cancel, and eventually we just stopped trying to even schedule our once-sacred gathering.

"Maybe we can see if Bryan's up for brunch on Saturday," Sasha suggests.

"Not this Saturday," I say glumly.

"Oh, right," Sasha says. "Fuck. Right. Wedding. Birthday. All of it."

"Yep."

"Eve, there's something I've been meaning to tell you…" Sasha says, and I know she's gonna tell me for the thousandth time that I should never have RSVP'd with a plus-one. The alcohol swimming through my veins has washed away every last drop of my patience. I can't hear the same old rebuke from her again, so I cut her off.

"I'm gonna ask him," I declare, pronouncing each word extremely carefully so I won't sound drunk. Which is an absolute dead giveaway that you're drunk. The more I try to articulate, the less my tongue seems to obey.

"Ask who?" Sasha says, eyelids struggling to stay at half-mast.

"Hajjash," I say.

"Who?"

"Hajjash!"

"Who—"

"Hot," I say, loudly and slowly, enunciating so hard I stretch the next word into two syllables: "Josh."

"Oh, right, right," says Sasha. "You were gonna ask the neighbor guy to the wedding. Yeah yeah, do that. Okay? Ask him. Ask him today. Might be awkward but it's definitely not the worst option."

"Right," I agree. "The worst option would be going alone."

"No," Sasha says softly. She sips from her empty glass, not seeming to notice the nothingness in her mouth, automatically swallowing before adding, barely audibly, "That's not the worst option."

If I were sober, I'd push her about this cryptic statement. Ask her what she means.

But I'm not.

So I don't.

"Well," I say. "Point is, I'm gonna ask him."

"May the odds be ever in your favor," Sasha says, pushing away her empty glass and seeming to step back into herself.

"They probably aren't," I say, swallowing a belch. "But I mean, what the hell, right? What do I have to lose?"

"Your dignity?" Sasha suggests.

I rise. Stumble slightly. As I right myself, I can no longer contain my massive alcohol-soaked burp; I let it loose in a mighty yawp, then make a big flourishing *voilà!* gesture with my hands.

"What dignity?" I ask.

"Fair point," says Sasha.

We close out our tab, embrace, promise to text each other when we get home safely. It's not even eight o'clock, but it's dark and cold. I'm on such liquid autopilot that I get on the train before I remember that I had a nasty encounter last night and also that I'm shit-faced and should probably have called a car.

Too late now, though.

Luckily, I make it to my stop without incident, although I do feel a little queasy. Jerky, motion-sickness-inducing train rides and too much alcohol are not a great combination. As I'm exiting the train, a dude in a Santa suit is waiting to board.

I stare at him, thoughts sloshing through my mind like a spilled drink.

Jesus Christ, what's with all the Santas and carolers and shit lately? Yeah yeah yeah, 'tis the season, blah blah blah. The decorations are nice but I mean, come on, is Chicago rebranding itself as Christmas Town USA?

The man in the Santa suit gives me a friendly wave.

I flip him the bird.

"Not today, Santa," I mutter, lurching down the platform.

17

When I make it home, I don't even bother going to my apartment. I just start pounding on the door across the hallway.

After a moment, the door opens, and Hot Josh looks at me, confused. He's wearing a nice sport coat and button-down shirt, paired with jeans, and barefoot. Working remotely, I realize dimly. Possibly still at work, even though it's pretty late. Maybe his office is on Pacific time. Or London time. Is London ahead of us, or behind us?

God, I'm drunk.

"All right, Eve?"

"Great," I say, brushing sweaty curls from my forehead. Why am I so damn sweaty again? It's freakin' December. Must be the booze. Ugh. Whatever.

"Is there something I can help you with, or...?" Josh asks.

"Yes, so look," I say, barreling forward before I can stop myself. "My little sister's getting married this weekend. Saturday night, out at Camp Heller-Diamond—do you know Camp Heller-Diamond?"

"Oh, er, actually—"

"Anyway I'm the maid of honor and that's a whole thing, but also kind of not a big deal because her best friend, Layla, is the real maid of honor, I'm more like a whaddayacallit…a fountainhead."

"A…what?"

"Fountainhead," I repeat, like he's stupid, until I realize that actually *I'm* the stupid one. I try to laugh it off quickly. "No, hahahaha, sorry, tang got tongue—I mean, tongue got tangled there. Not a fountainhead, a…a…a figurehead! That's it, that's what I was trying to… I'm a *figurehead*."

"You're a figurehead," he repeats, still just as confused.

"Yeah, total fucking figurehead. But anyway, that's not even the point. The point is, I've also been like super busy—*so busy, like so so busy!*—and this thing is just sneaking right up on me and long story short, I don't have a date yet, so do you want to go with me?"

Hot Josh stares at me.

I stare right back, unblinking. What's that they say in negotiations or deal-making or whatever? Whoever speaks first, loses? I'm not going to speak first.

I made my pitch, and now I'm gonna wait it out. And I think it was pretty slick, throwing in the whole I'm-so-busy thing, right? I don't have a date not because, like, I can't *get* a date. I'm just overscheduled, obviously. Haven't *prioritized* dating or sexing lately.

"Uh," says Hot Josh, swallowing so hard his Adam's apple bobs. "That's, erm… That'd be *this* Saturday?"

"Yep," I say confidently.

Then, reeling a bit internally and probably externally as well, I start to second-guess myself: *Wait, what's today? Maybe it's actually next Saturday? No, no, pretty sure it's this Saturday. Yes, it's this Saturday.* I am seventy-five percent certain that I manage to keep all of this in my head, but honestly, I can't swear to that.

"I…can't," says my alarmingly attractive neighbor, glancing down at his phone. Maybe checking the calendar. Maybe faking a text alert. Maybe just checking the time and wondering how he's wasted so much of it having this inane conversation with me. "I have, er, an appointment Saturday."

"An appointment," I repeat dully. "Saturday…night."

"Yes, actually," he says, somewhat defensively. Like he can tell I don't believe him. Which I don't. "Hey, Eve, are you all right, because—"

"Fine," I say, and I think I might be talking too loudly but I can't really tell. "I'm fine. I'm great. It's just also—it's also my birthday this weekend, so that just kinda makes it more, I don't know…like kind of a big weekend for me…"

Shit double shit, why did I say that?

"Oh," says Josh uncomfortably. "Well, ah, happy early birthday. After this weekend, perhaps we could—"

"No, no," I say, waving away whatever pity offer he's about to make. God, I'm so pathetic. "Don't worry about it, it's all good, all good—it is *all* good. Oh, and hey, I hope everything's great with your appointment. I mean—yeah. Appointment. I have lots of appointments, too. You know what? I have one right now."

My cheeks are burning as reality and humiliation begin to set in. I turn on my heel and walk the three steps to my own front door. I fumble for my keys, and, of course, jam the wrong one into the lock.

"Can I help you with—"

"Nope! Got it!" I yell without even turning around. I yank the wrong key from the lock, shove the right one in, half fall into my apartment, and shut the door firmly behind me.

Faaaaaaaaaaaaaaaaaaaaaaaaaaaaaaack.

I'm starving, but there's no food in my stupid apartment. I know I shouldn't have another drink. But my stomach is howling and I've never felt more humiliated in my life and if there's even a prayer of a chance that it'll take the edge off, I'm having another drink.

I stumble to the corner of my kitchen where a deep built-in shelf serves as my singleton liquor cabinet. It's bare bones in there. An empty bottle of gin, an empty bottle of vodka... What the hell's wrong with me, why do I have two empty bottles and nothing else?

I vaguely remember purging a bunch of stuff at some neighborhood give-and-take this summer. God, I wish I had whatever half-full jug of peach schnapps I must've given away. My kingdom for an old bottle of Smirnoff!

Reeling, I open up my fridge, hoping maybe I'm wrong and some food will have magically appeared there. A snack might chip away at all these awful feelings. But my fridge is almost as empty as I am, displaying only the same sad collection of condiments, empty bottles, and forgotten vegetables languishing since sometime before Thanksgiving. Despite my constant hunger, I haven't prioritized getting groceries in weeks now. One more item to add to my never-ending list of failures.

I slump down right there on the kitchen floor, defeated, stomach still noisily complaining. The ominous feeling is tugging at me again, cruelly teasing me in my altered state, making me see shadows in every corner. My head is already starting to throb with a dull ache that will split me wide open in the morning. The inventory of every bad thing I've got going on—what do you call that? A lint, a listy thing...no: *a litany.* My litany of woe—that's what those things are called—is rolling through my mind.

Alone.

Attacked.

They'll bomb us and come for us on the train.

No job, no partner, no self-respect.

Alone, alone, alone...

Hauling myself from the floor, I reach once more for the liquor bottles, confirming they're empty. They sure as hell are. Angry, I drop them into my recycling bin, hearing at least one of them shatter and feeling vague satisfaction at even that small destruction. I look back over at the corner of my kitchen where they came from, and spot something in the recesses of the old built-in shelf. I reach in and pull out a dusty bottle of Mogen David Concord grape wine.

I think I brought it to my parents' house for seder three or four years ago. I distinctly remember my father sending it home with me, assuring me lovingly but firmly that he would never drink that shit. *Worse than Manischewitz*, he told me, *and that's saying something.* I thought I'd put it directly into the trash. No one in our family has ever liked Mogen David. No one but Bubbe.

Bubbe, is this from you?

Hot, stupid tears spring to my eyes.

Dammit.

Can't have that.

I grab a bottle opener and pour myself some shitty, syrupy-sweet kosher wine. It truly is awful, cloying and heavy. I remember how Bubbe would drink glass after glass on holidays, until her eyes went dark and shiny.

As I gaze off into the middle distance, another memory bubbles up. A scene I haven't pictured in years. The first Hanukkah after Bubbe moved in with us, when she said something I never quite understood. Vision blurring, I close my eyes and drift toward a night I haven't thought about in years.

18

It was 1997.

I was thirteen, braces on my teeth, hair an uncontrolled cloud of dark puffy curls. At this tender age, I was somehow considered a woman by my people. I'd just celebrated my bat mitzvah. But I didn't feel like a woman. I felt like a child, and an awkward one at that.

I'd recently had to move out of my room, and into my little sister Rosie's room, so that my grandmother could have the space that used to be mine. I hated sharing a room with seven-year-old Rosie. But I was also fascinated, excited, and a little terrified to have Bubbe living with us.

Bubbe moved in the week before Thanksgiving, so by the time Hanukkah rolled around, we'd all had a little bit of time to settle in to the new arrangements. But it was still fresh, still strange. My father was polite and respectful to his mother-in-law, in spite of the fact that with my parents, Bubbe was difficult, her mood often sour, her tone sharp. But with Rosie and me, she softened. We were her *bubbelehs*, her little dolls. She adored us. She would do anything for us.

The first night of Hanukkah, I had the privilege of lighting the candles. I carefully lit the shamash, the helper candle, with a butane lighter. Then I used the shamash to light the first candle in the menorah. It looked so lonely, perched all on its own in the silver-filigreed hanukkiah. But at least the helper candle sat nearby, adding its light in solidarity.

We sang the blessings together: *"Baruch ata Adonai, eloheinu melech ha-olam, asher kidshanu b'mitz'vo'tav v'tzi-vanu l'hadlik ner shel Chanukah."*

"Happy Hanukkah!" Mom said, clapping her hands merrily. "Time for presents! David, help me with the big one…"

My parents exited the room. Rosie, eager for presents, grabbed a dreidel and sat on the floor, spinning it to distract herself until our parents returned. She was humming the old tune "I Have a Little Dreidel."

Bubbe's eyes were fixed on the flickering flames, but then she turned them toward me.

"You know, *bubbeleh*," she said in her thick Yiddish accent. "Hanukkah isn't really about presents."

I nodded solemnly, although I was pretty sure that Hanukkah was, in fact, very much about presents. Bubbe's face was lined and solemn, her lips narrow and well-defined. Her snowy hair was short, curling slightly around her ears, but not as tightly coiled as my mother's or mine. It was finer, like Rosie's, although before it went white, it was as dark as mine. By thirteen, I was already as tall as her; she was a short, round woman, but her posture was impeccable and she always seemed larger than she was.

"Bubbe," I said softly, "if…if it's not about presents, what is Hanukkah about?"

I winced as soon as I asked the question, feeling silly for asking such a stupid thing. I'd learned all about it in Hebrew school. I knew about the Maccabees, the fight for religious freedom, the victory over oppressors. About reclaiming the temple and rekindling the lamp, which had only enough oil to last one day but somehow lasted eight days, until more oil could be procured and the light sustained. I worried that now Bubbe would think I hadn't paid any attention at all to my Hebrew school education. (Which, to be fair, I mostly hadn't. But I did remember the Hanukkah stuff.) To my surprise, though, her answer mentioned neither Maccabees nor miracles.

"Survival," she said, her voice sharp and sure. "Hanukkah is about survival."

"Oh," I said.

"Not just Hanukkah," Bubbe continued, and for once, she didn't slip me a snack as she offered me her words. "*We* are about survival. Every holiday we celebrate, every story we tell—our people, our history, it's all about survival. That's what we do, *bubbeleh*. We survive. Never forget that."

"Yes, Bubbe," I promised.

"When we're attacked, we fight back," she said darkly. "We will always be attacked, and we will always fight back. We fight harder, and smarter. We do what we have to do. And in the end? We survive."

I shivered a little, because she was doing that thing she did, where she started to scare me by making things too real. When she alluded to all the darkness she'd been through, I could practically see the demons of her past slipping out of the shadows, catching hold of her, and threatening to reach out and grab me, too.

Most of the time, when she edged toward this darkness, my obvious discomfort would pull her back. She would see the fear in my eyes and hate that she put it there, so she would stop talking. Or at the very least, she would change the subject or tell me to run along, to spare me. To let me bask in my innocence for as long as possible.

But not that night.

"When they were coming for my family," Bubbe said, her voice so low I could barely hear it, "I had to do something. Had to make sure we survived. I knew what was being done to people. I knew we might be killed. And I was only one small girl, only a little older than you are now, but I had to do something, to save myself even if I couldn't save everyone else…and that's when I remembered the legend of the golem."

The golem.

Her voice lowered when she said the word, shaded with something like reverence. I didn't know what the word meant, but it made me feel cold. I blinked, shivering harder, wanting to hear whatever story Bubbe was about to tell, but also dreading it.

The Hanukkah candles were dancing lower now, and my mother had turned out the overhead lights before we lit them. Shadows stretched across the room. What was a golem? I couldn't form the words, but I didn't need to. All I had to do was listen as my grandmother kept talking.

"A man," she whispered. "But not a man—more than a man, and less than one. A creature made from earth. From dust, from clay…from desperation. He has a word on his head. Alef-mem-tav."

She lifted a finger into the air, adorned with the emerald ring, which glinted darkly in the flickering candlelight. She traced the outline of each letter, finger trembling slightly.

Alef-mem-tav.

"*Emet,*" she said. "It means *truth*. And as long as truth is on his brow, the golem will keep his people safe. And when he's not needed, we simply erase the alef."

She drew her palm through the air, as if wiping something away, and my tongue went dry.

"When you erase the alef, that leaves mem and tav. Which spells *death*. But taking him from truth to death, it doesn't kill our golem. It just lets him rest. Tells him to be patient. To wait. Until we need him again."

"You...made...?" I asked, my voice barely a whisper.

But she shook her head.

"I would have," she said. "I should have. But before I could, they came for us."

They came for us.

I felt the words in my bones.

"Bubbe," I said, shuddering and wanting comfort. Hoping she could make this thick knot of terror in my stomach dissolve by winking and telling me she was just joking. "That... that's just a story, though, right? It's not real? It's just a story—"

"'Just a story,'" she repeated, shaking her head. She was looking past me, the flickering lights of the candles snapping fire in her dark eyes. "As if stories are not the most powerful things we have."

"Presents!"

My parents burst into the room, turning on the overhead light, flooding the room with too much brightness and cheer all at once. Rosie squealed with delight, but I just sat frozen, staring at my grandmother, whose eyes were on the steadily declining candles.

"We survive," she whispered once more, or maybe I just imagined it.

19

I'm in the basement.

I don't remember coming down here.

My eyes land on the bags in the corner. The bags that some secret part of my mind remembered. Bags of clay.

And there's water, flowing from the drainage sink beside the ancient washer and dryer.

The other ingredient, desperation, shivers deep within me.

I'm fumbling in the dark, trying to do something I don't know how to do. One word keeps beating through my body, thrumming through my veins, singing under my skin.

Survive, survive, survive.

Grasping, holding tight, molding shape and form out of nothingness.

Survive, survive, survive.

My fingers scrape letters into wet clay.

Alef-mem-tav.

Survive, survive, survive.

Breathe in, breathe out.

Survive.
Survive.
Make.

THURSDAY

20

"Rockin' around the Christmas tree
At the Christmas party hop!
Mistletoe hung where you can see
Every couple tries to stop!"

I slam my fist on the clock radio. Usually I aim for the two-minute snooze button to make sure I don't drift back to sleep, but I don't know what the hell I hit this time. Maybe it's snoozed, maybe I turned it all the way off. I don't care.

I feel like death.

How much did I have to drink last night?

As I put my hand to my forehead, a small sound escapes me—something between a grumble and a moan. The pain slicing its way through my head is like a dull butter knife attacking stale bread, grinding slowly.

Shuddering, I pull the covers over my head. I lie there for a few minutes, just breathing, trying to make my head stop screaming at me. For the love of all things holy…what all even happened yesterday? It's coming back in bits and pieces, crumbs of memories sawed off bit by bit by the serrated edge of my hangover headache.

Bryan getting fired. Sasha and me going to the bar at the Heron Hotel, drinking way more than we should have. Me, taking the train home, stumbling into my apartment—no, oh shit, no. I remember now. I didn't stumble directly into my apartment.

I went to Hot Josh's first.

Oh no, oh no no no…

I invited him to the wedding, babbling like an idiot and… and did I call myself a *figurehead*? Can that be right? Understandably, he turned me down, which is when I finally stumbled my drunk ass into my own apartment.

Holy hell! How did I do so many stupid things in just one night? And for Christ's sake, did I really polish off that ancient bottle of disgusting Mogen David?

Feeling like I might throw up, I put my hand to my mouth. My fingernails feel strange against my lips. Holding my hand in front of my face and squinting at my nails, I can see that they're filthy, encrusted with pale dry dust.

What in the hell…?

Still feeling slightly sick, I hear my stomach rumbling hungrily.

Mrrrrrrrrrrrrrrrrrrrrrm.

I think it was my stomach.

Mrrrrrrrrrrrrrrrrrrrrrm.

It had to be my stomach.

Mrrrrrrrrrrrrrrrrrrrrrm.

I throw the comforter off my head and roll over onto my side, eyes still squeezed shut to ward off this awful morning. Finally, exhaling sharply, I open my eyes, and see two dark liquid eyes inches away from my own.

I blink once, slowly, not able to process what I'm seeing.

And then I start to scream.

The man beside me catapults from the bed.

He's fully naked, which makes my scream get even louder, my shriek rising in both pitch and volume.

The naked man is broad-shouldered and muscular, with skin

the color of golden sand. His hair and brows are sandy too, but darker, like wet sand after the tide rolls in. He's facing me head-on, standing at the edge of my bed while I clutch at my covers in terror. But even though he's a stranger, and naked, and in my bedroom, he doesn't look threatening. There's something weirdly familiar about him.

When I take a breath and stop shrieking, I can't help but notice that although he's not, well, standing at attention—he's big.

And circumcised.

"Mrrrrrrrrrrrrrrrrrrrrrrm," he says, and I know now that the low grumbling sound is coming from him. It's all he says, but it somehow conveys more. His eyes are fixed on mine, his hands up, palms toward me.

"Mrrrrrrrrrrrrm, mrrrrm." *I would never hurt you. Please, don't be scared.*

I nod, slowly. I should be absolutely terrified. But I'm not. The fact that I can understand his gravelly growls, which do not in any way resemble actual words, must mean we have some sort of connection. Or that I'm just straight up hallucinating. Either way, I was startled when I first saw this naked man. Obviously. But for some reason, when he indicates that he means me no harm…I believe him.

Until he takes a step toward the bed, and then panic seizes me by the throat. I don't scream this time, but the logical part of my mind kicks into survival mode. I have to get out of here. I have to call for help. I fumble around automatically for my phone—*yes, that's what I need, I need my phone*—scrambling my fingers around my sheets, my bedside table, searching for the damn phone. Is it on, or off? Did I plug it in last night? It should be right by my radio alarm—

"…will get a sentimental feeling when you hear
Voices singing, 'let's be jolly,
Deck the halls with—'"

The sound blaring out of nowhere makes me nearly jump out of my skin. Before I even know what's happening, the naked man is leaping toward me, then past me, to the radio alarm, which he slams with his open palm. The room goes completely silent.

The naked man turns to look at me, hand still pressing the alarm clock flat.

"Mrrmmmmmmmm," he says. *I stopped the threat. Are you all right?*

I stare as he slowly lifts his hand from my bedside table. The radio alarm is shattered into a thousand pieces, sharp shards of which are embedded in the naked man's hand. But he doesn't flinch, doesn't seem to feel any pain. He wipes his hands together, sending bits of plastic and wire falling to the floor, along with something else. Something smaller. Finer. Grainier.

Dust.

Clay?

No.

It can't be.

Something in me snaps into action. I roll away from him, practically falling off the other side of the bed. Flailing my way to my feet, I grab my robe from the open door of my closet and throw it at him.

"Put it on," I say.

Obediently, the man wraps himself in my robe. The arms of the silky purple garment barely come to his elbows, but at least he's no longer nude. He's looking at me expectantly. Like he's awaiting a next command.

Oh, shit.

Is he awaiting a next command?

From *me*?

The thought is terrifying.

And thrilling.

But mostly terrifying.

"Hold still," I say, practically squeaking.

He instantly goes rigid. I stare for a long, long moment, and the mysterious man doesn't move a muscle.

Shaking so hard I'm afraid I might chip a tooth, I walk the long way around the bed, slowly making my way toward him. I don't know what I'm about to do until I'm standing right in front of him, but when only inches separate us, I reach up. I brush the shock of brown hair from his forehead, and gasp.

Three Hebrew letters, engraved on his brow.

Alef. Mem. Tav.

"No way," I whisper. "No…way…"

I must be hallucinating.

This can't be real.

He can't be real.

I absolutely cannot have made a damn golem.

It's impossible.

Besides, a golem wouldn't look this human—weren't they clumpy, muddy monsters? Aside from the distinctive lettering on his brow, this thing—guy, golem, whatever he is—looks like a man. A well-formed, attractive man. Tall and towering, but not unnaturally large—other than his well-endowed southern region. The edges of his hands and fingernails are dusty, but the rest of him isn't. He doesn't look like the lumpy mud-monster of golem lore.

Oh my God, Eve, get it together.

What does it matter what they hypothetically look like? There's no such thing as golems, and certainly no way in hell that I could have made one. Even if they did exist, wasn't creating them the purview of, like, old bearded rabbis?

But then I remember my Bubbe's words.

I would have. I should have. But before I could…

A pounding on my door interrupts my thoughts.

The golem—*holy shit, I'm really thinking of this guy as a golem*—swivels his head toward the sound. With a low growl, he takes a step toward the front of my apartment. I put my hands on his chest, stopping him. Beneath the silky robe, his pecs feel like chiseled rock. If I'm hallucinating, someone must've slipped me one hell of a drug.

"Wait here," I tell him.

He doesn't look pleased.

But he stands still.

I run from my bedroom to my living room, practically flinging myself against the door. My eye is so close to the peephole I have to blink a minute and let my vision adjust before I can see through it. There, on the other side of my door, is Hot Josh.

Exhaling shakily, I turn the dead bolt and open the door.

"Eve," says Josh, looking concerned. He's wearing a creamy cable-knit sweater and dark brown corduroys. He looks much preppier than usual, like he's about to teach a sociology class or something, and somehow this, too, is hot. "Are you all right?"

"Oh, yeah," I say, trying to sound casual but probably sounding manic. "I'm fine, why?"

"Thought I heard screaming," he says. "Were you—"

"TV," I say, jerking my thumb toward the small and utterly silent flat screen in my living room. "You know how like sometimes the whispery parts are so quiet, then you turn it up and then out of nowhere there's an action scene and BAM, suddenly it's like way too loud and ha, God, I'm babbling. Anyway, I'm sorry about the noise."

"Oh…okay," Josh says, not looking entirely convinced. "So you're…you're all right, then?"

"Yep, never better," I say, which is a lie for more reasons than I can count.

"Right," Josh says. "Good, then. Hey, uh, Eve. About last night—"

"Now's not actually a great time," I say, face practically bursting into flames. Even the presence of a handmade man/possible hallucination is not enough to overpower my humiliation at the memory of Josh turning me down last night. "I have a big meeting this morning, really, really big. So I've really got to get to work."

"Mrmmmmm."

The rumble from my bedroom makes both Josh and I start.

"The hell was that?" Josh asks, dark brows knitting into one thick worried caterpillar on his forehead.

"Radiator," I say, thinking fast. "It's been making the weirdest noises."

My heart is thudding so hard I'm afraid it's going to punch its way out of my chest.

Josh heard the golem.

Which means this isn't just a hallucination.

Holy shit.

"You should…probably get that looked at," Josh says. Then he looks at me, his big brown eyes earnest and searching. "Eve, I just wanted to say—"

"Okay, thanks," I say, nodding my head up and down like a maniacal bobblehead doll. "Yes, I will definitely get my radiator looked at. And I'll keep my TV volume down. Bye!"

I shut the door on Josh and whatever he was about to say. Then I lean against the door, breathing hard. Was Josh about to bring up my drunken appearance at his door last night? Honestly, even if I didn't have a golem in my bedroom, no way in hell did I want to talk to Josh about that conversation. Now. Or ever. Also, I wasn't lying when I said I have to get to work.

Especially if I'm taking tomorrow off—or "working remotely," whatever—to help Rosie, I really have to get my ass to the office today. On time. Which means I need to get moving. But what the hell am I going to do with the mythical monster standing guard at my bedside, wearing my purple robe? I can't leave him here. Out of options, I suppress a groan.

I'm going to have to take the golem to the office with me.

21

"Do you, um, want a coffee?"

I look up at the man—golem, creature, figment of my imagination that somehow my neighbor can also hear, whatever he is—and gesture toward the walk-up window at a trendy little coffee dive called The Other Chicago Bean. He looks at me curiously, uncomprehending. I wish he weren't so attractive, but the truth is, he's incredibly good-looking, even in his current ridiculous getup.

Clearly, we couldn't leave my apartment with him wearing my purple robe. So I'd hastily ransacked my room and managed to find some scrub pants I'd stolen from an ex-boyfriend in my twenties—can't remember who it was, but those magical one-size-fits-most scrubs were well worth whatever crappy breakup they came from. I also dug out an oversize T-shirt from the one and only 5K I ever ran, with a shoddy screen print of the Chicago skyline jutting up beneath the words Lakeshore Drive Feel Alive 5K.

When he had on pants and a shirt, I breathed a sigh of relief, then looked down and saw his large bare feet. There's literally nowhere I could take him if he was shuffling around barefoot. Thinking fast, I grabbed my flip-flops out of the shower. They've always been too big for me. They're a terrible December footwear choice, but that's never stopped Midwestern bros from exposing their toes all winter long. And I'm guessing the cold won't bother a golem much.

Not that he's actually a golem, some part of my mind still insists.

In my front hall closet, I'd managed to scrounge up a men's winter coat that someone had once left at my place after a party, back when I used to throw parties. I've been meaning to take it to a coat drive for three or four years now, but thankfully my lengthy procrastination means I can shove my unexpected visitor into a nicely bulky coat. I also discovered a knit cap in the pocket of the coat, but when I made the golem put it on, it didn't go low enough to cover the letters on his forehead.

I had to find a way to cover the alef, mem, and tav. Even in Chicago, where body art is celebrated and interesting ink is no big deal, ancient Hebrew script tattooed across the brow might draw some stares. I grabbed my father's old Cubs baseball hat, the one he gave me when I left for college, and shoved it over the creature's thick mop of brown hair.

The handsome golem blinks down at me now from beneath the pulled-low bill, awaiting further explanation.

"Coffee," I say, louder and slower. "Do you know what that is?"

He shakes his head. *No.*

His attractiveness is almost cinematic. There's something about the strong but lean build and the intense expression in his eyes. He makes my stomach flip-flop like the first time I saw *Clueless*, and Cher Horowitz's insanely hot stepbrother entered the scene. A young Paul Rudd, ageless before he was... well, before he was officially ageless. Lanky body, twinkling eyes, all those open flannel shirts over loose tees. He was the absolute ideal.

God, that movie is such a perfect preservation of the nineties. The outfits—the plaid, the suspenders, the miniskirts and boas! The Valley Girl intonation! And I always wished I could be a Jewish girl who looked like Alicia Silverstone, but that was never going to happen. The best I could hope for was to be the cute-enough nerdy new girl, like Brittany Murphy's character. What was that song they sang, in the party scene, when perfect Paul Rudd is singing with plaid-clad Brittany Murphy?

Rollin' with my homies…

My thoughts are pinwheeling so ludicrously, I almost burst out laughing. I am officially losing my mind.

This can't be happening. I can't be standing here outside my favorite local coffee shop thinking about my favorite nineties movie while I buy a coffee for the golem that I made out of some clay from my apartment's creepy basement.

Then again, is it any more ridiculous that I'm living in a world where my dad is dead, my sister is having a Hanukkah-themed wedding on my fortieth birthday weekend, my grandmother occasionally speaks to me through homeless people, random guys spit at me on the train, and we survived a pandemic by perfecting our sourdough skills?

This is the weirdest timeline.

"You putting in an order, or not?"

The barista at the walk-up window gives me a pointed look. Jade, I think, might be the barista's name. They sometimes host the poetry open mic nights at the coffee shop, which I used to go to now and then. Jade has short green hair and star tattoos running from their collarbone up their neck, looping around their ear. Three small silver hoops dangle from their left eyebrow. Only artists and baristas can pull off this edgy look with zero effort, and the trio of hoops in their raised eyebrow adds a powerful indictment to their stare.

Fair enough: there's a line forming behind me, commuters who need their caffeine fix before they catch a train downtown. The same train I need to catch, as soon as possible.

"Um, yeah…yeah," I say quickly, stepping up to the counter and pulling out a ten. "One peppermint mocha, one regular coffee."

"We don't do peppermint mochas," says Jade with such ire that I almost apologize.

"Oh, just, uh, regular latte and a coffee," I say.

"For the latte, you want soy milk, oat, almond—"

"Just regular milk is fine."

"You want cow milk," Jade says witheringly.

At this, I vaguely remember them wearing a shirt that screamed The Future Is Vegan!!! the last time I was in the shop. I wince and wish I'd gone with oat milk, so I wouldn't seem like the asshole who is not only holding up the line but also exploiting animals. But it's fifty cents extra for oat milk, and the lattes at The Other Chicago Bean are already over-priced, and I hate oat milk.

Behind me, I can feel the golem tense. He takes a step forward, looming over me. Jade, ever nonplussed, looks up. Their eyes do widen slightly at the intimidating presence towering over them.

"Yep, great," I say, smiling brightly. "Cow milk."

"Name for the cups?" Jade asks, eyes still on the golem.

"Eve," I say.

"And let me guess," Jade says, regaining a little of their edge as they nod up toward my supernatural bodyguard. "This is Adam?"

I interject before the golem can growl.

"No, uh, he's— This is…Paul," I say, the name tumbling from my mouth before I even know what I'm saying. "Paul Mudd."

22

I don't know much about golems, but it turns out they have a real thing for caffeine. In fact, I'm pretty sure that no creature in the history of history has ever fallen in love with coffee faster than Paul Mudd.

As we walked from the coffee shop to the train, he hesitantly sipped the compostable cup I'd handed him. Stopped in the middle of the sidewalk. Looked down at the cup, then at me, wonder overtaking his generally stony expression.

"Mrmmmm," he said. *Incredible.*

I agreed—*yep, yep, coffee's pretty great*—then shoved him toward the train station.

Now, sitting on the brown line as it rattles its way toward the Loop, he's reverently clutching his long-emptied cup, sitting straight-backed beside me. I glance down at my watch. Assuming no issues with the train, I should get to the office a little before nine. Mercifully, I have no actual meetings today; I'm just catching up on some web copy, and playing hurry-up-and-wait on some packaging feedback.

But even with a light load, I can't just play hooky today. I'm already planning to "work remotely" while running errands for Rosie tomorrow, and office tensions are so high right now. I can't look like I'm slacking. Or like I'm bringing a hookup to work. God, how am I going to pull this off? Hopefully, Paul Mudd—*God, am I really calling him that?*—can hang out in the breakroom or something and just stay out of sight until I figure out what the hell to do with him.

The train doors slide open, people exiting, people entering. It's becoming more crowded in the car as we get closer to the Loop. A woman with two small children enters at the Irving Park stop, balancing one on her hip while she yells at the other to stay where she can see him.

"Stand up," I tell the golem, indicating that we should relinquish our seats to the family.

The mother gives me a grateful look. I nod pleasantly as I stand and take hold of the cold steel pole. Paul Mudd stands, as well, positioning himself behind me. He wraps his thick fingers around the pole, a few inches above my own, and his protective stance ensures no one else will come into contact with me on the train. He's not quite pressed up against me, but every time the train lurches forward, the front of his body gently knocks into the back of mine.

I feel a little electric shock of excitement each time it happens. A strange shame swirls through me. He's not a real man. I shouldn't be attracted to him. I don't think this is how it's supposed to work with golems. They're supposed to be mindless, hulking mud monsters, inhuman and unappealing. A soldier built only for defense.

But there's nothing monstrous about Paul Mudd.

And I can't help wondering how rock-hard a man made of clay might get.

He thuds against me again, and I shudder with guilty pleasure. Before I know it, we've made it downtown. I exit at Merchandise Mart and the golem follows me wordlessly. He's like a shadow, matching me step for step, never leaving my rear un-guarded. He's not that tall, not really—six feet, maybe. But his presence feels all-encompassing. He doesn't stand. He looms.

When we reach my office building, I hesitate. I look at Paul Mudd, who came to a complete stop as soon I did. He's wait-ing to see what I want him to do. The brim of the Cubs hat barely covers the letters on his forehead; I think about reach-ing up to tug a few strands of his dark-sand hair down a little lower to conceal it more. Thanks to the coat, the top half of him doesn't look too ridiculous for an office visit. But the bot-tom half of him is totally unacceptable, even for an advertising agency. Scrubs. No socks. Ragged old flip-flops. It's a walk-of-shame outfit if I've ever seen one.

A low whistle makes me turn, and I can feel the golem tense.

"Well, well, well," says Bryan, strolling up the block. He gives me a wink, then turns his attention to the golem. "Josh, I presume?"

"Oh, uh, no, this is actually…Paul," I say, wanting to die.

"Paul?" Bryan looks genuinely confused, and more than a little amused. "And where did we find this one…?"

"Bryan, what are you doing here?" I hiss. "Weren't you just—"

"Fired? Yeah," says Bryan. "Well, laid off, technically. But funny thing, tomorrow's the last prep meeting for the big please-don't-dump-us pitch—yes, Java-Lo, *that* one—and sur-prise surprise, the minimum-wage temp they hired to finish up the deck fucked everything up, so Julie called me begging and pleading and I demanded an outrageous hourly rate and she somehow got it approved so voilà, your boy's back. For a day. Hi, Paul. I'm Bryan."

"Mmmmrmm?" *Do we trust him?*

The golem's question is aimed at me, not Bryan.

"Yes, Bryan is one of my very best friends," I say, way too loudly.

"Mmmrmm," says the golem, and nods at Bryan.

"Not much of a talker, huh?" Bryan says, and gives me an approving nod. "Nice. So, you two heading up to the hell-mouth, or...?"

Bryan gestures toward the front entrance of the August Building, and my mouth goes dry. Somehow Paul Mudd has managed to pull off a reasonably normal human interaction with Bryan, but that's because Bryan is a nonthreatening extrovert who can talk to a stick. Or, in this case, a mud man. If I take him up into the office, what will happen when Nancy starts trying to talk to him? Or one of the interns?

Or Sasha?

There's a reason that Take Your Golem to Work Day is not a thing.

"Actually, uh," I say, mind reeling. How could I have ever thought taking Paul Mudd to the office would work? This is insane. I have to find another way. "I'm going up to get my laptop. Gonna work from home the next couple days."

"Work from home, huh," Bryan says, looking at Paul Mudd and letting his gaze linger a little too long over the too-tight crotch of the scrubs. "Work from bed, you mean...?"

"Dude, you can't say that in the office," I say. "I'm pretty sure that counts as sexual harassment."

"We're not in the office," Bryan points out. "And we're not coworkers anymore."

"Don't say that."

"Truth hurts," Bryan says with a shrug.

"Seriously, are you okay?" I ask my friend.

"Yeah, I was actually kind of already considering—" Bryan hesitates, then gives a small shake of his head, like he changed his mind about something. "Never mind. Short answer is yeah. I'm fine. Doctor husband, remember?"

"Bryan, if there's anything—"

"Nah, nothing," he says, then holds open the door. "Shall we?"

"Yeah, I, uh…" I flail, trying to figure out how to make this work. How to pass off my impossible creation as a normal guy while I grab what I need from the office. "Just gimme a sec."

I grab Paul Mudd by the hand and pull him far enough away that I can talk to him without Bryan eavesdropping.

"I need you to stay out here," I tell him. "I'll be right back."

"Mrrmmm." *I go with you.*

"No, you have to stay down here."

"Mrrrmmmmm." *I'm here to protect you.*

"I'll be fine. This is where I work. I just have to get my laptop. You can just…"

I look around wildly. I need something that will keep him safely distracted, just for the twenty minutes it will take me to get what I need. As if in answer to a prayer, a shining beacon at the end of the block catches my eye. Café de Paris, the little patisserie on the corner.

"You can have a coffee while you wait for me!" I say. "A *really big* coffee."

The golem hesitates.

"Mmmmmrmmm." *I do like the coffee.*

Ten minutes later, I'm on the eighteenth floor of the building, hurrying to my desk. Spotting an empty printer paper box near the copy machine, I grab it. As I'm hastily shoving my laptop, charger, notebook, and a few supplies into the box, I hear a concerned gasp behind me. I whirl around and see Nancy with her red no-chip manicure pressed dramatically to her heart. She's wearing tight red pants and a low-cut shimmering green sheath top with red cuffs, looking like some sort of elfin prostitute.

"Oh, Eve!" Nancy cries in mock horror. Or maybe it's sincere; I legitimately cannot tell with her. "You didn't get laid off, did you?"

"What? No," I say, gesturing for her to keep her voice down. I don't want to call any attention to myself or get trapped in co-worker conversations. I just want to get the hell back downstairs before the golem I made starts mumble-growling at strangers. I force a cough. "I started feeling sick, on the train. Just grabbing stuff so I can work from home today."

"Oh, no," says Nancy, backing away to put six feet of distance between us. Fine by me. I should cough at the office more often. "I hope you're all clear for the party tomorrow night!"

I almost ask *what party?* before I remember the stupid harbor cruise.

"Yeah, me too," I say. "Well, see you later."

"But not if you're sick," she says sternly.

"But not if I'm sick," I promise.

"I have some masks, if you need—"

"Bye, Nancy."

I hustle past her, box in arms, and practically run smack into Sasha.

"Eve!" my best friend says, looking at the box in surprise. "You didn't get—"

"No, I didn't get laid off," I say, preempting every question I can think of so I can get the hell out of there as quickly as possible. "I'm just working from home, not feeling great, but oh, speaking of laid off, they brought Bryan back in to help with the big Java-Lo pitch, you should go check in on him, I think he's feeling weird about it, I'll text you later, bye!"

I'm talking so fast that I'm running out of breath, practically wheezing the last few words because there's no time to inhale. Sasha stares at me, dumbfounded. I take a breath, give her an apologetic look, and head for the exit. It's only when I step into the elevator that an odd thought occurs to me.

I'm not hungry. And I haven't eaten a single thing today.

23

I barrel into Café de Paris, sweaty and clutching the printer paper box full of my work stuff. As soon as I'm inside, my heart stops.

The café is charming, as always: golden-framed black-and-white photographs of Parisian street scenes; white trellises and flourishes everywhere you look; and its centerpiece, a long glass display case boasting pastel petit fours, buttery croissants, and a bright rainbow of shiny macarons. It's decorated for the season, not in garish red and green but in elegant gold and white, delicate baubles and lights illuminating the shop.

But all the charm is undercut by a panicked realization: the golem isn't here.

"Hi, hello," I say, flustering my way up to the counter, box of office supplies in hand.

"Bonjour," says the model-pretty woman behind the counter. Her honey-toned chignon is in perfect harmony with the patisserie scene. She's often the one ringing up customers when I come in here, and I think she might also be the owner. She's several inches taller than I am, but so slight I'm sure a strong breeze would send her flying across the pond, all the way back to France. I notice, for the first time, her name embroidered in delicate gold thread on the left bosom of her neat white apron: Karine. "How may I assist you?"

"I left my—friend here," I say, my fingers getting so slick with perspiration I nearly drop my box. I can feel panic rising in me as I try to imagine where he might be, and what he might be doing. Nothing good can come of a twelve-hour-old nonverbal muscled monster wandering through the Loop. "He's about six feet, brown hair, he was in scrub pants and, uh, flip-flops and a Cubs hat, and—"

"Ah, *oui!*" Karine says with a delighted smile. "Monsieur Paul, yes?"

"Yes," I say, stunned.

For a moment I'm caught off guard, wondering how the hell she knew his name. Then I remember giving it to her when I put in his coffee order—*Grande café for Paul, for here, thanks.* Now she's smiling like she has a crush on my golem, referencing him with the familiarity of an old friend.

Which is impossible, since he didn't exist before last night.

"Such a nice man," she says, beaming. "He enjoyed his first coffee so much, and so quickly, even though it was very hot!"

"Yep, that's him," I say. "So where did he go?"

"I offered him a second coffee, for him to take—how you say…'one for the road'—if he would help me to carry some heavy boxes out to the recycling, in the alley. He's very strong, no?"

"Uh, yes," I agree.

"Monsieur Paul should be back any moment—ah, and here he is!"

I crane to look over my shoulder, and see my golem walking into the café. He heads directly for me, and takes the heavy box I'm holding like it's nothing. He tucks it easily under one arm.

"Ah, merci, Monsieur Paul!" the Frenchwoman says.

"Mrrrrmm," he says with a shrug. *It was no trouble, coffee woman.*

"I bought a new machine, you see?" Karine says, gesturing to a chic stainless steel espresso machine. "A friend in Paris, she told me she uses one like this at home, and she sent it to me for my shop. The grind is so fine, and in the same machine, *voilà*, latte!"

"Yeah, great," I say, barely glancing at it.

But then the logo catches my eye: a deeply engraved *JL*, with three threads of stylized steam rising above the letters. I wasn't aware that Java-Lo made such small machines. The footprint was so much smaller than the industrial models we were usually featuring in our campaigns. This one looked like it was exclusively meant for use in a tiny café, or even at home. Not a mansion's massive chef's kitchen, either—this thing would even fit in my dinky kitchen. I wonder why they haven't been marketing that? It seems like such an easy sell.

"Out with the old, in with the new, as they say!" Karine chirps. "And merci again, Paul, for taking out so much of my 'old.'"

She hands the golem a to-go cup of coffee, his name scrawled on the side in scrolling letters, accompanied by a heart. With his free hand, Paul Mudd accepts his third coffee of the day—and of his life. He gives Karine an appreciative nod, and she practically swoons.

"Would you like a croissant?" she asks, trying to keep us—him—there. "Perhaps a petit four, or a macaron—"

"We have to go," I say, taking my companion by the elbow.

"Ahh, *c'est dommage*," she says regretfully. "Another time, then. Au revoir, Monsieur Paul. Happy holidays. We hope to see you again at Café de Paris!"

"Fat chance," I mutter, and hurry him outside.

"Mrmmm?" Paul asks me when we're on the sidewalk. *You didn't want to eat anything?*

It's a fair question. I haven't eaten today, and everything at Café de Paris is delicious. It's embarrassing to calculate how much money I've spent there over the past year; I have basically been a living embodiment of the I-deserve-a-little-treat philosophy. I've been there a hell of a lot (not that Paul's new buddy Karine had ever bothered to learn *my* name) and have never walked out without a beautiful box of sugary carbs. But oddly enough, when I was in the café just now, I wasn't even tempted by the array of pastries.

"I'll eat at lunchtime," I tell Paul Mudd. "Come on, let's get you some actual clothes."

It occurs to me only after we start walking toward the train that I have no idea where we should go to get him clothes. I've never actually been clothes shopping with a man. Not since I was a little kid and occasionally got dragged out clothes shopping with my father, who basically only ever shopped the sales racks at outlet stores.

My father was one of the most generous people on the planet, constantly donating to the causes he loved, picking up the dinner tab when we were out with friends, volunteering at the temple and the animal shelter and for our school events. But he hated spending money on himself. And I doubt he'd want me dropping serious cash on outfits for a man I made out of some basement-repair leftovers.

So when I see a TJ Maxx on the corner ahead, I don't even bother with the train. I grab the golem by his elbow and steer him into the store. I immediately know it's the right choice, because it's not the sort of place where friendly salespeople are breathing down your neck the whole time. It's just a security guard at each entrance making sure you don't shoplift anything from the endless racks of discount clothing. The clothing and the customers are mostly ignored by the rest of the employees.

I steer my clueless companion past the towers of impersonal last-minute gifts, boxes and boxes of bath sets and hot cocoas and gourmet hot sauces, perfect for the person you just barely know who for some reason invites you to their white elephant holiday party. I breathe a sigh of relief when we reach Menswear, which appears to be the least popular section in the entire department store.

"Here," I say, grabbing a few size-large shirts and pants from a rack and shoving them toward the golem. "Try these on."

"Mrrmmm."

Obediently, the golem begins removing his shirt.

"Not out here," I hiss, dragging him toward the fitting rooms as an elderly Indian woman raises her eyebrows in alarm.

After I've given Paul a crash course on the dressing rooms, and how to maneuver the small slide lock, and a very specific order of operations—*go into the stall, close and lock the door, take off your clothes, put on some of the new clothes, come out and show me, repeat*—the golem fashion parade begins.

His first outfit is simple: a ribbed sweater, dark navy, with well-fitting jeans. It's hard not to do a double-take when he walks out. He's still wearing the Cubs cap, which I'd told him to always put on before stepping out of the dressing room. But other than the hat, wearing clothes actually meant for someone of his build is transformative. He looks like he stepped out of a *Vogue* spread using the world's most beautiful people to sell a rugged-everyman look.

At my expression, the corner of his mouth twitches in what might be the golem equivalent of a smile.

"Mrrrrm?" *You are pleased?*

"The shirt and the pants work," I say, crossing my arms over my chest and trying to sound authoritative. "They, you know, uh, fit. But you have to wear a hat, and right now the only one we've got for you looks weird with the outfit, so here— try this next."

I grab for another shirt and shove it at him. He compliantly returns to the dressing room, and emerges a few minutes later in a plain dark green long-sleeve T-shirt.

I nod approvingly.

"Good basic piece. Keeper."

I hand him a few more things to try. Khakis are a no-go; they somehow emphasize his subtly sandy skin, which can't be good. I need him to look as natural as possible. When he comes out in the bulky white cable-knit sweater, I shake my head for that one, too. Way too country club. If there's one thing this guy isn't, it's a WASP.

I grab a couple of T-shirts and a pair of sweatpants, in case he needs something to sleep in. Then, as I'm hanging the rejected country club wear on the rack outside the dressing room, someone else's reject catches my eye. I snag the red-and-black-checkered flannel button-down and tell the golem to put it on with the first pair of pants he tried.

He emerges moments later, once again wearing the same flattering dark-wash jeans, now paired with the red flannel shirt. It's open, revealing his taut, tawny chest. I swallow hard. He looks like a hot Jewish lumberjack. Paul Rudd meets Paul Bunyan.

The golem gives me a somewhat sheepish look, his dusty fingers tapping at the buttons. He doesn't know how they work.

"I'll, uh, help you," I say, closing the distance between us.

My hands tremble slightly as I bring them to his chest, my fingers fumbling on the first button before sliding it into place. Cheeks burning, head down, I quickly finish buttoning his shirt all the way until I reach the waistband of the dark-wash jeans. At the waistband, I hesitate. I've closed all but the very last of the buttons. This shirt is long, meant to comfortably be tucked in or worn loose. Which means that it extends below the belt, the final buttonhole resting expectantly on the dark denim crotch of the tight jeans.

"Just…one more button," I say.

My heart is thundering, my stomach churning, a hot hurricane twisting through my insides. I take the fabric gently, my fingers just barely grazing the denim down below as I slide the final button into place.

Maybe I'm imagining it, but the golem seems to be holding very, very still. I try to keep my breath steady as I look up at him. He's gazing down at me, unblinking, his chest rising and falling with his steady, impossible breath.

"All done," I say.

The golem nods, and smooths the front of the flannel shirt. His palms leave behind a faint trail of dust, so slight you'd miss it if you didn't know to look for it. He keeps one hand on the fabric of his shirt, and rests the other lightly on my hip. My skin tingles at his touch, so gentle but crackling with so much power.

"Mrrmm," he says. *I like this one.*

"Yeah," I say, swallowing hard. "Me, too."

I take a stumbling step back and try to gather my thoughts—which is when it finally occurs to me that I have no idea how much of a wardrobe I should be purchasing for him. Is the golem going to stick around for a while, or crumble into dirt at sunset? My stomach churns, and the first bite of hunger I've felt in almost twenty-four hours starts nibbling at the edge of my gut.

I need him to go to the wedding with me.

That's why I did…whatever I did, isn't it?

Oh my God, is that really why I did this?

Did I really do this?

Focus, Eve. Focus.

One thing at a time.

Something in me decides that no matter what, Paul Mudd is meant to be at my side when Rosie and Ana get married. They need to see someone next to me; so does my mother. If nothing else, he needs to be here through the weekend. That means at least four days' worth of clothes. After the wedding, I have no idea what the hell will happen. But at least factoring him in for that long helps me decide two things, shopping-wise: we're going to have to go to another store at some point, to get him a decent suit.

And I'll hold on to all the receipts.

24

When we exit the store, the golem is wearing the red flannel shirt, the dark-wash jeans, and the Cubs hat. He looks like someone's fantasy of a nice Jewish boy who brings strong cowboy energy to the table. Which, as it turns out, is *my* new fantasy.

His arms are overloaded with two bulky bags of quality discount clothing, plus my box of work stuff. I should really find a coffee shop or someplace to hole up for a bit and check my emails. Distracting as this whole myth-come-to-life thing is, I can't forget the all-too-real prospect of unemployment. I'd told everyone I ran into this morning that I was working remotely. I can't look like a flake when my job is very much on the line.

Kicking myself for not telling everyone I had COVID or something, I finally feel the gnawing teeth of hunger nibbling at my stomach again. Looking around wildly, I spot a little Italian eatery called Amalfi, which I've been meaning to try for ages. And it has a friendly We Have WiFi! sticker in the lower right corner of the window. I steer Paul Mudd in through its narrow doors.

"Table for two?"

The hostess, a young brunette with a wide forehead and a gap between her two front teeth, beams at us. Like she's absolutely delighted, because we've so obviously done something right just by showing up as a party of two. No one ever gives you that exuberant a smile when you ask for a table for one.

"Yep," I say.

"Mrrrrm," Paul Mudd concurs.

"Follow me!"

As we follow the perky hostess toward our table, I glance at the other diners. Mostly couples, leaned in toward one another, stealing bites from plates and sharing amusing videos on their phones. There are also a few families with small children, mouthing apologies to the cheerful waitstaff, dabbing at spaghetti sauce stains that will never come out. There's absolutely no one here on their own.

I guess this isn't the sort of place you come by yourself. Maybe that's why I haven't tried it before. I feel a twinge, suddenly certain I've been missing out on all sorts of things because I haven't been part of a real, honest-to-God couple in so damn long. And I haven't had my Dad surprising me with deli-dates. And I've avoided what remaining family I have. My stomach briefly clenches.

"Here you go!" The hostess with the toothy grin plops our red, white, and green laminated menus on a two-top toward the back of the restaurant. "Your server will be right with you. Enjoy your lunch, and happy holidays!"

I slide into the red pleather seat, and Paul Mudd sits across from me, still awkwardly holding the bags full of newly purchased clothes.

"Oh—you can put those under the table," I say, pointing.

He nods, and carefully places the bags near his massive feet as I pull out my laptop. I get it fired up, but don't have the guest password for the WiFi. Looking around to see if it's scrawled on a specials chalkboard or something, I notice that Paul is just sitting stock-still, staring at me. Waiting. That's when I realize he doesn't know what the hell to do next.

He's never been to a restaurant. He's never been *anywhere*. But he doesn't look nervous, or even uncomfortable. He's just watching me expectantly. Trusting me to know what to do—a truly stupid move on his part. I never know what to do, which is apparently how I wound up molding a man from clay instead of just finding a normal wedding date like a sane human being.

"This is a restaurant," I say slowly, gesturing around the room and hoping that no one is listening in to our conversation. Maybe they'll just assume we're in some sort of language immersion program or something. "People come here to eat."

"Mmrmm," he says. *Restaurant.*

"Yes," I say. I pick up a menu. "And these are menus. They tell you, uh, what you can eat."

"Mmrmmm," he says, picking up his own menu, and regarding it solemnly. *These are the rules about what you can eat.*

"No, not rules," I say, shaking my head. "They're...choices."

"Mrmm-mrmm," he says, confused. *I don't understand.*

"Menus have lots of choices," I say. "Like, do you want spaghetti, or eggplant parm, or maybe some fish... What exactly do you eat?"

"Mmmm," he says. *Whatever you want me to eat, I will eat.*

"It's your choice," I say.

"Mrmm?" *What is a choice?*

"It's a...an option. A decision. This, or this," I say, grabbing the salt and pepper shakers in front of me and using the small glass objects in a bizarre attempt to explain free will to a man made of clay. I lift the salt shaker, then the pepper, each in turn. "You might like this one, or this one. Whichever one you want—that's your choice. You can have what you want."

I offer him both of the small glass containers.

"Mrmm?" *I should eat this?*

"No, don't eat it!" I say hastily, not wanting him to start crunching through the restaurant's glass condiment containers. "Just pick one. To hold for a minute. Whichever one you think looks... I don't know. Prettier."

He hesitates, then takes the pepper. I nod encouragingly.

"Good," I say. "So, it's the same with lunch. You can choose whatever you want."

"Mrmmm." *How do I know what I want?*

"Oh," I say, dumbstruck. Of course he doesn't know what he wants—he doesn't know what anything is: not pasta, not fish, not anything. The only thing he's ever had is coffee. Not that I can judge; after almost forty years on this planet, I still never know what I want, either. "How about this, then... I'll get the eggplant parmesan, you get the chicken Florentine pasta, and if you don't like it, we'll switch."

He nods, stone-faced. (Or clay-faced, I guess.) He's taking this so seriously I can't help but smile. When I do, he instantly smiles back. I'm not sure if it's a genuine reaction or if he's mimicking me, trying to get it right. Before I can dwell on this thought for long, a tall waiter with a forgettable face comes to take our order.

"Eggplant parm and chicken Florentine," I say quickly. "And can I get the WiFi password?"

I spend the next twenty minutes furiously responding to emails and cranking out a quick headline for a spring sales event. Every time I glance up, Paul Mudd is still gazing at me patiently. I feel guilty that he's just sitting there, but I can't help it. *He's fine*, I tell myself, and hit Send on another email.

When I've put out the hottest email fires, I pull out my phone. Steeling myself, I turn it on, then swear under my breath when I see that I have a dozen missed text messages. Four are from Rosie and three are from our mother, all wedding related; I don't even bother reading them. The remaining five are from Sasha.

Sasha: Hey, B says you were with a guy this morning. Who's the guy?

Sasha: And why were you busting through the office so fast?

Sasha: Playing hooky with Mystery Guy or is something up?

Sasha: Hello?

Sasha: Everything ok?

Before I can text her back to say everything's fine, my screen lights up.

Now Sasha is calling me.

"Ugh," I say aloud before I can stop myself.

The golem immediately looks concerned.

"Mrmmm?" *What's wrong?*

"Oh, nothing, it's just—Sasha," I say.

"Mrmm," he says, like he's learning the name. *Sasha.*

"Yeah, she's just—being a little overbearing. Gimme a sec." I sigh and slide my finger across the screen. "Hello?"

"So you'll answer your phone but not a text? This can't be the real Eve Goodman. Where's the pod?"

Where's the pod? has been a running gag for our entire friendship. It's a reference to an old horror movie called... I don't even know. *Invasion of the Pod Aliens?* Or maybe something like *The Godawful Body Snatchers?* I'm not sure, because I've never actually seen the movie, and neither has Sasha. But it's about aliens who come down to earth and hatch from pods and look identical to specific humans, and they take over those humans' lives. Or something like that. Who knows. It's just good shorthand for "why are you being so weird?" And thus Sasha and I are forever nostalgically referencing this film we've never seen, which feels like a deeply millennial thing to do.

"Ha," I say. "Sorry. Phone was silenced. Now I'm about to get on the train."

I wince a little, because I hate lying to Sasha. I can't think of another time that I've done it. Not even when I slept with Kirk the Firefighter one more time after promising Sasha I was really, truly done with him. I confessed my weakness, she rolled her eyes and gave me hell, but ultimately hugged me and got me through it. But this feels like a much, much bigger confession. Which is why, instead of confessing, I have to keep lying.

"Bryan said he ran into you with some guy. So who's the guy?"

I look across the table. There's clearly no way I can tell Eve the truth about Paul Mudd. There's no way I can tell *anyone* the truth about him. If I say that I'm out to lunch with a man I made from leftover basement renovation supplies, Sasha is going to think I'm out to lunch in another way—namely, the gone-completely-batshit-insane way. But if I avoid her question she's only going to get more suspicious. So the only thing I can do is lie to her a second time.

"He's, uh, my wedding date," I say.

"I thought you were going to ask Hot Josh."

"Yep," I say, because it's easier to give a one-word confirmation than concoct some made-up persona for the golem staring straight into my eyes. "That's him. Hot Josh."

"Bryan said you told him the guy's name was Paul."

Shit!

"Oh, uh, well it's Josh Paul," I say, reeling, totally off my game.

"Josh Paul," Sasha says flatly, one hundred percent onto me.

"Yeah," I say, squirming under her gaze. "Kind of like the Pope, but...not."

"Eve. What the hell's going on?"

"It's...complicated," I say, which is the first honest thing I've said this whole damn phone call. I should never have answered it. *Dammit, dammit, dammit.* I've got to end this conversation right the hell now. "Hey, um, I'm about to get on the train, so—"

"Eve, you gotta tell me what's up—"

"Sorry, you're kinda breaking up, the signal's bad here," I say, lying yet again.

"Are you serious with this 'you're breaking up, I can't hear you' routine?"

"I'll call you later, love you, bye!" I say, and hang up on my best friend.

"Mrmmm?" the golem asks. *Are you all right?*

"All good," I say, attempting a smile and turning my phone all the way off once more. "And you're going to love the chicken Florentine."

Turns out, Paul Mudd does indeed love the chicken Florentine. He also loves eggplant parmesan—I'm full after only a few bites, and when I offer him my plate, he practically swallows it whole. Then he grins at me, red sauce rimming his lips like bright blood.

I hand him a napkin; when he doesn't know quite how to use it, I wipe the sauce from his mouth myself. He's so attractive, I almost want to just lick his lips clean.

Calm down, Eve, I tell myself. *He's not real.*

But he sure as hell looks real. And feels real. And by now, he's interacted with so many people that unless I'm in a hospital bed somewhere dreaming all this up while in a deep-ass coma, there's no way I can write him off as a figment of my imagination.

So even if he's not a regular old guy, in the traditional sense, does that have to mean he's not *real*?

"Mrmmmmmmmm," he says when the table is bare between us. *Thank you for making good choices.*

"Don't mention it," I say, a slight discomfort gnawing at me.

Was he thanking me for my choice of entrées, or my choice to bring him to life?

I hastily signal for the check.

After lunch, we get back on the train—mostly so I can convince myself that my lie to Sasha about boarding a train was halfway true. We have the whole train car to ourselves, all the way from the Loop to Lincoln Square, which feels like its own kind of holiday miracle. Paul Mudd keeps his eye on the train doors every time they slide open, constantly on guard. I stare out the window, still somewhat convinced that I've lost my mind.

When we get to my apartment, it's a relief to drop the bags of clothes and box of office stuff we've been lugging around. It's also a relief just to have somehow made it through the morning. I start to pull my laptop out again, then hesitate.

I'm already out of the office. I'm probably about to be laid off, just in time to turn forty. My baby sister's getting married this weekend. I've just lied to my best friend for the first time.

But weirdly... I've also had kind of a nice day.

Clothes shopping. Going out to lunch. Introducing Paul Mudd to concepts like free will. Not exactly a conventional first date, but there's something about being around the golem that makes me feel good. Safe. Seen. Consequences be damned, I just want to enjoy this bizarre day before it all goes up in flames. Instead of opening my laptop, I turn on my phone. Ignoring all the new alerts, I text my boss, Amy.

Me: Not feeling great. ☹

Amy: Oh no! Need to take the day?

Me: Ugh probably

Amy: Ok keep me posted

Me: Thx will do [soup emoji]

"Come on," I say to Paul Mudd. "I'll show you the Square."

Lincoln Square on a Thursday afternoon in December is almost too perfect. Shoppers flit from one artisanal store to the next, wearing long woolen camel coats and bright puffy parkas and slim black ski jackets. The sun sets so early at this time of year that the first lights are already beginning to twinkle in the tree branches. When the holidays have passed and the doldrums have set in, their bare limbs will look sad. But in this moment they look elegant, sharp pencil lines reaching for the sky, holiday lights clinging to them like luminescent dew.

"Mrmmm," says the golem, looking at me thoughtfully. He seems unimpressed with the charming scenery, studying only me. *You like it here.*

"Yes," I say. "This is my neighborhood."

"Mrmmm?" *This is where people like you live?*

"This is where…all kinds of people live," I tell him, taking him by the elbow. "Here, I'll show you my favorite spot."

I walk us into The Book Cellar, a bookstore with its own coffee-and-wine café. Literal literary heaven on earth. The smell of unread pages and fresh-ground beans welcomes us into the cozy space, full of possibility. I glance at my phone to see what time it is, but my phone is off. At the thought of getting another call from Sasha or text from a family member, I decide there's no way I'm turning it back on.

"I'm getting us some wine," I say.

"Mrmm," Paul Mudd says, intrigued.

I get a glass of Malbec for each of us, the warm and slightly spicy one I had here just last weekend when I came in for their blind-date-with-a-book event. It's one of my favorite little treats—every few months, the bookstore staff wrap a bunch of books in plain brown paper and scrawl a few words on the packaging: "sleeper hit," "surprise romance," "mystery with a twist." You buy the book without knowing its actual identity, in hopes of falling in love.

Who would've guessed that less than a week later I'd be sipping the same Malbec, but instead of being on a blind date with a book, I'd be on an entirely different kind of pseudo-date, teaching a golem about wine?

"It comes from grapes," I say, gently swirling my glass and praying I don't splash any over the rim of the glass. Then it occurs to me that *grape* is probably just as meaningless a word to the golem as *wine*. I wonder how he can be so calm, knowing so little. Then again, knowing as much as I know about love, loss, politics, climate change, and on and on and on certainly doesn't do anything to ease my anxiety. Maybe he's the one living the ideal existence. Still, he should at least know what wine is, where it comes from, how delicious it can be. "Grapes are a fruit, which you can eat—"

"Mrmm," chimes in the golem, an eager student. *You have the option to eat grapes. It is a choice.*

"Yes," I say. "But you also have the option of letting someone crush them and make wine out of them, and I think that's an even better choice. Here. Raise your glass."

I raise mine, demonstrating, and Paul instantly raises his as well, the liquid inside sloshing precariously. He's even clumsier than I am.

"L'chaim," I say, shivering a little as I recall the meaning of the toast.

To life.

We clink glasses, my golem and I.

When he sips the wine, his eyes go wide and he holds absolutely still. For a long, long moment, he doesn't say anything. Doesn't move. Doesn't breathe.

My throat seizes with a momentary panic, my own sip of rich Malbec turning to fire in my stomach. What if wine is somehow poison to golems? What if his body can handle caffeine, but not alcohol? What if that little sip just cost me everything?

"Mrmmm," Paul Mudd says, swallowing and raising his glass again. *That's almost as good as coffee.*

I feel weak with relief.

"Depends on your mood," I manage to say, exhaling shakily. "Sometimes it's better than coffee."

He's still holding his glass aloft, waiting. Does he want permission? Do I need to tell him to go ahead and keep drinking? Then I realize what he's actually waiting for, and I can't help but smile.

"We don't have to toast every time," I say.

"Mrmm," he says, disappointed.

"But hey, one more time won't hurt," I say quickly, and bring my glass to meet his. *"L'chaim."*

"Mrmm!"

We drink.

After we've each drained our glass, we head back outside. I stumble a little on a small patch of ice, and the golem effortlessly catches me. His arm is beneath my elbow, just like that, and I'm steadied. Held. I look up at him.

"Thank you," I say, and he nods dutifully.

It must be close to four o'clock by now. I think about turning on my phone, seeing what the damage is—how many work emails I've missed, how many angry calls from Sasha, how many texts about the wedding from my mother and my sister. But I don't want to know.

I don't want to let the real world back in. Not when it's so loud, so crowded, so painful and full of expectations I can never meet. Not when instead, I can keep existing right here in this incredible fantasy world. Drinking wine in the afternoon. Gazing up at the beautiful lights, everything feeling festive and hopeful for the first time in a long damn time. And most of all, having a handsome man catch me, instead of stumbling through everything alone and falling flat on my face as usual.

"Mrmmm?" *Are you all right?*

"Yes," I say. "I'm fine. I'm good."

We stroll through the neighborhood, gazing at the beautiful holiday window displays. When a well-meaning canvasser approaches us with a petition about some worthy cause, the golem growls and the petitioner retreats without saying a word. I suppress a laugh. I'm easily guilted into signing petitions or giving some small donation to the cause, but it's kind of a relief to have someone else make a different choice for me this time.

Maybe it's the wine, maybe it's exhaustion, maybe I'm just delirious, but I'm feeling really good. I shouldn't feel this good, not about spending time with some mud man I wrought with my own two hands. I look up and see the first stars winking down at me, like they know my secret. The sky is pink, purple, and silver, the sun already dipping out of sight behind low-hanging clouds that might sprinkle snow over the city while we sleep. The holiday lights are glowing even more warmly now, daring anyone to resist the intoxicating siren call of a sweet holiday mood.

There's a promising chill in the wind as it whistles through the lit branches above, and I shiver. The golem holds me up against his side, shielding me from the breeze. I lean in to him, buzzing a little from the wine and the heady surrealism of this whole day. It's been so good already, and I want it to be perfect.

I think about taking my golem downtown, so I can show him his first-ever sunset majestically placed in the middle of the city's striking lakeside skyline. There's something achingly romantic about the idea of taking him to the top of a skyscraper and letting his first day on this earth end with a view from the top of the world.

Then again, it's getting cold, and the man beside me feels so tantalizingly warm. He shouldn't feel this warm, this cozy, this tempting. He's not really flesh and blood, is he? If anything, he should feel cold and hard. Shivering at the thought, I realize I'm really only interested in finding out if one very particular part of him is hard.

"Paul," I whisper. "Let's go home."

25

We walk from the square to my apartment, the golem's arm draped protectively across my shoulders the whole time. It's cold, although there's still no snow. The proximity to him keeps me warm, although I'm not sure if there's any actual heat coming from him, or if it's all emanating from my own body. Either way, I barely feel the temperature drop as winter asserts herself in the rapidly darkening night. All I feel is him—the weight of his arm on my shoulders, the solid bulk of his body beside mine, the steady reassurance of his footsteps as we walk. Being this close to him, I can't deny it any longer. I want to feel more of him. To feel *all* of him.

I don't even know if any of the wild fantasies heating my body are even possible. Is he actually human enough for what I want? My surging hormones are screaming, *There's only one way to find out*, but I'm trying to maintain some self-control.

As we approach my apartment, a white minivan pulls out of the alley from behind my building. We halt our steps on the sidewalk, waiting for the vehicle to pull out onto the street.

The tires crunch on the pavement as the van comes to a stop, pausing to check for pedestrians before slowly edging out toward the road. When I see who the driver is, I press myself up against Paul to make sure I'm hidden from view.

It's Hot Josh.

But what is he doing in that van? He's lived here for long enough that if the van was his, I would've seen it by now. I've never seen that van parked anywhere around here. And I've certainly never seen Hot Josh driving it. I would have clocked that, because it's weird. What kind of single guy over thirty drives a minivan?

I've only known one dude who fits that description: Ricky, the skeevy dealer who lived just off campus when I was in college. The one who was cruising toward the latter half of his thirties while still spending all his time with nineteen-year-olds. His entire income came from selling skunk weed to any kid with twenty bucks cash. My gut twists a little as I wonder if my cute British-Jewish neighbor is, in fact, just some low-life drug dealer.

"Mrmmm," says the golem. *You're upset. You're scared.*

"No," I say quickly. "I'm fine. Let's just—get inside."

Pushing Josh from my thoughts, I hurry the golem through the courtyard. I roughly shove my key into the building's exterior lock, trying the wrong one first, as usual—*why do I always do this?*—and lead us upstairs. I lock the door, and tell the golem to wait in the living room. I need a minute to catch my suddenly erratic breath.

When I shut myself into the bathroom, for a half second I'm afraid I might start crying. My emotions are all over the place. I don't know what I'm feeling, what I'm thinking. My mind feels like a coffee grinder, obliterating once-whole thoughts into dark powder. Splashing my face with cold water, I stare into the mirror, shaking my head.

There shouldn't be anything unfamiliar in the reflection:

same dark curls, big eyes, round cheeks. But somehow I barely recognize myself. Everything is off-kilter, altered and askew. There are purplish shadows beneath my eyes, an odd angle to my jaw. I look like an alternate version of myself, unsettled and unsettling.

The magic of the day is rapidly fading. For some reason, seeing Hot Josh totally killed my mood. I don't feel good and consequences-be-damned giddy anymore. Instead of feeling hot with desire, I feel flushed with embarrassment. The more I think about this twisted and impossible scenario, the more deeply uncomfortable I feel. Like I've been messing with things I shouldn't have messed with, and nothing good can come of this. Awful reality is snaking its way back toward me, hissing indictments and disapproval.

My mind flashes back to the memory of Bubbe, first telling me about the legend of the golem. It wasn't a story she was taking lightly; in her telling, the stakes were life and death. Making a golem wasn't something done on a whim. Taking such drastic action was only justified by imminent danger.

But isn't there imminent danger in my life?

There are threats all around me, all the time.

That's not just in my head. It's real. The whole world is a dumpster fire. There's war, pandemics, climate change. Women still have to walk around with our keys between our fingers. Antisemitism is on the rise, yet again. Crime in the city is out of control. The person you love most can suddenly vanish, and then you're alone to deal with all the nightmares.

There's no one to keep me safe, or even check in on me. There's no one on earth who loves me more than anything.

Not anymore.

Still, it's hard to feel like I'm not just being selfish. Maybe I need to just close my eyes, click my heels or whatever the hell, and see if Paul Mudd just disappears. See if I can do the right thing, and drag myself back toward my actual obligations. My hand drifts toward my pocket, ready to pull out my phone, turn it on, and accept my fate. I can't run away from it all any longer. I have to read the emails, respond to the texts, answer the calls, deal with my actual life.

"Eeeeeeve."

I see it happening in the mirror—cold shock sliding over my face like ice forming on a lake. Somehow, looking utterly surprised makes me look more like my old self again. My eyes are still staring into their own reflected depths, blinking slowly, as I try to piece together what I just heard.

Was that…?

It couldn't have been.

I slowly open the bathroom door and look up to see the golem staring down at me, his handsome face chiseled with concern.

"Eeeeeve," he says again.

"Did you just say…my name?" I ask, and when he nods, I gape. "But I thought… I thought you couldn't…"

"Eeeeeve," he says. "Safe."

He moves toward me, slowly opening his arms. Like he wants to enfold me. Wrap himself around me like an impenetrable wall, and make sure nothing and no one can hurt me. At the sight of his open arms, something in me begins to crack.

Here is someone who wants to keep me safe.

Here is someone who cares about me more than anything.

I take one tentative step closer to the golem.

"Yes," I say. "I feel…safe with you."

"Safe," he says again.

"Yes," I say. My voice becomes a trembling whisper. "I want to be safe."

"Want," says the golem, slowly.

"You…want…?" I ask, unable to form the word *me*.

"Eeeeve want?" Paul Mudd says, and I realize he wants this to be *my* choice.

Here is someone who will not pressure me, no matter what he might want. An increasingly human protector who wants what *I* want.

What do I want?

Do I want to do this?

Do I want this to be the first time I get into bed with a man in over a year—finally breaking my dry spell with someone who might not even be real?

When he gets close enough to me that I can breathe in his earthy scent, I know the answer. Whether or not he's real is beside the point. Desire is rarely based in reality, and I'm ready to release myself into this fantasy.

Yes.

This is what I want.

I kiss him, immediately forgetting all the angst of a few moments ago. His lips are rough, but tender. I taste fine grains of sand on my tongue, and there's something delicious about the granulated sensation. It's like sugar, melting instantly in the humid heat of my mouth. When I place my hands under his shirt to feel his body, there's no film of dust. Only flesh and blood, warm and taut. I kiss him again, rising on my tiptoes to press myself against him, and then I'm not having to reach at all because he's lifting me. The simple feeling of his arms around me is enough to make me shudder, my emotions caught somewhere between lust and pure relief.

This is what I want.

I wrap my legs around his waist and he kisses my mouth, my neck, my collarbone. Keeping one hand firmly against my lower back, in one smooth motion he pulls my shirt off. With a rumbling sound, he nuzzles into the lace of my best black bra. His jaw feels lightly stubbled, like soft sandpaper against my breasts. Not enough to hurt, but just enough to make me ache.

Our pants are still on as we begin moving against each other, and it's the most erotic thing I've ever felt. The slim separation of the fabric allows an already-ecstatic sensation that promises, with increasing fervor, all the pleasure that still awaits. The feel of him makes my whole body catch fire. He's hard and strong, straining against the denim that can barely contain the oversize contents. He thrusts forward and up, and I cry out in primal delight. I can feel him already, through every layer. He's right there, finding his way with his perfectly shaped key, ready to slide into the long-neglected lock of my desire.

"Eeeeve want?"

"Yes," I whisper. "Yes…"

All my inhibitions are gone. The sensations sizzling through my body are all I know. I'm moving against him, head rolling back, breath coming fast and heavy. Everything else is falling away, forgotten. All I want is him, and all that exists is this movement, this feeling, shifting up and down, up and down, my thighs tight around the sides of his body. So close, so close.

Even through the tight new denim of his fresh jeans, I can feel every solid inch of him. But it's not enough anymore. I need him inside me. I push against him, harder. Fireworks are already sparking between my legs as my whole body begins rhythmically contracting and releasing, slow now, slow but not for long. Already eager for the pace to increase, wanting to go harder, faster, craving the escalating thrill of friction, our bodies chasing that final satisfaction.

I want to devour this feeling.

I'm hungry.

So hungry.

And finally—*finally*—my craving isn't for food, or sleep, or the past. It's for this moment, right here, right now. I want to be in my body, to experience and revel in whatever is about to come.

"More," I whisper. "Now."

His grip on me tightens.

I start to unbutton his jeans, but he stops me. For a terrifying moment I'm afraid everything is going to stop. But then he's lowering me onto the bed, pinning my arms down with one of his muscular hands while the other does everything for me. He has his pants off in an instant, then somehow with just one hand, smoothly removes mine while I remain pinned. I'm trembling with desire as he sinks his full weight down on me. I reach up for him, scraping at his strong back with my fingernails.

"Eve wants," he breathes against my ear, before sliding his mouth lower.

"Yes," I say, arching my back as he bites at the lace of my bra, tearing the fabric away with a rough, electrifying rip of his teeth. His sandpapery mouth closes around my nipple and I gasp with unrepentant pleasure. "Yes, Eve wants."

FRIDAY

26

My grandmother is looking at me, reaching for me. Her fingers are bare now, but in her liver-spotted hands she's clutching something that used to adorn them. A ring, gleaming emerald. She's taken it off, she's trying to give it to me—but something won't let her. The ring is trapped in her hand, and she can't get rid of it.

The air between us thickens. Everything grows darker, a wall of shadows rising to divide us. The shadowy shape is looming, hulking, threatening to hide my grandmother from view. Her eyes widen in terror.

"Make..."

I sit up, my oversize T-shirt drenched in sweat. I look around, disoriented, trying to still my racing mind and heart. I'm alone in my bed. My alarm hasn't gone off yet, and I quickly unplug it, because I'm not in the mood for Christmas carols. I press my palm to my forehead, trying to figure out what the hell is going on.

Was yesterday all a dream?

The golem, my grandmother's warning, all of it? Weird

back-to-back dreams, brought on by the stress of this week-end's big family wedding?

Probably so.

Obviously so.

Which is a huge relief, and also, incredibly disappointing.

Meanwhile, it's Friday. I groan inwardly, remembering Rosie's unequivocal demand that I take the day off today to help with final wedding errands. And that I basically screwed myself by instead requesting to work remotely, so now both my little sister and my boss will be expecting me to get shit done for them. It's going to be a day full of pent-up emotions, hastily composed emails, and explosions of bridal anxieties.

The whole day plays out in my mind like a bad movie mon-tage: I'll have a full workload on my plate, but will be trying to hide it from my family. I'll be juggling my family's neuro-ses, and trying to hide that from my boss. My sister will ask to borrow my car. My mother will insist on salads for lunch. None of us will mention the man who used to ease all family tensions. I'll endure it all in a lingering haze of weird dreams and repressed existential crises, and will undoubtedly stub a toe or trip down a few stairs at some point. Just to bring a little physical comedy to the montage, of course.

What a way to spend the penultimate day of my thirties.

And I have no date. Because Hot Josh—who may or may not be a drug dealer, or was seeing him in a white van also one of my wacky dreams last night?—turned me down. So I'll also have to explain to my mother and sister that I will not be bringing my mysterious plus-one, because he doesn't actually exist. There's just no end to the humiliation.

I ease myself out of the bed, shuffling into the bathroom. Everything about my morning routine is automatic: pee, wash hands, wash face, brush teeth, think about showering, decide I need coffee first. I walk down the hallway, into the living room, where pale December sunlight is filtering through my eyelet curtains. Before I make it into the adjacent kitchen, I glance over at the door, and stop dead in my tracks.

There's Paul Mudd, fully nude and stone-faced, standing in front of the door like a stripped-down king's guard at Buckingham Palace.

He turns to look at me.

"Mmmmm...orning, Eve," says the golem.

I don't know if I'm more freaked out by his unapologetic nakedness or his ongoing acquisition of language. Or just the fact that he's there at all.

In a flash, last night comes tumbling back to me with inescapable clarity. It wasn't a dream. I remember him saying my name. The first word he'd ever spoken. Eve. How hearing him say my name made it feel all right for me to invite him into my bed. How he was indeed flesh, not clay; how we had ravaged one another. At the fresh and flaming-hot memory, I shiver with both guilt and desire. As I glance at his nude body, a wild part of me suddenly wants to take him into the shower with me right then and there.

But even though he held up all right last night, what if that's a fluke? I mean, he seemed like flesh. He felt like flesh. But is it worth the risk? What if all that pressurized water...undoes him? What if he starts falling apart in muddy clumps in the shower?

This horrific thought quickly zaps my arousal.

"Morning," I squeak.

"Kaw," he says, slowly. "Fee?"

I stare at him, finding that I'm suddenly the one without any discernible words.

"Kaw-fee?" Paul Mudd says again.

"Coffee!" I yelp. I start to turn to the kitchen, to point to the coffeemaker, but I can barely form a sentence and know that brewing a pot will be beyond my current abilities. "Yes, we can— We'll go— Um, I'm just going to take a shower and then we'll head out to get...coffee."

I turn and flee down the hallway, back into the bathroom, shutting the door behind me.

What the hell have I done?

Yesterday wasn't a dream; it was an entire day spent with a man I made out of clay. Followed by a night of sleeping with him. And now a morning where he's guarding my door in the buff and asking for coffee.

And today I have to see my family.

Crappity crappity shit crap.

Okay. Okay. One thing at a time. First, I'll shower. Then, I'll make myself turn on my phone—oh God, that's a big ask. After that, I'll figure out how to juggle a day full of my mother, my sister, wedding errands, and a golem.

A golem I slept with after more than thirteen months of celibacy.

I did not have that on my bingo card for this year.

I peel off my sweaty sleep shirt, and tremble at the fine grains of sand clinging here and there to my skin. Paul Mudd doesn't look or feel as if he's made from dirt, but the fine film of dust from his fingertips seems like an important reminder. Maybe even a warning.

He looks like a real man, but he isn't.

But what makes a man…a man? Isn't everything a construct, even reality? If Paul Mudd is someone who breathes and walks and now even talks…it's nontraditional, sure, but couldn't he be…real?

Or am I just trying to justify having slept with a hunk of clay?

I take the hottest and fastest shower of my life. I scrub with such ferocity that I emerge raw and red, steam rising from my tenderized skin. I wrap myself in a periwinkle towel and practically run from the bathroom to my bedroom, not wanting to deal with the golem again until I'm fully dressed and feeling slightly more human myself.

Picking up my lacy black bra from the floor, I see that it's ripped to shreds. Shuddering with a sort of horrified pleasure, I throw it in the trash. Wishing good bras weren't so expensive, I take my phone off the charger. When I turn it on, I wince, bracing myself. There's one brief, blessed moment of silence.

Then it starts dinging like it's having a seizure.

Dozens of text messages, voicemail alerts, and other notifications are pinging and vibrating and setting my phone ablaze. I want to throw the damn thing across the room. Instead, I do a quick inventory.

Three missed calls from Rosie.

Four missed calls from my mother.

A dozen texts from each of them.

One text from Bryan.

An email from Amy, my boss, asking if I'm feeling any better (oh right, I called in sick yesterday to play hooky with the golem), seeing if I'll still be working remotely today (oh damn, I'm still supposed to work remotely today), and asking for a quick turnaround on a hot task "if I'm up for it" (this feels doubtful). She needs me to pen three to five headlines with big-picture concept campaigns for Java-Lo ASAP.

I vaguely recall Bryan mentioning the all-hands-on-deck status for Java-Lo, right before he got fired. Still, it seems like odd timing to pull me on to the account. I quickly respond to confirm: I'm on Java-Lo now?

Amy responds immediately to say yes, congratulations, I'm now on Team Java-Lo. She's attached the creative brief and a link to the folder with all the work done to date in a follow-up message with the subject line "This Is Not a Drill."

Shit.

I also have a missed call from Sasha—along with *twenty-two text messages* from her, which I definitely can't handle reading at the moment. Especially since, like it or not, the family ones are probably more urgent right about now.

Before I can bring myself to open the unread messages from my mother, the phone lights up: HOT MAMA RENA.

Gritting my teeth, I answer.

"Hi, Mom."

"Oh, good, you're alive!" Mom says, then yells for dramatic effect, probably to Rosie, "Eve answered! She's alive!"

"Okay, calm down—"

"I was worried—starting to get really, *really* worried," Mom says, and her voice almost sounds shaky.

"I'm sorry, Mom," I say, meaning it. "It's just—"

"Eve, Jesus Christ!" Rosie says, having grabbed the phone from our mother. "We've been trying to reach you forever—we're at The Other Chicago Bean—"

"What? Why?"

My mother and sister are at *my* local coffee shop, just a few blocks away?

I immediately break into a cold sweat.

"Um, because the salon and half our other errands are nearby," Rosie says. "But also because we're about to come storm your apartment building—"

"Don't!" I yelp, panicking at the thought of them barreling in here and seeing a naked golem guarding my door.

"Why, you got a guy over or something?" Rosie asks suspiciously, and when I say nothing for three full seconds, she howls, "Oh my God, that's what it is. She's got a guy over there, Mom!"

"Is it the mystery wedding date?" I hear my mother ask, muffled but unmistakable.

"I don't know. Eve, is this your mystery wedding date? Because I totally thought you were bullshitting me with that it's-a-surprise thing."

"It's—yep," I say, voice squeaking. "It's, uh, my wedding date. Paul."

"Paul!" Rosie squeals. "Mom, his name is Paul!"

"Okay, look, I'm going to need a few minutes," I say.

"Sounds like it," Rosie says, then snaps into business mode.

"But for real. I'm happy you're getting laid and all but I'm getting married, *tomorrow*. So I need you, *and your car*, five minutes ago. We have to pick up the flower arrangements, and then I'm sending you to get the wine while Mom and I get the candles. And then we'll all meet up at the salon for the mani-pedis—"

"Rosie," I interrupt, my mind racing. There's no way I can leave the golem alone for all that time, and I'm not ready to introduce him to my mother and sister. Not yet. Although apparently, they'll be meeting him very, very soon. "How about we divide and conquer. Just text me the flower and wine pickup info, I'll go get that taken care of—"

"Yeah but like it's a lot of stuff to carry out to the car—"

"Paul will help me," I say.

"Oh, he will, huh," says Rosie. "That sounds serious. This new guy is already running errands for you?"

"*With* me, not *for* me—"

"So are you also bringing him to the rehearsal dinner tonight?"

Fuck, I think.

"Yep," I say.

"Wow. This must actually be something, Eve. *He* must be something."

"Yep," I say again, this time so weakly I'm sure Rosie's going to know there's something I'm not telling her. "He... something."

"Anyway. If you think divide-and-conquer is best, we'll do that," Rosie says, a little whiny, but also desperate to get her to-do list checked off. "We'll just see you at the salon, then?"

"I'm not sure I'm making it to the salon," I say. "I never texted Layla back, so..."

"Eve! What the hell! Why didn't you text Layla back? I *told* you to text her—"

"And anyway Paul needs me to help him buy a suit," I say quickly.

"He— What?" Rosie says. "He doesn't own a suit?"

"Not one that fits," I say, biting my lip and wanting to get off this call so bad I'm about to explode. "Sorry, Ro, but he really wants me to help him out with this, and obviously I want my date to your wedding to be looking his best, so…"

"Ugh, fine," Rosie says. "Does this mean we're not seeing you until the rehearsal dinner?"

"Yes," I say, trying to keep the relief out of my voice.

"This Paul guy better be unbelievable," says Rosie, and hangs up.

"*Unbelievable* is a good word for him," I mutter.

Throwing my phone onto the bed, I dress as quickly as I can. I select my best dark-wash jeans, the ones that make me look a good ten pounds lighter, as long as I don't slouch. I also grab a deep maroon sweater, nice and bulky, and in a flattering color. As I pull it from the closet, I notice the empty hanger beside it and close my eyes, swearing under my breath.

The missing item is my beloved tacky Hanukkah sweater. It's still in the basement, on the drying rack. It's been down there for two days now. I have to go get it before some irritated neighbor throws it out. The thought that someone already might have trashed it momentarily worries me. Because it's not just a shirt; it's one of the only things I have from my father. I have to go get it before we get all the stupid errands underway.

I make a quick pot of coffee to meet the golem's need for caffeine—since obviously, I'm not taking him to The Other Chicago Bean this morning, when my family might still be there. After taking a few sips from my own steaming mug, I start heading downstairs to the basement to collect my drip-dried Hanukkah sweater. Paul Mudd tries to follow me out the door, but I stop him.

"I'll be fine," I tell him. "I'll be right back. Just have some coffee, take a breather. Okay? Stay. Here."

His expression is impassive, and he holds his ground. I'm

not sure if he always has to obey me, or only when the odds are decent that I'm not in actual danger. Or maybe he doesn't have to listen to me at all. Maybe he can make his own decisions, as long as he thinks they're in my best interest.

I'm not sure if I like him calling the shots that way.

But it does make me feel better about sleeping with him.

No matter what, I don't want the golem coming down into the basement with me. Taking him to the ground zero of his own creation feels inherently risky. Like returning to the scene of the crime will break the spell, and he'll just crumble into dust.

Shuddering at the thought, I make my way down into the creepy basement, hoping it's empty. Lots of people in the building work remotely these days. Mornings have become a popular time to pop in a load before hopping on a video call, and I'm not up for casual chit-chat today. When I enter the laundry room, the washer and dryer are both running, so I must have just missed someone, but thankfully no one's there. I'm also relieved to see my sweater still waiting expectantly on the drying rack.

I grab it, whirl around to head upstairs, and almost run smack into Hot Josh.

"Jesus," I say, clutching the shirt to my chest in a vain attempt to get my heart restarted.

"It's 'Josh,' actually," he says, and almost gets me to laugh.

"All nice Jewish boys look alike, I guess," I say, and when Josh chuckles, I feel like I've won the lottery. Then I remember that he might very well be a drug dealer, and also that I have a golem waiting for me upstairs. I mentally un-cash the lottery ticket.

"Really, Eve," he says, shaking his head. He has another heaping basket of laundry in his arms. This one appears to be mostly towels. How the hell does this guy generate so much laundry? It can't all be his. Does he have a side gig as a wash-and-fold service? If he does, I should hire him. "We have to stop meeting like this."

"Ha," I say.

"Shouldn't you be at work?"

"I'm taking the day off."

"Oh, right, family wedding and all," he says, nodding.

My cheeks go hot. In the delightful ease of this morning's banter, I'd momentarily forgotten about inviting him to the wedding while extremely drunk. And getting turned down flat.

"Yep, that's right," I say.

"You, er, excited for it?"

"Thrilled," I say, an iciness in my voice that wasn't there a minute ago.

"You look nice," he says.

"Thanks," I say, self-conscious and not really believing him. I'm not wearing any makeup, my hair is still damp, and under normal circumstances I'd never want Hot Josh to see me like this. But at least I'm in my good jeans and my pretty maroon sweater. And maybe I have some sort of postcoital golem glow going for me. The thought makes me blush. "Anyway, I have a bunch of errands to run, for my sister, so I should really get going. Um, have a good weekend—"

"Eve, I meant to explain..." Josh begins, then stops when his phone buzzes in his pocket. "Sorry, I need to see if it's—"

He awkwardly sets down the laundry basket and takes out his phone. Several towels fall to the floor from the overflowing basket. When he sees whoever's calling on his phone, he quickly answers it.

"Hey. Yeah, everything's ready... Well I don't know why you would have assumed... No, actually, that doesn't work for me..."

Josh turns from me, hunching down over the clearly upsetting call. He's getting agitated, which seems to be out of character for him. But then again, what do I know?

I narrow my eyes, picturing him in the white van last night.

Because that call sure sounds like it could be someone jonesing for a fix. Maybe my imagination wasn't overactive. Maybe he really is a dealer. Wouldn't be the strangest revelation of this week.

"...next weekend, then... Well, it's not as if I have much choice, so—fine."

Whatever this call is, it's none of my business, and I don't want to leave the golem alone any longer than I have to. So I start to walk around Josh, heading for the stairs. He sees me out of the corner of his eye as he's ending the call.

"Sorry about that," he says. "That was... Never mind. Anyhow, I just wanted to say, about the wedding— You said it was at Camp—"

"Yep," I say, cutting him off at the pass. "Sorry, I really have to get back upstairs, so...have a good weekend. Hope everything goes well with your—appointment."

"My...? Oh. Right, yes. My appointment. Well...right, thanks."

I'm more certain than ever that he was lying to me about having an "appointment." He's definitely hiding something. Well, I'm not going to be charmed by some con artist. Especially not when someone whose motives are entirely transparent is waiting for me upstairs.

"Sweater's getting wrinkled," Josh says, nodding down at the tightly balled fabric in my arms. "Wouldn't want to waste all those days you spent, leaving it down here to dry flat."

I know he's teasing me, but for some reason, it stings.

"If you noticed it down here 'for days,' you could've brought it up to me," I snap.

"Oh," Josh says, looking genuinely taken aback. "Sorry, I didn't figure you'd want me messing about with your clothes, or I'd've—"

"Either mind your own business, or don't," I snap.

There's an awful silence, and I know it's my fault. There

was no reason for me to go after him like that. I'm the one who shifted us from bantering to berating. I should have just gone upstairs and left well enough alone. But his remark felt rude, and I'm not in the mood for an attack of any kind, joking or not.

Honestly, why did I think this guy was so appealing? He's just some random snotty British dude who lives in my building. He generates more laundry than any normal human being on the planet. He has a secret dealer van he parks off-site, probably so none of the neighbors will suspect he's the one doling out addictive drugs to innocent minor children. Who knows what kind of stuff this asshole is really doing? And he's not even that cute.

"Wasn't intending to be snide, Eve," Josh says, thick brows knit together apologetically. He blinks huge, dark-lashed brown eyes at me, looking like a sorrowful puppy dog.

Okay, fine, he's that cute.

But he's still probably a drug dealer, I remind myself. *And I have a golem waiting for me. Who might decide to come looking for me if I don't get my ass back upstairs.*

"Yeah, all good," I say. "See you later."

"I got a little something for you." Josh fumbles in his pocket. "It's just a bit of a—"

But I walk past him before he can pull out whatever it is from his pocket. If it's a joint, a number for a dry cleaner, or whatever else he might think I need, I'm not interested. He can keep it, and also keep whatever smart-ass commentary might come with it.

When I open the door to my apartment, it hits something hard, and I gasp. Paul Mudd is standing directly in front of the door again, a guard at his post, although thankfully fully clothed this time. The interior knob must have hit him right in the crotch when I threw the door open.

"Sorry," I say.

He gives me a confused look. I guess he didn't even feel it when I rammed him in the business section with a solid brass door handle. Which briefly makes me wonder if he felt anything at all last night, when my body was experiencing ecstasy for the first time in far too long. He keeps looking at me like he's trying to divine something from my expression.

"Eve," he says. "Mad?"

"No, I'm not mad," I say, too quickly. But I am mad. Not at the golem, but at Josh. Or at myself, maybe. I don't even know. "We just have…a lot to do today."

"Help," he says, touching his chest, indicating his willingness to serve.

"Yeah," I say, a weird lump forming in my throat. "Thanks. Um, I'll be right back."

I head once more for my bedroom, blinking back tears I don't even understand. I close the door behind me and look down at the wadded-up shirt in my hands. Josh was right. I wrinkled it badly, squandering all those days (*just two days*, I think defensively) of allowing it to line dry in the basement. I also still don't know if I've fully ruined it by washing it and possibly killing the battery. I hope not. I really, really want to see those ridiculous lights light up again.

The memory of my father handing this shirt to me swims before my eyes. His grin, so sincere beneath that walrus mustache of his. Brown eyes beaming. So pleased to have found something so perfect, and to be able to present it to me.

As with any recollection of my father, the warm scene is framed in cold despair. These moments of memory are welcome, but dangerous. I don't want to forget him. But if I let myself think about him for too long, I run the risk of slipping back into the darkest depths of my grief. The sharp edge of the memory warns me away, giving me just enough of a pang to remember the larger pain threatening at any moment to be unearthed.

When you lose someone as suddenly as we lost him, there's no chance for goodbye. He had no final words, no tender farewells. I don't have a parting gift from him. All I have is everything he gave me over the years, most of which is hard to quantify—my sense of humor, my love of deli sandwiches, my unironic Jewish worship of Christmas. It's everything, yet somehow still doesn't feel like enough. I want something I can grasp, something I can show other people to prove that he existed.

But Dad wasn't much of a "stuff" guy. This stupid sweater is one of the only gifts I can remember him giving me that was just from him, just to me. Not from him and my mother, not as part of some set of gifts Rosie and I both got. This sweater is something he saw, purchased, and presented to me, without anyone else getting involved.

I'm not ready for it to be gone. If it's broken, the battery pack ruined…I don't want to know. Not yet.

I'll deal with it if I have to, but not right now. There's already too much else to do. I can't get distracted by something like this.

So I shove the sweater into a dresser drawer, and head out to run some wedding errands with a golem.

27

Three hours later, thanks to the tireless muscles of Paul Mudd and my mad packing skills, all of Rosie and Ana's flowers and wine bottles have been carefully loaded into my sky-blue Subaru. The hatchback trunk looks like a little greenhouse, crowded with gorgeous snow-white roses (*of course* Rosie would have all the flowers at her wedding be roses) and the back seat is packed with neat rows of boxes full of wine. Bottles of red on the seats, bottles of white on the floorboards, everything so tightly positioned they don't even rattle when I drive over a pothole.

Turns out if you have someone to help you with some of the heavy lifting, running wedding errands isn't so bad. I thought my whole day would be eaten up meeting my sister's various demands, but it's barely noon and we've made it all the way through her to-do list. Looking at the clock, I realize I could technically make it to the salon in time for mani-pedis. All the rest of the bridal party will be there, and as maid of honor, I should probably at least make an appearance.

But I said I wasn't going. And it's not like I actually want to go, or they actually want me to be there.

Besides, there's still another item on *my* to-do list.

"All right," I say, looking up at the golem as I turn the car into the parking lot of the Men's Wearhouse in Skokie. "Time to get you a suit."

I didn't feel like dealing with downtown traffic on a Friday, so I'd aimed for a nearby suburb instead. It's often easier to go from my corner of the city to a northern burb full of parking lots than fight traffic and hunt for parking closer to the Loop. Besides, the burbs are best for generic box stores anyway. I was pretty sure Men's Wearhouse was home of the hundred-dollar suit or something like that. One more question I would've asked my father, if I could.

Hey, where do you get a cheap suit? I'd ask.

Are you asking me because my suits look cheap? he'd say.

You said it, not me. I'd wink, and we'd both laugh.

Thankfully, even without being able to verify the information with the man I trusted most, this place does turn out to have affordable suits. It also has incredibly hokey holiday decor, including a sad fake Christmas tree weighed down with Chicago sports team ornaments. The pathetic little tree makes me smile, though. This is exactly the sort of place my father would have bought his suits. Maybe even this very location, fifteen minutes from my childhood home.

The home Mom is about to sell, I think, and my smile fades.

A team of salesmen descend upon us like hungry wolves when we enter, but wisely back off when Paul Mudd snarls at them. On our own, we find a plain charcoal suit that fits the golem like it was made for him. As I fuss over it in front of the mirrors outside the dressing room, a reluctant salesman approaches us. They've all avoided us ever since the growling. But someone's got to get the commission, and I guess this guy drew the short straw.

BETH KANDER • 209

The salesman aims his timid wave at me, making no sudden moves. He has lips so dry they're flaking, a nametag that reads Fred, and either a really bad dishwater-blond toupee or a truly horrible barber. He could be fifty or eighty. The hair makes it hard to tell.

"How's it going?" Fred asks deferentially. "I see you two have good taste."

The golem curls his lip, but I put a reassuring hand on his arm.

"We'll take this one," I say, since the suit Paul is wearing seems perfect.

"We can have it tailored," Fred says, since it's his job to say things like that. Even when it's obvious that the suit fits the snappish customer like a glove. "We send out for alteration, but we can usually turn it round in just a couple days—"

"It fits fine, and we need it for tomorrow," I say, handing him my credit card as another thought occurs to me. "Um, one other thing. Do you have any, like…dress hats?"

Cutting a dashing figure in the suit, Paul Mudd is also still wearing the Cubs hat. He looks like a frat boy forced to attend a formal dance. But we can't have his Hebrew-tattooed forehead on display at the wedding. Especially since some of the guests at a Jewish lifecycle event might actually be able to read it. Not that they would ever assume he was an actual golem, since that would be insane. But seeing the Hebrew word for *truth* on Paul's forehead would understandably raise questions like whether or not he's some fundamentalist cult weirdo.

"Dress hats?" the beleaguered salesman asks, chewing at his chapped lips.

"Yeah, like, I don't know, like a…a…"

For some reason, a top hat is the only fancy hat coming to mind. And a top hat is obviously one hundred percent out of the question. I don't want it to look like I'm so pathetic that I hired a magician to be my date to Rosie's wedding.

"A fedora?" Fred suggests.

"Yes!" I say. "A fedora!"

"I'll go look in the back," Fred says, bewildered.

Apparently, no one has requested a fedora since the days of Al Capone.

The golem wears the suit and fedora out of the store, and I smugly notice several women in the parking lot openly gawking at him as we walk toward my car. They're probably wondering if he's some sort of celebrity, since no mere mortal could pull off the midday suit-and-fedora look with this much unironic ease.

We make it back to my place in twenty minutes. When we park in the lot behind my building and get out of the car, the golem immediately opens the door and begins removing a box of wine bottles.

"No, wait," I say, and he freezes. "Those are for the wedding. We're just here to get ready, then we're going to take those with us—put it back in the car. Please."

Slowly, the golem puts the box back in the car. Then he turns to me and lowers his head.

"Sah-ree," he says, rumbling an apology.

"What? No, you don't have to apologize!" I say quickly, moved by his sweet chagrin. "You didn't know. It's fine. Come on, let's...let's go get ready."

There's nothing he needs to do to get ready. He's already in his sharp new charcoal suit and the matching fedora Sad Salesman Fred managed to dig out of a time capsule. So he just stands in front of my door while I retreat into the bedroom to get gussied up.

Entering my room, I see my computer and groan inwardly. *Shit.* I still haven't written the headlines Amy asked for, nor have I written the speech I'm supposed to deliver at the wedding tomorrow night.

I grab my laptop off my bed and open the document with the paragraph I'd written at the office about breaking the glass in the Jewish wedding ceremony. I stare at it for three full minutes and have no idea where to take it next. Even though they're constantly on my mind, I have no idea how to put into words what my father and my grandmother meant to me. To Rosie. To my mother.

I close that document and open up a new file. I stare at the screen for a long moment, paralyzed by the pressure of writing these particular headlines. I read the brief, but it doesn't feel like I have enough to go on yet. Java-Lo isn't my client. I don't know their culture, don't know their quirks. What I do know is that if we don't keep them happy in these next few days, we might lose their business. Just the *threat* of them pulling out has already cost Bryan his job. The idea of shirking on this task and having it cost someone their job—Sasha, someone from our art department, even freaking Nancy—turns my stomach.

The computer screen blurs before my eyes. And then I remember Paul Mudd in the Parisian coffee shop, accepting a second cup from the Frenchwoman's sleek Java-Lo home model. There was something so inherently charming about a big, strong guy sipping the delicate brew. Something that busted through any stereotypes of Java-Lo only being for big businesses or corporate-type environments. I quickly reread the creative brief, and pop over to the Java-Lo website to confirm what models they sell.

Sure enough, when I scroll all the way down, they have an entire line of home and "small shop" coffeemakers with dual grind-and-froth action. It's ridiculous that this is at the bottom of the pile—and based on the copy, mostly aimed at the European market. Why didn't these products become front and center during lockdown? And even now, with so many folks working from home, seeking flex schedules…why wouldn't this coffee contraption behemoth be raising their public profile, and trying to sell directly to consumers instead of only to the still-struggling hotels, conference centers, and massive catering operations?

Something clicks, and I bang out a half-dozen headlines:

Daily Grind. Favorite Find.

Escape the Daily Grind.

Hi, Lo.

Java-Lo: To Stay or To-Go

Work from Home. Drink from Heaven.

Make Home-Work Taste Better.

I'm on a roll, and I swiftly write up a tight rationale for the headlines. Some of them won't make sense on their own; a few are admittedly hacky. But with the right rationale and supporting art, some of these could really sing.

So I don't just write up the headlines. Instead, I draft a new document to attach with it, and suggest updating the whole creative brief. I make a case for Java-Lo showcasing their industrial coffeemaking products and home versions at the same time, giving them the opportunity to create real brand loyalty so that people come to crave that same fine-ground experience at home, work, and in their favorite local coffee shops. I even throw in an internal logo proof of concept, with the three threads of stylized steam above the letters *JL* each assigned a market sector: home, retail, corporate.

When I'm done with the flurry of activity, I blink at all the neat little files on-screen. I never generate whole-campaign overhauls like this, let alone for a client that isn't even mine. It's not what Amy asked for, but it's good. I know it with a certainty I rarely feel. It might even be good enough for us to win back Java-Lo's affections before they break up with us for good.

Or maybe it's all crap, I think, stomach churning as my confidence slips.

"Eeeeve?" the golem calls from the other room.

Fuck it, I think, and hit Send.

After the email is on its way to Amy, I exhale a sigh of relief. Then it occurs to me that I also still need to write the damn wedding toast. But I'm out of steam for the moment. I have things to say about coffee, but nothing to say about love.

So be it. I might be a terrible maid of honor, but at least I'm still a decent copywriter with a graduate degree in marketing. I used to work at a small shop where I had to do all this shit, and I was good at it. It feels nice to flex this muscle, and show my boss that maybe the Mercer & Mercer team should see me as a burgeoning brand strategist.

Glad to have taken care of at least one of the obligations hanging over my head, I figure I should probably check in on the golem before resuming my rehearsal-dinner dress-up routine. When I open the door, he's still standing just outside it, but his head is inclined toward the window. Like he's listening for something.

"Everything okay?" I ask.

He gives me an unreadable look.

"Loud outside," he says.

I wonder if he means the constant street sounds, the train in the distance, people chatting on the sidewalk, all the normal city sounds. He looks so troubled that I'm worried he's tuning in to something darker, but I can't worry about that right now. I just nod and shut my bedroom door again, leaving him to eavesdrop on whatever evil golems are on the lookout for when they stand guard.

"Here," I say, leading him down the short hallway and back into my small living room. I turn on my television, and hand him the remote. He'll figure it out, or not. "Just focus on this for a few minutes, ignore whatever's going on outside."

I return to my bedroom and pull out the dress I'd decided to wear for the rehearsal dinner. I knew I wanted to wear black tonight, since tomorrow I'll be one of six women wearing the same magenta pantsuit Rosie selected for her bridal party. (Ana's brides-people are wearing charcoal blazers, and whatever they like under them: suits, dresses, flattering denim. It's hard not to wish I was standing up on her side of the wedding.) The thing is, I only own one black dress: the one I wore to my father's funeral last year. Maybe it's morbid, but it feels somehow fitting to don it again tonight. A tribute to our loved ones missing from the celebration.

As I drag eyeliner across my lids and twist my curls into a bun, I try not to think too deeply about the golem in my living room. What would my grandmother say if she knew what I'd done? When she told me the story of the golem, it was lore. A rabbi grasping clumps of earth, invoking truth and death and elemental forces; cobbling together a creature with clay and desperation. The legend of a powerful protector of our people, conjured to safeguard Jews when the whole world had turned on us. When she considered building one, the Nazis were coming for her. These were all stories where the stakes were literal life and death.

Summoning the power and protection of a golem so I'd have a wedding date feels pathetic in comparison.

I wasn't thinking of anyone but myself when I made him. In spite of all the shit going on in the world, when push came to shove, I didn't create a protector like the golem of Prague. I built myself a pseudo-boyfriend, my own personal bodyguard and companion. I was applying ancient wisdom like a cheap Band-Aid.

But is it wrong to want someone to care about me?

And isn't Bubbe the one who told me to make…something?

*Something, but probably not some*one…

My stomach rumbles.

I want to eat something, to take the edge off. But for the first time, it occurs to me that maybe I'm not even actually hungry. It's just habit. Something to want when I can't have what I really want. A way to fill the rapidly expanding black hole of loss, questions, fears, and doubts constantly metastasizing within me.

I lift a tube of lipstick to my mouth with trembling hands. In the distance, a siren wails outside. I barely notice the sound, since my apartment is around the corner from a hospital and sirens are constantly cutting through the air around here. But a second after the siren, there are three loud thuds in my hallway, which I barely have time to identify as heavy running footfalls before the golem bursts through my bedroom door. He wraps his arms around me, cradling my head in his hands, and takes us both down to the floor.

"What the hell!"

"Eve safe," says the golem.

The pity party I was just throwing ends abruptly. Instead of staring in the mirror and spiraling into despair, my perspective has quite literally shifted. I'm flat on my back on the bedroom floor, the golem covering my entire body with his. My hair is probably ruined, and I'm definitely going to need to redo the lipstick I was applying when he tackled me. But instead of feeling irritated, I feel relieved. Knocked off course from reality once more, held tightly by someone hell-bent on taking care of me.

"Eve safe," the golem repeats, looking up as the siren wails once more in the distance.

"It's just a siren," I tell him, trying to reassure the ever-vigilant Paul Mudd that there was no actual threat he needed to worry about in this moment. "No danger—not for us, anyway. Someone else might be in trouble, or something, but… but I'm fine. I'm safe."

And then, because he's right there, I kiss him.

He doesn't kiss me back. He's still on alert. But the siren is fading in the distance now, and whatever danger he assumed was heading our way appears indeed to have passed. He blinks, slowly.

"Hey," I say, and kiss him again.

This time he kisses me back.

"This is what makes me feel safe," I say, stroking his arm, his chest, then shifting beneath him, pressing my lower body against his. I realize the truth of my words as I say them. Being close to him, having someone I can trust with my body, and maybe even with my heart, makes me feel safer in the midst of this unstable world. "I want to feel safe. Please."

He moves against me in response, and my whole body thrums with anticipation and relief. His rough mouth finds my neck, and I close my eyes, slipping my hands beneath his starched white shirt and letting everything else fall away.

28

After our tryst on the floor, I quickly redo my hair and makeup. I'm still slightly disheveled and I don't even care. I'm kind of into it, to be honest. When's the last time I showed up somewhere flush-faced and wild-haired? It's exhilarating.

Looking at the time, I swear under my breath and hurry us toward the door. In the living room, I see that the television is still on. Some Dick Wolf show set in Chicago. Two cops making out. In the background, there's a siren, which makes the TV cops pause. I wonder what the golem saw on-screen before he came leaping protectively toward me. Did he see a siren on the show, and learn what it meant from the action on-screen?

I turn off the television, and grab our coats.

"Let's go," I command.

The rehearsal dinner is downtown, which means normally I'd take transit to get there, because traffic and parking anywhere in the Loop sucks. But since I have a Subaru full of bottles and blooms to transfer to my sister, the golem and I drive into the heart of the city.

Parking in the garage connected to the restaurant costs forty dollars, which makes me curse under my breath when I read the posted pricing. But at this point, we'll be late if I take the time to look for cheaper parking. So I punch the button, take the ticket, and park the car. Shoving the ticket into my cute little clutch purse—an early birthday gift from Sasha—I pause. I still haven't even read any of Sasha's messages from yesterday or today. Whenever we cross paths, she's absolutely going to murder me.

Good thing I have a golem to thwart her efforts, I guess.

As soon as we walk into the restaurant, I hear a shriek.

"Safe?" Paul Mudd asks, tensing beside me.

"Oh, that sound isn't technically a threat," I say, although my shoulders have gone so rigid they're practically touching my ears. "It's just my sister."

Rosie comes barreling over, dragging Ana behind her. Rosie is wearing a bright red cocktail dress, her honey-blonde hair done up in a sleek chignon, showing off her narrow neck. She is fit, thin, and vibrating with misdirected energy. Ana, sturdy and curvy, is in billowy black pants and a white sleeveless shift shirt. Her dark hair hangs heavily to her chin on the right side of her face while the left side is pulled up and back to reveal the clean lines of her sharp, freshly shorn undercut.

I also notice their matching perfectly manicured nails, and feel a small pang, guilt commingling with regret over not making it to the salon with the rest of the bridal party. I should probably check my own nails for dusty debris. I have to remind myself that while it would have made my nails look nice, I wouldn't have had fun at the salon. I would have been the old spinster sister, whispered about behind polished hands, miserable and resentful. At least, that's probably how it would have gone. I resist the urge to bite my colorless fingernail.

"Where do I even start—" Rosie says, wide-eyed.

"How about 'hello'?" I mutter, but she's talking right over me.

"Did you get everything? Is your car here? Where did you

park? Not on the street, I hope. I don't want someone to break in and steal everything. Is everything in the car?"

"Rosie, take a breath," I say. "Yes, everything's in there. All the flowers, all the wine. I parked in the garage attached to the restaurant."

"Good," Rosie says, finally exhaling. "And you locked the car?"

"Thanks so much," Ana says, with a genuine smile, putting an arm around Rosie and giving her a squeeze that clearly means *chill out, dude.*

"Happy to help," I say to my future sister-in-law, and not to my sister.

"We really appreciate it," Ana says. "And tomorrow night, the toast—I want you to know, it means a lot to both of us that you're doing that. We're just really glad you can help make the night special."

"Yeah, of course," I say uneasily. Not wanting either of them to ask me anything specific about the nonexistent draft of the epic speech, I quickly add, "Hey, you really look great. Both of you."

"Thanks, you too," says Rosie, but she's not looking at me. She's looking at the golem. "And this must be Paul."

"Paul," repeats the golem, startling me, since that's the first time I've heard him use the stupid name I gave him. He just stands there, not extending a hand or anything, which is when I realize that perhaps I should have attempted some sort of crash course in basic etiquette.

"So nice to meet you, Paul," says the ever-gracious Ana. She's an attorney, skilled in the art of talking to strangers and engaging in redirection. "We're so glad you can be here to celebrate with us."

The golem nods gravely, like he's just been asked to testify at a murder trial and is committed to telling the truth, the whole truth, and nothing but the truth.

"Nice hat," Rosie says.

Paul touches the brim of the fedora, which I insisted he pull down as far as possible. Tonight, he's only wearing the hat, a crisp white shirt, and the suit pants. Tomorrow he'll wear a blue button-down shirt and we'll add the suit jacket, keeping the same hat and pants. Hopefully, no one will notice. It's kind of fun, figuring out what to dress him in with these mix-and-match pieces. Like having a hot Mr. Potato Head.

"So, how did you two—" Ana starts to ask, and I plaster a huge smile on my face and interrupt her before she can finish the question.

"This place is *so* nice," I say, looking around, desperate to get Rosie and Ana to stop directly engaging with the golem.

The restaurant's decor is modern, with high ceilings, chrome accents, black walls. It's the polar opposite of "Hanukkah camp vibes." But apparently, the parents got to pick the rehearsal venue, since they're paying for it. Some parts of a wedding weekend are for the couple, and some parts are for the benefactors.

I guess my mother and Ana's parents must have a similar aesthetic. The holiday decorations here are minimal but striking: a tall, slender, silver-tinsel tree in the center of the dining area, red poinsettias on the larger tables, and a single elegant menorah placed near the hostess stand. I wonder if they set that out just for us.

"Yeah, it's fine," says Rosie, gesturing for us to follow her, and in the same motion waving away a maître d' that had just tentatively approached us. "Come on, the rest of the bridal party's already here. We're going to do a quick walk-through of the ceremony. We're doing it on the rooftop bar—it's heated, it's covered, *it's fine*—and then we'll meet the rest of the guests in the private room for cocktails and dinner."

"The rest of the guests?" I say. "I thought the rehearsal dinner was just for the bridal party—"

"And a few out-of-town guests," Rosie says.

"Rosie and I have different definitions of 'a few,'" Ana warns me.

Rosie ushers us all into a clear glass elevator. When it begins lifting us skyward, the golem flattens against one of the glass walls, pressing his palm over my hand. I recognize his posture as defensive, but my sister assumes he's afraid.

"Scared of heights?" Rosie asks, raising an eyebrow.

"I'm not a huge fan of heights myself," Ana says, nodding sympathetically.

The golem says nothing.

I'm relieved when we make it to the roof, six floors up. The rooftop bar is lined with tiki torches, which have made me uncomfortable ever since they made headlines as the accessory of choice for white supremacists. But otherwise it's nice, evoking the same clean lines and elegant feel of the restaurant while adding the glamour of the sparkling Chicago skyline into the mix.

The bridal party is scattered across the wide-open space of the roof, laughing and talking in small clusters of two people here, three people there. I recognize most of them as Rosie and Ana's camp and college friends, including Layla, the bridesmaid serving as maid of honor in all but name. And there are a few silver-haired folks chatting in a far corner with the rabbi.

This group includes my mother.

"Okay, we're just about ready!" Rosie calls, clapping her hands together to get everyone's attention. "Five minutes 'til we run through this thing!"

Mom turns around at the sound of Rosie's voice. Her eyes land on me and she hurries over, smiling brightly. She gives me a hug, tighter and longer than I'd expect, before turning her gaze to Paul Mudd.

"Hi, I'm Rena," she says. "Eve's mother."

"Mother," he repeats.

"Bit early to call me that," she jokes. "But I like the sound of it."

"Mom," I say, horrified.

"Oh, I'm only kidding," she says with a wink, but she also

has a beaming ear-to-ear smile that means she is absolutely *not* kidding.

Then Rosie has me by the elbow.

"Sorry, Mom, sorry, Paul, I've got to borrow her," Rosie says.

She drags me over to the rest of the bridal party, which doesn't include our mother. Or Ana's parents. They're not having anyone walk them down the aisle; the parents will be seated the whole time in a place of honor in the front row. Seems a little odd, if you ask me, but Rosie always has enjoyed keeping the spotlight on herself.

I look over my shoulder, apologetically mouthing *I'll be right back* to my mother and the golem, praying that nothing weird happens while I'm away.

"Okay, I want to introduce you to Ethan," Rosie says. "He's the brides-man who's going to walk you down the aisle. He's Ana's cousin. Her *only* cousin, so her parents were kind of insistent that he be included, but whatever. He's got a big personality, but he's harmless, I swear. Okay? So *be nice.*"

"I'm always nice," I say, but my sister isn't even looking at me.

"Ethan!" Rosie yells.

A short guy with a thinning faux-hawk turns around and lifts one hand in greeting. He has a pint of beer in his other hand. He's somewhere in his mid-thirties, a few years younger than I am. He's wearing tight black jeans and a leather jacket, a bad-boy look that's not quite working for him. But truly, it's the faux-hawk that's throwing me. I wonder if they're back, or if this guy just hasn't updated his look since high school.

"You must be Eve!" Ethan says, giving me a wet kiss on the cheek that makes me flinch. "Ethan, Eve, E and E! That's, like, a perfect name-match."

"A perfect name-match would be Adam and Eve," I say automatically, since people have been making some variation of this joke for my entire life.

"Good one," Ethan guffaws.

"Not really," I say.

"You two are gonna be great together," Rosie says brightly, already backing away from us like we're a bomb about to explode. "Okay, I'm going to tell the rabbi we're ready to roll. Oh, and I'm live streaming the whole rehearsal, by the way, so like—keep that in mind."

I suddenly remember Bryan raving about my little sister's million TikTok followers. Is she really streaming this whole thing for all those strangers to see? I try to shrink a little deeper into my long-sleeved dress.

"She should make people sign a waiver," I mutter.

"So, you're Rosie's sister?" Ethan says. "Are you into girls, too, or...?"

"Or," I say curtly, glancing over at Paul Mudd.

My mother appears to be talking his ear off. I wonder what she's saying. I wonder what *he's* saying. I wish I could go over there to drag those two apart before one or the other of them says something dangerous.

"Sweet," says the chatty brides-man. "And you're not married, huh?"

"Not last time I checked."

"Ooh, and she's funny," says Ethan. He takes a swig of his beer, which is obviously not his first of the night, and leans in closer toward me. He smells like a sports bar. "So, do you have plans tonight?"

"Apparently I'm supposed to be at a wedding rehearsal."

"Ha, no, I mean, like, when we're done here," Ethan says, with a wolfish smile. He drains the last of his beer, gesturing with the sudsy glass as he talks. "We should get into a little trouble after the rehearsal stuff's done. I mean, bridesmaids, groomsmen, it's, like, a whole thing, right? Tradition?"

"There are no groomsmen in this wedding," I say, only half listening, mostly just trying to steal glances at my mother and the golem.

"What? Sure, there are—"

"No, there's not," I say, officially irritated. "Because there's no groom."

"Oh, right!" Ethan laughs, like what I just said was a riot.

Why is Ana allowing this prick in her wedding party? I know they're cousins and her parents made her ask him, but Jesus Christ. Shouldn't the brides have veto power?

"...so at least we should have a little fun, is what I'm saying," he says.

"Uh-huh," I say, barely aware he was still talking.

"Cool," he says. "So when we're all done here—you want to mess around right away, or wait 'til their actual wedding night?"

At my startled expression, he laughs.

"Just playing," he says. "I'm not actually an asshole, you just kinda seemed like you were, I dunno, tuning me out. I was just seeing if you were listening. But for real, if you wanna—"

"I don't," I snap.

"Oh," he says, looking genuinely surprised. "Got it. Well. I'm gonna grab another beer."

"Bridal party, line up!"

Ethan manages to snag another sweaty bottle of craft beer as we walk to where the rabbi is waving everyone over, at the other end of the rooftop bar. Suddenly we're all just cogs in a wedding machine. There are some brief introductions before we begin our orchestrated movements. I'm side by side with Ethan, who doesn't say anything else to me. He just swigs his beer, swallowing quiet burps and exhaling sour breath.

Disgusted, I look around to see if my mother and the golem are still nearby or if someone has shuffled them away from the rehearsal. I spot them, still standing in a rooftop corner. My mother is gazing at Rosie and Ana. The golem is looking in our direction, too. But he's not looking at the brides, or at me.

He's looking at Ethan.

29

As soon as we're done with the rehearsal, I peel off from the bridal party. I want to put as much distance between myself and Ethan as possible. I quickly make my way back to my mother and the golem. They're sitting at a little café table now, tucked into the corner of the rooftop bar. The golem has positioned himself so he's facing me. His eyes are moving steadily from my mother, to me, to somewhere behind me—wherever Ethan is, I'm guessing. My mother's back is to me, and when the golem gives a slight nod, she turns to look at me and I'm stunned to see that she's crying.

She's not making a big show of it. As she dabs at her eye, anyone else passing by might assume she was just experiencing some mild allergies, or maybe some sweet wedding-related emotions. But the red rimming the interior of her lids, the slight drop of her nose, and the wet sheen to her eyes tell another story.

"Mom? Are you okay?"

"Oh, I'm fine, I'm fine," she says, giving me a watery smile. "Paul, here—well. I tell you what. He's a very good listener."

"Mrmmm," says the golem, reverting to his original rumbling, since he probably doesn't know any words appropriate to this situation. He looks at me, assessing. I want to assure him that I'm fine, and not to go into protector mode, but I find my attention drawn to my mother.

"I'm—glad you two had a nice chat," I say. "Is there anything you want to...?"

I trail off, and she shakes her head, eyes already drying. When neither of us takes the conversation any further, I feel disappointed. Like I just missed out on a significant moment. A moment that somehow Paul Mudd was able to experience, instead of me. My mother grabs for her purse, checks her makeup, reapplies color to her lips.

"We should head to the dinner," she says, twisting the cap back on the lipstick.

The guests at this rehearsal dinner all fall into one of three distinct and equally terrible categories: people I've never met (Ana's guests), people I've met once or twice and should know their names but mostly don't (friends of Rosie's, Ana's immediate family, and so forth), and a wider swath than I'd anticipated of my own extended family, most of whom I haven't seen since Dad's funeral.

Absolute nightmare.

Servers are floating around with flutes of champagne on elegant silver serving trays. I take a glass for myself, and one for the golem. When he shakes his head, I'm confused. He liked the wine at The Book Cellar. Why doesn't he want a drink now? I try once more to offer him the glass, but again, he firmly shakes his head. I consider telling him he *has* to drink it, to see if he'll follow my orders, but what would be the point?

So I hand the glass to my mother, who takes it but doesn't sip. She's looking around, her expression impossible to read. I wonder if she's looking for someone in particular, a cousin she was hoping to see here tonight, someone from her synagogue maybe? Whoever she's hoping to spot in the crowd doesn't seem to be there. After a moment, she turns and smiles at me and the golem.

"Well, you two should mingle," she says.

"Mingle?" I say, confused.

"Yes, yes, go on," says my mother. "Introduce Paul to people."

"I don't know half the people here."

"Oh, you know most of the people here."

"I really don't."

"There's Layla, you know her."

I try very hard not to roll my eyes. Yes, I know Rosie's best friend. The beautiful fitness instructor who dropped out of a doctoral program, meaning she's smart and pretty. Maybe her fatal flaw is that she's bad at follow-through, being a dropout and all; then again, she was really on the ball with all the bridal party stuff. She hasn't just been my sister's go-to person for the wedding, but for *everything* lately. All things considered, I'm pretty sure I hate her.

But before I can protest, my mother has shoved Paul and me toward Layla.

"Eve, hey," Layla says when she sees me, offering a tentative smile. Then she aims a more genuine grin at my golem. "And I'm sorry, I didn't catch your name…?"

"This is Paul," I say. "Paul, Layla."

He nods. She beams.

"Nice to meet you, Paul," she says, then gives me an almost-friendly wink. "The surprise wedding date, huh?"

Evidently Rosie must convey her every annoyance with me to her best friend.

"Yep," I say. "He's quite the surprise."

"Hard to believe the big day's really here, huh?" Layla asks. "I love your dress, by the way."

"Thanks," I say, biting my tongue to keep from telling her

it's the same dress I wore to my father's funeral and seeing what that might do to her perky smile. "I love yours, too."

In stark contrast to my long-sleeved black wool "spinster sister" number, Layla is wearing a bright blue cocktail dress with one large white flower flowing across her sculpted brown shoulder. It's probably designer, but the girl would look good in a sack. Being a fitness instructor is one of those convenient careers that allows you to get in your own workout while earning your money, all at once. No need to hit the gym after the office, when your office *is* the gym. Her shining black hair is in an elegant low ponytail, the sort of style that would look messy on me but is elegant without being fussy on her. She delicately touches the flower on her dress.

"Oh, thanks, I borrowed it." Layla looks around, like she's trying to find someone. Eyes landing on her target, she starts frantically waving at a handsome Indian man standing in line at the bar. "Sorry, that's my husband, Amir. He's just— Honey, are you almost...?"

He gestures that he's about to put in an order for the both of them, and that she should just wait there. A brief look of panicked disappointment crosses Layla's face. She doesn't want to talk to me, either, I realize. But she's better at faking it than I am, and within a fraction of a second, she's recovered and is beaming at us again.

"Hey, so Paul! Tell me everything! What do you do, how did you two meet—"

"He works in security," I say quickly, providing a reasonably accurate answer to one of her questions. "And oh, hey, I think I see my great-uncle over there. Wow, I haven't seen Uncle Ira in years! If you'll excuse us, so sorry—"

"Oh no, totally fine," says Layla, clearly relieved at our parting.

I drag the golem toward my imaginary uncle until we're far enough away from Layla that I can drop his hand and grab a cloth napkin at a nearby table. I dab at my temples, and resist the urge to swab my armpits. I'm so sweaty. The combination of nerves, wool dress, and overheated venue is deadly.

"I've got to get out of here," I say aloud.

"Eve...safe?"

Paul Mudd is looking down at me with expressionless black eyes.

"I... Yeah, I'm safe. It's just..."

It's just that I never feel safe, I think. *Not on trains. Not at work. Not around my family. Not anywhere, not ever.*

But then I look up at the golem, and something clicks into place. My fears are unfounded, at least for the moment. He's not going to let anyone hurt me. With him at my side, I don't have to fear anything—not even others' judgment of my life. He's passing at this party far better than I thought he would— he's charmed my mother, managed not to set off my sister, been civil to everyone...hell, he's doing better here than I am.

I'm safe.

I have Paul.

A server passes by, and before she can even say *Would you care for a*— I've grabbed two glasses of champagne from her tray. I turn as if I'm about to hand one to the golem, then down them both myself.

An hour later, we're the life of the party. Well, I am, any-way, and my golem is unwaveringly at my side. I've chatted with relatives I barely remember—it turns out I *do* have an uncle Ira!—and made nice with all five of the other women in Rosie's bridal party. I even scored an invitation to one of their summer cabins in Wisconsin.

While I'm a little lightheaded from the champagne, I'm still clear-eyed enough to avoid Ethan. I don't want to find out what would happen if he made another pass at me while the golem was in earshot. I also mostly avoid my mother and my sister, because I don't want either of them to give me any static about how much I'm drinking.

But when I turn around in search of another friendly tray-bearing server, I instead find myself nose to nose with Rosie.

"Eve," she says. "I need your keys."

"Excuse me?"

"Your keys," she says impatiently. "I want to take your car to Mom's place tonight. It'll be safer to park it in Winnetka than in the city—I don't want someone to break in and steal all the wine. Besides, it doesn't seem like you should be driving tonight anyway."

I glare at her.

"I'm fine to drive," I say, even though I know I'm not. And I wouldn't drive drunk, but I also don't like being called out by my baby sister.

"No, you're not," says my mother, appearing out of nowhere.

She looks up at the golem, then leads me away from him. Being courteous, trying not to shame me in front of my date, I guess. Rosie follows, hot on our heels and mad as hell.

"You're drunk," says my sister.

"I am not—"

"Have you even had anything to eat tonight, Eve?" Mom interrupts.

"Since when do you want me to eat?" I ask, and my mother looks slapped.

"Maybe Paul can drive them home..." Ana says, appearing out of nowhere. I hadn't even noticed her approaching this confrontation. Bad choice on her part to get involved. This has nothing to do with her.

"Paul doesn't drive," I snap.

"And we need all the stuff in her car anyway," Rosie says to Ana, before returning her petulant gaze to mine. "So get a Lyft home, or take the train, whatever. But give me your keys. You're not driving."

"And how exactly am I supposed to get to the wedding to-morrow without a car?" I ask. "I can't take a Lyft out to the middle of fucking nowhere. There's no train that goes out to the camp. You want me to just stay home? Skip the wedding? I will, if that's what you want."

Rosie stares at me, wide-eyed.

"Eve," my mother says softly. "That's enough. I'll come get you tomorrow."

"I still don't think—" I start to protest, but my mother is already leading me back to the golem, who has been watching our entire exchange from a respectful distance.

"Paul, it's getting late," says my mother, gesturing him over. I glower at her. It's barely six thirty. "I'm going to head to services, and I'd appreciate it if you could just go ahead and get our girl home safe."

"Don't talk about me like I'm not here," I snap.

"Safe," the golem agrees, putting a heavy hand on my shoulder.

"Are you seriously sending me home? The room's booked for another hour," I say. "The party isn't over. I should be here. I'm the maid of honor."

"*Now* you're the maid of honor," Rosie mutters.

"I think you should get some rest," says my mother, giving a quick glance to my sister. At first I think maybe she's glaring at her on my behalf, for her sarcastic remarks. But when I look at Rosie, I see that she's crying. What the hell is she crying about?

"Fine," I say, digging around furiously in my little black clutch. I shove the keys at my sister. Then, with a small stab of satisfaction, I also toss the garage ticket at her. "You have to pay when you exit."

I turn on my heel, knowing the golem will follow me. When we get outside, the cold air sears my lungs. I realize I left my coat in the car, and won't be able to get it until my mother comes to collect us from my house tomorrow. I wrap my arms around myself, shivering.

Then I feel the golem envelop me, protecting me from the cold. His embrace is sturdy, muscular, providing a solid barrier against the elements. I lean my head against his chest, breathing in the earthy scent of him.

Emotions are surging through me, but they're too raw for me to even categorize. I'm not crying, and I don't want to cry. It's so rare that I just let loose and enjoy myself. I'd been having a good time up until my mother and sister staged their mean little intervention. I'm not ready to call it a night. I want to keep having a good time. I'm all dressed up. I have a date. I don't have my car, but I have my Ventra card and we're only a block from the train. I want to go out. I want to have fun.

And that's when I remember the office river cruise.

30

It takes almost no time at all to get from the restaurant to the harbor. The night is cold and crisp. I wish it would snow, but at least the clear skies make transit and walking easy. Even though we made good time getting there, I was worried we might have literally missed the boat. But when I checked the invitation—which Nancy had conveniently emailed, as well as distributing hard copy posters to every desk and plastering them all over the breakroom—it said that there would be a cruise from five to seven, followed by "docked debauchery" until midnight. It's just past seven now.

Perfect.

"Ahhhh! Eve, you came!"

Nancy is, predictably, the first person to greet us upon arrival. She's wearing a red beret and a bright green peacoat, and looks like a tipsy French boat elf. When she throws her arms around me in an enthusiastic drunken hug, I don't recoil.

"We came," I agree, and I even smile at her.

"And who's this?" Nancy asks, gazing blurrily at my golem.

"This is Paul," I say, and he nods at Nancy.

"Well hello, Paul!" Nancy beams. "Okay, you both need to get some Dirty Santas—that's the signature drink tonight. It's cookies-and-cream liqueur with rose bitters and a maraschino cherry...you know, like in the poem, how 'his cheeks were like roses, his nose like a cherry'?"

"Um, yeah, of course," I say, since she seems to be expecting a response. I'm pretty sure she's referencing "'Twas the Night before Christmas," but who knows.

"I knew you'd get it," Nancy enthuses. "You can also 'pop Santa's cherry' if you want to make it a real dirty drink!"

"That sounds disgusting and I can't wait to try it," I say, and Nancy guffaws. I grin, satisfied. This is more like it. I'll be appreciated here, unlike at that stupid rehearsal dinner.

Paul and I each grab a drink, although he merely carries his around while I slam mine. It's just as disgusting as I imagined it would be, but I don't even care. When I've finished my Dirty Santa, I grab a bottle of Old Style from one of the many drink tables and make a quick circuit, introducing Paul to my coworkers, enjoying their appreciative assessments of my handsome date.

I don't see either Bryan or Sasha, and I've been on the boat for almost an hour before it dawns on me that Bryan isn't here because he was laid off. I bet Sasha skipped it in solidarity, and I'm the only asshole who showed up.

But then I hear a familiar voice behind me.

"So this is the famous Josh Paul."

I turn and see Sasha looking at the golem, arms folded across her chest.

"It's...just Paul, actually," I say, without explaining further.

"Nice hat," she says, eyeing the golem's fedora. "Kinda windy out here, better make sure you don't lose it."

"Pull it down further," I snap at the golem, low enough that my best friend won't hear me. We can't have the wind carrying his hat away. He obediently pulls it down low, and keeps one hand on the brim for good measure. I raise my voice to say with forced cheer, "Hi, Sasha."

"Sasha," the golem says softly, remembering this name.

Hearing him say her name, Sasha looks startled. She takes a step back, then turns and looks at me. Her eyes are radiating concern. She's not really dressed for a party, which is unlike her. She's wearing jeans and her nice winter boots, a big down coat, a warm hat. No makeup, no bling. Like she was just sitting at home on her couch, then decided to bundle up, take out the trash, and continue on to the office holiday party for no apparent reason.

"You didn't get very dressed up tonight," I say.

"I wasn't planning on coming, but then…"

"But then…?"

"Nancy texted me to say that you were here," Sasha says, with a momentary nose-wrinkle at the office gossip's perpetual overreach. "I guess she thought that might make me show up."

"Come for the friends, stay for the Dirty Santas," I say, shaking my empty glass in her direction.

"Eve," she says, uninterested in my tipsy banter. "You wanna tell me why you've been ignoring me?"

"I'm—sorry," I say, but I mostly feel annoyed. Whatever big conversation Sasha wants to have, now isn't the time. I just want to enjoy myself. Besides, *she* ignored me for most of the last year. "I've been busy. The wedding's tomorrow, and it's been, like, nonstop—"

"And there's—" Sasha looks nervously at the golem, and when she says his name it sounds like it tastes bad in her mouth "—Paul."

"Yeah, but it's not like—"

"Did you even read my texts?"

"I mean, some of them…" I mumble.

"No, you haven't," Sasha says. "Are you still keeping your phone off?"

"Sometimes," I admit, although *almost always* is the actual truth.

"God, Eve. Okay. Okay, can we just— Can I just talk to you alone for a minute?"

"What do you mean 'alone'?" I say, looking around.

We're standing toward the front of the party boat, and no one else is within earshot. They're all laughing and distracted, anyway, every single one of our coworkers drunk on holiday cheer and Dirty Santas. No one is paying any attention to me, my best friend, and the golem.

"I mean, without..." Sasha drops her voice, casting a furtive look at Paul Mudd. She almost looks scared of him. "Without him around."

The golem takes a step forward, standing directly beside me.

"Is there something you have to tell me that he can't hear?"

He takes another step forward, so he's just slightly in front of me now, his body between mine and Sasha's. She takes a step back, looking angry and a little bit frightened. Which is ridiculous. She has no reason to be scared of my date. Paul would never hurt her.

Still, there's an undeniable fear in her eyes. She lowers her voice, and the intensity in it takes me by surprise.

"Eve, please," she says. "I'm worried about you."

"Why are you worried about me?"

"Can we just talk—"

"We're talking—"

"Alone, please, we really need to—"

"Now you 'really need' to talk?" I say, hot embers of resentment finally bursting into a furious flame in my chest. "Remember all last year, when I was going through hell, and wanted to talk, and you were— Where were you again? Oh, right: with your shitty boyfriend. Right?"

"Eve," Sasha says. "That's not exactly—"

"And then you were sad about *not* having a shitty boyfriend anymore," I say, temperature rising. "And now *I* show up with a date, and suddenly you don't just want to talk, you want to pull me aside, get me to yourself, end my fun. All I wanted tonight was to have a good time. And every time I start to enjoy myself, someone shits all over it. And I'm sick of it. God! I am *sick* of it. Come on."

I aim those last two words at the golem, who lurches after me as I head for the exit, making my way to the stairs leading to the dock level of the boat. When Sasha calls out after me, I ignore her.

When Sasha broke up with her boyfriend and decided to reenter our social circle, I welcomed her back in with open arms. So did Bryan. No questions, no punishment—we were just glad to have our friend back. It had hurt when she ignored me and Bryan and everyone else in her life; especially the weeks she spent holed up with her boyfriend while I was mourning the fresh loss of my father. Maybe I'd been too quick to forgive her for all that, especially with how weird she's being now. Where was she back then, when I *actually* needed her? Why the hell is she concerned now, when I finally have someone looking out for me?

She's jealous.

The thought is a bee sting, small and sharp, then swelling into something I can't ignore. Jealousy, that must be it. Sasha has never had any reason to feel jealous of me before, and it doesn't look good on her. She's used to being the one who has all her shit together, while I'm the disaster bestie. She's the allstar at work, the fashionable one, and, usually, the one with a boyfriend. She's currently single, sure, but she's still shining in every other area of her life. It shouldn't be such a big deal for me to have a plus-one when she doesn't.

Why can't I have this one thing?

Sasha should be happy, now that I finally have someone

who's actually treating me well. Instead, she's freaking out. So I didn't respond to her texts for a couple days—so what? That's no reason to get this upset.

"Eve, please, just listen…" Sasha calls from behind me.

Clutching the golem's hand, I don't even turn around when I finally answer her.

"Go to hell, Sasha," I say, and leave the boat with my golem in tow.

31

The golem and I walk toward the L stop in silence. I'm grateful to be with someone who won't push me to talk. Someone who will just stay beside me, no matter what. No one has made me feel this secure in a long, long time.

Maybe the golem is all I need. Maybe we should just go home. Maybe we should never leave the apartment again.

The thoughts whisper their way through my mind with such ferocity, they don't even feel like my own. I shiver. No. We're not going home. Not yet. I'm not ready to call it a night. I'm all dressed up, I have a date, I'm buzzed, and I want to keep the buzz going.

The neon lights of a bar on the block before the train station catch my eye. I look up at the golem, who hasn't had a drop to drink all night. Is it because he was on guard at the rehearsal dinner? Picking up on my tension? Maybe we both need to loosen up.

"You want to have a drink with me?"

The golem shakes his head.

"Not safe," he says.

"Not safe for me to drink?" I ask. "Or for you to drink?"

At first I think maybe he wants to keep his hands free, like a good bodyguard. Then it occurs to me that maybe he's trying to stay sober in case the alcohol does to him what it's been doing to me. I feel a little ashamed, and try to remind myself that he can't judge me. He's not even a real person.

Then why did you sleep with him, Eve?

I shove the question from my mind, wanting to dull my thoughts with more liquor but feeling like that option is off the table now.

"Let's just go home, then," I mutter.

A train approaches the station as soon as we reach the platform. When we board, the car is packed. It's ten o'clock on a Friday night, holiday season, relatively mild weather. Everyone is enjoying their evening, laughing as they enter and exit the train. The crowd finally thins by the time we reach Belmont. When we change from the red line to the brown line, we're the only ones aboard.

But then, at the next stop, someone else gets on the train. A slender white guy in a denim jacket. Short blond hair, no hat.

Nazi, I think. *That's the same fucking Nazi who spit at me earlier this week.*

Terror instantly clogs my throat, and beside me, I feel the golem stir. I try not to look at the pinched face of the man in the denim jacket, but my eyes steal his way—and instantly lock with his pale blue ones.

I feel like a deer caught in the headlights, about to be slammed by an oncoming vehicle. Surely he'll recognize me, the girl he spit on and leered at less than a week ago. I tense, waiting for the wicked smile or wad of spit.

But his eyes are dull, uninterested. There's not even a glimmer of an acknowledgment of our past interaction. Nothing whatsoever seems reflected in his ice-blue eyes.

He doesn't recognize me, I realize with a start.

Because the last time he saw me, he didn't see me as an actual person. He saw me as a woman riding alone on the train with a big Jewish beacon on her chest. An easy target for someone who harbors hatred in his heart for people like me. Jews. Women. But right now, there aren't such obvious marks of victimhood clinging to me. I'm just another person on the train, wearing a plain black dress, sitting beside a big, hulking man.

Except the big, hulking man isn't sitting beside me anymore.

"Paul?"

I look up and see that the golem is rapidly closing the distance between himself and the man in the denim jacket. And then, before I even know what's happening, he's slamming his powerful fist into the man's nose.

"What the fuck!"

The guy reels back, stumbling, falling heavily into one of the empty seats lining the train car. The golem advances on him again, fists raised.

"I'll call the cops!"

At these words, the golem rips the fedora from his head and snarls. His victim stares in terror at the Hebrew letters bearing down on him. There's blood coming from his nose, a dark scarlet trickle, staining his teeth, running down to his chin. He scuttles backward like a wounded animal, whimpering. The golem takes another step toward him.

I leap to my feet, grabbing him by the elbow and pleading with him to stop.

"You can't do this," I say. "You'll get arrested."

The train lurches to a stop, the PA system announcing the next stop. The preppy racist vaults to his feet. For half a second I think he's going to take a swing at the golem, who I'm still restraining. Instead, he gives my protector a look of terrified hatred. Then, clutching his bleeding nose, he bolts from the train.

"Oh shit," I say, heart thudding and head pounding in a painful preview of the hangover I'll be experiencing tomorrow morning. "Oh shit. He's going to call the cops, he's going to be back here with the police, there might be a camera on the train, oh shit..."

But then the train rumbles forward again. No one else gets on or off it. At the next stop, I tense, certain police are about to board and attempt to handcuff the golem, which won't go well for them. To my shock and relief, no cops come for us at that stop, either. The only people to board the train are a middle-aged couple, laughing about the holiday improv show they just saw.

We make it all the way to my stop without incident. I hurry us home, up the stairs, into my apartment, locking the door and the dead bolt before finally turning to face the golem. My heart is pounding, my breath coming in rapid gasps. All my more complicated emotions have been burned away, leaving only this fresh shock.

"Why did you do that?" I ask my protector.

"Man was enemy," said the golem simply. He thudded his chest with his fist. "Keep safe."

"Oh," I say, everything within me blooming and unfurling into a garden of blissful relief. It was so straightforward to my protector, so black-and-white. The man was a threat. Paul neutralized the threat. He wasn't going to wait until I was being harmed; he was going to prevent me from being attacked. He's not just a reactive protector, but a proactive one. Is there any better way to stay safe?

Grateful and buzzing, hungry for the earthquakes of pleasure this safety could bring, I throw myself at the golem like I'm going to swallow him whole.

32

Sasha: Please call me

Sasha: I'm worried about you

Sasha: Eve I'm serious

Sasha: I don't want to do this over text

Sasha: There's something I have to tell you

Sasha: Maybe I'm wrong but idk, I just have this feeling

Sasha: Jesus Eve CALL ME

Sasha: The way Bryan described the guy he saw you with, the way you've just ghosted us, this feeling I have in the pit of my stomach… God I really wish you'd just call me

Sasha: Or I could come over

Sasha: This would be easier in person

Sasha: Fuck

Sasha: Eve

Sasha: RESPOND

SATURDAY

33

I'm so hungover I'm awake before dawn, exhausted but unable to sleep. I read through the slew of texts Sasha sent last night, but there's no way I'm going to respond to them. Instead, I drag myself into the shower.

The hot water feels good, melting away the angriest edges of my pounding headache. I lean against the wall's chipped ceramic tiles, inhaling steam, just trying to breathe.

Today's the wedding.

Shit.

Dragging myself out of the shower, I want to go lie down again and not get out of bed until the very last possible minute. The wedding isn't until evening, so maybe I can spend most of the day under the covers...but then I remember Rosie has my car, and my mother will be over at some point to drive Paul Mudd and me out to the damn summer camp. And I also have to keep my phone on, since my mother's going to call when she gets here.

Ugh.

I put on my robe, swallow a few aspirin, and shuffle into the living room. I'm no longer startled by the sight of the golem stationed at the door. He's not naked this morning. He's wearing a T-shirt and sweatpants, which I vaguely remember encouraging him to put on before I passed out. With the luck I was having last night, if I hadn't made him wear pajamas, a fire alarm would have gone off and I would have been forced to put a bare-assed golem on display for all my neighbors to see.

Wonder what Hot Josh would have to say about that. Bet he would've been at a loss for a snappy comeback for the first time in his snide little British-Jewish life.

"Coffee?" the golem inquires politely.

"Yeah," I say. "Let's go get some coffee."

On our way to The Other Chicago Bean, I pull out my phone and idly open TikTok. The first video in my feed is from @GoGo-RoRo. I watch with the sound off as she shows her adoring audience a sneak peek of her wedding shoes, her bouquet, and her party nails; the wedding dress, of course, will be a surprise until the live stream of the ceremony.

I notice that the video, posted only thirty-two minutes ago, has more than eleven thousand likes, and nine hundred comments. My little sister, the internet celebrity. When she starts blowing kisses to the screen, a new comment pops up, from a user called AltMight07: "There's still time to change your mind, Rosie—you know you need a real MAN."

God, TikTok is full of weirdos.

I click from the video over to Rosie's actual profile, which I hadn't even bothered to look at when Mom made me follow her. I'm surprised to see that Bryan's claim about Rosie having "like a million followers" was barely an exaggeration: she has almost four hundred thousand, and lots of clearly popular pinned videos of exercise tips and bike-ride-alongs. One of the pinned posts boasts two million views. Who knew my little sister was a genuine social media influencer?

Everyone but me, apparently.

We're walking back from The Other Chicago Bean when my mother calls. It's not quite ten o'clock, and I know she's going to want to be at camp early to make sure everything's in place and Rosie's feeling supported. Hopefully not too early, but it's totally out of my control at this point. We'll be on her timetable. I've really screwed myself over by getting roped into driving there with my mother.

And a golem.

"Good morning," I say, answering the phone.

"How are you feeling?" Mom says by way of greeting.

"Fine," I say, even though my head is still pounding.

"I'll be at your place in an hour," she says.

"An hour? The wedding's not until five—"

"I assume Paul will already be at your place?"

"That's quite an assumption."

My mother waits.

"Yes," I admit grudgingly. "He'll be here."

"See you at eleven," she says, and hangs up.

At eleven on the dot, my mother rings the buzzer. I shove the Cubs cap onto the golem's head before letting Mom upstairs.

She makes quite an entrance: her makeup is fully done, and her silver curls are practically shimmering. She's already wearing her mother-of-the-bride attire, a very flattering sea green pantsuit with a sequin-lined pocket square.

"You're already dressed," I say.

"I like to get ready at home," my mother says, eyeing the golem and me. He's still in a T-shirt and sweatpants. I'm in a hoodie and track pants. "I see that you two will be getting dressed out at the camp."

"Seeing as we're going to be there five hours early, might as well."

"There's nothing wrong with being early."

"Agree to disagree."

"You know who else hated being early," my mother says, and then stops abruptly.

We both know that the answer is my father, but neither of us says so. We could have shared a smile about his perennial *I'm on Jewish time, sorry!* excuse for being late. Instead, I mumble something about getting our stuff together.

"Eve, last night…" my mother begins, then shakes her head and looks away. "Let's have a better day today, okay?"

I give a noncommittal nod, and head to the bedroom to get everything assembled. I throw some toiletries into a bag and grab the magenta pantsuit from my closet. It's still in the dry-cleaning bag from when I had it altered to fit me. A week ago, I was afraid it might be tight, since I'd put on a few pounds since the fitting. But I'm pretty sure I've dropped those same few pounds just in the past few days, eating as little as I have been, sweating so profusely, and being constantly on the move to keep up with this unexpected week.

"You're awfully quiet this morning," my mother says to the golem as we load everything into her compact little red Fiat 500.

"Yes," he confirms.

Paul Mudd climbs into the back seat of the car. I've hated this thing ever since my mother bought it. The spring after Dad died, she traded in both of their cars—his ancient Jeep, her reliable Camry—and got this utterly impractical little thing. She can't even drive it when it snows, which means she's about to realize what a stupid purchase this was, but she's so damn proud of it.

On top of being useless in the snow, it's also not great golem transport. He's so cramped in the Fiat's back seat that his knees are jammed up in front of his nose. I'd offer him the front seat, but it wouldn't be a much better fit, and the tight squeeze doesn't seem to bother him. As I look into the back seat to make sure he's all right, he just sits there, patiently waiting.

"Oy—Eve!"

As I'm getting into the car, I hear a distinctive voice calling my name. I turn and see Josh jogging up to me, waving. He's in a track suit, which I normally would have found endearing, but after recent events just kind of make him look like a low-level Sopranos affiliate.

In other words, a drug dealer.

"Who's that?" my mother asks from across the top of her little sports car. She was about to get into the driver's seat, but is now quite obviously not going to do so until she gets to witness this interaction.

"My neighbor," I mutter.

Shielding my eyes against the sun, I look over at Josh. The parking lot of our building has exterior stairs that go below-ground to the basement laundry rooms. He seems to have bounded up those stairs and jogged half the length of the parking lot, but slows as he approaches.

"Heading out for the wedding?" Josh asks.

"Yep," I say. "Do you need something, or...?"

"Hi!" my mother says loudly. To my utter humiliation, she walks out from behind the car and marches straight over to Josh. "I'm Rena, Eve's mother."

"Pleasure," Josh says, taking her hand.

"Good grip," says my mother.

"*Get* a grip, Mom," I say, accidentally-on-purpose loud enough for them both to hear me. This earns me an eyebrow lift from Josh, and a subtle glare from my mother. "Josh, what's up?"

"Right," he says, his hand still awkwardly clasped by my mother. "I just wanted to say, er, have a nice time. At the wedding. And—did you say it's out at the summer camp? Heller-Diamond?"

"Yeah," I say, grudgingly impressed that he remembered the name.

"It's a Jewish summer camp," my mother says unnecessarily.

"Right," Josh says, nodding like he actually knows all about Camp Heller-Diamond. He smiles politely down at my mother, who has yet to let go of his hand. "Well, I just... I just wanted to say... I hope it's a lovely event, and honestly I thought I couldn't get out of—"

"Well, thanks, yeah," I say, fast and loud, to bury him sharing the fact that I'd invited him to the wedding and he'd turned me down flat. That's something I definitely don't need my mother to know, now or ever. "We've really gotta get going, so..."

I flick my glance over to the back seat of my mother's car. The windows are tinted, completely hiding the golem from view. I'm weirdly relieved that Josh can't see him in there. Then again, wouldn't it be great for him to know I'm not dateless after all? That I'm not as pathetic as he must think I am?

"Oh, so now you're in a rush?" Mom says, and the twinkle in her eye makes me want to scream. My expression must be murderous, because she reluctantly releases Josh's hand. "It was nice to meet you, Josh."

"You as well, Mrs. Goodman," says Hot Josh.

"Charmed," my mother says, putting a hand to her chest. With a meaningful glance my way, she finally gets into the car.

"Er, Eve," Josh says, looking back at me. His big brown eyes, so thickly lashed and hooded under those heavy brows, intensify his every expression. His gaze seems apologetic, almost regretful. "I just wanted to say, I really do wish I could've—"

He touches my arm, gently, and there's a spark.

Literal static electricity snaps between us, and we both spring back, startled. Then Josh chuckles, laugh lines crinkling around his dark lashes, and against my better judgment I'm smiling like an idiot right back at him.

"Sorry about that," he says. "It's those damn old dryers downstairs. Swear to God, every shirt I have has been weaponized in that thing. I'm a bloody electro-man these days, just zapping shit all the time. Every hero needs an origin story, I suppose."

"And every villain," I say, wiping the smile from my face and forcing myself to remember that this guy is probably a criminal.

My mother honks the horn of her car. Apparently now that she's no longer got her talons in my hot neighbor, she's remembered how eager she was to hit the road out to camp. I shake my head, lifting my head in a half wave as I turn away from him.

"See you around."

"Right," he says. "Oh, wait—I got you a little something…"

"What? Why?"

"You said it was also your birthday this weekend?"

I'm startled. Had I really mentioned that when I banged on his door, drunk, and asked him to the wedding? I must have, but am genuinely shocked that he'd remembered that detail, even after turning me down.

"You didn't have to—" I start, but he cuts me off with a little wave with one hand as he digs in his pocket with the other.

"It's nothing, really," he says. "Truly nothing. Two dollars' worth of nothing. Swear. It's just a little something that— well—it's just a silly little something."

He hands me something small; an oddly lumpy wad of bright blue Hanukkah wrapping paper.

"Thanks," I say, taking it gingerly from him.

"Sure," he says. "Well, er, right, then. See you."

Shoving the unexpected gift into my coat pocket, I get into the passenger seat of my mother's car. I buckle myself in and hunch down as far as I can, not wanting to accidentally lock eyes with Josh as we pull out of the small parking lot. Behind me, I hear the golem grunt.

My mother looks over at me, her eyes hidden by the giant rhinestone-lined cat's-eye sunglasses she's wearing. Yet somehow I can still see the obnoxious twinkle behind the dark shades.

"When it rains it pours, huh?" Mom says, tilting her head first toward the parking lot, then toward the back seat.

"Mom, just drive."

She shrugs and obliges.

I briefly wonder if I should open the little present from Josh. Before I can decide, we're on the highway. Immediately, I'm grabbing for the oh-shit handle, swearing under my breath and praying that the golem's protection somehow extends to preventing motor vehicle accidents. Somehow I'd forgotten that my mother graduated with honors from the Bat Out of Hell driving school.

"Mom, maybe slow down a little," I say as I watch the speedometer creep past eighty. "It's not like we're going to be late."

"I'm not going that fast," my mother insists, swerving across three lanes without so much as glancing at her mirrors or tapping her turn signal.

A high whining wail of a siren begs to differ as flashing blue-and-red lights barrel up behind us.

"Tell it to the cops," I mutter.

Jaw clenching, my mother puts on her turn signal for the first time in decades and pulls over by the side of the highway. An officer approaches her window. She rolls it down and blinks up innocently.

"Good morning," she says.

"Ma'am," says the officer. He's a Black guy with a neat mustache and a paunch. From my position in the passenger seat, I can't read the name glinting from his chest. "License and registration."

My mother nods for me to grab the registration out of the glove box, and she fumbles with her purse to get out her license. In the back seat, the golem shifts, letting out a low, inquisitive rumble.

"It's fine," I hiss to him as I hand my mother the registration.

"You aware of how fast you were going?" the cop asks my mother as he takes the documents from her.

"I'm sorry, Officer," she says. "I don't know, actually. I was just going with the flow of traffic."

This is obviously bullshit, since there are very few cars out at the moment. The officer has noticed this as well, as evidenced by the simultaneous lift of his brow and quirk of his lips. He looks briefly over his shoulder at the quiet strip of highway just behind him, waiting a full twenty seconds before a car goes by. In a sprawling metropolitan area frequently plagued with wall-to-wall traffic, this Saturday morning is practically car free.

"I'm on my way to my daughter's wedding," my mother adds, offering a small but hopeful smile.

The officer leans down a little and looks at me, as if to confirm she has a bride in the car.

"My *other* daughter," says my mother.

"Well, congratulations," he says. "I'm still gonna have to write you a ticket."

"What?"

My mother is genuinely stunned. Despite her lead foot, I don't think she's ever gotten a ticket. Dad was always the one parking where he shouldn't, rolling through stop signs, racking up a pile of violations, and driving their insurance through the roof. It infuriated Mom, and now here she was getting a speeding ticket.

The officer walks back to his car, and my mother grips the steering wheel so hard her knuckles go white.

"Fuck," she spits, furious. "Fuck, fuck, fuck!"

I'm gaping. I don't think I've ever heard my mother drop the f-bomb before. Hearing her fire off four at once takes me aback. Even the golem seems astounded, ceasing his shifting to watch my mother's display of rage.

"Mom," I say. "It's no big deal—"

"Eve, please just be quiet."

"Mom, come on—"

But before I can say anything else, I feel the golem gripping my seat. I'm not sure what he's doing at first, then I realize he's trying to figure out how to get out of the cramped back seat of this car without plowing through me in the process. He's looking over his broad shoulder at the police officer, his jaw set. I turn around and mouth for him to be still, but the golem blinks at me, uncomprehending.

"Threat," he says, pointing out the back window at the officer.

"No, not a threat," I whisper, hoping my distraught mother can't hear me.

"Enemy," insists the golem.

"He's not our enemy," I say, louder. "He's just doing his job."

"Just doing his job," snorts my mother, who apparently heard that part, at least. "That's what they said about the fucking Nazis."

"Mom," I say, horrified.

At the word *Nazi*, the golem practically goes through the roof. Like it triggered some sort of automatic deployment, and now he's in full-on destroy mode. Not good. I crane my neck, trying to meet his eyes and convey to him that this is not a situation that warrants him going berserk.

"Sit down," I hiss. "He's not a Nazi. He's just a cop, and he's not even doing bad-cop stuff. My mother was speeding, she's getting a ticket, it happens."

Even though he's supposed to listen to me, the golem still looks like he wants to get out. If he decides to do it, to disobey me, I'm not sure how I could stop him. He outweighs me by a hundred pounds—okay, fifty—and his strength is supernatural.

But he'll listen to me.

He has to...doesn't he?

My intestines begin quietly knotting themselves into a writhing mass of uncertainty. I can't even imagine what would happen if the golem confronted the cop. Would he hurt the policeman, or would he get shot? What would happen if a bullet pierced the golem's flesh? Would blood pour out? Would dust?

I don't want to find out.

I glance over at Mom to see if she's clocking our conversation. But she's still hunched over the steering wheel, eyes now closed, face taut. Why is she so upset about a stupid speeding ticket? She clearly needs comforting but I'm not sure what to do, or why she's overreacting like this. I'm caught between my distraught mother up front beside me, and the itching-for-a-fight defender in the back.

The officer returns to my mother's window, handing her back her license and registration, now with a speeding violation atop the pile. My mother takes it with a shaking hand, unable to conceal her consternation. Once again, the golem tries to rise, and I shake my head at him furiously, praying that he just stays put for two more minutes.

"Drive carefully the rest of the way to that wedding, now," the police officer says. "Just watch that speed, get there safely, all right? Enjoy the day."

My mother says nothing.

When the cop saunters back to his squad car, my mother shoves the paperwork into her purse with such violent energy I'm afraid she's going to hurt herself.

"Do you want me to drive?" I ask.

"No," she seethes, and starts the car.

The remaining forty minutes of our drive are spent in total silence. My mother uses cruise control to ensure no further speeding. The tension in the car is thick enough to choke on. The golem fumes in the back, my mother fumes in the front. As for me, I'm beginning to fear I don't understand the depths of their rage—or, if I'm being honest, my own.

But it's fine, I tell myself. *We're all good people.*

Or good golems. Whatever.

Everything's going to be fine.

34

Rosie had requested the bridal party arrive at three, and the ceremony itself is scheduled for five. It's noon when we get there. My mother parks her little red Fiat in a small lot between the theater building and the cafetorium. I recall Rosie mentioning that the ceremony would be in the theater, the reception in the cafetorium. There's only one other car in the lot right now, and it's my Subaru. The hatchback is open, the flowers almost all unloaded.

After a minute, Ana emerges from the cafetorium, wearing overalls and a bright yellow puffy winter coat, unzipped. Her hair is down for once, maybe because it's too cold outside to leave her undercut exposed. Or maybe she's about to get it done by a stylist, for the wedding. She waves a tentative hand in greeting when she sees us.

"Hi, honey!" Mom calls out to Ana, perky as ever.

I look at her, astonished by her skillful transformation. She's smiling, cheery and bright. There's no indication whatsoever that less than an hour ago she was pounding her steering wheel and swearing like a sailor and having a total breakdown over a speeding violation. I didn't know she was capable of that kind of cover-up.

"Hi, Mom," says Ana. It still weirds me out that Ana calls my mother "Mom," but I guess she's officially becoming a daughter-in-law today, so maybe it's normal. "You guys are early. Like…really early."

"Just wanted to be here and help out, if there's anything you need," says my mother.

I hear a rumbling and realize the golem is still stuck in the back seat of the Fiat. I tip my car's seat forward, and he awkwardly pulls himself out of the tiny vehicle like the last giant clown emerging from a clown car.

"Oh—Paul!" Ana says, surprised. "Wow, you're here, too. Okay, well, as long are you're all here—you want to grab the wine from the Subaru, bring them into the cafetorium? There's a bar set up toward the back of the room."

She points, and he nods, lumbering to the open hatchback of my car and grabbing a box easily. When he heads into the cafetorium, Ana looks back at my mother and me. She seems unsure what to do next, which is relatable.

"Is Rosie here?" my mother asks.

"Oh, um, no," Ana says. "She didn't want me to see her before the ceremony. She's getting ready with the girls—" Ana looks guiltily at me when she says this, since apparently today's get-ready-with-the-girls invitation hadn't been extended to me "—and, um, they'll all be here around three."

"But if you're here, there must be some setup, or…?"

"I'm just here to unload the car," Ana says, with another glance at me. Because, of course, the car in question is *my* car. The one they confiscated last night. My cheeks heat. Maybe I shouldn't have had so much to drink. But also, maybe it's no one else's business. "And I have to check in with the facilities manager and stuff… Anyway, my parents' house is only a half-hour drive, so I'll head over there to get ready in a bit. Drive back with them. I can, um, leave the car at their place, whenever you want to get it, Eve—"

"Sure, sure," says my mother, nodding, smiling, doing her damnedest to radiate joy. "Well, if there's anything we can do to be helpful, just say the word. Put us to work."

"I put the flowers on the tables, but maybe you can arrange them a little?" Ana suggests to my mother. Then she eyes me carefully. "And, Eve, why don't you come with me to find the facilities manager?"

I nod, even though I'm reluctant to leave the golem and my mother alone again. I'm not worried that he'll hurt her, but I am a little nervous that if a janitor looks at my mother funny, Paul will pound him to a pulp. The scene on the train flashes through my mind; the single-minded, unapologetic fury with which the golem's fist smashed that man's nose. When the cop pulled us over on our way here, Paul looked like he wanted to exact the same punishment. But I wasn't the one feeling threatened by the officer; only my mother had been upset by him. Before that, I'd thought the golem was only protective of me. But his vigilance seems to extend to my mother, at least.

Understandable, I guess, but my stomach is starting to knot with thick, uncomfortable ropes of worry. How far does his protection extend? And if it's not only on my behalf, what happens when I'm not around to keep him in check?

The golem returns to heft another box of wine, and my mother follows him into the cafetorium. Ana turns toward the main office, which she says is about a quarter mile up the winding dirt road of the campground. It's cold, but dry and sunny. Not a bad day for a little walk. Ana waits until there's some significant distance between us and anyone else before she clears her throat and looks over at me.

"So. How have you been?"

I shrug. I haven't had a great answer to that question in over a year. I don't know why anyone even asks it anymore.

"You?" I ask instead.

"Well, I'm marrying the love of my life today, so, net positive," Ana says. "But there are some bumps, too. I mean, there's all the obvious stuff from the last year, and then, you know. Life keeps throwing you more."

"Yeah," I agree.

Ana looks at me, considering.

"Did Rosie tell you about any of the weird stalker stuff we've been dealing with on her TikTok account?" she finally asks.

"No," I say, surprised.

"Yeah, guess not," Ana says. "It's probably nothing, and, you know. It's not like you two talk a lot."

I wish I could argue with her on this point, but I can't.

"And then, last night…" Ana says, grimacing. "I mean… that was a tense little conversation."

I blink, caught off guard once more. I guess I forgot that Ana had briefly interjected when my mother and sister were sniping at me. She zips up her puffy yellow coat, and the metallic whine of the zipper seems to echo through the forest of leafless trees.

My silence in the wake of her direct statement stretches out awkwardly between us. I don't know how to respond. Even though this woman has been the most important person in my sister's life for the better part of two decades, I barely know her. She's been at every family event, including Dad's funeral and unveiling, but we rarely have any conversations of substance. She's like a lifelong next-door neighbor, someone who knows our family's rhythms and habits but whose home I have never entered.

I should know you better, I think. *But you don't know me, either.*

"I guess," I say, hearing the defensiveness in my voice.

"Rosie was upset," Ana says, not looking at me. "Really upset. She really looks up to you, Eve. You know that, right?"

I find this hard to believe, but say nothing.

"I know this past year has been awful, for all of you," Ana continues. "For all of us. Rosie and I, we both...we both just really want today to be special. Not just for us. For our families."

"Of course," I say automatically.

Ana gives me another sidelong glance.

"Do you mean that?"

"Yes," I say, testily. "It's just... I have a lot going on right now, too. Sorry if I've been a little, whatever. Distracted. I'm here, and I'll be here. Okay? Whatever I'm supposed to do, I'll do it. I ran my errands yesterday. I did everything she asked me to do. I loaned you my car. I got the wine. I got Rosie's roses."

It's hard to keep the bitterness out of my voice, and Ana doesn't miss it.

"You know," she says, eyeing me, "I was the one who picked the flowers."

"You did?" I ask, genuinely surprised.

So it wasn't Rosie picking roses as the flowers to continually position herself in the spotlight. It was Ana, in a sweet gesture about what *she* wanted in the center. I feel a bit cowed by this, although I won't admit that aloud.

"I did," she says.

"Oh," I say. "Well. That's nice."

"Yeah," Ana agrees.

And then she waits.

Like she knows I'm going to say something else.

Which I shouldn't, but I do.

"I'm trying hard, I really am," I say. "But it's a two-way street. Rosie and I—it's complicated. I'm not trying to be a jerk. I'm not. But it's not like she goes out of the way to be nice to me, either. She doesn't want me around. My mother told me that you two went over to her place for Shabbat last week. I live nearby. You could have invited me."

"We did," Ana says.

"No, you didn't," I insist.

"We tried to," says Ana. "Rosie called you, but you never called her back. Your mother called you, and got your voice-mail, which was full. We're not trying to exclude you, Eve. Do you know how many times—" She stops, takes a breath, and says coolly, "Your family has reached out to you, Eve. We've reached out to you a lot. But when someone knocks, you have to open the door. And also, sometimes? You should try being the one who knocks."

We walk for a moment in silence, Ana's Timberland boots crunching along the path, my impractical sneakers shuffling soundlessly. I want to snap back at her, but I can't. Because she's not actually my sister—and she's not actually wrong.

My phone is always off. Part of me suddenly wants to tell Ana why, but when I open my mouth, it goes dry and silent. I feel too guilty to speak. Because I probably did miss the invitation to Shabbat dinner. Of course I did. And the sad truth is, if I'd seen a text or listened to a voicemail about it, I probably would have turned them down. Or just ignored them completely. Maybe Ana's right. Maybe my family's been knocking more than I've given them credit for, and I've been the one with the bolt on my door.

"I'll do better," I finally mumble.

"Yeah," Ana says, and I'm not sure if she believes me or if she's being sarcastic.

"I'm not the only one who's been difficult," I can't help but add, even though I immediately regret this move. "I'm not the only one who makes mistakes."

Ana stops walking.

She turns and really looks at me.

"True," she says. "We all make mistakes."

I think for a half second she's going to leave it there. But she doesn't.

"I'm holding on to things too hard," Ana says. "Can't let things go. I should probably work on that. Meanwhile your mom's letting everything go and upgrading it all for shinier models. Rosie's taking something from here, there, and everywhere to try to make it meaningful. And then there's you— God, it's like we're the somethings old, new, borrowed, and blue at this wedding. Jesus. Yes. You're right, Eve. We all make mistakes. We've all been difficult. This year's been difficult. I'm not saying any of us have been handling it well. But can you please just step it up for today?"

"Yeah," I say. "Sure."

She's not buying it.

Her eyes narrow.

"Let's make a deal," Ana says. She's wearing her successful lawyer hat now, brokering the best compromise she can manage. She's always treated me so gently, keeping the peace. But now I'm officially the opposition, and she needs to handle me. "Just for today, let's put away all the old skeletons, okay? All of them. Lock them in the closet, we'll deal with them later. I'll tell Rosie you feel bad about last night and showed up early to help with setup to make up for it. And that you'd never actually skip our wedding, and you feel like an asshole for suggesting you might."

Oh my God, I forgot that I said that.

I visibly wince. I hadn't meant it. But I said it, and the memory is like a knife sliding into my side. Which is probably what it felt like to my sister last night when I said such a hateful thing. I'd told myself that Rosie wouldn't really care if I was there or not, but that seems ridiculous now. Rosie wasn't the one pushing me away. I was the one being a total bitch. Under Ana's scrutiny, I feel awful.

"I wouldn't," I say quickly.

"I know," Ana says, and she actually seems to mean it. I'm relieved that she believes me for once. "But I want to make sure that Rosie knows it, too."

"Okay," I say. "Yes. For sure. However I can make today special—just tell me. I'll do it."

"That's a good start," Ana says encouragingly. "And showing up to help with setup, that's good, too. I think the biggest thing is just…just act like you're happy to be here, even if it's hard, okay? And, of course, the toast."

"The toast," I repeat slowly.

Shit.

One more thing I haven't done. And I didn't even bring my laptop with me. It's sitting useless in my bedroom, the one half-assed paragraph I'd written inaccessible to me from here. I have literally nothing to read in front of all the guests tonight.

"You're giving the only official toast of the evening," Ana says. "It's really important to Rosie."

"Oh," I say, my dread deepening.

I'd assumed that there would be other toasts.

"You know Rosie wants to make sure you mention your Bubbe. And Dad."

"I will," I promise, the ropy knots of worry in my stomach tightening so much I want to throw up.

"She misses them, too, you know," says Ana.

Not that she ever mentions them, I think. *She expects me to handle that for her. Just like Mom. I'm the only one who ever brings up anything real.*

I nod stiffly.

"Okay," Ana says, exhaling. Her breath hangs in the air in front of us. I don't know when we started walking again, but we're outside the camp's main office now. Ana nods, dismissing me. "Right, so. Obviously I don't actually need you to talk with the facilities manager. I just wanted to—get that off my chest. Make sure we're on the same page about today. So…yeah.

You can go check in with Paul or whatever. Maybe try talking with your mom. Or Rosie. See you for the cocktail hour."

She walks into the camp office.

Feeling helpless, I turn around and look up the desolate dirt road. The grounds of the summer camp look ghostlike in winter, and I feel like a forlorn spirit floating through the scene. I take a deep breath. I'm not a ghost, although it turns out I might be an asshole. An asshole who made a literal monster.

But I made him for protection.

I made him because I don't have someone to come to my defense, when push comes to shove. Someone who always has my back.

Someone who would do what Ana just did for Rosie.

This realization stops me in my tracks. I stand there for a long moment in the cold, jealousy and admiration and loneliness swirling within me as I contemplate what a true protector—someone who will guard your heart, your reputation, your life—can actually look like.

Then I start trying and failing to compose a speech in my head as I resume my walk up the lonely road, shivering the whole way.

35

I hate this magenta pantsuit.

The brief introspection triggered by my conversation with Ana has swiftly been replaced by irritation at my assigned attire for the day. Since I didn't get dressed at home and wasn't invited to get ready at the hotel in the city with the rest of Rosie's party, I had to shove myself into my bridal party getup in the bathroom of the camp's drafty theater building. The pantsuit is unflattering as hell, in spite of the tailoring. The pants flare wildly at my already-wide hips, the blazer smooshes my boobs, and the color converts my olive-toned skin into a pallid shade of sickly winter yellow.

It's hard not to feel like Rosie chose this just to make me look bad.

Tugging a little at the bosom of the blazer, then sighing because there's nothing else I can do, I go to find Mom and the golem. Turns out "Big Paul" was swiftly put to work by the facilities team. He earned the affectionate nickname by towering over the rest of the facilities staff and being able to move whole long tables by himself.

When I walk from the theater into the adjacent cafetorium, I'm amazed at the transformation. Lace-covered tables fill the room, each adorned with a beautiful arrangement of white roses and silver-encased tea lights. String lights loop like cursive letters throughout the room, telling a twinkling love story. At the front of the room is the bridal table, with a giant filigree menorah rising from the center, awaiting the lighting ceremony planned for sunset.

"You look…nice," says my mother, looking up from a centerpiece she's needlessly rearranging. "Doesn't she look nice, Paul?"

Across the room, the golem nods.

"Anything I can do to be helpful?" I ask.

Secretly, I know the answer is that I should be writing the toast I'm supposed to give this evening. When composing it in my head proved useless, I'd briefly taken a stab at it on my phone. But I've always been an awkward phone typist and quickly gave up. Plus, I had to keep dismissing messages from Sasha. I finally gave up and turned my phone off again.

"Oh, wow," says a voice behind me, and I turn to see my sister.

Rosie's hair and makeup are impeccable, but she's not in her dress yet. Instead, she's donning a dark purple quilted down coat, open over a pair of painter's overalls and her big winter boots. Looking around the summer camp cafetorium now converted into a Hanukkah wedding wonderland, she puts a hand to her heart. Beside her, Layla squeezes her other hand.

"It looks beautiful," Layla says, taking in the scene. She looks surprised when she sees me there. "Did you help with this?"

"I was more like moral support," I admit, much as I wish I could claim to have done one maid-of-honor thing better than Layla. "Paul and Mom, though—and Ana—they really worked some magic."

Layla nods approvingly, like I finally got something right. I look away, my gaze landing on the golem. He's standing on the far side of the room, looking from one corner to the next. Memorizing the exits, I suppose. We should probably be paying him for providing event security.

I walk over and slip my hand into his. It feels cold, much colder than I've ever noticed before. He doesn't look down at me when I clasp his hand, just keeps surveying the scene.

"Thanks for all your help," I say.

The golem says nothing.

I return my attention to my sister, who is walking around, lightly touching the tables, the centerpieces, marveling at the twinkling string lights above it all. For a moment, my heart softens, seeing how genuinely charmed she is at the carefully assembled ornamentation. Then she pulls out her phone, glittering in its silver case covered in sequined roses. She aims it first at herself, then all around the room, and I realize she's sharing the whole scene with her TikTok audience.

My heart hardens once again.

Why does Rosie always have to make everything into a show?

I look back up at the golem, whose dark eyes have narrowed. He's still in his T-shirt and sweatpants, the Cubs cap shoved low over his distinctively lettered brow. He looks like a plain-clothes officer, watching Rosie carefully, his fists curling and uncurling. Apparently his protective inclinations extend to her, as well. Or maybe he sees her as a threat, since she so clearly gets under my skin.

I squeeze his cold hand, remembering my conversation with Ana. I don't want to ruin the wedding, and I don't want my date to be a distraction. I need to make sure he's not so on guard. I want him to just be the man I spent the last two days with, drinking coffee and wine, buying clothes, pulling him into my bed. The pleasant memories warm me, reassuring me that everything really will be all right. I need to give the golem that same reassurance.

"Everything's fine," I tell him. "Let's get you into your suit."

An hour later, the camp has come alive with jubilant wedding guests. The cocktail hour before the wedding is in full swing. Instead of hiring cater-waiters, Rosie and Ana asked camp friends to volunteer for the role. They were really getting into it, wearing tuxes, putting on various accents—God, I forgot how many of their friends were aspiring actors—making everyone laugh as they served up the evening's signature drinks.

One of their bartender friends had concocted the duo: both had a base of high-end potato vodka. One was blended with apple liquor, the other with cream and bitters. Unlike the Dirty Santas on the cruise ship last night, both of these were surprisingly delicious. I take a sip of each, just to know, then set them at the table where Paul Mudd and I will be seated later. After last night, I'd probably better take it easy on the alcohol tonight. But I do appreciate the thematic humor: the drinks are called Applesauce Vodka Latke versus Sour Cream Vodka Latke.

Their wedding is also a phone-free event. There's a giant white wicker basket beside the guest book, with a looping-cursive sign tied to its handle:

We request your full presence, to help us celebrate right;
please leave your phone here 'til the end of the night!

It's totally hokey, not to mention superfluous; people could just keep their phones off, like I do. But apparently folks are charmed by this element of the event, and the lacy basket is full of phones.

I'm clutching the golem's hand, determined to keep him at my side all evening. After a while, I forget that part of my motivation for doing so is to ensure he doesn't go into defensive mode— because having him beside me generally makes everything more pleasant. Everyone is just so damn delighted to see him.

Paul Mudd had won everyone over at the rehearsal dinner and was now being greeted like a celebrity. Uncle Ira, who I'd forgotten even existed until the night prior, gives "good ol' Paul" an enthusiastic handshake; my mother tells everyone how helpful he was with the tables today. He's the mayor of Wedding Town.

No one is suspicious of the handsome golem. Only one person questions anything about him at all—my aunt Rochelle, who points at his fedora and asks incredibly loudly, "So what's with the hat? Is he religious?"

When no one answers her question, I guess Aunt Rochelle decides that he must be observant, and she shrugs her approval before taking an applesauce latke cocktail from a nearby pseudo-waiter.

"Here's your coat."

I turn and see my mother holding out my winter coat to me.

"What?" I say, confused.

"You left it in your car last night," she says. "Ana saw it when we were all leaving the rehearsal dinner, I brought it with me this morning when I came to get you. I didn't want you to get cold. But I guess that cute neighbor was heating things up—"

"Mom," I hiss, cheeks instantly aflame.

"Anyway, I forgot to give it to you earlier—here, take it before I forget again."

Just then, there's a loud clap.

"If you can hear me, clap once!"

Almost everyone in the room immediately claps.

Mom and I look around, startled. Layla is at the front of the room, standing on a chair, resplendent in her magenta pantsuit. Somehow, on her, it looks couture. As it should, given what we paid for them. She yells again.

"If you can hear me, clap twice!"

Everyone laughs, and claps twice. My mother and I hesitantly join in, along with our confused older relatives. It dawns on me that this is a camp thing, a cute way of counselors getting kids' attention. Rosie told me about it at some point, I think; maybe she was saying she also used it when she was teaching fitness classes or something?

But Layla never went to this camp. How would she know about this schtick?

"Okay!" Layla says, grinning like a Miss Universe contestant. "All you campers, how'd I do?"

All the former campers in the room whoop and cheer, Ana and Rosie loudest of all. That's when I realize that Layla knows about the trick because Rosie told her about it, too, and Layla is the sort of friend who pays attention.

Of course, I think darkly, *it's easy for her to pay attention to her friend's random little stories; she's a pretty fitness instructor who dropped out of grad school when it got too hard. It's easy to pay attention when your life is stress-free.*

"Bridal party, we need you in the tay-a-tron!" Layla says, reading the word from a notecard and absolutely butchering it. Her skewering of the Hebrew makes me feel a little better. At least I could've bested her on that front. "Everyone else, enjoy your latke vodkas for another twenty minutes and then we'll really get this party started. Let's hear it for Rosie and Ana!"

Everyone claps and cheers.

"I don't know what to do with this," I tell my mother, awkwardly clutching the winter coat she shoved into my hands. "I have to go with the bridal party."

"They made the green room into a coatroom," she says, nodding toward the theater building. "Drop it off on your way."

"Fine," I sigh. I look up at the golem, whose eyes are still roving the room. Pulling him aside, I whisper, "I'll find you as soon as the ceremony's over, okay? Everything's fine, I'm safe, I'll get you a coffee with dinner."

"You can sit with me, Paul," says my mother, sliding her arm around his elbow.

I hurry with my heavy coat toward the *tayatron*, not wanting the rest of the bridal party to be waiting on me. They're all still milling around, hugging folks on their way out of the cafetorium, moving slowly. When I open the door to the theater, it, too, is beautifully decorated. Dozens of rows of white folding chairs with aisles between them, all oriented toward the chuppah—the wedding canopy rising majestically on the stage at the front of the room.

The chuppah looks expectant, ready to fill its matrimonial purpose. The canopy is lace, with creamy pale roses adorning each corner—Ana's choice, I remind myself. Beneath the chuppah is a table with a Havdalah set. The thick blue twisted candle, silver wine goblet, and matching silver spice box are dainty and make me think of my grandmother. I haven't marked the end of Shabbat with a Havdalah ceremony in years, but I can still hear the crisp *kssh!* sound of Bubbe extinguishing the braided candle into the wine glass, and smell the sweet spices intended to ease our way from the holiness of the sabbath to the mundanity of the rest of the week.

I hear laughter behind me and know the rest of the bridal party must be right on my heels. Figuring the green room is probably behind the stage, I walk up the stairs on stage left and duck behind the thick blue crushed-velvet curtains. Sure enough, there's a room back there, crowded with racks to transform it into a makeshift coatroom.

There's also a man in the room, young, with bad posture, angry acne sprawling across his forehead and chin, and a beginner's beer gut rounding the bottom of his black sweatshirt. His thinning shoulder-length hair is pulled into a low ponytail, the same dulled-brown color as his eyes.

"Hey," I say.

At the sound of my voice, he jumps. I don't recognize him, and he looks a little underdressed for a wedding. Maybe he's one of Ana and Rosie's friends who volunteered for cater-waiter duty but drew the short straw and was sent to work the coatroom instead, and dressed down in protest. Or maybe he's another one of Ana's weird family members.

He's still just staring at me.

"Um, here you go," I say, handing him my coat. "Figured I should hang this up before we get rolling. Thanks."

It takes a second before he wordlessly takes my coat.

"Oh, wait," I say.

I pull my phone from my pantsuit pocket. I can't keep it in there during the ceremony; the whole outline of it is visible through the tight sateen fabric. Plus, it's supposed to be in that stupid basket anyway. Might as well leave it here.

I shove the phone into my coat pocket, and hand it to the guy again. He takes it more quickly this time. It feels weird not to offer a tip or something. But everyone working here is a friend of Rosie or Ana, doing it as a wedding gift. They probably wouldn't want my cash. If I even had any on me, which I never do. I recall my recent contribution of a mere quarter to the woman panhandling on the train, and can't help but cringe. I vow to start carrying small bills on me. Taking some steps toward being a better person, starting Monday.

"Thanks again," I say to the coatroom guy.

"Wedding about to start?" he asks.

His voice cracks like a nervous teenager's, and I feel kind of bad for him. What an awkward dude. I wonder again where the brides know him from, since he's so unlike the rest of their bubbly, extroverted friends—if he's not some random family member, maybe he's from Ana's office? He seems young, but I think they have interns there sometimes. Or maybe he just works for the camp.

"Yeah, in like ten minutes," I say, realizing I need to get moving before I get yelled at by someone. The bridal party is supposed to start lining up right now.

He nods, and gives me a thin-lipped smile.

"Thanks," he says. "Wouldn't want to miss it."

36

I'm hurrying toward the *tayatron* hallway, worried I'm going to be late for the processional lineup, when someone grabs me by the wrist. My pulse quickens. I whirl around and see that the person confronting me is my sister.

"Can I talk to you for a second?"

Rosie's question instantly puts me on guard. I eye her warily. She looks beautiful, with her dewy makeup, golden chignon, and elegant long-sleeved white-lace eyelet wedding dress. But she's still just Rosie.

"What's up?" I ask. "Aren't you about to get married?"

"That's the plan, yeah," Rosie says. "I just... Before the ceremony, I just want to say... I really want today to be special. I really *need* today to be special."

"Okay," I say, wondering what this has to do with me.

"You know how much family means to me."

"Sure," I say, even though I find her words trite. Rosie's the one always gushing about "chosen family," making sure we all know how important her friends are to her. Since when has she

prioritized her biological family? I'm feeling impatient, wanting this conversation to be over with, wanting the wedding
to be over with, wanting to crawl back under the covers with
my golem and never emerge again.

"I know you don't want to be here," Rosie says softly. "But
if you could pretend, at least for Mom's sake...I'd appreciate it."

"What are you talking about? Of course I want to be here,"
I say, since that's what I'm supposed to say.

"No, you don't," says Rosie. "You never call me back—
not about wedding stuff, not about anything. You skipped the
bachelorette party—"

"I had a work conference that week—" I protest, but Rosie
just keeps going.

"You bitched and moaned about the pantsuits. You didn't
come get mani-pedis with us, even though Layla picked a spot
in your neighborhood. You've made very, very clear that you
don't give a shit about my wedding. And it really sucks, especially because...especially because since Dad can't be here, it
would be nice if my sister tried a little harder."

The mention of our father lands like a punch in the chest.
Rosie almost never references Dad, and just hearing her say the
word forces me to actually hear everything else she just said,
too. To take it in, and let it hurt the way it should. Realizing
how disappointed Dad would be to see this widening chasm
between his daughters genuinely guts me. But I don't know
how to acknowledge that. I feel cornered, and instead of con-
trite, my response is curt.

"I'm here," I say. "And I didn't mean to make it seem like I
don't care. I care, okay?"

"Yeah," she says. "Sure."

She's making me feel so selfish, and it's not fair. I want to
point out all the ways that she's been selfish, too. But it's her
wedding day, and we're three minutes from walking down the
aisle. So I should keep my damn mouth shut.

Instead, I surprise us both by asking, "Why isn't Mom walking you down the aisle?"

"What?" Rosie asks, blinking.

"Why is she just sitting in the front row?"

"Because that's what she wanted," Rosie says.

"What are you talking about?" I say, because that can't be right. Mom loves the spotlight. Loves weddings. Loves Rosie. Why would she request to be sidelined?

"I asked her to walk me down the aisle," Rosie says, voice wobbling a little. "But she said that was something Dad always wanted to do, and she...she didn't feel right doing it. She'd do it if I wanted her to, but she'd prefer to just...to just get to watch me walk. When Ana's parents heard that, they offered to sit with her, too. So none of the parents are in the ceremony. No 'giving the brides away.' Stupid archaic old tradition anyway. Back from when women were property. Kind of gross, if you think about it."

But the tears in her eyes tell me she doesn't really feel that way, at least not completely. Maybe she really wanted someone to walk her down the aisle. Dad. Mom. Someone. But since our father couldn't, and our mother wouldn't, she found herself without any parental escort. And instead of pressuring Mom into it, Rosie decided to do what made our mother comfortable.

I never would have predicted that. Which makes me feel proud of my little sister, and shitty about myself. I'm also incredibly envious that Rosie and Mom were able to have a conversation like that at all. One where they directly referenced our absent family.

"You two...talk about Dad?" I ask, voice tight. "You and Mom, you...you talk about him?"

"We're figuring out how to," my sister says. "She's really angry, you know. At God, at the doctors, at everyone. She doesn't want to be sad. So she's mad. But she's also really good at hiding it, most of the time."

Fuck, fuck, fuck, fuck! I remember my mother cursing when the cop pulled us over—and remembering, just as clearly, her picture-perfect smile by the time we arrived at camp half an hour later.

"Oh," I say.

"Anyway," Rosie says, dabbing her hand lightly across her nose, trying not to smear her makeup. "I don't know why I even tried to say anything right now, I just... I just felt like I had to try to... I don't know..."

I want to tell her *I know.*

I want to tell her *I'm sorry.*

I want to tell her *I love you.*

But there seems to be a wall between me and those words. I can't get over it, can't get around it. I just stand there on the other side of the wall, resenting everything and everyone, myself included.

Then the moment is over, and my sister lowers her head and turns away from me.

37

The wedding party is shuffled out into the cold, waiting out-side in pairs for our cues to walk in. As soon as the rest of us are moved outside, Ana is supposed to make her entrance. She'll walk up the aisle, stopping to kiss her parents and my mother in the front row. The front row, where my mother *requested* to sit. I wonder if there will be an empty seat beside her. I squeeze my eyes shut, willing away the awful image.

After she kisses the parents, Ana will walk up onto the stage, and wait alone beneath the chuppah. I wonder what it feels like for her to be there, on her own, all eyes on her for once as she awaits her bride.

Her beloved, our grandmother would say.

Ethan is beside me, rubbing his hands together and blow-ing on them for warmth. His faux-hawk looks frozen stiff, and even though he's barely my height, somehow the sleeves of his rented tuxedo are too short for him.

"Man, we must really love those girls to freeze our asses off out here, huh?"

"Yep," I say, not bothering to look at him. I just want the ceremony to be over, so I can go check on the golem and get on with my life. Not that I know what getting on with my life will entail, or how long the golem will be a part of it. I shudder at the uncertainty of everything, wondering how much decision-making power I really have.

A friend of Ana and Rosie whose name I've already forgotten is in charge of sending each couple out as the processional gets underway. The friend is consulting a wedding program, tapping people when it's their turn to start marching. I watch from behind them as Layla and her husband, Amir, walk into the theater. Amir takes a seat in the audience; Layla alights to the wooden stage with the rest of the bridal party. Amir is just as fit and attractive as Layla, and an evil part of me hopes that he's secretly gay or something. No one's life should be that perfect.

"Hey," Ethan says. "I was super wasted last night, so if I said anything, like, out of line, please just—"

"No worries," I say, not wanting to have this conversation. "We've all been there."

And then Ethan and I are walking down the aisle, arm in arm. Ana is under the chuppah, eyes shining. She's wearing a tailored suit, black, with a creamy silk shirt and a rose blooming from her pocket square. She's already flanked by the rest of the bridal party, since Ethan and I are the last ones to precede Rosie in the processional. Just as we part ways at the stage, Ethan stumbles a little; righting himself, he grabs my breast instead of my arm. I flinch, but he gives me a look that seems legitimately apologetic.

"Sorry," he whispers. "For real."

I nod, then look into the audience, and see the golem starting to rise.

"Not at this part of the ceremony, dear," I hear my mother whisper, tugging at his hand.

Sit down, I mouth. *Now.*

For a moment, the golem stands there defiantly.

Then, slowly, he sits.

Exhaling a sigh of relief, I hurry up onto the stage.

The rabbi, a woman with a sleek silver bob haircut and warm eyes, makes everyone feel welcomed into the wedding ceremony. I think she's one of the newer rabbis at my parents' synagogue, but I can't be sure—I haven't been there in so long. I should probably go. Especially if they're getting bomb threats. It would be an act of solidarity. Although I guess if it's my people being targeted, it's not really an act of solidarity. It's just showing up.

I keep glancing back at the golem, wanting to make sure he stays put. But at some point, I get swept up in the ceremony, and everything else falls away. Ethan, the vigilant golem, my secretly emotional mother, the guests known and unknown— they all disappear. In the twinkling of the string lights above the chuppah and the Havdalah candle beneath it, all I see is my sister and her bride.

Ana and Rosie look so happy. The rabbi is talking about building a life together, starting with a solid foundation, and building upward into a true and lasting partnership. It all sounds like such a nice fairy tale. Rosie circles Ana, then Ana circles Rosie. Rosie's elegant old-world lace wedding dress and Ana's sleek black suit make them look like two halves of a whole as they circle one another—yin and yang, day and night, calm and energy.

Blessings are given. Rings are exchanged. Layla places a glass beneath each of their feet, and each bride enthusiastically stomps. The in-stereo sound of two shattered cups cues the entire audience to yell, "Mazel tov!"

The brides kiss, and I feel the unfamiliar sensation of hot tears stinging my eyes. None slide down my cheek, but they're there. Reassuring or threatening, I can't tell. But they're there, reminding me I'm still human.

Then the ceremony is over. We exit the stage, this time walking down the aisle and taking up positions at the back of the room. It's nice not to be out in the cold, but awkward to stand there greeting everyone as they exit the theater and head back to the cafetorium for the reception. Ana and Rosie are absolutely glowing. Layla greets everyone with a radiant smile, as does the rest of the wedding party. Almost as soon as the greeting line begins, Ethan announces that he has to take a piss, and disappears.

As I shake hands and get hugged by family and strangers alike, the whole time I'm keeping my eye out for the golem. My mother is part of the greeting line, as are Ana's parents, who walked with the bridal party from the stage to the rear door. But Paul Mudd wasn't with my mother when she joined the line, and I haven't had the chance to ask her where he might be.

Soon, all the guests have cleared out of the theater. But the golem still hasn't made his way through the greeting line. And now the stage-manager friend is ushering the bridal party back toward the cafetorium, and before I know what's happening, Layla is beckoning me over to her. There's a microphone in her hand.

Oh faaaaaaaaaaaaaaaaaaaaaaaaack.

"Everyone, we are so excited to officially introduce you to the new Mrs. and Mrs. Berger-Goodman!" Layla cries. From their seats at the table of honor, Rosie and Ana wave. Then Layla turns to me. "And before we do the candle-lighting ceremony, Eve Goodman, Rosie's big sister, is going to offer a toast for the couple."

To my horror, Layla hands me the microphone and walks away. She takes a seat beside her handsome husband, and gives me a smile that somehow manages to convey bright joy to everyone else while conveying *Don't fuck this up* to me.

Sweat beads in my armpits and runs down my back, for-ever ruining the magenta pantsuit. I look this way and that, my mind blank as a sea of expectant faces stare at me, smil-ing. When I lock eyes with Ana, her smile tightens. She, too, is willing me not to fumble this one.

I clear my throat and raise the mic to my lips.

"I, uh, had some trouble figuring out what to say today," I begin, voice cracking. "I thought about saying something about the symbolism of the broken glass, joy alongside grief...but that speech didn't...didn't quite come together. Instead I just kept thinking about... I just keep thinking about..."

I close my eyes, praying that something will come to me.

Bubbe.

Dad.

Someone.

Help.

I open my eyes.

There's no one who can help me.

There's only me.

"I keep thinking about how much of life is outside of our control," I say, looking around the room. A few people nod, in agreement or encouragement. "Almost all of it, really. Which is kind of terrifying, to be honest. I know, I know...the big sister has issues with not being in control? Stop the presses."

There are a few chuckles.

Heartened, I go on.

"But even though we may not have a lot of control—we do have a lot of choice. We make choices every day. Choices about who we invite into our lives, and how we treat them. Choices about the kind of people that we want to be. Choices about whether to root for the Cubs, or whether to be wrong."

More laughter.

I take a deep breath.

"Rosie and I were very close with our grandmother—our

bubbe, Leah Klein. We were also very close with our father...
David Goodman." I thought saying their names would make
everything harder, but despite the lump in my throat, I feel
strengthened. "If we had control over it, they would both be
here with us today. To see how happy Rosie and Ana are. To
raise a glass in their honor. We don't have that kind of control...
but we do have a choice. We can choose to live our lives in a
way that honors them: by being fiercely loyal survivors, like
Bubbe; and by being funny, joyful cheerleaders, like...Dad."

I close my eyes.

You've got this, Evie.

"In Jewish tradition, when we lose someone, we say, 'May
their memory be a blessing.' And when it comes to us, and our
loved ones...no one has been more blessed than we have. Ana
and Rosie, I hope you know how loved you are—by those who
aren't here, and by those who are. So please, raise a glass with
me, in honor of the loved ones we've lost, and in honor of new
family members gained. Most of all, to the beautiful brides.
We wish them health, and love, and every happiness. *L'chaim.*"

"*L'chaim,*" everyone says, and I see a few people dab their
eyes.

Including Rosie.

Weak with relief, I make my way to the bridal party table
and slide into my seat. That's when I notice that one of the
seats at the long table is empty. I do a quick inventory of the
wedding party.

The missing one is Ethan.

Heart thudding, I look around the room, hoping against
hope to find the face I'm looking for, safely seated beside my
mother or stationed at one of the doors.

But the golem is gone, too.

38

"Eve, that was...that was really wonderful," says Ana, squeezing my shoulder.

I look up, wild-eyed, and try to compose myself. My improvised speech has already blurred and faded away. I can barely remember what I said. The only thing on my mind now is finding out where the golem has gone, and making sure he hasn't done anything stupid.

"Thanks—thank you," I say, rising and giving her a quick hug, looking over her shoulder as I do so, trying to still scan the room. Rosie is behind Ana, looking almost shy.

"I— Yeah," Rosie says, taking a tentative step toward me. "What Ana said."

Heart thudding so loud I can barely hear myself think, I give my little sister a quick hug, too. I know I should make more of this moment, but I can't. All I can think about is the missing golem and the missing brides-man.

"Be right back," I say. "Bathroom."

I hastily bolt from the bridal table before either of them can say anything else. I make it into the cafetorium hallway, where I remember seeing the bathrooms. Thankfully, all the bathrooms have been designated gender neutral, so I'll easily be able to check both without raising any eyebrows. I'm about to push the first door open when a hand lands on my shoulder.

I whirl around and find myself face-to-face with Layla.

Her dark eyes are shining, her lips trembling. My sister's best friend shakes her head, like she's trying to say something but can't quite get it out, the words trapped somewhere between her mind and her mouth.

"I…" She clears her throat, then says, "I wanted to say— good job. With the speech."

"Thanks," I say, looking past her in case the golem rounds the corner. "Look, I really have to—"

"I haven't known what to think, sometimes, but your words just now—they were really lovely. Especially that thing you said about memory being a blessing—"

"Yeah, uh-huh," I say, completely distracted.

"It was so moving, I mean really—"

"Yep, it's a good line," I say, eyes darting everywhere in search of the golem, in search of Ethan, in search of any sign of trouble. "I mean, if you don't have your memories, what's the point, right?"

Layla looks stricken.

"Is that supposed to be funny?" she asks, eyes snapping with sudden fury. I don't understand how the conversation took such a sharp turn, and I don't have the time to figure out why this woman is suddenly getting in my face. "Seriously, what's wrong with you?"

"Oh my God, Layla, I don't know what your damage is, but I really have to go," I snap, because while maybe under other circumstances I'd try to figure out how I accidentally ticked off my sister's bestie, I don't have time right now. The golem has been glowering at Ethan all night, and now they're both gone, and the dread gnawing at my gut is too much to ignore.

I dart into the first bathroom, praying Layla doesn't follow me inside.

She doesn't.

I hastily check each stall, and they're all empty. I burst back into the hallway, relieved that somehow Layla has already disappeared. I barrel into the second bathroom. Empty. My heart is banging against my ribs like a deranged woodpecker. Thinking fast, I remember that we were actually still in the theater when Ethan said he had to piss, so I take off at a dead run for the second set of gender-neutral bathrooms.

The first theater bathroom I barge into is empty, lights off, completely dark. The second one, when I open the door, greets me with buzzing fluorescent lights. The buzzing sound fills my ears, so loud I'm not even sure it's just the lights anymore. My whole body is humming with fear because I don't know what I'm going to find in here.

For one merciful moment, I think the answer might be nothing. It's quiet. Still.

Then I hear a soft moan.

Terror clutching at my stomach, I push open the door of the accessible stall at the far end of the bathroom.

There, stretched face up across the toilet, is Ethan.

His face is purpled and swollen, blood dripping from his nose. His hand is holding his side, like he's trying to keep himself from falling apart. I'm paralyzed with horror, seeing what the golem has done.

What *I've* done.

Ethan is so still that for a moment I'm afraid he's dead, but then he takes a wheezing inhale, exhaling another low moan. The sound jolts me into action, and I lurch forward, putting a trembling hand on his forehead.

"You're going to be okay," I say.

"Eve," he wheezes. "Your... boyfriend..."

"Don't talk," I say. "I'm calling an ambulance."

I reach into my pants pocket, but there's no phone there. With a sickening feeling, I suddenly remember shoving the phone into my coat pocket.

The coatroom.

"I'll be right back, I swear," I tell Ethan, who barely exhales in response.

I race to the coatroom. It's empty when I get there—the coatroom attendant must be off shift, getting to enjoy the party with his friends. Blissfully unaware of the devastation in the theater bathroom, and the angry monster on the loose.

My angry monster.

I paw at rack after rack, finally finding my coat, jamming my hand into the pocket and pulling out my phone. My fingers are shaking so hard I barely manage to turn it on. I hit Send on the emergency call.

It doesn't go through.

No!

Reeling, I vaguely recall guests lightheartedly complaining about the terrible cell service out at camp. I hold the phone in the air, divining for signal, and hit the emergency call button again. This time, miraculously, the call goes through.

"911, what's your—"

"Someone's been attacked," I say. "He's hurt, badly, we need an ambulance—"

"Slow down, ma'am. Where are you located?"

"Camp Heller-Diamond," I say. "Off exit thirty-six—"

"One moment, let me call up your location... Okay, ma'am, it's going to take about half an hour for us to get an ambulance out that way."

Shit.

"Please just get someone here as fast as you can!" I scream, then run at breakneck speed back toward the *tayatron* bathroom.

I don't want Ethan to be alone for the half hour it's going to take for help to arrive. He might be a low-grade schmuck, but he didn't deserve to be brutalized like this. I have to wait with him until—

A shriek from the cafetorium stops me in my tracks.

For one impossibly long moment, I stand frozen in the cold, empty theater. A few yards to my left, Ethan is in the bathroom stall, bleeding and broken. The cafetorium is one building over, to my right. And somewhere out there is the golem, possibly wreaking havoc, all because of me and my selfish choices.

I don't know what to do. I don't know which way to go. Every choice I've ever made has been the wrong one. I don't trust myself. I don't trust anyone.

Then there's a second scream from the cafetorium, and my heart ceases its beating, because I recognize the screamer. She had the same shrill shriek when we were children and she was scared or angry.

Rosie.

I turn and race toward the wedding party.

When I burst back into the cafetorium, the whole room is abuzz. There's more confusion than fear, as everyone looks around to see where the screams are coming from. The anxiety in the air is palpable, but it's tempered with the hesitation that often talks our potential hysteria off the ledge.

Maybe everything is okay.

Maybe it's just a kid screwing around.

Maybe it's some kind of joke.

But Ana is standing up behind the bridal table, eyes darting all across the room. My mother is standing beside her, trying to calm her down, although she looks stricken herself. Rosie isn't with them.

"Rosie," Ana says, panic choking her voice. "Where's Rosie? I heard her screaming, but I can't tell where it's coming from."

I run over to Ana and my mother. All of our heads are swiveling, eyes searching, looking for any clue as to what's going on. That's when I notice something strange. There's a smaller secondary stage at the rear of the cafetorium, right by the entrance to the kitchen. It must be something the summer camp uses for small services or song sessions.

The guy from the coatroom is standing on the platform.

He's holding something in each of his hands. The object in his left hand I quickly identify as a cell phone. I can't tell what the other thing is, because the right sleeve of his ill-fitting black sweatshirt is hanging over it, past his slim wrist. Whatever it is, he's using it to beckon someone from the kitchen.

"What the hell is the coatroom guy doing up there?" I ask.

"What coatroom guy?" Ana replies, utterly bewildered.

That's when Rosie stumbles from the kitchen, terrified.

Even from all the way across the cafetorium, I can see the thick streaks of mascara running down her cheeks like polluted rivers. Her face is contorted with fear, and she has her hands up, and edges forward slowly, like someone is beckoning her toward someplace she doesn't want to go.

Ana screams.

The coatroom guy turns to face us, and I go rigid with horror.

Because the object in his right hand is a gun, and it's pointed at my sister.

39

"Say hello to GoGo-RoRo's whole fucking audience," screams the coatroom guy, who is not actually a coatroom guy.

He's pointing the cell phone at all of us, scanning the room with the phone's camera as he clutches it awkwardly in his left hand. The phone is in a shiny silver case with glittery sequins. It's Rosie's phone, I realize.

He's broadcasting live from her TikTok account.

Whatever is about to happen, he wants people to see it. He's here to make some sort of statement—or worse. My blood turns to ice in my veins. Rosie is trembling, forced to cower and weep in front of her own beloved audience.

This can't be happening.

"Oh my God, no," Ana whispers. "No, no, no…"

"Who is he?" I whisper back, subtly trying to fish my phone from my pocket, wondering if you can text 911. "He was in the coatroom, he took my coat, but he—"

"Streaming live from the bullshit 'wedding' of your favorite fitness bitch," barks the sociopath with the gun. "Oh, what's the matter, RoRo? Surprised? Nah, come on. She shouldn't be surprised! Y'all know I warned her. I told all of you, didn't I? And now you're all going to see what happens when— Fuck, did I just lose signal…?"

"It's Alt-Might-Oh-Seven," Ana says, her voice thinned by dread. "That's gotta be him, but I never thought…"

"Who?" I ask, terror clawing at my throat, barely letting the word escape.

"I don't… I don't really know," she says. "He's…this troll, obsessed with Rosie… She always told me it was no big deal. She takes a lot of shit online. But I kept flagging his posts because they were freaking me out—I even tried to get a restraining order, but we didn't know his real name, and of course the platform assholes never got back to us, so we couldn't get it handled that way but…but I never actually thought— Oh, Jesus…"

Why isn't anyone calling 911? I wonder, looking around the room with growing panic. *Why isn't anyone filming him, why isn't anyone—*

But then my eyes land on the lacy basket, where dozens of phones are uselessly piled atop one another. I see several other guests eyeing the basket, too. Wondering if they should make a grab for it. It's risky, though, because it's positioned near Rosie.

Then the gunman, too, notices the basket, and screams at the top of his lungs.

"Anyone I see with a phone gets shot!"

Everyone freezes.

Swallowing hard, I click my phone off and pocket it. I stare at the gunman, whose face is contorted with purple rage. Veins bulge from his ropy neck. I look around wildly, because if ever I needed a protector, now is the moment.

Where's my golem? I wonder, my mind screaming for some sort of solution. *Did he run off after hurting Ethan, who wasn't even an actual threat? Now that we really, truly need him, where the hell is he?*

The armed ponytailed man swings the phone and the gun around the room, making people gasp and duck.

"I'm the only one with a goddamn phone right now, you hear me? I'm the only one with a goddamn phone, and I'm in charge!" He looks down at his phone once more, and smiles a wolfish smile at the small screen. "Hello, audience, we're live again. Sorry, sorry, are you only here for GoGo-RoRo? Don't worry, don't worry, the flower herself is right here. Come on, Rosie, say hello to your fans."

He points the camera at Rosie again. She sobs harder.

"Oh, now you're sad?" The mock pity in his voice makes me feel sick. "Well, a lot of us were sad when you decided to step away from your fitness videos and 'inspo' and start putting up all your dyke-kike bullshit instead. You went from health and fitness to something fucking sick. *That's* what's sad. Am I right?"

He's vacillating wildly between addressing Rosie and addressing the phone screen. I pray that thousands of people really are watching this live stream, and that at least one of them will figure out how to send help our way. If he figured out where the wedding is, other people must have, too, right? Rosie had shown images of the camp more than once.

But they won't get here soon enough, I think, feeling sick. *Even the 911 dispatcher said it would take half an hour for an ambulance to arrive.*

"Oh my God," whispers my mother.

"I told her to stop with the wedding streams," Ana whispers, hoarse, stiff, and still but unable to stop the words tumbling from her mouth. "That even if she didn't mention the camp's name it would be way too easy to find out where we'd be, but I never in a million years thought he'd… Jesus Christ, we have to stop him, we have to…"

"See, Rosie? I told you. I TOLD YOU," shrieks the man, who's barely more than a kid. I'd seen his acne up close, and can now see the youthful awkwardness of his movements. He can't be more than twenty-two, twenty-three.

The thought adds to my terror. He doesn't know what he's doing. He's never felt the weight of consequences, doesn't know how permanent death would be. He's just some desperate kid whose misguided beliefs might get someone killed.

"It's not like I didn't warn you, and warn you, and *warn you*," he spits at Rosie, waving the gun at her in a way that makes the whole room flinch. "I messaged you. I tagged you. I even called your synagogue last week."

"Oh God," my mother whispers again, like these are the only words she has anymore. "Oh my God, *oh my God...*"

"Just say the word *bomb* and everyone freaks out," he says, shaking his head, like he's amazed at how easy it is to terrorize people. "But there's just no getting through to you."

"Please," says Rosie. "Please, stop, you don't have to do this—"

"Oh, I sure as hell have to do this," snaps her stalker. "You didn't leave me any other choice, Rosie. I gave you every chance. I gave you every fucking chance. But you just ignored me. Blocked me. That kike-dyke lawyer you're pretending to marry threatened to get a restraining order on me? Bullshit. Bull. Shit. Does she think I didn't see her comments, too? I saw everything. *Everything.* And if she ever tries to come after me, I swear I'll—"

But the screaming stalker never gets to finish his threat, because there's a huge crash from the side of the building. Every head in the room swivels toward the sound.

The golem had evidently entered the room holding an armful of metal, dropping it to the ground with a massive clatter. Now, moving faster than humanly possible, he hurls himself at the gunman, knocking him to the ground. The gunman doesn't even have time to react before he's pinned to the floor by my avenging angel.

Rosie bolts toward us, not stopping until she's in Ana's arms. My mother and I take a defensive position in front of the brides, eyes on the golem and the gunman, waiting to see what will happen.

From somewhere nearby, I dimly hear people digging through the lacy basket, securing cell phones and calling the police. I stand there, my back to my sister and her wife, hands balled into fists, breath coming in short gasps. The threat has been taken down before anyone was seriously hurt. For one long moment, I'm so grateful to the golem for saving us all that I forget that not everyone has made it through the wedding unharmed.

Then I remember Ethan, alone and injured in the bathroom. *Shit.*

Do I stay here, do I go back to Ethan, do I check on the golem?

What do I do?

Before I can reach a decision, a commotion at the other end of the room catches my attention. Paul Mudd, still clutching Rosie's alt-right stalker, is getting up from the floor. There's a collective gasp as the golem slowly rises.

The fedora has been knocked from his head, and even from across the room I can clearly see the Hebrew letters emblazoned on his brow. They almost seem to glow, like they're written in angry fire. He has one hand around the white supremacist's neck; in the other, he holds the gun. He crushes the weapon with his bare hand, then throws it to the ground. He tightens his grip on the gunman's throat.

"Please," wheezes the attacker. His face is purpling, eyes bulging. He can't catch a breath, and barely manages to croak out his plea. "Please…"

"Stop!"

A new voice cuts through the chaos. For the third time that night, everyone's attention is hijacked by an unexpected arrival. This time, it's not a gunman, or a golem.

It's Sasha, and she's pissed.

40

Sasha hurries past me, eyes locked on her target. She slows as she approaches the golem, stopping a few yards away. She begins speaking in a calm but firm tone. Her back is to me, so I can't see her expression, but I can hear the fear behind her strong words. Everyone in the ruined wedding scene has gone quiet, watching her.

"Put him down."

The golem continues to impassively choke the ponytailed assailant, whose legs are kicking feebly. He's no longer able to choke out words, only sickening gurgles. Sasha takes another stride toward them, raising her voice.

"You stopped the threat. Let us take it from here. Please."

Something on the ground catches her eye. She picks it up, and I see her spine stiffen. Sasha turns from the golem to me, eyes wild.

"Tell him."

I stare at her in utter confusion. Why should I tell him to release the gunman?

But Sasha's face is hard and certain.

She's not asking.

"Paul," I say, but my voice is caught in my throat and no sound escapes. I feel trapped in one of those dreams where you're screaming but no sound comes out of your mouth. I try again, and this time the word comes out a scream: "Paul!"

The golem slowly turns his head toward me.

"Put him down," I say.

The golem blinks, and drops the gunman, who doesn't move. There's a moment of shocked silence.

Then all hell breaks loose.

Everyone is screaming, exclaiming, making calls, fumbling for keys, trying to get out of there. Sasha drags me away from my mother and sister, away from my golem. I stare at him over my shoulder, but he's just standing there for the moment. Watching. Waiting.

"This isn't over," Sasha says, dragging me toward the golem.

"Wait...wait," I say. I have a thousand questions for her, and don't know which one to ask first and then one just tumbles from my mouth of its own accord. "How did you get here? You don't have a car!"

"*That's* your first question?" Sasha exclaims, and almost looks amused. "Jesus Christ. Bryan and Carlos drove me."

She locks eyes with me, and for the first time in a long time, I look at her. *Really* look at her. And then the next question I should ask becomes irrelevant, because when I see the sorrow and regret and worry in her eyes, I already know the answer to why she's here. Even if I hadn't read all of her texts, even if I hadn't noticed her apprehension earlier, even if I didn't have all the pieces to the puzzle that are finally sliding into place, the look in her eyes tells me everything I need to know.

"Holy shit," I say. "You made a golem, too."

"Yeah," she says.

"Is this one of those things every middle-aged Jewish woman does, and they just never talk about it?"

"I don't think so," Sasha says. "It's just that you and I share the same brain, remember? And hey, fuck you for calling us middle-aged."

"Sorry," I say. "I think I'm in shock."

"You are."

"Emmet was a golem?"

"Yes."

"The whole time—"

"Yes."

"Wait," I say, shaking my head in disbelief. "You literally just called him the name on his forehead. Alef-mem-tav— 'Emmet.'"

"What can I say," Sasha says. "I'm not the creative type, re-member? I'm the account executive."

"Sasha, how the hell—"

"Eve, I love you, but you've got to shut up," Sasha says. "This is not a where's-the-pod moment, okay? Save the questions. We've gotta end this thing."

"What do you mean 'end this thing'?" I ask, nervous. "I know this looks bad, but I need him."

"You don't," Sasha says.

"I do—"

"No," she says firmly. "Babe, I get it—trust me, I get it. But this is not the sort of thing we should be messing around with. It's dangerous. And the longer you have him…the more you'll feel like you need him. And like you don't need the rest of us. Your family. Your friends. It changes you, Eve. It…it changed me. You start to lose yourself. You start to think you *only* need the golem."

"No," I protest, but some part of me knows she's right.

Ever since I created the golem, I've been even more of a monster. But if I'm being truly honest, it didn't start with the

golem. He was only the culmination of my fear, my misery...
my grief. My sorrow blinded me to so much, shoved me into
a corner, kept me from connecting with my friends or engaging with the world. My grief led me to make a monster. But
worse, my grief made *me* a monster.

My God, I've been awful. I've justified things that defy jus-
tification. I've retreated from the ones whose pain was as deep
and raw as mine.

My mother.

My sister.

But I can't get rid of my golem.

"No," I say to Sasha again, shaking my head, not wanting
to admit how wrong I've been. "I can't get rid of him. I need
him, and he's good. Can't you see that? He just did a good
thing. He saved my sister. He saved all of us. Paul is fundamentally good—"

"He's fundamentally *a golem*," Sasha says. "They're not good
or bad. They're only protective. And they're not big on nuance."

"But he just saved us," I insist. "If it weren't for him, someone could've been killed."

"Not this time, actually," Sasha says, and presses something
into my hand.

I feel the plastic object in my palm before I see it. When I
look down, I can't help but gasp. It's the thing she picked up
from the ground—the stalker's gun.

Only it isn't actually a gun, it's a *toy* gun.

From across the room, it had us all fooled, but up close, it
doesn't even look real. The whole time, Rosie's TikTok troll
was pointing a toy weapon at us all. It doesn't make what we
went through any less traumatic, but it does change the story.
The intention. The potential for harm.

"But that's..." I say, shaking my head, shocked but sill certain that taking the kid down was the right thing to do. "I

mean, okay, so it's fake, but we had no way of knowing, and neither did Paul..."

"Right, which is why the golem might've just killed him," Sasha says. "Like I said, no nuance. A golem's not a judge or jury, Eve, he's only an executioner. An executioner you summoned—"

"Because there are real dangers," I say. "We're constantly under attack—"

"Eve," Sasha says, gently but firmly. Her eyes won't let mine go. "Does that mean *we* should be constantly attacking?"

"I don't... I don't know," I say, throat thickening.

Because I don't know how to answer her question. I don't want to be a monster, but I also don't want to be a victim. It's not just my grief that drove me to this. It's the man who spit at me on the train. It's the memories of my grandmother who survived the horrors of actual genocide. It's actual genocides still happening today. It's the news, the bomb threats, the inherited trauma, the ongoing conflicts. My fears aren't based on nothing. They're real.

"We can't let our pain convince us to cause more pain," Sasha says softly. "I'm not saying there's not bad shit out there, and I'm not saying we shouldn't fight it. I'm just saying if we become the ones who always run in, guns blazing, no questions asked—we become the bad guys."

Something twinges in me. I remember sitting across the table from my mother at the Walnut Room, just a few days ago. She was telling me about the bomb threat, but that wasn't the only important part. I suddenly remember what she said about the security decision. Why they weren't going to default to always having armed protection on-site.

We wouldn't want someone getting hurt, just because someone else felt nervous.

I look down at the plastic gun still sitting in my palm. Rosie's internet stalker deserves to get in trouble for storming her wedding reception, threatening her with this fake weapon, doing truly horrible things.

But did he deserve to die for it?

Do I want that on my conscience?

I look at Sasha, and nod slowly.

She exhales and puts her hand over the fake gun, squeezing my fingers in hers.

"Now look," she says. "We have to move fast. A golem has only one purpose: protect his people. Not just you. It starts out that way—you're his first priority, for a while. But he evolves toward his true purpose, which is guarding us. All of us. We're his people, and he's perceiving a big-ass attack right now—right or wrong. And that means—"

A blur of motion catches our attention, and both of us snap our heads toward the golem. He's no longer standing beside the crumpled gunman. Instead, he's collecting the massive pile of scrap metal he dropped earlier. He selects one of the longest metal bars in his arm. Carefully setting down the rest of the pile, he twists the metal around the door handles of the cafetorium's rear exit, locking it securely.

"What is he doing?" I ask, utterly bewildered.

"Keeping us safe," says Sasha grimly.

As confused partygoers approach the door with keys in hand, the golem snarls, warning them back. He picks up another hunk of metal and lumbers to the other exit, the side door, swiftly disabling that one, too. When he sees someone making a break for the kitchen, he roars, stopping them in their tracks, then positions himself in front of the kitchen door, blocking the last of the exits from the cafetorium.

"I don't understand," I say.

"Like I said," Sasha explains, eyes narrowing as she stares at the monster. "He only has one purpose. One job: keep his people safe. The golem was always a desperate-times, desperate-measures creation. And I'm not saying our times aren't desperate. They are. Of course they are. But golems aren't built for this world. All the social media, the nonstop news cycle, the constant threats, all the time...they can't handle it. Did you ever let him watch any television?"

I flash back to him tackling me, when he heard the wail of a siren in the distance.

After he was watching cop shows on television.

Oh, no.

Someone tries to dart past the golem, and he blocks them with ease. He doesn't hurt the person trying to flee—Layla, I realize; it's Layla, sobbing and terrified—instead catching her in his arms and gently returning her to the middle of the room, then shaking his head firmly and returning to his guard post.

"He's been taking it all in the last few days," Sasha continues. "Little threat here, little threat there. Stuff specific to you, then more broad communal threats. Always taking it all in. I saw him doing it on the boat. It took a lot longer with Emmet, because I almost never took him out into the world. He didn't kick into overdrive until we went to a march downtown, and...that's a story for later. But you had some shit luck tonight with Rosie's stalker showing up, Eve. A golem only gets more vigilant, the more danger he sees approaching us. He feeds off our fears. The more scared we are, the more protective he gets. He'll do whatever he thinks he needs to do."

"But I still don't understand," I say. "What's he doing—"

"He's blocking the doors," Sasha says. "He wants us to stay here. At this camp. In this room. The outside world is too dangerous. He wants this little corner—this little shtetl—to be under his protection. If we all just stay here, he can keep us safe. And that's all he wants to do. It's all he'll ever want to do."

"For how long?" I ask.

Sasha looks from the golem to me.

"Forever," she says.

41

"He can't keep us here forever," I say, watching in sick horror as the golem seals off another door. It feels like an iron fist is slowly squeezing my heart until it's about to burst. "Why would you say that? How could you know for sure that he'd try to—"

"Remember when I disappeared?" Sasha says softly. "When I wasn't going out, wasn't returning calls, wasn't part of your life anymore...?"

I have a sudden vision of Sasha in her apartment, sitting on her bed, a golem barring her exit. Believing the world outside was too dangerous for her, and he couldn't risk allowing her to move freely through it.

"Oh God," I say. "Sasha...then how...how did you...?"

"It's hard," she says. "It's really fucking hard."

Sasha reaches into her pocket, and pulls out something small, sharp, and silver. It takes me a moment to identify the object as a chisel.

The chisel looks expectant in her palm. There's dry dust on the end of it, remnants from when she must have plunged the thing into Emmet's forehead. I don't know how she summoned the strength to do it then, and I don't know how she's going to pull it off this time.

"Fine," I say, trembling. I look at my best friend, chisel in her hand. She looks like a warrior. "If you have to take him down...I won't stop you."

She gives me a sad smile.

"I already took care of my monster," she says. "This one's yours."

"What?" I gasp. "No, I can't."

"You can, and you will," Sasha says. "You have to be the one to stop him. You're his creator. You have to destroy him. Erase the alef from his forehead. Then he's just left with mem and tav, and that spells—"

"Death," I whisper, remembering my bubbe's story. "But he won't... I mean he won't really *die*, right?"

"Close enough," Sasha says.

She takes the fake gun, and presses the chisel into my palm.

The cold feel of the metal against my skin makes me shiver. I curl my fingers around the chisel, but something in me rebels at the feeling of the thing in my hand. I don't think I can do this. I don't think I can destroy Paul Mudd.

Besides, what if the golem is right?

Sure, locking us in here seems extreme. But how often have I joked about running away to Canada, or starting a commune, or building a bunker? Is that so different? What if everything really is too hard, too sad, too broken? What if this whole world really is mostly a dangerous and overrated place, and it's better to just never go out again?

I can feel the monster within me fighting for the monster I created. Drowning out the better part of me, the pleas of my best friend, the screams of the terrified wedding guests. I close my eyes, stuck. Like always.

"Eve, what's going on?"

My mother, Ana, and Rosie all crowd around me, their faces painted with terror.

"What's wrong with Paul?" Mom asks.

"He saved me," Rosie says, grateful but confused. "But now he's...he's blocking the doors, and I don't understand... Eve, what's going on...?"

My eyes are still closed, but something is coming into view. A familiar face, looking weary but hopeful. Her eyes, steel gray and solid, seek mine. Her mouth slowly forms a word, as if with great effort: *Make...*

"Bubbe," I say, opening my eyes with a gasp. My guilt and fear and grief are crushing me, making it hard to breathe. "Bubbe wanted me to...to make..."

"To make what?" Rosie asks, blinking back tears.

I lock eyes with my sister. My breathing steadies, just a little. She's so familiar. I can still see the child she used to be.

"Do you remember the first Hanukkah that Bubbe was with us, after she moved in?" I ask. "The year she told us that story...?"

"I don't remember a story," Rosie says, shaking her head. "But do you mean...do you mean the year my music box broke?"

And with those words, in a flash, the memory of that night comes racing back to me. But it's not exactly the same memory. There's a piece of it I'd forgotten.

Rosie's piece.

Bubbe lifted a finger into the air, adorned with the emerald ring, which glinted darkly in the flickering candlelight. She traced the outline of each letter, finger trembling slightly.

Alef, mem, tav.

"Emet," she said. "It means truth. *And as long as truth is on his brow, the golem will keep his people safe. And when he's not needed, we simply erase the alef."*

She drew her palm through the air, as if wiping something away, and my tongue went dry.

"When you erase the alef, that leaves mem and tav. Which spells death. But taking him from truth to death, it doesn't kill our golem. It just lets him rest. Tells him to be patient. To wait. Until we need him again."

"Presents!"

My parents burst into the room, turning on the overhead light, flooding the room with too much brightness and cheer all at once. Rosie squealed with delight, but I just sat frozen, staring at my grandmother, whose eyes were on the steadily declining candles.

"We survive," she whispered once more, or maybe I just imagined it.

Rosie was practically vibrating with joy, opening her first present. It was a delicate jewelry box, and when you opened it, music played and a tiny ballerina dancer spun in a small circle. She was so excited, she lifted it into the air to show Bubbe and me—and it slipped to the floor, shattering.

Rosie began to wail. My mother was instantly beside her, on her knees to gather the broken shards of glass. A shining edge sliced through her palm, and she cried out. Bubbe placed an emerald-ringed finger on my shoulder, squeezing gently.

"Make sure she's all right," she said, urging me out of my seat. She shoved a cloth napkin into my hand. "We have to make sure our girls are all right."

I went over and gave the napkin to my mother, who wrapped it hastily around her bleeding hand. Then I awkwardly put my arms around my little sister, who shoved me away in her fury. I looked up at my grandmother, indignant. I'd done what she said, and my care had been rebuked.

"Try again," said Bubbe.

I didn't want to. But I also didn't want to disobey my grandmother. So I went back over to Rosie. This time, instead of putting my arms around her, I just squatted next to her. I sat there while my mother finished binding her hand, then swept up the mess, and my father brought out another round of presents. I handed her a tissue so she could wipe away her snot, and she finally stopped crying. When she opened a new present—a game of Candyland—she asked me if I wanted to play it with her. I didn't, not really, but I played the game anyway.

"Good," said my grandmother. She was standing beside my mother, the arm on the small of her back. Almost like she was holding her up.

Making sure her girl was all right.

The golem roars again, nearby, blocking someone else from leaving the camp cafetorium. He might be a protector, but he looks like something else. His care has become something deformed by extremism. In his unrelenting mission to shield us from all pain, he's shoving us toward new dangers—and hurting people while he does it.

Everyone is terrified. Most of the wedding guests have gone from escape mode to taking shelter, ducking beneath tables and chairs, trying to stay out of sight of the monster. Some are quietly weeping, others clawing at the ironclad doors.

I look from my sister to my mother and back again. Beyond the terror in their eyes, I finally see something else. Their aching hearts, their grief, everything they've carried for this past year. All the pain I've avoided asking them about, always waiting for one of them to be the first to broach the topic.

Suddenly, I know what I have to do.

I have to make sure that they'll be all right.

And so I walk over to the golem.

42

The golem looks down at me as I approach. I keep the chisel behind my back so he won't see it. I don't know if he will identify it as a weapon. Do golems engage in self-defense? Will he see me as a threat? I swallow my fear and gaze at him.

As I look into the handsome face of my monster, uncertainty flutters through me. We had so many good moments. He was attentive, intrigued by new experiences. He drank coffee. He learned new words. He slept with me, for Christ's sake, and finally made me feel something again. Which is, obviously, not something I can ever tell anyone about.

But all things considered—I can't just destroy him. Not without giving him a chance to change his ways. Not without making sure I'm not about to make a terrible mistake.

"Paul," I say, voice trembling. "You have to let these people go."

"Safe," he says firmly.

"That's not your call," I say. "Maybe some of them...some of us...don't feel safe. Maybe we're afraid, every day. But we still choose to go out into the world. To take risks. It's our choice. And you have a choice, too. You can choose to let us go."

"Safe," Paul repeats.

The fiery Hebrew letters on his forehead pulse slightly.

Alef, mem, tav.

I remember their meaning: *truth*.

"I'm telling you the truth," I tell the golem, hoping he'll believe me. "Do you remember...do you remember when we were at the restaurant? When we had the eggplant parmesan, and the chicken Florentine...?"

The golem nods.

"And I explained to you about options," I say. "About choice."

"Choice," he repeats.

"Yes," I say, hope rising in me like a balloon. "Choice. *You* have a choice. One option is to keep us here, against our will. Trapped. Prisoners. The other option is to use your free will, and make a different choice. Let us go."

The golem slowly shakes his head.

"No choice," he says. "Not safe."

"Not safe," I agree, "but there's still a choice."

"No choice," he repeats. "Not safe."

The balloon of hope in my chest deflates. This won't work. He looks human. He feels human, sounds human, sometimes acts human. But he has no free will. Because that's how he was built. He can't make a different choice even if he wanted to; all he can do is protect his people, at all costs, without compromise, forever.

And he's already very nearly killed two people in doing so.

Real harm is being done, and more harm will be done. He won't be able to stop himself from hurting people in the name of saving people. He doesn't have a choice.

But I do.

You've got this, Evie.

My father's voice echoes through me. My grandmother's strength urges me forward. With a cry that comes from my very soul, I lunge at the golem, aiming the chisel for the alef on his brow.

In one effortless move, the golem catches me by the wrist.

He takes the chisel and tosses it across the room. It clatters uselessly across the floor.

From somewhere nearby, I hear Sasha let out a strangled scream. The golem still has my wrist, and his eyes are boring into mine.

"Eve," he says sternly. "Not safe."

"Put her down, or I'll take you out, I swear to God."

The golem turns to look at my slim, silver-haired mother.

Her manicured fists are raised, and her ready-for-a-fight posture in her mother-of-the-bride pantsuit would be hilarious if our situation wasn't so dire. My mother is flanked by Rosie, Ana, and Sasha, all of them with fists balled and eyes radiating determination.

A surge of love and loyalty burns through me. I pull my wrist from the golem's grasp, stumbling toward the most important women in my life. I wrap my hand around one of my mother's fists, and as I do so, I feel something sharp and hard.

Bubbe's ring.

Emerald, diamond, and gold.

Small enough to fit in my palm.

Harder than solid rock.

I tug at the ring, then release my grip and position myself in front of my mother, hoping she'll understand. I put my hand behind my back, waiting. In an instant, my mother slips the ring from her finger onto mine, all out of view of the golem.

I flex my fingers, feeling the heavy weight on my ring finger, unaccustomed to wearing anything there. Now all I have to do is figure out how to get close enough to the monster of my own creation to finally destroy him.

I take a hesitant step toward the golem.

"I know you just want to keep me safe," I say.

"Safe," he agrees.

"I'm grateful," I say. "Grateful for everything. For all the times you kept me safe. For saving my sister. For…everything. Honestly, these past few days have been… They've been life-changing, Paul."

I take another step toward the golem.

So close I can almost touch him.

"Eve," Sasha whispers from behind me. "What are you doing?"

"Paul," I say.

Another step.

And then I say the magic words. The ones I wish I could say to my father, but will instead whisper to the other protector I can no longer hold on to.

"Thank you," I say, closing the distance between myself and the golem. *Thank you.*

And then I kiss him.

The kiss is rough, but the force is coming from me, not him. It's always been me kissing him, I realize. He has never initiated a thing. He can't want, or not-want. He's not here to love me or hate me. He's only here to keep me safe. And after so much loneliness, that briefly felt like enough.

But it's not actually enough.

Then, my mouth still pressed to his, I drag my bubbe's ring across the first letter on his forehead. Scratching against the surface with all my might, I erase the alef.

The golem shudders and reels back.

I put a hand to my mouth, tasting sand.

Tears are pouring down my cheeks now, as I watch the light go out from behind my protector's eyes. Doubt and guilt lance their way through me, perforating my heart, seizing my lungs.

I know it's the right thing to do, but destroying my shield feels vulnerable, and cruel, and dangerous.

"Eve," says the golem, eyes momentarily widening in shock and bewilderment.

Then his lids fall down like curtains, and he takes one step backward before sitting down heavily on the floor, then falling all the way to his back. Dust flies up in a cloud around him, golden and shimmering.

He remains on the floor, motionless.

For a moment, looking at him lying still and supine on the cafetorium floor, I'm convinced I've done the wrong thing, yet again. I've never been good at making decisions, and this one has left me alone and unguarded.

But then something breaks open within me. All the pent-up emotions of the last year, emotions I tried to just ignore, or submerge in alcohol, or fend off with a golem, wash over me. Not drowning me, but immersing me. Cleansing me, like a ritual bath. Reminding me of the whole person that I am. Alongside my grief, I feel a resurgence of everything else, too. All the things my father, grandmother, and everyone else I've ever loved would want me to feel. Hope. Strength. Love.

And then my stomach lets out the loudest rumble of my entire life.

Sasha lets out a triumphant cry, and in a rush of relief and joy, they're all embracing me: Sasha, my mother, my sister, my new sister-in-law. Arms wrapped around me, all of us crying and sweating and dirty and alive.

I was wrong. I'm not alone.

I'm surrounded.

"Your father would be so proud of you," my mother whispers in my ear.

I half laugh, half sob. Because it's so wonderful for us to be acknowledging my father again, and how much we miss him. But also because if my father found out that I destroyed a golem only after first bringing it to life and wreaking utter havoc, I'm not sure if he'd be proud or absolutely appalled at my stupidity. Both reactions would be fair.

But in the end, he'd still tell me, *You've got this, Evie.*

All around us, wedding guests begin emerging from under tables and behind chairs. I don't know how many of them saw my final battle with the golem, and I don't care. Whatever we tell people about tonight, no one will believe us. And they don't have to.

We know, and that's enough.

Maybe this whole time, Bubbe really was trying to get a message to me—but maybe it wasn't a warning. Maybe she was trying to give me something even more important: a reminder. Because there will always be threats, and the most important thing isn't to be on guard. The most important thing is to go out there and dare to live anyway, even in a world full of danger. To be there for the ones who matter most to us— and let them be there for us, as well. That's how we overcome the threats.

That's how we survive.

"What in the bloody hell...?"

I look up, and the most surreal night of my life gets even stranger.

Because there, in the midst of the rubble and tumult of what was once my sister's wedding reception, is Hot Josh.

43

"What are you doing here?" I ask.

"I was… God, this sounds so stupid, but I was going to surprise you," Josh says, looking around the room. "But, er, looks a bit like you've had quite enough surprises around here…"

I see the chaos anew through his wide brown eyes. The string lights are still twinkling cheerily above us, but every table is on its side, roses litter the floor, and there's a motionless monster at the edge of it all. Ana is gently examining Rosie's hand, which the gunman twisted when he grabbed her phone. Sasha and my mother are eyeing Josh and me. Bruised and bewildered guests are checking in on one another, divining for signal with their phones, trying to pry the golem-bent metal from the main entrance and side door.

"How did you get in here?" I ask, remembering the exits being cut off.

"Kitchen," Josh says, indicating behind him with a jerk of his thumb. He doesn't seem to notice the golem slumped up against the wall near the no-longer-guarded door. "I tried both of the main doors, but they were locked, then two blokes in a sports car told me to try the kitchen door 'round back..."

Two blokes in a sports car?

Bryan and Carlos!

I wonder how much Sasha had told them before making them schlep her out to summer camp. There are probably a hundred thousand things I'll be left wondering about for a long, long time.

"So what happened here?" Josh asks. "Is everything— Is everyone— Are you okay?"

"I'm fine," I say.

"Who's this guy?" he asks, gesturing toward Paul Mudd. "Is he pissed?"

It takes me a moment to realize by "pissed," Josh means *drunk*.

"He's... Don't worry about him," I say, clutching Josh's hand and leading him away from the fallen golem. "You wanted to...surprise me?"

"Er, yeah," Josh says, adorably sheepish. "But if you've another date—"

"I don't," I say, a little too quickly. And then my stomach rumbles again, somehow even louder than a minute ago. Honestly, it sounds louder than it ever has in my whole damn life.

"Hello, tum," Josh says, unfazed. He gives me a brief smile, then knits his brow again. "Eve, I..."

"Got out of your appointment early and just decided to pop by the camp in the middle of nowhere?" I suggest helpfully.

"What? No. Well...sort of," he says. "My appointment got a bit shifted around, and since you mentioned the wedding was at Heller-Diamond, I figured, well, that's not a bad drive—"

"Wait...you know Camp Heller-Diamond?"

"Yeah," he says.

"But you didn't go here," I say. Because if he did, Rosie

would know him. And besides, he grew up in England. There's no way he went to summer camp in rural Illinois.

"Nah, I didn't," he says, then hesitates and adds, "but my kids do."

It takes a moment for these words to sink in.

I am, as the Brits might say, gobsmacked.

"Your…kids?" I ask.

"Yeah," he says. "My girls. That was—that was my appointment. They were coming in from Milwaukee for the weekend. I've been going to see them every weekend these last few months, while we all got settled in the new situation. This was going to be their first time staying with me at the new apartment. Which is why I had to do all that damn laundry—had to get the sheets and towels all cleaned and ready, had to clean up all my bachelor-flat mess, even rented a damn minivan… Anyhow, indoor soccer, last-minute game, and their mum wanted to take them, so…"

"You're a dad," I say, still incapable of processing the latest in an evidently never-ending list of unexpected revelations.

"Seems to be my situation, yes," says Hot Josh, reddening. "I'm a dad. I didn't know how to mention any of it—I never quite know how to bring up the divorce, or my girls, but… Well, let's just try this: hello. Single dad here. Nice to meet you. Sorry to show up uninvited."

"Technically, you were invited," I say.

My bantering muscles feel weak, like they've atrophied over the last few days. But cracking wise makes me feel like my old self again. I wasn't always a temperamental monster, and I don't have to be one now. It feels surreal, flirting with my neighbor in the messy aftermath of this overturned wedding reception.

But is it any more surreal than waking up to find a golem in my bed?

"Technically, I was indeed invited," he agrees. Then he looks around again. "Christ, though. You sure you're all right?

It looks like a bloody war zone in here. Is this some mad, American-battle-themed wedding party? Because I'm not quite dressed for it…"

"There was a…situation," I say. "But everyone's okay."

As I say these words, I realize they may be overly optimistic. With a sinking feeling, I remember Ethan in the bathroom, and Rosie's stalker still lying motionless on the floor.

Just then, I hear the blessed wail of sirens approaching.

"Is that an ambulance?" Josh asks.

"Yeah," I say. "Actually… Sorry, but things here are…kind of a mess. I have to go talk to the EMTs, you'll probably just want to head home, so—"

"Nothing of the sort," says Hot Josh, taking off his jacket and rolling up his sleeves. He's wearing a navy blue suit, a little old and faded, but still flattering. "I'm here. Let me help."

"Okay," I say, and we go to meet the ambulance.

My stomach is rumbling the whole time as I lead the medic team to Ethan. To my relief, he's still conscious; even manages to crack a thought-you-forgot-about-me joke. I smile weakly, unable to explain the delay. I feel awful, knowing this guy took a thrashing because of me.

But the golem didn't kill him.

He could have, but he didn't.

I wonder if it's because Ethan wasn't actually a threat—not to the community, not even really to me. I wonder if the golem really was just jealous. The thought reaffirms how dangerous he really was, but also sends a sharp stab of guilt through my heart. What if he really had feelings for me, and I betrayed him?

"You all right?" Hot Josh asks, and I make myself nod.

Everything's a blur of flashing lights and EMTs calling out questions and numbers. But I hold on to the important take-aways: Ethan's vitals are good as they load him into the ambulance. He didn't pay the ultimate price just for being kind of a drunken douchebag, and I'm glad about that. No one deserves to be killed just for being an idiot. If they did, well, I'd be a dead girl walking.

AltMight07 is also going to survive. Turns out his name is Tim Reeves, and he's only nineteen years old. There's no doubt he'll be facing some serious consequences when he gets out of the hospital. But at least he's alive, which keeps the blood off my hands.

The better angel within me hopes he'll have the chance to get better—hopefully not just physically, but also that he can unlearn whatever twisted lessons taught him to carry so much hate around. Meanwhile my darker angel hopes he has chronic pain, is too scared to ever start shit again, and also that his stupid broadcasting of how it all went down in the end will discourage any would-be copycat artists out there.

The police take statements from everyone, and I'm sure they're getting conflicting accounts of the night's events. Hopefully no one's able to pin me as the unhinged woman who brought a golem to her sister's wedding.

When all the hubbub finally dies down, only a small handful of us remain: Rosie, Ana, my mother, Sasha, Josh, and me.

"Well," Rosie says. "I always wanted my wedding to be memorable."

"So now do we just…go home?" Ana asks, kissing Rosie's cheek.

"I'm going to need a ride," Sasha says, having sent poor Carlos and Bryan home an hour earlier with very little explanation.

"I've got a van," says Josh helpfully.

"We could light the candles before we go," says my mother, and we all stare at her.

She's holding the delicate silver menorah from the bridal party table.

"Are you serious?" Rosie asks.

"Why not?" Mom says.

"It's not even actually Hanukkah yet," I point out.

"Lighting the lights early would honestly be the least weird thing about tonight," Rosie says, almost-smiling.

"It actually...kinda sounds like a suggestion Dad would make," I add.

"Are you kidding?" Mom huffs. "You know I love him, but you girls always give him all the credit. *I'm* the one who made sure we lit the Hanukkah lights every year. Your father always wanted to go out driving around looking at the damn Christmas lights."

Rosie laughs first.

Then I laugh, and finally, Mom joins in, but her laughter swiftly dissolves into tears. I feel my own shoulder shake dissolve into sobs, and Rosie puts her hand on the small of my back to join in.

Then all three Goodman women are crying.

And it feels really, really good.

SUNDAY

44

The next day is a blur that somehow also brings clarity my way for the first time in a long, long time.

It's my birthday.

I'm forty.

My little sister is married.

My mother is putting her house on the market.

My father is still gone.

But he'll also always be here.

My best friend is sleeping on my couch.

My crush is just across the hall.

There is no golem in my bed.

There are no easy answers.

My apartment is a mess.

Everything is a mess.

And I'm just happy to be alive.

I don't know why I struggled so much with this milestone, with this number. Yesterday I was in my thirties; today I'm not, but what changed? I should be proud of every step I took to get here. I learned a few lessons along the road—most of them the hard way—but God, I still have so much to learn. This isn't the end of anything. It's just one more beginning, like every damn day can be if we just let it.

Exhaling and resolving to let this day be a good one, I pull open my middle dresser drawer. I reach in, fingers stretching out in search of something soft, something to wear to welcome myself into this new dawn. This new decade.

Instead, my fingers close around something hard, and for a moment I freeze.

Then I pull my crumpled ugly Hanukkah sweater from the drawer.

Still clutching the battery pack encased within the fabric, I find the little switch, and turn it on. For a second, nothing happens. Then every twinkling flame on the menorah begins blinking off and on, good as new. It feels like a birthday greeting from my father.

Maybe that's exactly what it is.

I press the tacky sweater to my face and sob. Sorrowful, grateful, hopeful, everything all at once. For the first time ever, I'm comfortable with the messy, authentic reality of myself. I don't have to just be sad, or just be happy, or just be on auto-pilot. I can start to remember how to feel all the things. How to be there for myself, and for my loved ones.

It's just going to take a little time.

ONE WEEK LATER

45

"We're doing Dry January," Rosie says, a dainty gin and tonic clutched tightly in her fingers. Her nails are still pretty, although the wedding manicure is beginning to chip at the edges. My own nails are unpainted, but clean. "Ana thinks it'll be good for us. So this is my last hurrah."

We're at Boka, one of my favorite neighborhood spots for a fancy cocktail. It's New Year's Eve, but only two in the afternoon, so it's not too crowded. When Rosie and Ana were still on their mini-moon in Malibu (their full honeymoon will be this summer, backpacking through Europe), Rosie had texted to ask if we could meet up for a drink. They flew in and out of Chicago, and she wanted to squeeze in a one-on-one visit before they returned to St. Louis.

"Dry January, huh?" I say. "You really are an old married lady."

"I really am married, apparently," Rosie says, smiling brightly. But then an odd expression passes across her face. "But... God, this so embarrassing... The thing is... I barely remember the wedding reception."

I give her a funny look. I can't tell if she's joking or not. After a lifetime of intermittent bickering, and a very fresh commitment to improving our relationship, I don't want to respond incorrectly to whatever she's trying to tell me.

"What do you mean?" I ask carefully.

"I mean..." Rosie shakes her head, seeming genuinely baffled. "It's just, like—I remember the morning, getting ready, all of the decorations. I remember the ceremony, mostly, although I think it all felt like a dream even in the moment. And I remember your speech, which really was wonderful. But...that's it."

"That's...it?"

"Pretty much, yeah," says Rosie, almost embarrassed. "It's funny, so many people told me, 'Your wedding day will just be a blur,' but I had no idea it would be a *complete and total* blur. The weird thing is, it's the same for Ana. She says it's a blank for her after your speech. That's why we're doing Dry January, honestly. Seems like we overdid it."

"Oh," I say, mind reeling as I try to keep up with what she's telling me.

She—and Ana—really don't remember anything?

About the golem?

The gunman?

Any of it?

"What about Ethan?" I ask.

"Ethan!" Rosie's eyes widen, and she nods. "Oh my God, yes! Someone mentioned Ethan getting into a fistfight with your date. Apparently Ethan really got his ass handed to him. I don't know how I missed that. What the hell happened?"

"I...don't know," I say, then add, "Ethan made a pass at me, maybe that's why—"

"Ugh, what a prick," Rosie says, taking a sip of her drink and seeming relieved to ease in to more familiar conversational territory. "I hate that he's going to be front and center in all the wedding pictures. Sorry you had to walk down the aisle with him."

"No worries," I say, still utterly confused.

How can Rosie and Ana have blacked out on the whole debacle?

"So is that why you and what's-his-name split?" Rosie asks, almost shyly. We're not used to talking like this: sharing secrets, digging for details. It takes me a minute to realize that by what's-his-name, she means Paul Mudd. "Because he had a temper?"

"Basically, yeah," I say, feeling a brief return of my stomach-clenching anxiety.

"Well, then, good riddance," says Rosie. "You deserve better than that."

"I… Thanks," I say, smiling tentatively at my sister. "Hey, you want to maybe share an appetizer or something?"

An hour somehow flies by, which never happens when we're spending time together. It's a pleasant surprise to realize Rosie is someone I can actually enjoy spending time with. But right after I signal the waiter to request our check, my sister turns to me with a slightly nervous look. All of a sudden I'm worried the nice little house of cards we've been stacking all night is about to get blown over.

"Hey, there is this one other thing," Rosie says. "Layla—who really did go overboard at happy hour; she barely remembers a thing, either—she said the one thing *she* remembers from the wedding is you said something shitty about her mom."

"About her mom?" I ask, lost again. "I don't even know her mom."

"But you know she's her caretaker," Rosie says. When I shake my head, she goes on, "Layla's mom was living with her and Amir for the past two years. That's why Layla had to leave her doctoral program."

"Oh," I say, feeling awful. "Is it cancer, or…?"

"Alzheimer's," says Rosie, shaking her head. "Layla wanted to keep her mom at home with them for as long as possible, but the dementia was getting so bad, they had to move her into a

facility, like, a month ago. She said you made some comment
about without memories, what's the point...?"

"Oh, God," I say, remembering the moment in the hallway. While everyone else seems to have blurred out that awful
night, every moment of it is rushing back to me now. "I think
I did say something like that, but like—that's totally not what
I meant. Honestly, I didn't know anything about her mom. I
didn't know Layla was dealing with all that."

I had, in fact, assumed that Layla was a beautiful and spacey
grad school dropout who decided to focus on fitness instead
of sticking with school. She was one of the many people I'd
written off without knowing their whole story, because I was
wallowing so miserably in my own. It's yet another awful realization.

"I think the fact she's gone through hell, too, is why she was
able to show up for me so much," Rosie says, voice cracking
a little. "She's been...she's been a really good friend to me."

I remember how Layla came to the funeral, and to shiva. I
think of all the times Rosie texted me, and I didn't get back
to her—but Layla probably did. I feel guilty, and also grateful.
I'm glad my sister has a friend like that.

"Please tell her I'm sorry," I say, stomach grinding uncomfortably. "I didn't mean that. At all."

"You tell her," Rosie says. "We'll have both of you over
when you come visit St. Louis."

"Oh, am I coming to visit you in St. Louis?"

"Yeah." Rosie smiles. "Winter's beautiful in Missouri."

I chuckle, warmed even amid all the confusion.

"Okay," I say.

"She'll forgive you," Rosie says. "Layla's pretty great."

"I'm actually kind of—jealous of her," I say, surprised at my
own honesty.

"Why are you jealous of Layla?" Rosie asks, her delicate
brows drawing together in confusion.

"Because you two are close," I say. "And because…she has her shit together. Same reason I'm jealous of you, honestly."

"That's wild," says Rosie. "The idea of *you* being jealous of *me* for a change."

"Wait, what?" I say, baffled. "When have you ever been jealous of me?"

"Um, my whole life?" Rosie says, cocking her head. "You're my big sister. You were always so good at everything I wasn't— school, Hebrew school, having a 'real career' and whatever. How was I supposed to compete with any of that? Plus, you always had all the inside jokes with Dad…" Rosie hesitates. "I know how much you miss him."

It comes out of nowhere, but it also comes out of everywhere. An instinct to protect my sister shudders through me. I can see how much she's hurting, and I'm done looking away.

"I know how much you miss him, too," I say, reaching for her hand.

"I really do," she says, eyes going glassy. "And, like… I don't know. He was just—like, he was the one person who could always make me laugh. Like when he did his impressions of Bubbe."

"Oh, God," I say. "Those impressions were terrible."

"But so funny," she says. "Honestly, I think that's why I always thought of Bubbe as kind of funny. Because the way Dad saw her, she was. All her *spielkes* and weird stories and everything was…endearing, the way Dad saw it. The way he saw everyone made them seem a little better, or easier, or funnier than they actually were. I miss that."

"I miss that, too."

We sit there for a moment, just holding hands. At first, all I can think about is the man we're missing. How relieved Dad would be, to see us together like this, working on our relationship. But then everything else Rosie just told me tugs at my thoughts again.

"You really don't remember your wedding reception?" I finally ask. "Like, at all?"

"I wish I did," she says.

Don't be so sure, I think, still perplexed but not wanting to press the issue.

After we tab out, I text my mother and ask if she's up for a quick visit. Half an hour later I'm curled up on the couch in her Winnetka living room. Mom is in a track suit, folding laundry, a task she continues throughout our conversation.

"How was your happy hour with Rosie?"

"It was good," I say, grateful to be able to answer honestly.

"I'm glad," says my mother, folding a fitted sheet in a way I'll never understand. "It's so important to me that you two... have each other."

"Yeah," I say, and even though I came over to ask her something else, I find myself finally giving voice to a question that's burdened me for more than a year: "Mom, when Dad...when Dad died. I never asked...how it all happened. Was he awake, were you able to...?"

I trail off, unable to go on.

My mother presses the fitted sheet to her chest, and closes her eyes.

"He was still awake when we got to the hospital," she says. "We were both a little worried, but still joking, just talking. Neither of us knew how bad it was yet. We had absolutely no idea."

I tremble, watching her.

I want to know, and I don't want to know.

"They took him back for some tests, and that's when...that's when his heart started failing. There was all this activity, I had a sense even from out in the hallway that something was going on, and then they brought me in and his eyes were closed and they told me they had lost his pulse for several minutes. That he was there, but that...he probably wouldn't ever wake up. But they told me he might be able to hear me..."

The air in Mom's warm living room feels so cold.

A single tear slips down her cheek—mine, too.

"I knew there wouldn't be time for you and Rosie to get there," she whispers. "So I told him how much we all loved him. You. RoRo. Me. Everyone. And when I ran out of words, there was this kind young man—I don't know if he was a nurse or an aide or a what, but he said we could put on music for a few minutes. He had a little Bluetooth speaker, and when he turned it on, it started playing Christmas music. He said I'm sorry, I know the paperwork says he's Jewish, let me change it—but I said no. He loved Christmas music. He and his baby girl, they both always loved..."

My mother's voice gives out, her eyes still closed.

I stand up, and wrap my arms around her.

Our tears are silent, and so are we.

I wish I had been there.

But now I know, some part of me was.

Just like some part of him is always, always here.

"Thank you for asking," whispers my mother.

"Thank you for telling me," I whisper back.

"You know," she says, "I love you just as much as he did."

I nod.

I know.

It's different.

But I know.

"And I know you don't like having your phone on," she says. "But if you could maybe keep it on a little more often? For my sake."

"I'm working on it," I promise.

"Okay," she says.

I wind up staying for dinner. Salad, unsurprisingly, but it's actually pretty good. For salad. After we've cleared the plates from the table, I reluctantly tell my mother that I should go before the holiday traffic gets terrible. And then I make myself ask the question I'd initially come to pose.

"Hey, Mom—this might sound weird, but…how much do you remember about Rosie's wedding reception?"

"You know, it's the funniest thing," my mother says. "Everything after your speech is a little fuzzy. I guess champagne hits me harder now than it used to. I remember how I felt, though. So proud. It was a good night. Rosie and Ana, they looked so happy. That's the part I'll never forget."

"Yeah," I say, feeling like I'm losing my mind.

"Oh, speaking of forgetting!" Mom says, and sets a neatly folded towel down beside me on the couch. "You left your coat at the camp, it wound up in my car. Here, let me get it for you before I forget—that one you wore here today, it's not warm enough, you'll catch cold."

She walks to her front hall closet and hands me my coat.

I shrug it on, hugging my mother before slipping my hands into its pockets. My fingers brush something crinkly. I pull out a small, crumpled gift.

"Your cute neighbor gave you whatever that is," Mom says, eyes sparkling. "I found it in my car and put it in the pocket for you."

"Oh," I say, cheeks warming. "Thanks."

"Josh, right? You should have brought him to the wedding."

I tried, I think, but I obviously can't tell my mother that. I almost ask her how much she remembers about the guy I *did* bring, but decide maybe it's best to let this particular sleeping dog lie.

"What is it?" Mom asks, nodding to the little present.

"I don't know," I mumble, shoving it back into my pocket. "I'll open it later."

If it's something mortifying, I don't want to open it in front of my mother. Somehow the golem incident seems largely erased from people's minds, but I can't count on that kind of luck in other situations.

Suddenly, a thought occurs to me: Sasha.

I have to ask Sasha what she knows about all this golem-forgetting stuff.

We're already supposed to have brunch tomorrow, with

Bryan. The long-awaited return of Bestie Brunch. I decide to text her and see if maybe she can meet me half an hour early so we can talk alone.

The next morning, I take the train toward Lakeview for brunch. My thoughts are all over the place. Sasha agreed to meet me early, so we could talk. But I'm still not sure exactly how to ask her about what's on my mind.

Hey, remember how we both built monsters instead of dealing with our shit? Did everyone forget about yours? Or did you actually never make a golem, and I'm just fully losing my mind and made up that part, too?

"Baby, cover your mouth when you cough, please."

The words come from a woman with coppery hair piled atop her head. She's standing across the aisle from me, wearing a tiny infant in a moss-colored linen carrier, and also holding the hand of a little boy. He's maybe two or three years old, and he's the one who coughed. He obediently lifts his little elbow, coughing into its crook, and his mother crinkles her nose at him.

There's something familiar about her. Then I remember: I'd given my seat up to her two weeks earlier, when she was exceedingly pregnant. The same strange day I'd seen both Santa and the ghost of my grandmother on the brown line. I wonder why she's already back on the train, with such a young baby, and the coughing toddler. Are they going to the doctor? Something routine, or more worrisome?

The young mother catches me looking at her, and gives me a tired smile. But there's no recognition in her eyes. She doesn't remember me having given up my seat for her, nor should she. I hope a thousand people gave up their seat for her when she needed to get off her feet. I hope so many small favors are done for her that they all just blur together. Suddenly, my fierce hope is that *most* good deeds go unnoticed, because their frequency makes them commonplace. That feels like the sort of world my dad was trying to help create, and I want to do that, too.

We'll keep each other safe, I want to tell the woman with the two small children. *I want your kids to be okay.*

But instead, I just smile back at her, and get off at the next stop.

Sasha is already seated at our table when I arrive. The brunch spot is packed; only a handful of places were open on New Year's Day, and we were lucky to get a table at this one. It's called Shine, and it will probably be closed before the next New Year rolls around, but for now it's full of sparkling lights and bottomless mimosas.

"I have to ask you about something," I say before I even sit down.

"Let me guess," Sasha says. "Everyone's forgetting your golem."

"How?" is all I can manage in reply.

"No idea," she says. "I wanted to give it a few days, make sure it happened for you, too. But I think it's just a thing. If you think about all the legends of the golem, which of course I used to think were just stories...they're all told by the rabbis who built them. No reference to random rampaging Jew-saving monsters in the history books. Golems are a shadowy thing, and they just sort of become shadowy in people's memories. Maybe that's why they're depicted as mud monsters. No one remembers what they really look like. If it's anything like it was for me, people will kind-of remember you had a date named Paul, but that'll be about it. How much do you remember about Emmet?"

I try to remember Sasha's ex-boyfriend—her golem, I remind myself—and find that I can't. Not really. I just kind of remember a quiet, tallish guy in a baseball cap.

"Basically nothing," I say.

"Bingo," she says.

We order mimosas.

It doesn't take long for us to piece together how easy it is for all evidence of the golem to be erased. A white suprema-cist named Tim Reeves was arrested on the campus of Camp

Heller-Diamond that night, but none of the guests remember him being there, and his concussion gives a reason for him forgetting everything, too. The cell reception at the camp sucked, so the whole time he was live streaming his actions...nothing actually made it to TikTok. Everyone else's phones were in the lacy basket until the main action was over. Ethan was hospitalized with a broken nose and some busted ribs, and remembers *getting shit-housed and hitting on some muscle-bro's girlfriend*. Everything having to do with the golem has blurred at the edges for everyone.

"So we really got away with it," I say, bewildered.

"I mean, kinda," Sasha says. "I don't feel great about it."

"Me, neither," I agree. "I mean...we're two smart, capable, grown-ass women. How did we think it was okay?"

"Because everything's hard," Sasha says. "Being a smart, capable, grown-ass woman is hard. Living on this planet is hard. The world's a dumpster fire. Your dad died. I got mugged on the way home from work—"

"You what?" I ask, horrified.

"Yeah. Dude took my phone and wallet, twisted my wrist when he grabbed it from me."

"Why didn't you tell me?"

"I honestly don't know," Sasha says, exhaling sharply. "I just hit a wall, when that happened. Being a woman, being Black, being Jewish, living alone, staying late at work, pandemics, protests, blah blah blah. It was just all more than I could handle for a minute there. So I, you know. Thought outside the box."

"Creative problem solvers, that's us," I say weakly.

"Yeah," Sasha says, shaking her head. "But like. Everyone's got shit they're dealing with, all the time. Can't use that as an excuse to become part of the problem. At some point you just realize...*oh, so that's life.*"

"Yeah," I agree. "It's like...if you're not the saddest one in the room right now, you will be someday."

"Right," says Sasha. "So let's go easier on people. And on ourselves. And, you know. No more making golems. Deal?"

"Deal," I say quickly. Then, voice trembling: "I really thought it was only me."

"Me, too," says Sasha. She sets down her mimosa, leaning back in her chair. For a moment, the old look of exhaustion crosses her face, adding angles to her already-high cheekbones. "Worst lie we tell ourselves."

I nod, swallowing the thick knot in my throat.

"But we don't have to feel so alone," Sasha adds, leaning forward again. Closing the distance, making sure I can see just how serious she is about this. "Not when we know we've always got backup. Right?"

My stomach tightens, but doesn't make a sound. Like it doesn't want to tell on me; not this time. But I do want to reassure Sasha, to let her know beyond the shadow of a doubt that she does have backup. Whenever she needs it. To let her know how serious I am about this, too.

"Right," I say at last.

She smiles, reaching again for her mimosa. Her shoulders ease, her face softening once more. I wait another few seconds.

And then I ask her the other thing I've been dying to know.

"Um. Did you sleep with Emmet?"

Sasha raises an eyebrow.

"Did you sleep with Paul?"

"I asked you first."

She sips her mimosa, then gives the slightest nod.

I sip my mimosa, and give her the same sly nod.

"…It was good, huh," Sasha says.

"Yeah," I say, flushing at the memory. "It was really good."

"But also bad," Sasha adds quickly.

"Oh yes, obviously, very bad."

"Like you got the world's best vibrator, but after you use it, it starts randomly electrocuting other people," Sasha muses.

I laugh.

She laughs.

And that, too, feels really, really good.

"Hey, what are we laughing about?" Bryan says, entering red-faced and rubbing his hands together. "It's cold as shit out there, by the way. But at least it's finally snowing."

"It is?"

I look outside, and sure enough, fat, silvery flakes are floating from the sky. After all these cold, dry months, the sight of snow warms something deep within me. I smile at my friends.

"Just talking girl-talk," Sasha says.

"I love girl-talk," says Bryan. "But I do have some actually huge news, like massive, and I don't know how to ease in to it so I'm just going to say it, okay oh my God, here it is: Carlos and I have been trying for almost two years to adopt and we don't bring it up because it's hard and scary and jinxy but we got picked by this woman who just had her baby and we're picking the baby up tomorrow and she's going to be ours and her name is Chela and Carlos is researching formula right now and I can only stay for like an hour because we have to build a crib but Carlos told me I had to come and tell you in person and I'm so happy and excited and terrified because *holy shit you guys I'm gonna be a dad.*"

Sasha and I are silent for less than a nanosecond, and then we scream with joy and pounce on him, everything else forgotten. Bryan's crying and we're crying and our server comes by and then says he'll be back if we need a moment. We're laughing and wiping our eyes and asking a million questions.

The whole time, I'm wondering, how did I not know about the most important things going on with my friends? It's like we've all been taking the publicly shared headlines of each other's lives at face value instead of digging deeper. Like cranky Boomers cruising Facebook and sharing posts without checking sources, blissfully riding the waves of confirmation bias. My friends didn't know how much I was really dealing with, but also, I didn't know how much they were really dealing with, because it's so easy to just keep things surface level. Do a cursory check-in, hit the proverbial like button, and just move on.

I don't want to do that anymore.

"So anyway," says Bryan. "I'm just really hoping I don't screw this up."

I look at my friend, awed that he's about to become a father. A warmth spreads through my chest as I think of my own father. I miss him so much; it's an ache that will always be with me. But I am so grateful that out of all the dads in the world, he's the one I got. And thanks to him, I know exactly what to say.

"You've got this, Bry."

As I'm leaving brunch, the snow begins falling more heavily. I put my hands in my pockets, and feel the unopened little gift once more. When I'm seated on the train, I open it. Nestled in the crinkled wrapping paper, there are two small plastic rings—one green, one yellow—and a note: "Maybe these will help you open the right door the first time around from now on."

Color covers for my keys, I realize. The gift is so small, but somehow manages to be clever and thoughtful and useful.

I haven't talked to Hot Josh since the wedding; he left town the next day to spend the week working remotely from Milwaukee, to get in some time with his daughters since he missed seeing them over the weekend. But he should be home by now.

Covered in a thin film of snow, I'm nervous when I knock on his door. But when Josh opens it, the nerves begin to shift into something more like excitement. Hope.

"Hey," I say, holding up the color covers. "Thanks for these."

"You're welcome," he says. "You're, er, supposed to put them on your keys, you realize."

"I thought maybe you could help me with that."

He smiles, brown eyes twinkling at me, and opens the door wide enough to invite me all the way in.

ONE MONTH LATER

Epilogue: February

Some people hate February, especially in Chicago, because it's when the long, dark slog of actual winter really settles over the city. The holidays are all in the rearview mirror, with endless cold nights stretching out ahead. I used to be one of those people. But not anymore. Now, I appreciate all those long, dark nights. They give you an excuse to stay in, and reflect, and maybe even find ways to keep yourself warm.

Bleary, still blinking away the sleep, I pick my phone up from my bedside table where it's still plugged in. It's 6:58 a.m., which means in two minutes, my alarm is going to go off. But it's Sunday, and I don't have anywhere to be. So I slide my finger across the alarm, canceling the seven-o'clock wakeup, and roll over.

Josh is staring at me, eyes comically wide.

I yelp, and he laughs.

"Morning," he says.

"I thought you were still sleeping," I say, digging my fingers into his ribs and tickling him. "Don't stare at me like that, it's creepy!"

"Sorry, luv," he says, still chuckling.

"No, you're not!"

I like this side of him, the one that's still so new to me. The goofy, endearing side, so much warmer than the banter that first drew me in. I love how when it's just us, he's so playful. I would never have guessed that this man was the king of terrible dad jokes. He's also tender, and incredibly attentive. He rubs my back and asks about my day. He remembers my co-workers' names. When I took him out for drinks with Carlos, Bryan, and Sasha last week, he was engaging and animated, but when we slipped into bed that night he asked shyly if I thought they liked him.

I know they matter to you, he said. *I want that best-friend seal of approval.*

I assured him that they liked him. Which they very much did. Bryan had even texted post-drinks to say *I adore your Jewnicorn*, but I kept that detail to myself.

"Hey," Josh says. His accent paired with his intensely serious face makes every word sound so formal. "I've been meaning to say... I still think about what an idiot I was early on, not telling you about my kids and all that. Sorry I didn't tell you earlier. Don't know why it's still sometimes so hard to just... just say it, you know?"

"It's okay," I tell him, meaning it. "I get it."

There are things I didn't tell you, I think. *Things I never can.*

"I just didn't want to... I don't know," he says, taking my hands in his, kissing my knuckles. "Scare you off, I suppose."

"I don't scare easy," I assure him.

"I want to be real with you," he says.

"That's my favorite thing about you," I tell him. "You're real."

"Yeah?"

"Yeah."

"All right, then," he says. "Well. In the spirit of being real. I really have to piss."

"So romantic," I say, rolling my eyes.

While Josh is in the bathroom, I quickly scroll through my phone. Bryan sent Sasha and me a midnight text, a selfie of him with little Chela.

Bryan: She does not sleep. But God, she's cute.

I heart the image.

I miss having Bryan and Sasha at the office. But sleepless nights aside, Bryan loves being the stay-at-home dad who can take on a freelance gig here and there. And the new senior account executive position at Ogilvy has been great for Sasha. Seeing how much happier they both are makes me wonder if I should jump ship soon, too. But for now, I'm riding the wave of being seen as the Java-Lo account savior.

Amy loved the headlines and rationale I'd sent her right before the wedding. She took them to the group creative director on the Java-Lo account, who immediately brought none other than Bryan in to draft some visual concepts. They took them in to the big pitch before the holiday break, and the client went absolutely bananas for the simple *Hi, Lo* headline, paired with the concept of seeing Java-Lo everywhere you go. It's inspiring them to push their home line and their corporate standbys simultaneously, which they've never done before. They're buying up billboards nationwide. Amy made sure everyone knew that it was my ideas that saved the day.

It's nice not to feel like the anonymous new kid at Mercer & Mercer anymore. No one calls me Neve anymore, and I chat with all of my coworkers, instead of only my little clique of Sasha and Bryan. I even have lunch with Nancy once a week or so, which isn't something I ever would have predicted.

At our first lunch together, she told me about her messy divorce just over a year ago. *I really lost it for a while there,* she said. *I even made this voodoo doll of my ex, like with some of the hair I found on his old comb. And I swear when I poked it, bad things really did happen to him. Like, he got COVID and stuff. Do you think that's crazy?*

No, I told her. *I actually don't.*

She smiled, and it occurred to me again that everyone gets hurt, and finds their own—sometimes legitimately insane— ways to cope. No one's perfect, and certainly not me. I'm working on it, but I have a long way to go. I can admit now that I'd written Nancy off way too early. She's just a person piecing her life back together, like most of us. And her energy is kind of infectious, and there are some definite perks to befriending the office gossip.

Like being one of the first to hear when that godawful Barry from corporate got fired right after the New Year, which was enough to make me want to stay with Mercer & Mercer a little while longer. I know eventually I'll leave advertising. Maybe take on a nonprofit role, something that pays less but makes me feel like I'm making a difference in the world. But change doesn't happen overnight. Even when I know what I need to do, it takes me a hot minute to do it, and that's probably going to be true for a little while longer.

"I'm back," says Josh, slipping under the covers and shimmying up against me. "And your bathroom floors are cold as faaaaaaaaaaaaaaaaaack."

He puts his icicle toes on top of my warm feet. I squeal, shoving him away. But then he pulls me close and kisses me, and soon, everything's warm again. More than warm. Hot. I kiss him slowly, intentionally. I love how soft his lips are. He pulls me up against him, and I love the hard part of him, too.

"Faaaaaaack meee," I say, in the worst British accent ever.

"You makin' fun of me?" Josh says, and somehow his Brooklyn accent is worse than my British one.

"Per'aps I yam," I say. "But I'm also puttin' in a request. Guvnah."

He laughs so hard that he snorts, then kisses me with such intensity that I melt right into him. When we're done ravaging each other in the bed, I lead him into the shower. There is no fear of him disappearing or falling apart when the water touches his perfectly human flesh. He washes my hair, massaging my head with his strong fingers, slick soap and hot water running down our bodies.

"Hey," he says, wrapping one of my periwinkle-blue towels around his waist after stepping out of the shower. I admire the dark curls of his robust chest hair, the lean muscles of his arms, the slightly soft curve of his stomach. *Hello, tum*, I think, grateful for how accepting he is of my appetite—which is no longer ravenous, but still significant. And even more grateful for the other appetite he awakens in me. "I'm starving. Want to go get some bagels?"

"Ugh, yes," I say, nodding and slipping into my purple robe. "Bagels sound so good. I'm starving."

"I'll pop across the hall and get dressed," he says.

"You're going to go out in the hall like that?" I ask, tugging at the edge of the towel covering the lower half of him. "What if one of the neighbors sees you?"

"Lucky them," he says with a cheeky grin, waggling his thick, dark brows. "Meet you in the hallway, then?"

Josh leaves, and I can't stop smiling the whole time as I get dressed, put on deodorant, and towel-dry my hair. I skip the diffuser for time's sake, instead twisting my curls and piling them on top of my head in a scrunchie. I grab my warmest hat and inelegantly jam it down on top of my hair. It's going to be a puffy, frizzy mess later, but I don't even care. I'm making progress in *some* ways, if not in *all* ways.

There's so much I'm looking forward to now. I'm taking Josh with me when I visit Rosie and Ana in St. Louis next month. If Mom has her way, we'll be joining her for Shabbat services the week after that. Bestie Brunch will be the following weekend. Then, for what would have been my dad's seventy-fifth birthday in April, my mother and sister and I will go have giant overstuffed sandwiches with garlic pickles at his favorite deli.

My calendar has gone from empty to full, and I'm grateful that this season is so much warmer than the last. It's cold outside, though, so I'll need my new winter coat. The one I bought on sale right after the holidays. Yet another lesson from my dad: snag the deal without skimping on quality.

When I get to the front hall closet, I hesitate before opening it, just for a second. Then I exhale, twist the handle, and pull open the door. Front and center, I see my good winter coat. It's an evergreen North Face jacket, nestled in among many other, less-worthy coats.

And there in the far corner, hidden from view by all the silently hanging winter wear, is the reassuring form of my slumbering golem.

His eyes are closed, his forehead still smudged. He's not destroyed, only dormant. He won't hurt anyone, because this monster will never move or breathe again.

Unless I need to wake him up.

★ ★ ★ ★ ★

Acknowledgments

This book began as a movie pitch. The essence of the pitch was "*Broad City* meets *Shaun of the Dead*," which I still think is a solid way to explain this story. I first shared the concept on my now-defunct blog back in 2018. A few years later, I submitted it to the *Hey Alma!* Hanukkah Movie Pitch competition. Winning the *Hey Alma!* competition was absolutely the genesis of this novel finding its way to readers, and that's where I need to begin my gratitude tour for this thing.

Thank you to everyone who voted for the movie pitch—this is your win, you beautiful and hilarious people, especially users like @rabbijfroco, who said, "If this isn't green lighted for Hanukkah 2023 I will riot"; @stellalunabat, who commented, "Pretty sure Rabbi Loew supports this use of the golem"; and @jmomseattle, who asked, "How can we manifest this into existence?"

We did, in fact, collectively manifest this into existence.

Huge thanks to the entire savvy *Hey Alma!* team, especially Molly Tolsky, Evelyn Frick, and Avital Dayanim, whose eye-popping movie poster featuring Paul Rudd as Paul Mudd went on to inspire the cover of this book. Related: Oh, hi, Paul Rudd! Thank you for having a great golem parody name! Want to be on this story's real-life movie poster someday?

Speaking of the cover of this book, thank you to Elita Sidiropoulou and the design team at HarperCollins for bringing such gorgeous detail and storytelling to the cover art. Everyone I've met and/or worked with at MIRA Books, HarperCollins, and Harlequin have been as friendly as they are professional, and the team's clear love of books and sharing good stories made me feel right at home. The most special thanks to editor extraordinaire April Osborn, who knew what I was trying to do with this story from the very beginning and made sure it deepened in truth (and spice). Deep gratitude as well to Leah Morse, who swiftly felt less like a publicist and more like a friend and co-conspirator determined to make folks fall in love with this story.

And how do I even begin to thank Allison Hellegers? Alli, you aren't just an agent, you're an ally, brilliant reader, my long-lost camp buddy (not for real, but in our hearts), and a champion for all your authors. I'm so grateful to collaborate with you. My gratitude, as well, to all the all-star team at Stimola Literary Studio.

While this novel is a true debut, I have a very dramatic writing history...which is a super hokey way of saying I've been a playwright for a long, long time. I am incapable of writing a story that isn't shaped by my theatrical upbringing. Knowing that I'm leaving way too many people off this list, I do want to thank some of the theater collaborators who made me the writer I am today: Kyle Haden, John and Diana Howell, Denise Halbach, Richard Lawrence, Amy Szerlong, Ian August, Minita Gandhi, Betty Hart, Tim X. Davis, the Mississippi University for Women MFA community, and all my colleagues from the gloriously ill-timed Chateau de Poigny Goldfinger Residency in March 2020.

Transitioning from playwright to novelist was made easier and a lot more fun thanks to the 2024-Ever debut authors group with all their wit and wisdom, as well as the 2019–2020 PitchWars community—especially my keen-eyed mentor, Sam Taylor. Special thanks as well to the friends who always, always believed in my writing, even when I didn't, and gave generously of their reading, guerilla marketing, and encouragement: Kara Lewis, Leah Alvarez, Debra Kassoff, Tammie Ward Rice, Exodus Brownlow, Brent Hearn, Delia Kropp, Shira Muroff, Chela Sanchez, Meg Donahue, Jenna Jo Pawlicki, the Chicago Buddies Escape Room Discord crew, and so many others.

When I wrote the first full draft of this novel two years ago, centering it around a woman unable to process the trauma of losing her father to a sudden heart attack, I had no idea that one year later, that exact thing would happen to me. I didn't build a golem, but I did wrestle with my own grief demons. Personally and communally, the losses of the past year were overwhelming. But being able to tell this story, and trust that others would read it, provided essential solace. Sometimes people refer to sorrow as being "in the muck." If *clay* can also be called *muck*, well, maybe the title of this book has yet another layer of meaning. I'm making it out, with the help of my community. My gratitude is endless. To everyone who showed up when the earth crumbled beneath me, thank you. For the meals, the hugs, the quiet walks, the poems, all of it. Thank you. Thank you. Thank you.

Mom, Jake, Adam, Claire: It's been the hardest year. You have all provided strength, grace, love, and humor in spite of everything. That is a gift I will never take for granted.

E & M: You bring me joy every single day. I love you so much. (But sorry you can't read this book for, like, a decade or so, sweet kiddos.)

Danny, thank you for seeing me, and for seeing me through each day. No golem could be a better protector, and I could not ask for a better (or funnier) love story than ours.

And he was mentioned in the dedication, but *this* is the section where I wanted—and still want—to acknowledge my father. The man who loved everything I ever wrote and who I still can't believe will not be reading this, but whose story will echo throughout my life. I miss you every day, Dad.